W9-BMO-114

REAPER

REAPER

K. D. McENTIRE

PYR®

an imprint of **Prometheus Books**
Amherst, NY

Published 2012 by Pyr®, an imprint of Prometheus Books

Cover illustration © Sam Weber
Cover design by Grace M. Conti-Zilsberger

Inquiries should be addressed to
Pyr
59 John Glenn Drive
Amherst, New York 14228–2119
VOICE: 716–691–0133
FAX: 716–691–0137
WWW.PYRSF.COM

16 15 14 13 12   5 4 3 2 1

Library of Congress Cataloging-in-Publication Data

McEntire, K. D., 1980–
    Reaper / by K. D. McEntire.
        p. cm.
    Summary: After being forced to destroy the twisted and diseased soul of her mother, known in the Never as the White Lady, Wendy must guide the spirits of the dead into the afterlife all by herself, while across town her best friend Eddie lies in a coma, his soul mysteriously separated from his body.
    ISBN 978–1–61614–632–0 (cloth)
    ISBN 978–1–61614–633–7 (ebook)
    [1. Supernatural—Fiction. 2. Soul—Fiction. 3. Death—Fiction. 4. Future life—Fiction.] I. Title.
PZ7.M478454238Re 2012
[Fic]—dc23

                                                        2012006471

Printed in the United States of America on acid-free paper

For my mother.

Thank you
for all those Sundays we spent
at the bookstore
and Taco Bell.

ACKNOWLEDGMENTS

As always, this book wouldn't exist without a truly fabulous group of people. I'd like to thank the consistently awesome Joe Monti and Lou Anders. Both are super busy guys who always make the time to talk plot and all things geektastic. I wouldn't be half the writer I sort of am if it weren't for you two. Thanks also go to the spiffy Gabrielle Harbowy who sifts through my gobbledygook for the good stuff. Thank you so much!

Thank you to Karen Ramsey and Jennifer Day, my glorious beta readers. Other dudes who rock include Sam Weber, the amazing cover artist (http://sampaints.com/). Check him out!

Of course, I would be utterly remiss if I were to forget the fabulously talented George Levchenko—not only is he an amazing photographer and web designer (http://www.glnet.tv) but he very graciously accepted 9 p.m. translation request texts without grumping at me. Thank you, George. You rock.

Last but not least, thanks go to my husband Jake. Without you I'd never have time to write, especially now that we're juggling a toddler and a newborn. Thank you.

PROLOGUE

When the slow, steady beeping turned shrill, every nurse on the floor rushed into the room. Wendy, dozing at her best friend's bedside, shoved back from the mattress and staggered to her feet. Beside her, Eddie's machines continued to beep steadily. His roommate wasn't so lucky.

Despite the bustle of the hospital staff and the long, intricate dance of defibrillator and medical personnel, the shrill tone stretched until a doctor pushed back from the body on the bed and said, "Call it."

"Seven-oh-two," a short, stocky nurse murmured, tugging the dangling pen at his neck free of its cord, clicking it open. As he passed Wendy the nurse patted her on the shoulder. "You okay?"

"Yeah," Wendy said, watching the spirit of Eddie's departed roommate step away from her cooling body and hesitate at the curtain separating their beds before reaching out a tentative hand and sliding through. "I've seen it before."

Biding her time, Wendy waited until the orderlies had carted the body away and stripped the bed before she waved to the ghost. Even dead, the girl was all bones and sallow skin, long lank hair and large, protruding eyes. She'd been admitted to the ward three days before but Wendy had known that she wouldn't last; the silver cord dangling from her navel that connected her soul to her body looked as if moths had been at it even then. Now, as she stood near the bed that had once been hers, her cord was barely more than a desiccated string.

"Am I dead?" The ghost approached and ran her hand over Wendy's plastic chair. Like with the curtain, her fingers passed smoothly through the back. "I don't feel dead."

"I know. Weird, right?" Wendy settled on the edge of Eddie's bed and glanced around the room. It had been at least half an hour since the girl had died. The Light should have appeared for her by now. "But you're not hurting anymore, so that's good."

Wendy hated this part; making polite conversation with the dead strangers that filled her world until their Light arrived. She wasn't good at small talk with the living; why she felt compelled to keep the dead company right after their deaths was beyond her. Perhaps because it was the sort of thing Piotr did.

It didn't help that the script rarely varied: they asked if they were dead, she confirmed, she pointed out that at least they weren't in pain, they agreed. Sometimes there were protests or further questions, but the act of dying was enough to stun the average human soul into a slight fugue for a while, often long enough for their Light to appear.

"Yeah," the girl agreed and shuffled her feet. The remnants of her cord dangled like shifting seaweed from her navel. She noticed it and gingerly plucked at the cord, lifting it up and tentatively poking her index finger into one of the holes like a toddler examining her belly button. She winced as if she expected the poke was going to hurt but then relaxed, pinching the thin, tattered end of the cord curiously. "So . . . what now?"

A talker, huh? Wendy took a deep breath, sighed, and stood. "Well, when your Light gets here you step into it. No more mortal coil. Boom. Done." Wendy grimaced and pushed a frizzing red curl out of her eyes; getting a haircut and a fresh dye job was on the perpetual To Do list. "So if you've got any, err, final-final words, any secrets you feel compelled to spill to a friendly ear or a message you just have to get to someone, now would be the time to share." She grimaced. "I don't do revenge stuff, though. Just sayin'."

Dropping her cord, the girl squatted down beside Wendy's chair and prodded a chair leg, marveling at the way her hand slipped in and out of the metal. "Then what?"

"Then . . . I don't know. You pass on." Wendy shrugged, uneasy with the way the conversation was turning and uncomfortable with the way the girl was experimenting so easily with her environment. Normally the newly dead just wailed or wandered about in confusion; this girl seemed to be actively trying to figure out the physics of the Never. "I don't know what happens after the Light. Not really my jurisdiction."

Behind the spirit the room was beginning to lighten, a delicate whispering hum rose from nothing, and a tangy scent of ozone and hickory filled the air. Wendy grinned, thrilled to see the familiar sight though her nose itched at the aroma. "Looks like your ride's here."

A thin shaft of Light, no wider than a hair's breadth, broke through the hospital ceiling and struck the tile floor. Then it began to widen, filling the room with heat and Light, and the hum became a high, plaintive siren song like tinkling bells—a pleasant, sweet sound.

Rising fluidly out of her squat, the girl glanced over her shoulder at the Light, at Wendy, and at the Light again. Her hands twisted together; all of a sudden she was on the edge of tears. "Are you an angel?" she whispered plaintively. "Because I never . . . is that Heaven? Was I wrong? Before? Or is there . . . I mean . . ." She wildly gestured at the Light. "Is it my fault that I didn't know?"

"Not an angel," Wendy hurried to say, glancing down at her inartfully shredded fishnets and mud-caked motorcycle boots. No corset today, just a faded black tee over her favorite plaid mini, but she'd borrowed Eddie's ratty old motorcycle jacket and it was slung over the end of the bed, across his feet. No matter how goth her look got, they always wanted to know if Wendy'd been sent from some higher being. The angelic assumptions never ceased to amuse her.

"Not an angel, I promise. I don't know if there even *is* a Heaven, okay? The Light . . . that's . . . ." Wendy paused, looking for the right way to explain the Light. Her fall-back description always seemed inadequate, but it was the closest thing to truth she could muster.

The Light was getting stronger and stronger, the music rising to a lovely crescendo. Soon it would begin to fade, and Wendy didn't want to stall the girl; she settled, once again, on the pat reply. "It's like your elevator home, okay? Your one-way ticket to peace—call it Heaven, call it Nirvana, call it whatever you want—but it doesn't discriminate and it doesn't wait, so don't hang around here too long. Take my word for it. The Light goes away after a while. After that, well, you've got to find your own way home."

Wendy thought of the month before—how the White Lady, Wendy's own mother, driven insane by the sundering of her soul, had tricked Wendy and Piotr into a showdown in the basement of the Palace Hotel. There had been a dozen huddled Lost chained to the walls, drained and weak and crazed with hunger. In order to return to her body, the twisted thing Wendy's mother had decided to sacrifice Wendy. She'd almost succeeded, but Piotr had held Wendy's—even now, Wendy wasn't quite sure what to call it, but the easiest explanation was thinking of the orb of Light as her "power"—in the palm of his hand. He'd stubbornly refused to give the Light over and had instead allowed it to break.

Of those in the room, only Wendy and Piotr survived the blast of Light; Elle and Lily had escaped the basement and subsequent explosion by the skin of their teeth. James, Lily's love, had been one of the unlucky ones. Wendy still felt badly about his passing.

Wendy abruptly shook her head to clear the painful memory from her mind. "Believe me," she urged, "that when I say finding your Light a second time isn't easy, I mean it. It's not simple, it's nothing like this. Not at all."

"Oh. Okay." The girl, shivering, glanced between Wendy and the Light. Longingly, she looked at the chair another moment, marveling at the way her hand slid through the back and how her fingers wiggled out the other side. "I guess . . . I guess I'll go, then. Thanks for keeping me company."

Uncertain still, but her decision made, the girl started backing toward the Light. Worry for the girl niggled at the back of Wendy's head. She looked so small and young. She couldn't be much older than Wendy or Eddie. "You never said if you wanted me to pass a message on," Wendy reminded her quickly, listening as the siren song reached its peak. "Last chance."

"Nah," the girl said, nearing the edge of the Light. She tilted her head back and smiled sweetly, inhaling the scent and shivering with joy. "It's better this way." Then she paused and examined Wendy closely. "What about you? You seem like a girl who's known a lot of dead people in your time. You want me to pass a message on to the great beyond?"

"For me?" Startled by the unexpected offer, Wendy struggled for a reply. "I . . ."

"Last chance," the girl said and grinned, showing a sudden flash of humor. Smiling, resting in the outer nimbus of Light, she was no longer pale and wan, but slim and subtle and lovely, her hair backlit with Light. "But if you want me to punch someone in Heaven, sorry, I don't do revenge."

Glancing down at Eddie, Wendy chuckled softly. "Tell you what, if you see this guy's dad out there—name of Matt Barry—let him know I'm keeping my promise." She touched Eddie's knee and smiled sadly. "I'm trying to, at least."

"Matt Barry," the girl repeated and nodded once. She held her hand up to her Light and sighed deeply, a slow, grateful smile curling across her face. In the warm wash of Light her face appeared fuller, her hair brighter. Wendy realized that this was how she must have looked before whatever illness she'd had had begun to eat away at her body, to chew the edges of her willpower apart.

"Got it. I'll pass it on."

"Thanks," Wendy said.

The Light winked out and with it went the girl. Only a faint, charred circle on the tile spoke of what had happened to the spirit. No normal living soul would be able to see it, but Wendy was used to simultaneously peering into the afterlife and the living world. To her, the circle outlined in the Never was as clear in all its grim grayness as the bright orange chair she'd been sitting in.

Settling back in the bedside chair, Wendy took one of Eddie's cool hands in her own, rubbing small, soothing circles into the webbing between thumb and index finger.

"I'm trying, Eds," she said, turning her face away from the circle and trying not to picture Eddie vanishing into the Light, his teasing grin and crinkled smile gone forever.

Unbidden, an image of Piotr stepping into the Light came instead. Frowning and silently cursing her overactive imagination, Wendy pushed the unwelcome picture away and concentrated on her friend. Piotr was strong and he had Lily and Elle with him. He didn't need her. Eddie did.

"I promised your dad I'd take care of you," Wendy said, voice pitched low so the nurses wouldn't hear, her eyes stinging from weariness and unshed tears. She leaned forward and rested her forehead against Eddie's, noses touching, her fingers threaded through his.

"I'll find you," she whispered. "I promise."

CHAPTER ONE

Night in the Never fell slowly, a flag of silver-tinged darkness uncurling in a steadily rising dusk. Before meeting Wendy it had been centuries—no, more—since Piotr had seen real, living twilight. Most of his memories had been eaten by time and by death-workers like Wendy's mother, but he could still remember the way the stars would emerge in the fading light one by one, mysterious pinpricks dotting the sky. All else had been swallowed by vast stretches of time where the years piled up like cobwebbed shadows in the corners of his mind.

Then he'd met Wendy.

Now? Now he could catch the light of hazy twilight between flickers, though it wasn't nearly the same thing. Concentrating on the light did no good—he'd gaze out into the Never if he actively attempted to see the living lands—but when Piotr relaxed and went with the flow, sometimes the quality of the light would shift and change: brief, powerful flickers allowed him to see the world as Wendy must, in all its solid, living glory.

Though it had been only a little time since the White Lady's demise, Piotr had already realized that he'd been permanently altered by the encounter. The changes in his vision were one thing, the urge to strike out and discover his own origins another. The real question had become what to do next, how to live his afterlife, or if he even wanted to do anything special at all. Before, he'd had the Lost to protect, his duty as a defunct Rider to keep, but now he had nothing but Lily and Elle and his own ambition to guide him.

It wasn't enough.

Out of habit, Piotr wandered the familiar span of turf between

San Francisco and Mountain View, killing time by catching rides in the back of taxis and trucks and keeping a lookout for spirits in danger. Dark things wandered the city at night—Walkers and worse, who'd traded their humanity for the certainty of continued existence, even if it cost them their very souls—and Piotr had spent too many years as a protector, as a Rider, to willingly walk away from another ghost in trouble, be they Shade or Lost or anything else.

It was late though, past midnight, and rides were starting to grow scarce. He could have taken Caltrain, but by doing so he would have run the risk of being brushed by a passenger. Living heat burned fiercely and, after the explosion of Light that burned away most of the White Lady's army but left him intact, Piotr was finding himself far more susceptible to the touch of the living than he had been previously.

Without one of the Lost to help speed the healing process, it now took weeks to heal a burn from straying too near one of the living; for something as basic as an aimless train ride from point A to point B, Piotr was unwilling to risk the pain. Daring the unknown backseats of random cars, with the potential for infants in bucket seats or teenagers stretched out in the back, was risk enough.

Flashing red-blue-red stuttered through the darkness, and the SUV he'd hopped into at the last on-ramp slowed and changed lanes in deference to the sirens and light. Piotr, spotting the pile-up up ahead, rolled neatly out of the car through the side door and came to his feet in the breakdown lane. Glass was everywhere—some had even crossed over into the Never—and Piotr stepped over the glittering mess and made his way to the pile-up.

A child, no more than six, huddled on the side of the road. He was small and blond and sported a plain white tee over grass-stained jeans. He worried a baseball cap between his hands and rocked back and forth, forehead pressed to his knees. Piotr knelt beside him.

"I like that comic," he said gently, referencing the emblem emblazoned across the front of the cap, a large stylized *A*. "The hero is very quick, *da*? What I would give for a shield like a Frisbee. You see a bad guy and *whoosh*!" He made a grand swooping gesture with one hand, miming taking off an enemy's head with a flick of a wrist.

The kid snorted but didn't look up. His fingers clutched the cap tighter.

Piotr was familiar with this give and take. "I am Piotr," he said kindly, trying again. He waited.

Several minutes passed before the boy turned his face in Piotr's direction and looked him up and down. "Jamie," the boy said. "And you talk weird."

"To me, Jamie," Piotr said, grinning broadly now that he had the little boy's attention, "perhaps it is you who talks weird, *da*?"

"What does *da* mean?" Jamie straightened.

"Ah. It means 'yes,' yes?"

"Yes?"

"*Da*." Piotr flopped onto the ground beside the boy, stretching his legs so that his knees popped. "You know, Jamie, I think your name, it does not suit you. Heroes always have secret identities; I think we should pick out a hero name for you, hmm? Would you like that?"

Jamie's answering smile was tentative but sweet. He crossed his legs underneath him; his frightened rocking ceased. "Yeah? Like what?"

"Oh, I do not know. Perhaps Cap?" Piotr nudged the cap in Jamie's hand. "It is a good name. We could find you a matching star-spangled shield for your enemies."

Jamie shook his head so that his hair drooped over his eyes. He'd needed a trim before he'd died. "I can't do that, Cap's already taken!"

"Ah, so, true enough." Piotr positioned himself between the boy and the tiny twisted body the EMTs were now lifting out of the back of the car. A small, grimy hand, still clutching a Captain America baseball cap, flopped over the edge of the gurney before an EMT considerately tucked it and the cap back beneath the sheet.

"They took my mommy away," Jamie informed Piotr, leaning past him to watch as the EMTs loaded his body into the back of the ambulance. "The airbag went *poof* and she bounced all around. She's got a broken head and arm but I think the rest of her's gonna be okay."

"That happens," Piotr said, nodding. He glanced around for Jamie's Light but the telltale rays were nowhere to be seen. "You weren't buckled in?"

"I was," Jamie said and then blushed. "I dropped my cap," he confessed. "Mommy turned to yell at me for unbuckling my belt and *crash*! *Bash*! *Boom*!" He made a series of drawn-out grinding and crinkling noises to outline exactly what had happened to the rusted Mustang he and his mother had been riding in. Then he frowned. "It was loud."

"I see," Piotr said, and he did. This wasn't his first time sitting at the side of the road while the police cleaned up glass and oil. It wasn't even his thousandth.

"Well," Piotr said, realizing with quiet relief that he was on Rider duty once again, "I know a very nice place we can stay for a while until your Light appears. Will you come with me?" He rose to his feet and offered Jamie a hand. It was nice to be doing good work again, he mused as the first of the police cars drove away. It was wonderful to not feel so aimless and lost.

"My Light?" Jamie hopped to his feet and tucked the bill of his cap into the back pocket of his jeans before resting cool fingers in Piotr's open palm.

"I'll explain on the way," Piotr promised. As he walked and talked he saw Jamie's steps grow more confident, and his pace sped up. The after-death double vision must be fading, he realized. The living land was receding for Jamie, the Never pressing to the front. Soon Jamie would only see the grey and brooding Never as the bulk of the bright living world entirely faded away.

Piotr explained how sometimes, if you concentrated, you could faintly hear the shrillest, loudest living noises through the bulk of years, but they were muted, hardly more than faint whispers in the Never. He spoke of phasing through walls, thin in the Never, that were solid in the living lands, or how if a building or object were witness to enough powerful emotion, even after it had been destroyed in the living world a solid wall could remain in the Never, blocking passage.

The trip toward the abandoned steel mill Piotr's old clan had dubbed "the Treehouse" was much shorter than he remembered. Underfoot the road shimmered and shifted between buckled concrete and warped bricks, the striation of the roads that had existed before being layered on top of one another like packed sand on the beach.

They were almost to the Treehouse when he heard the scrape of stone on stone, the tumbledown sound of gravel shifting nearby. Immediately on edge, Piotr grabbed Jamie's wrist and yanked the boy behind him. When Jamie began to protest Piotr shushed him sharply, shoving a finger against his lips so hard he knew he'd bruise the next day.

"Walker," Piotr whispered, realizing only then that while he'd explained what Jamie would have to expect from being dead in the Never, he hadn't had the time to explain about the bogeymen that were the Walkers. Now was an inopportune time to learn.

"Stay back," he murmured, and fumbled at his hip, unsheathing the old bone dagger one-handed. Jamie hissed in surprise but Piotr didn't turn around. Just ahead, a few feet past a copse of skeletal oaks, Piotr watched the shadows shift.

Moving forward in the sliding hunter stalk Lily had taught him ages ago, Piotr balanced on the balls of his feet and shifted his toes under the crackling debris of the street. This slow stride made no noise and the relaxed stance of the shadow at the edge of the alley left Piotr confident that his presence had not yet been noted; he would easily be able to sneak up on the unwelcome visitor.

Rounding the corner, Piotr found himself face to rotting face with a black-robed Walker. The beast was, like all Walkers, grotesquely tall, slim, and bone white. Sections of its face were beginning to stretch against its bones, the desiccated flesh pulling taut against the ridge of cheekbone and jaw. Yellowing teeth clicked in a rough staccato as Piotr leapt forward, knife thrust outward, and stabbed the Walker in the shoulder.

"It dares!" hissed the Walker, swatting Piotr aside as if he weighed nothing. "The useless Rider flesh tries to sneak up on me!"

Unable to catch his balance, Piotr slapped hard against the side of the building, and cursed as the jagged bricks of the corner cut his left cheek in an irregular swath from nose to ear. He swiped the back of his hand against the wet spill of essence that sluiced down his chin and soaked his collar. Luckily his short flight and abrupt landing hadn't jarred the knife out of his hand. The bone blade wasn't even nicked.

"*Ny ti i svoloch'*," Piotr ground out, tightening his grip on the dagger, feeling the well-worn heft of it shift perfectly in his palm. "Of course, you must excuse me, but I just have this thing about foul dogs dropping in uninvited."

"You left this territory, flesh." The Walker stretched to its full height and swayed above Piotr menacingly. The hem of its robe fluttered about the yellow-bone shins, dangling hunks of rotting flesh slapping against its calves as it swayed left and right, left and right. "Riders are all gone. This land belongs to Walkers now."

"Over my dead body," Piotr snapped and dove for the Walker again. This time the once-man didn't even bother flinging him off— it merely let out a sound like grinding glass over asphalt, the best its stripped vocal cords could make of a laugh, and stood there while Piotr stabbed and stabbed and stabbed. Then it lifted its arms to reveal the swiss cheese he'd made of its cloak . . . and the skeletal frame beneath. None of his swipes had broken the taut, stretched flesh.

Piotr fell back a step to analyze the situation. This Walker was far tougher than he was accustomed to, and smarter. Usually a solitary Walker would run rather than risk its precious skin in a fight. So why was this one staying, mocking him? Since there were no Lost nearby, there was no reason to . . .

Stilling, Piotr went cold all over. It'd been weeks since he'd had a child, a Lost, to protect, and he'd forgotten all about Jamie in the heat of the fight! Spinning on his heel, Piotr rushed back around the corner to where he'd left the boy.

Jamie was gone. Only his cap, rapidly fading, remained.

Growling, Piotr scooped up the cap and scanned the area, hoping against hope that he'd hear a distant scream that would lead him in the right direction. The last of the cap, the tiny bit of Jamie's spiritual essence remaining, lost coherence. His fingers pressed together, and it was gone.

Jamie was gone.

Sick to his stomach with guilt, Piotr staggered a few steps away from the building, paying distant attention to the shadow at his back. The Walker was still laughing as it turned the corner and rested against the wall, the edges of its frayed hood trembling with glee.

"Rider loses something? So sad!" crooned the Walker. "Perhaps he is waylaid. It happens." The Walker was *too* nonchalant. It wasn't afraid of him in the least, which meant it had either recently fed well or it wasn't alone—or both.

"You are working in pairs," Piotr said, fingers clenching for the handle of his knife. Anger pulsed in a hard, steady beat behind his eyes, giving the clearing a stutter-flash look similar to what he saw when he let the visions of the living world sneak up on him. His fury felt like it was lighting up the night. "You haven't gone back to your old ways."

While the ghosts of adults and those of younger people, like the ones the Riders gathered in large, protective groups, tended to congregate where they'd had the most fun while alive, the Walkers had shed their silver cords and their souls in order to ensure their own sort of hideous half-life. For centuries they had been solitary, mistrusting creatures that avoided not only the light and heat of the living but also the other dead.

Until the White Lady came.

"Hunting alone?" The Walker waved a negligent hand as if to say *that is so yesterday*. "Why should we do so when it is so easy to draw foolish Riders away from prey?"

"Not all Riders are like me." Piotr put his back to the closest wall. "Most Riders go in packs. They're strong in will. Much stronger than a *beast* like you."

"Yes, we learn from the flesh!" The Walker cried, clapping its bony hands together. "She healed us, made us stronger, and taught us well! Many good lessons from the White Lady, yes! She says for us to work together, like flesh, like Riders do, like the other spirits do. It is hard at first but the White Lady had ways of making us follow her orders."

It touched its face, where the taut skin beneath the hollow eyes was crisscrossed with twisted ropes of scars and crosshatched brands burned into the flesh.

Despite his hatred of the once-man before him, Piotr winced in sympathy. He'd been well acquainted with the White Lady's persuasive methods. She'd been a master of healing the Walkers with a kiss or, if they angered her, stripping them to bare bones with a swipe.

It was no mystery why the Walkers had flocked to the White Lady, while they willingly subjected themselves to all sorts of agony in her employ. Living in the Never required a constant influx of willpower, the ability to keep slogging through the dim, gray days of eternity without looking too hard at the shadow of the world around you. The younger a person was when they died, the easier it was to keep going on in the Never. The young seemed to have an inexhaustible supply of willpower and hope.

Not so for souls who'd lived a longer life before passing into the

Never. It was often a struggle just to keep going, and adult spirits who found their will weakening had a limited number of choices— they could allow themselves to fade away, as the Shades did, or they could follow the path of the Walkers.

Being a Walker was to willingly become a monster; Walkers chose to cannibalize the essence, the unlived years, of other spirits. Those unlived years were most plentiful in the ghosts of children, the Lost. They could get nothing from the Riders, but the Lost were like ripe peaches, sweet and juicy and filled with life.

No one could remember when it had all begun, but it had been this way for eons. The Riders grouped together and protected the Lost from the Walkers, the Walkers did everything in their power to steal away the child-spirits every chance they got.

Then the White Lady—Wendy's mother—had come into the Never and everything had grown further twisted and wrong. The Walkers, normally untrusting and near feral, began to work together. And the Riders, normally a tight-knit group dedicated to the Lost's cause, had fallen apart.

Part of this, Piotr knew, was his fault.

"Jamie's gone," Piotr said, holding out his hand to show the Walker that the cap had vanished. "But you're still here. Didn't you want some of your prey?"

The Walker patted its midsection. "I eat when I eat. Tonight is not my night for prey. Tonight is my night for talking to the Rider. We knew you would come back if we waited long enough." It licked its lips. "You stink of female flesh, Lightbringer flesh, still. We knew you would come."

The anger drained away and Piotr was swept with sudden chills. *Lightbringer*. Wendy.

"We have parted," Piotr said carefully, certain now that he could hear rustling in the deepest, darkest shadows. He counted the individual movements that he could make out and was dismayed. Piotr's conversation with the Walker in front of him had allowed the others to sneak rather close. He put the count at somewhere between two and five more, each taking turns shifting closer.

"Maybe you part from living flesh, maybe not." The Walker leaned in from its ridiculous height, bringing with it a puff of air stinking of maggoty meat and pond scum roasting in the summer sun, and said, "The Walkers who are left think not. We talk about flesh, we talk about Lightbringer, and we say to ourselves, 'Why would they part?' It makes no sense, flesh. It is senseless."

For a moment, just the briefest of seconds, Piotr was tempted to laugh. Senseless indeed. He'd struggled with the decision to leave Wendy the entire time she lay comatose; endless hell. She'd looked so small and fragile in her hospital bed, childlike with her black-tipped curls tangled damply against her cheeks.

Piotr had loathed himself in those long hours, watching her sink deeper and deeper into the twilight-world of her own mind with no way to reach her, no way to draw her into the waking, burning heat of the living world. He knew; he'd tried everything he could think of to reach her soul, even once going so far as to kiss her, hoping it would be like a fairy tale, that she would wake in his arms and love him. He'd failed.

"I left her," he said to the Walker stiffly, "for her own good." And it was the truth, so far as truth went, even if there was more to it. Wendy had found herself in the hospital because he'd been unwilling to step away from how he felt about her, because he wouldn't allow her to become her mother's pawn; he'd been unwilling to sacrifice the Lightbringer's soul for his fellow Riders or even the Lost. He'd sworn to protect them and, when faced with a choice of losing Wendy or the Lost, had let an explosion of Light obliterate everyone in the room instead.

Somehow, out of them all, he alone came out unscathed. How he'd survived . . . well, that was still a mystery.

"The Lightbringer needs the likes of you?" The Walker chuckled again and its bones rattled in mirth. Piotr felt a wave of cold come off the Walker, a chilly breeze that reminded him not to let the Walker get too close lest it freeze his very essence and trap him there to be shredded apart. "Rider flesh has a high opinion of itself."

"You said you were waiting for me," Piotr snapped, annoyed now and revving up for a fight, trying to stay out of the cold air pockets but feeling pressed upon on all sides. He glanced left and right, trying to pinpoint exactly where the others would come from, or how he might turn their numbers to his advantage. "So what is it that you want? Some sort of deal, like the White Lady had with you? You wish this territory?"

"Want? Flesh wants to bargain with us?" Rocking back on its heels, the Walker shook its head and laughed its gravelly laugh. "There is no bargain with Walkers, flesh. You have bothered others too long."

"Others?" Piotr asked. "What others?"

"Others matters to flesh? Now? How funny! We come for you now because it is time. We are paid, we take care of you. You are example. To other Riders. To Lost. To Lightbringer. I am bored. We are done here. Goodbye."

The rustles had grown very close now. He could feel the encroaching cold, the ice that clung to branch and rock wherever Walkers trod. Now his breath frosted the air. Piotr knelt down.

He was tensed, preparing for the attack, when a long, yodeling war cry cut the air. Twin blades flashed as a slim, dark-haired woman darted from behind a nearby bush and leapt at the Walker.

A second shape darted by and Piotr found himself thrust aside into the rough-hewn wall by a familiar blonde figure. Slowing only a split-second to make sure Piotr was unharmed, Elle flashed him a quicksilver grin and leapt into the fray.

Watching the girls fight was like watching a ballet. Elle, who'd died a rich society girl in the late 20s, had been an only child of two world-jaunting glitterati. Her parents had no time for their darling only child but spared no expense when it came to her education,

interests, or hobbies. Fencing, archery, horseback riding, dancing—
Elle had tried it all and was good at most of it.

Lily, on the other hand, had lived the quiet life of a plains-dwelling
tribeswoman, a girl so long dead she couldn't even reliably recall the
various names of her tribe and only occasionally the names of her gods.
Her range of talents wasn't quite so varied, but the lithe brunette
unerringly wielded her twin bone daggers with lethal precision.

In moments the pair was flanked—five Walkers, all towering
above the tiny girls, all armed with their claws sharpened to razor-
fine points and stunning, slowing ice-breath.

The Walkers surrounded the girls and pressed forward on one
side, attempting to nudge them into a less advantageous position so
that they'd be overwhelmed, slowed by the cold. Piotr expected Lily
to fall back—she was adept at strategizing, especially during close
combat such as this—but instead she shrieked and flung herself forward, slashing high at the nearest Walker's face with one dagger and
punching low with the other.

Hissing, the Walker fell back, clawing at his hood, which
dropped to reveal the last few remaining wisps of sparse white hair
across his crown. His features were a desiccated maw of teeth and
rudely stitched-together twine frayed at the edges and seeping yellowing pus-like essence.

Elle, likewise, was aiming for the eyes or, at least, where the eyes
used to be. The Walkers fought hard but the girls fought harder,
recklessly ignoring the chill and dodging the sharpened hands.
Within minutes all but one Walker had fled the scene, bleeding and
cursing, leaving the pair facing the Walker who'd distracted Piotr
earlier. They stalked around and around, moving toward him as the
Walkers had circled Piotr, slowing only when Piotr stepped forward
and cleared his throat.

Though intimidated by their strength and skill, Piotr was also
pathetically glad of their support and his unexpected salvation.
Trapped in a group like that, he never would have thought to go for

the eyes, much less been willing to take on such heavy odds, even with another Rider at his side. Lily and Elle had hardly blinked before wading in and saving his skin—again.

The first Walker, backed up against a wall at this point, held still and silent, a ruined rabbit in a terrible snare. Looking between the three of them, it chuckled, seeming to appreciate the irony of falling prey to the fate it'd initially intended for Piotr.

"You seem to be at a disadvantage," Piotr told the Walker before crossing his arms over his chest and smiling thankfully at the girls. "But Elle, Lily, I am grateful for your intervention. *Spasibo*. You have my great thanks."

Elle shrugged. "You think we'd let a poor little bunny like you duke it out all by your lonesome, Petey? Some friends we'd be." She crouched a little lower and her skirt rode up, exposing a length of strong, tan thigh. The Walker shifted, claws twitching, and Piotr knew it was imagining punching through Elle's exposed flesh with its fingers, tearing her leg from her body. "These dizzy palookas were taking you for a ride."

"Indeed," Piotr agreed gravely, interspersing himself slightly between the Walker and Elle. "I noted that myself."

"We were too late to save the boy," Lily said coolly, lifting her daggers shoulder-height and easing back on the ball of her left foot. Piotr had seen her relax into this stance before; it allowed for a fluid, viper-fast movement to the left or right with only a slight shift in weight. "But rest assured, he is avenged."

"This is good," Piotr said and looked to the Walker. "Did you arrive in time to hear our talk?"

Elle snorted, rising so that her skirt once again covered more of her thigh. "Yeah, but why are you bothered about beatin' your gums at this one, Petey? What's the point? He's all balled up."

Now that she wasn't as exposed and vulnerable, the Walker chuckled and turned its face away from Elle. Slightly between them, Piotr relaxed.

"The flesh speaks in riddles. Always the talky-talky." The Walker flapped his fingers in a quacking motion. "Either do for me as you did before or let me walk, flesh. I live on short-time, the dawn comes."

"Ol' white and creepy here's right. We oughta stop futzing around and bump off the hood already." Elle rested one fist on her hip and leered darkly at the Walker. Then she glanced at Piotr and groaned, irritated. "Jeepers creepers! I know that look."

Lily, peeking at Piotr, sighed and relaxed her pose. The entire set of her body radiated disapproval. "As do I. Piotr, you do not wish us to finish this beast off? Why? What use does this abomination hold for you?"

"Patience," Piotr cautioned mildly, picking up the hilt of his shattered knife from the ground. "Something he said earlier struck me. He was asking about the Lightbringer. Then he suggested that he'd been sent by others. That he was, perhaps, taking the orders?"

Lily frowned. "Sent by others? Surely, I do not comprehend. The White Lady has been dispatched. Who is there to send such as these after you?"

"That's what I'm wondering. What genius would send this dew-dropper to give ol' Petey the bum's rush?" Elle narrowed her eyes at the Walker and, shoving Piotr over, waved her knife beneath the Walker's neck. "Come on, palooka. Talk and maybe we'll just take your teeth instead of your whole head."

"She speaks true. This is your last chance at salvation, beast," Lily agreed coldly, striding up to the Walker and holding the point of her dagger to his left eye. "Speak what you know and by Piotr's willing grace we shall allow you to continue with your poisonous ways. This time. Speak not and I promise the sting of my knives shall be but the first pain you feel tonight."

The Walker seemed to take her seriously. It hesitated and then shrugged. "Flesh is . . . persuasive. Perhaps it is the poison it coats over this blade."

Piotr glanced sharply at Lily. Poison? This was new. He made a mental note to ask her about it later.

The Walker, holding one bony hand outward in a gesture of peace, dug through its robe with the other until it found what it was looking for. He passed the object, a small sheet of tightly folded paper, to Lily and stepped back, putting plenty of space between her daggers and his face. Elle took the sheet from Lily's hand and unfolded it.

"Oh Petey," she whispered. "Have they got the goods on you." She held up the paper and Piotr was stunned silent when it turned out to be a sketch of his own face staring back at him. It was clumsily made, true, but he recognized the hand that'd done it. One of his Lost, Pandora, had been a budding artist and had been fond of drawing anyone who'd sit still long enough for her to capture the essence of their features. Piotr had often been a subject.

Piotr turned away, choked up. Dora was gone, obliterated in the same explosion that had put Wendy in the hospital and destroyed the White Lady. Seeing her art in such an unexpected way was like a punch to the throat . . . and heart.

"Those on Nob Hill send their greetings," the Walker said and, before Lily could react, slashed outward with sharpened fingertips. Yelling, Lily fell back. Elle, several feet away, spun on her heel to take the Walker on, but the creature fled through the closest thin wall, disappearing from sight with a flutter of grimy black fabric and a hollow, mocking laugh.

"They want ol' Pete delivered up to Nob Hill," Elle mused, plucking the drawing from Piotr's nerveless fingers and skimming it. "Hey Pocahontas, I'm having problems remembering, but ain't Nob Hill part of Council turf?"

"Last I recall the Council frequents the Mark Hopkins hotel, yes," Lily agreed. "I have hardly had dealings with them but it is wise to know the lay of the land when possible, especially regarding those more powerful than one's self. Yet then the question becomes this: why would they seek Piotr? He has always kept to himself along the canal and has not aggravated them. Why seek him out? It makes no sense."

"Petey? Hey, flyboy! Up'n at'em!" Elle snapped her fingers in front of Piotr's face. "You got a clue why the daddies and debs up Nob Hill way would want you floating on the Styx side of the Never?" When Piotr, frowning, didn't answer, she threw up her hands. "Useless."

Piotr's frown deepened into a scowl and he waved a hand in Elle's direction, aggravated at the interruption. His vision was flickering wildly. One moment the Never was clear as a bell; in the next, the living world lay over it like a film of shining plastic. "I am thinking, Elle. Be patient."

"Thinking like a glacier moves," she grumbled, but dropped to the ground and stretched out, tucking hands behind her head and gazing up at the stars. "Ugh, you'd think with all these calluses that my feet wouldn't hurt so badly after just a little hoofin' it."

"Wendy," Piotr said finally. "They mentioned that I stank of her still."

"Well you're no sweet summer morning, but you don't exactly stink either," Elle quipped. "Lightbringer, huh? Should've figured we weren't done with that dizzy dame."

"Hush," Lily said and was quiet for some time before approaching Piotr's side. "If you are in danger, Piotr, there is a chance that the Lightbringer is as well." She bit her lip and eased in front of him, making sure she had his full attention before continuing.

"It would be a great disservice to Wendy to ignore this warning. They sent a half-score of Walkers for you. How many would they send for one such as the Lightbringer? We are here, at your side, to fight with you, but the Lightbringer is alone. Is she even aware that some Walkers escaped the skirmish with the White Lady?"

Abruptly, Piotr shook his head. "*Net*. Such thoughts are a waste of energy and time. Wendy is strong, capable. She can take care of herself, no matter who the enemy or the number sent. On this you have my word."

He could see Lily struggling with the decision of whether to debate him further or not; after long moments her eyelashes drifted down and she nodded once, brusquely. "As you say, Piotr. You are familiar with the Lightbringer and her capabilities and I am not. For now, I shall follow your lead." Frowning, she reached out and gripped his wrist until he winced. "For now."

Lily stepped aside as Piotr, scowling and rubbing his wrist, moved to kneel beside Elle, still stretched out on the ground and flexing her tired feet. She raised one hand as if shielding her vision from the moonlight and winked at him.

"Hello Pete. Have a seat?"

He ignored her flirting and got straight to the point. "Elle, you are familiar with the Nob Hill, *da*?"

"I swung around the juice joints in that neck of the woods a time or two, sure." She closed her eyes and grinned at the memories. "Alive *and* dead, mind you."

"I believe I sense what Piotr may be contemplating," Lily said, settling cross-legged next to Elle. "It only stands to reason that you are well known on Nob Hill, due to your familiarity with the Pier."

"Pier's my turf," Elle grumbled, opening one eye with a scowl in Lily's direction. "Was my turf. Whatever. Familiarity ain't even close. Those lollygaggers tried sending a mulligan down my way a time or two early on, before they knew who they were futzing with. I made 'em get a wiggle on, *toute suite*. But I hadn't heard hide nor hair of them in months, so I figured they'd skeedaddled when the White Lady started sniffing round. Apparently not."

"Exactly," Piotr said, encouragingly. "You are the perfect emissary for me, then."

"Emissary?" Elle sat up. "You want me to crash a Nob Hill shindig? You've gone daffy!"

"Elle," soothed Lily, "if anyone can discover why the Council is sending Walkers after Piotr, it is you. You were born to affluence, you speak their language."

"Hell, guys," Elle groaned, "it ain't like you can drop a c-note on the ground and get that bunch of big cheeses to sing a pretty tune! There's *rules* up Nob Hill way! They don't just let any mook off the street up at the Mark Hopkins, and to them I'm just some wacky kid with arrows a'plenty!"

"All the better," Lily interjected smoothly, "for they are wise to recognize your prowess in battle. Elle, you know as well as I that Piotr would be worse than useless in this scenario, especially if the Council truly does wish him harm. He needs you. *We* need you."

"Thank you so very much," Piotr snapped, not bothering to hide the bitterness in his tone.

She flapped a hand at him. "I speak only the truth, Piotr. There is no room for your false pride. It took you long enough to believe our words when your memories were lax. Believe me, as you are now you would be naught but meat for their dogs."

"*Da*," he agreed, sighing heavily. "You are right. But I do not appreciate being called useless."

"'Worse than useless,'" Elle quoted with a dark grin. "Get it right, Petey, or I might not get all dolled up and rub elbows with the high hats up Nob Hill way."

"You will do this, then?" Lily touched Elle lightly on the knee, her expression concerned but cool. "Despite the potential danger?"

"What're a few goons to me?" Elle hopped to her feet and winked broadly. "Let's get a wiggle on. I've gotta be off my nut to wanna crash a Council brawl, but . . . for you two? I'd do anything."

CHAPTER TWO

T he sash of her window was stuck. Irritated, Wendy popped the side of the glass with the heel of her hand. It shifted with a shudder and she slid the window up without further problem.

Sliding one leg through the window and into her bedroom, Wendy paused to muse on how ridiculous she felt. Her father was out on assignment again—he was one of the best efficiency experts in Silicon Valley, sent in as a hatchet-man to strip down companies and build them back up again—but reorganizing behemoth mega-corps usually took weeks at best and chances were that he wouldn't be home for another week. There was no logical reason why she should be sneaking home through her window like a thief again.

Since the death of her mother, her curfew had been lifted. Wendy could have stayed out until dawn and sauntered in at break-fast without earning herself so much as a raised eyebrow. Still, it just felt *right* to be coming in this way, no matter if it made sense or not.

"Just go with it," she muttered under her breath as she closed the window behind her and drew her curtains down. The twins were both still up—as usual, she could hear them arguing about something in the kitchen.

Wendy had no more than sat on her bed and begun unlacing her right boot when thunderous steps pounded up the stairs and a fist hammered at her door.

"Yeah?" she called, making a face at the door and stifling a groan. She was exhausted. Couldn't refereeing Chel and Jon's bick-ering wait until morning?

Chel opened the door and stuck her disheveled blonde head

through the crack. Wendy was amused to see that her sister had only slathered on part of a facial mask; half her face was fluorescent pink, the other splotchy with acne. "We need you."

"You need me," Wendy repeated dryly, glancing at the ticking cat clock on the wall. "Right now. At midnight."

Narrowing her eyes, Chel thrust the door open the rest of the way. In addition to the half-done mask, she wore one of their mother's tattered old robes, once a vibrant red and now a washed out, streaky pink, and a much-mended pair of Wendy's old Hello Kitty PJ bottoms frayed at the knees. Jon's favorite yellow slippers were comically overlarge on her feet.

"Yeah, you sanctimonious butthead, now is when we need you." Chel glared at Wendy, ignoring her older sister's smirk at her appearance. "You don't have to be an ass about it."

"I don't care about whatever you two are arguing about, Chel," Wendy sighed, unlacing her boots and toeing them off. She wriggled her feet in the carpet and sighed appreciatively. "I really don't. Kill each other, for all I care. I'm not getting in the middle of another fight."

"Oh please," Chel said, rolling her eyes and running a hand through her hair, pushing the bleached blonde back so Wendy could see the untouched red roots beneath. "Jon-shmon, we don't want you to judge a debate, this is important."

"Fine. Fine!" Wendy stood, crossing her arms over her chest and resisting the urge to kick her sister in the shin. "What is it?"

"Lose the skirt, grab some jeans, and shut up," Chel snapped and waved for Wendy to follow. Wendy stuck her tongue out at Chel's back but shimmied quickly out of her mini, yanked an old, grungy pair of jeans off the top of the mend pile, and, hopping on one foot as she donned the pants, followed her sister downstairs. Chel waited in the kichen with the heater on and the back door open. Jon hovered in the doorway, distressed, crossing and uncrossing his arms and shifting nervously from foot to foot.

"I wasn't sure you were home," he said apologetically as Wendy, grabbing a pair of their father's old sneakers from beside the door, turned the corner. "But Dad said you were in charge and . . . well, you just seem to be *better* at this sort of stuff than we are."

As Wendy joined him in the doorway, he shifted his bulk out of the way, and Wendy bit her lip to keep from mentioning the fresh plate of cookies on the counter. Jon was supposed to be on a diet, but he was a stress-eater and the last few months had been stressful as hell. She ought to say something, she knew, but Jon was so mournful about bothering her and edgy in general that Wendy didn't have the heart to get on his case about it. *Besides*, she reasoned, *maybe they weren't for him.*

"What sort of stuff? And shut the door, you're letting all the warm air out." Curious now, Wendy glanced around the kitchen. Nothing, besides the cookies, *seemed* out of the ordinary.

Blocking Jon from shutting the door with her arm, Chel shook her head. "Can't you *hear* it?"

"Hear what?" Wendy froze and listened, but she couldn't understand why Chel was so agitated. Everything was still and silent.

"Deaf as a post. Come on." Chel grabbed Wendy by the wrist and dragged her into the black backyard. Jon shut the door behind them, blocking the light from the kitchen and leaving them in chilly darkness. He tripped heavily following them down the stairs.

Allowing her sister to haul her across the yard, Wendy shivered. It was uncommonly cold out, even for Northern California, and the air smelled like a mixture of sharp ice shards and the last of the rotting, unplucked oranges drooping from their neighbor's citrus trees.

They had reached the back shed before Wendy heard it. Soft, muffled keening sounds. Pain, very clearly pain.

"It's a raccoon," Chel whispered, fumbling in the robe pocket and coming up with a palm-sized LED flashlight. She passed the light to Wendy. "Look."

"A raccoon?" Wendy took the light but didn't turn it on. "You dragged me out here for a raccoon? Can't you call Animal Control or something?"

"This close to New Year's?" Chel's voice dripped derision. "We tried that already and the automated system thingy said no one will be in the office for another three days."

Startled, Wendy shook her head. "Isn't that illegal? Aren't they supposed to have someone on call for crap like this? What if it's rabid or something?"

"I don't know if it's rabid, but it's definitely hurt. Look, already. Use the frickin' light."

Nervous now, Wendy pressed the face of the flashlight into her palm to dim the brightness and slowly turned the body of the light until she heard a click. It was a powerful light for being so small; her palm lit up pink and she could make out the veins in her hands easily.

"I don't want to piss it off," she whispered to Chel.

"I think it might be past the point of getting pissed off," Chel whispered back.

Jon touched her shoulder and Wendy almost yelped out loud. *Stupid, stupid, stupid,* she berated herself savagely. *You can face down a bunch of Walkers with their faces rotting off with hardly a blink but you come across one hurt animal and you jump like a little girl? Seriously? You big baby, get it together!*

Gingerly, expecting the raccoon to leap out at her like a chest-burster from a horror flick, Wendy lifted the light to the filthy shed window. What she saw broke her heart.

The raccoon, so far as Wendy could tell, wasn't the huge grizzled veteran of forest and highway she'd been expecting. It was younger, a juvenile, and twisted into a ball in the corner of the shed. Half of its body was black with dried blood; one forearm had been torn nearly off, and half of its face was matted with clumps of missing fur and jagged, weeping gashes. The stump that had once been a perky ear waved weakly as Wendy lit the shed; Wendy turned her face away, heart pounding.

It was still alive.

"Oh, poor baby," she whispered, handing the light to Jon and slumping down the side of the shed to bury her hot face against her knees. *Don't cry, Wendy*, she thought fiercely, *don't you dare cry*. "What happened?"

"Dog? I don't know." Chel's voice quivered. "It doesn't have three days to wait for help, Wendy."

"At this rate it doesn't even have three hours," Jon said. "Not in this cold." He twisted the flashlight until the LEDs flicked off. "What do we do?"

"I can call the 24-hour vet," Chel suggested, rubbing her hands up and down her arms. "Mom's rolodex is still in the cabinet, right?"

"I don't think they take wild animals," Wendy said, wracking her brains for the right course of action. Why did Dad have to be out of town? Why now, when they needed him?

"Then what do we do, Wendy?" Chel knelt beside Wendy and pushed a hank of Wendy's hair off her face. "Because we're out of ideas over here."

Now, up close to the shed, Wendy marveled that she hadn't heard the raccoon before. Its pain was whisper-bright, like silvery bells chiming in the Never, audible in an unexpected way, like slivers of ice against the back of her neck.

Wendy remembered her mother's cat Jabberwocky, how he'd hung around after his death and kept Wendy company in the lonely months after her mother had been hospitalized. Jabber'd been spying on her for the White Lady but Wendy hadn't known that at the time; she'd been grateful for his ghostly presence, no matter how touchy he could get at times, and even if it was weird to hang out with a dead cat. According to Piotr, animals could communicate in the Never, she remembered. Hopefully this one wouldn't be the exception to the rule.

"Go see what Google has to say," Wendy told Jon, holding her hand out for the flashlight. "See if there's any other company we can call." She pushed off the wall to stand and looked at Chel. "You phone the vet. See if they're willing to take him. It. Whatever. I'll stay here for a minute, see if I can figure something out." She waved her hands at her siblings. "Go. Shoo."

Silently they followed orders, slipping inside the house like ghosts themselves. Wendy waited until she saw Chel's shadow moving around in her bedroom upstairs to call upon the Light and slip through the thinnest side of the shed in the Never rather than waking the neighbors by risking the noisy, rusted squeal the shed door usually made. Once inside she coalesced back into her living shape, eyes open to the spiritual realm.

The spirit of the raccoon huddled in the same corner as its body. Thankfully its incorporeal body was in much better shape than its physical one. The physical shell hardly twitched at her approach; up close Wendy could see the narrow gap in the back of the shed. Where the shed pressed against the overgrown hedge and honey-suckle at the back of their yard, some animal—perhaps this raccoon, perhaps something else—had carved out a sizeable tunnel to allow easy passage from yard to yard, making their shed a nice, cozy haven.

"Hi," Wendy said nervously, kneeling down. "Do you under-stand me?"

The soul of the raccoon sniffed at her hand and Wendy *felt* what it meant to convey rather than heard what it was saying.

It was like a waterfall of images, nothing like what she'd ex-pected after discussing animal communication with Piotr. He'd described it as words in your head, but this was more like a rapid-fire slideshow shot directly into her brain, accompanied with tastes and smells that left Wendy momentarily shaking and overwhelmed.

Moldy bread. Apples. Open bags of Cheetos, jagged Sonic bags with hot dog remnants. Carrot tops and onion roots and dead squirrels and half a garden snake. A bent can of tuna fish. Cold, salty fries out of greasy card-board cups. Licking days-old sauce off of In & Out wrappers.

"No, I don't have any food right now," she apologized, stunned by the depth of the raccoon's expression. "I'm sorry. What happened?"

Separated from its mother, from its family. Tried to follow the smell but found a cat. Big cat. In the hills. Dog. Smelled the blood. Chased the raccoon. Sleep. Exhaustion. Pain in face, pain in ear. Another dog, this one bigger, meaner, no shiny around its neck. A stray. Big. Black. Teeth, nails, pain. Then . . . people smells.

Not supposed to go to people smells, stay near woods, stay near shiny cans with good food at edge of woods, but never people. People are mean. People hurt with big sticks. But pain. Dog won't go into people places. Run, limp, hide. Pain in neck. Pain in face. Pain. So thirsty. Front leg hurts lots. Paw doesn't work. Back leg doesn't work, drag it. Found old tunnel. Thirsty. So thirsty, but finally found good smells, this people house smells like tunnel, like woods. This people house smells like peace. Rest. Sleep. Quiet. Safe.

Slowly it dawned on Wendy what the raccoon was trying to get across. She knelt down beside him, swallowing deeply, and fought the tears pricking the corners of her eyes.

"You came here to die," she whispered. "You can smell . . . you know what death smells like?"

The raccoon's spirit ears flicked and Wendy got a clear image: the raccoon's father crawling away from the highway, back legs crushed and covered with the blood-rust-salt smell of death, one of the raccoon's sisters—only a pup—clutched in his mouth. She tumbled safely down the embankment into the rich loam at the edge of the woods, stinking of death, and then, after a long, long time, their father died, curled on the side of the road while the people sped past.

The others went into the woods but this raccoon didn't; he waited until his father died to rejoin his family. He sat vigil. He waited. Anger, helplessness, frustration, sorrow. But most of all, the overwhelming feeling of *want-to. Want-to-help. Want-to-fix. Want-to-make-the-pain-stop. Want-to-want-to-want-to.*

Wendy swallowed thickly, a tear tracking down her cheek as she thought of all the hours she'd spent at her mother's bedside, talking to her mom's unmoving body, ignoring the beeping machines and savagely wishing that whatever had happened to her had just finished her off in one fell swoop rather than leaving her mother a slowly degrading shell of her former, fiery self.

"I . . . I can't," Wendy said, scrubbing a hand along her face. "You're going to die anyway, right? So I don't have to . . . to do this. Right? Right?"

The raccoon blinked.

Wendy shivered. "Don't look at me like that."

A tap on the window made Wendy jump and stagger back, cracking the back of her head against the dusty shelf lining the side wall. A watering can tumbled down and smacked the raccoon on the haunches. He stirred in the living world and a flood of guilt left Wendy shaking.

"I'm so sorry!" she gasped, snatching the can up and setting it aside as Chel and Jon forced the shed door open. It squealed just as loudly as Wendy had suspected it would.

"How did you get in here?" Chel panted, watching the raccoon curled in the corner sadly. "More importantly, either one of us could probably bench you one-handed, so how did flimsy little *you* close it again?"

"Not important," Wendy said, handing off the flashlight to Jon again. "What did they say?"

"No one is answering," Jon said as he turned the flashlight on and set it on the shelf Wendy'd smacked her head on. "I Googled as hard as a guy can Google and it's all voicemail and 'Have a happy holiday!'" He scowled, the shadows lying darkly across half his face. "Figures."

"The vet?"

"They don't handle cases like this," Chel said, scorn dripping from each word. "The night assistant said to just let it curl up and die and not to approach it. Rabies." Chel glanced down and shook her head. "Though you shot that right out of the water, huh?"

Nervously, Wendy licked her lips. "It's in pain, guys. Real, serious pain. And it's going to die anyway. We all know that, right?"

"Duh," Jon said, not unkindly. "But what do we do about it? I don't think there's any way we can make it more comfortable before it dies. And hauling a heater out here to keep it warm before it dies might start a fire."

His legs were completely crushed but he finished crawling across the highway, Wendy thought. *When I'm a mom I hope I'm half as good a parent as that.*

"I have an idea," she said softly. "Jon, is Mom's old spade-fork-thing in the garage? And the rake and shovel?"

Jon paled. "Yeaaah," he drawled. "Why?"

Wendy forced a sad smile. "I'm going to put it out of its misery. Go get the fork and a pair of Mom's old gardening gloves. And a garbage bag. Two. No, three."

"Wendy, I don't know—" Jon began but stopped when Chel grabbed him by the arm.

"You sure?" Chel studied the raccoon. "It's going to be bloody. And it really *might* have some kind of disease. There's no foam or anything, but—"

"If it were me," Wendy said, "I'd want to be put down. Okay? I wouldn't want to linger."

Jon stiffened. "This isn't about Mom, Wendy—"

"Just get the damn fork, Jon!" Wendy snapped. Then she winced, regretful of her tone. "Sorry. Sorry. This is hard. Just . . . please, Jon. Please. Get the fork. And the plastic. Especially the gloves and maybe a latex pair from under the sink too, just to be safe. Okay?"

Softening, he nodded. "It's okay. This is rough. I'll get all the stuff, but I just want you to know that you don't have to do this."

"If not me, who? You? Chel? I saw those cookies, Jon. You both have been doing so well with your personal stuff, neither of you need to be freaked out right now. I can take care of it." She smiled wanly.

"That's what I'm here for, to do the tough stuff. I've got this. I promise."

Jon opened his mouth to reply but thought better of it. "Okay. Point taken. You're just trying to look out for us. Thank you." He hugged her briefly with one arm, turned, and left, leaving Chel and Wendy huddled around the raccoon's body.

"We could maybe bundle it up in a blanket instead," Chel offered softly. "I bet if we showed up at the vet they could give it a shot or something, even if it's not policy. No one likes to see an animal in pain."

"They won't," Wendy said. "You know they won't."

"This sucks." Chel rubbed a hand across her mouth. "I wish Mom was here."

"Me too," Wendy said softly, still brooding on her mother, on the Walkers, on the past few months and Eddie wasting away in his own hospital bed, the girl one bed over slipping into the Light that hadn't yet come for him.

How long would Eddie lay there because his mother couldn't do what Wendy was about to do? And what would Wendy do if Mrs. Barry decided to grow a pair and pull the plug before Wendy found Eddie's soul and his cord? She shivered. It was too much to think about right now. Better to concentrate on the mute, agonized animal at her feet. Better to handle one thing at a time.

"Hey Chel?" she said softly. "I meant it, by the way."

"You mean it?" Chel's hand on her wrist was humid and hot, the skin damp from nervous sweat. She may have quit cheerleading, but her fingers were still strong, her grip still sure. Their mother's cracked and ancient floor-length mirror leaned against the opposite corner; Chel, faintly lit by moonlight, looked ghostly in its silvered reflection, all color bled away, a shadow of a girl in grey and white. "What do you mean, Wendy?"

Wendy turned her face away from Chel's reflection. Lights from the street were reflecting strangely in the depths of the mirror, red dots, probably streetlights, floated over Chel's left shoulder like hanging eyes, giving Wendy an uneasy feeling deep in her gut. Crazily, she wished Piotr were here. He'd been around forever, right? Maybe he'd tell her the easiest way to do this, the easiest way to kill another living being, even if it was some dumb animal whose best idea of security was pillaging rest stop trash cans for refuse.

"If . . . if I'm like this . . . in pain and wounded, please, please pull the plug," Wendy whispered, scrubbing her hands across her face. "Don't let me suffer, okay?"

"Eddie's going to be okay," Chel said, misunderstanding Wendy's nervous energy.

"I know he will," Wendy agreed. "I'm going to make sure of it. But this isn't about Eddie. If I go under again . . ."

"I'll let Dad know," Chel promised. Then, softly, "You ready? Here comes Jon."

It took only a moment to prepare; Wendy donned the thick gloves and claimed the long-handled spading fork, which had been used to turn their mother's compost heap before she'd bought the tumbler two years before. The tines weren't as needle sharp as she'd have liked, but they weren't dulled by years of use, either. Their mother had been conscientious about her tools. She'd been conscientious about most things, actually; a fact Wendy had only recently really started appreciating.

"Jon, take the shovel," she ordered nervously. "Chel the rake. Jon, point the light this way, okay?"

In the Never, the raccoon moved away from them, avoiding their living heat by huddling behind the mirror and peering around the edge. He bared his teeth at the mirror for a moment, and Wendy wondered what the reflective surface looked like to the spirit. She knew that she could ask, but there were more important tasks at hand.

"I'm sorry," Wendy said out loud, both for the raccoon to hear and for Chel and Jon. This was going to suck.

Chel used the rake to turn the body onto its back as best as she could; Jon used the shovel to press the head as gently as he could into the floor. Chel pressed the rake into its belly, so they were effectively holding it down. The raccoon, so far gone, whimpered only a little.

Shaking wildly, it took Wendy four tries to line up the tines with the animal's chest, centering the middle tines over the heart as best as she could. "Sorry," she whispered again. "Sorry-sorry-SORRY!"

At the last "sorry," she shoved down with the fork with all her weight, feeling the metal prongs punch through fur and flesh and jab themselves into the rotting floor beneath, the squish of the heart squelching around the tool, and the hot splatter of blood gushing against her shins. The raccoon keened once, twice, and jittered for a moment against her boots before going limp and still.

"I'm going to be sick," Jon said, and retched on the raccoon. The backsplash joined the blood on Wendy's jeans.

"Mom," Wendy said, turning to look up at the ceiling as her brother and sister staggered out of the shed, both gagging, "if you're out there somewhere . . . please make sure that these gloves don't have holes in them."

Though they'd helped with the death, neither Jon nor Chel was able to bundle the body up in the garbage bags. They took turns digging a hole in the corner of the yard instead, nervously joking about ground water contamination while Wendy eased the stiffening corpse into the garbage bags by herself and scrubbed the floor down with a bucket of bleach-water.

The raccoon vanished in the Never; no Light came for it. One moment it was there, watching Wendy dispose of its body, the next it was a flick of a tail over the edge of the back hedge and rapidly running along the fence toward the highway. Wendy sent good thoughts its way and kept scrubbing, letting the swish-dunk-scrub-scrub-scrub keep her body occupied, and sank thankfully, mind-lessly, into the zen of cleaning.

It was past one when the deed was done, the dirt was tamped down, and the only other evidence of their deed was crusting on Wendy's pants. She didn't even wait to get inside the house before stripping off her jeans and her father's sneakers, flinging them both into the garbage can beside the door to the kitchen. Jon took a cookie from the stack as they entered; Chel, surprisingly, did so as well. Wendy, stomach churning, bounded pantslessly up the stairs, ready to call this terrible day a wash and go to sleep.

Stripping off the remainder of her clothes and flinging her top at the closet and herself on her bed, Wendy smacked her knuckles against the seatbelt buckle she'd tucked between her pillows that morning. Whimpering in pain, Wendy yanked the buckle out and glared at it; her first instinct was to chuck it against the far wall, but the buckle had been Eddie's. It was a seatbelt buckle from his father's car, scavenged for Eddie after the wreck that took his dad's life and woke Wendy to her Lightbringer duties and the Never. He'd given it to Wendy a few weeks prior, just as school had let out for the holidays, along with a love letter and a promise to bide his time and wait for her to love him as much as he loved her.

Now, sitting on her bed, Wendy turned the buckle over in her hands again, weighing its heft in her hands, her subconscious mind ticking aimlessly along as she stared at the edges of the buckle and depressed the button in the middle with her thumb. The buckle was jammed, locked, stuck in one spot. Like Eddie.

"Eddie," Wendy mused, letting her eyes relax, letting the Never swim in and out of view. "Eddie, Eddie, Edd—"

She suddenly broke off. Wait a second. Wait just a second . . .

Before, Piotr had brought her items from his kidnapped children. Pieces of them that stayed solid as long as the children were safe and in one piece. A hat, a cloak, spectacles, all firm and solid in the Never so long as the children they belonged to still existed in the Never.

Just like Eddie's buckle.

Examining the buckle in the Never was something Wendy had never thought to do before; she opened herself up and was happy to see that her impulse had been correct.

The buckle was as solid in the Never as it had been in real life. Wendy poked it and the clasp clicked, coming apart slightly in her hands before catching on some inner cylinder and jamming. With a little bit of force, Wendy was able to click it shut again.

Excited, Wendy flung herself off her bed and hurried to her closet, grabbing the closest comfy outfit and dressing as fast as she could. Her boots were on a minute later and Eddie's jacket was in her arms before she was out the door, bounding back down the stairs and speeding past the twins as she burst out the front door and sprinted toward the car.

"Where are you going?" Chel called from the front stoop as Wendy revved the car and slapped it into reverse.

"Hospital!" Wendy yelled back. "Be back soon!"

Thankfully it was the middle of the week—even the cops seemed to be resting after the excesses of the holidays, and the highway was nearly empty as Wendy hurried up the familiar route toward the hospital and Eddie. Christmas was over, but KOIT-FM was still playing holiday tunes; Wendy cranked a jazzy *Jingle Jingle Jingle* remix and tapped the steering wheel as the 101 spun out beneath her tires.

CHAPTER THREE

The air of the Never was thick tonight, filled with the cold of the bay and heavy with fog. In the distance foghorns called across the water, their echoes dimly heard even as far as Nob Hill. Piotr, lounging on the sidewalk below the huge hotel, tilted his head up. The foghorns weren't the only echoes reaching the street. Tonight the Top of the Mark rooftop bar was jumping with spirits—though the restaurant had closed to the living at midnight, the party for the dead had barely begun.

A faint movement to his left revealed Lily and her blades. As she approached she sheathed the bone knives and held her hands wide, welcoming him. "The perimeter is clear," Lily murmured, brushing a thick black braid over one bare shoulder.

Tonight she'd formed her essence into a lightweight version of the cotton *manta* and deerskin moccasins she'd worn in life; generally Lily kept her clothing nondescript, but Piotr had known her long enough to tell that she, like Elle, felt that tonight, visiting the Council, was a night to honor who they had once been. Faintly jealous, Piotr glanced down at his own basic shirt and black pants. If only he could do the same. Lily didn't notice his comparison. "No Walkers roam these streets."

Piotr was glad. He was still shaken up over the previous night's encounter, and tangling with Walkers this close to downtown was never a good idea. The White Lady's territory hadn't been too far from here, cunningly hidden amid the lush vastness and living heat of the city; there was no telling how many of her trained Walkers had escaped that deadly fight and still haunted her old locale.

"*Prekrasnah*," Piotr declared, grinning and leaning against the balustrade. His gaze flicked up to the top of the hotel again and he fancied that he saw thin, white faces looking down. "This news is very good, Lily. Have you any word from Elle?"

"None yet," Lily said, sliding beside him to stand in the shadow of the matched columns guarding the entryway. In the dappled moonlight she was as still as a doe, wary and watchful but peaceful nonetheless. "The moon is high, yet she is still speaking with the *cacique* of this place."

"I wish she would hurry."

"In time all things come," Lily soothed. "We shall journey on to the great wide world soon enough, and then," she spread her hands out, as if encompassing the city, "then you shall miss this and wish we had stayed."

When Piotr did not rise to the bait, she touched his shoulder. "The words of the Walker last evening concern me. You claim that you and Wendy have parted, but I wonder. Have you spoken yet with the Lightbringer, Piotr? Have you truly said your goodbyes?"

"*Da*," he snapped, pulling away from his old friend. Some days, he fancied that Lily had a healer's soul; she was gifted with a knack for prodding his sore spots, exposing festering pain, both physical and mental. Normally he allowed her the little jabs and probing, as he almost always felt better after speaking his mind to her, but Piotr was protective of his feelings for Wendy. He didn't want to discuss the Lightbringer with her. "Wendy and I are through; she understands what I must do."

"What you must do, yes, but Piotr . . ." Lily glanced up at the riotous rooftop. "What about what help you swore to her? If it were not for her—"

"If it weren't for Wendy then James would still be with us," Piotr said through gritted teeth, ignoring the way his stomach clenched at the low blow. Lily and James had been together for decades until Wendy's Light had destroyed James. With him gone, Lily had fallen into mourning for days. No matter who spoke to her, she was unwilling to do more than sequester herself amid the lush thickets of Apatos Village Park and pray to her gods for James' safe passage into a kinder afterlife than the Never. When her praying was done, Lily left the park with her head held high and a refusal to speak of her pain on her lips. It was her way, and until now Piotr and Elle had respected it, but if mentioning James' death moved her to silence, Piotr was willing to broach the topic.

"Perhaps," Lily said mildly. "Perhaps not."

Unwilling to get into a fight with his oldest friend over Wendy, Piotr turned his back on Lily and scowled out into the darkness. Though the fog was thick, he could still make out the shapes of lighthouses in the distance and the thin moonlight drifting down. Shapes moved at the base of the hill—humans and the dead alike. It was late though, past one, and there were no crowds milling about to burn the weeping, wandering Shades with their searing, living heat.

If Wendy were here, Piotr thought, she would send the Shades on into the Light. In truth, the act would be a blessing. Their minds were long gone.

These past few weeks, Piotr had tried to avoid thoughts of Wendy, but it was difficult to do when Lily insisted on continuously poking his pain. He would never admit it out loud but he missed the sight of her, the electric fire of her touch. He and Wendy had parted ways amicably, but all Lily seemed to see was that they had parted.

Piotr knew that it had been the right decision, leaving Wendy. It *had*.

"It was James' time, as it was time for the Lost," Lily added coolly, dismissing his moody silence outright. "Piotr, it is as if you think I do not know the ways of the Never! After these many years? For all my love for James, his will to continue existing was weakening. In truth, he was very lucky that the Lightbringer came along when she did; Wendy saved him from great pain." She looked at the Shades below and shook her head, expression grave. "The Light washed over him and he moved on. It is as it should have been. It is done. It is good."

Piotr crossed his arms over his chest. He did not like where this conversation was going or how thoroughly Lily was derailing his points. "That is not how Elle sees it."

"Elle is angry," Lily said, frowning. "Her emotions are not the Lightbringer's concern."

"Nice," Piotr snorted.

Lily gestured to the Shades below. "Look at them and know that I speak the truth. Piotr, for all your protestations, you *know* this in your heart. It is not Wendy's duty to keep the dead and our relationships with one another intact. It is her job to send suffering spirits on—spirits like them, spirits like you, spirits like myself, and yes, even spirits like the Lost or James."

Startled, Piotr glanced at his old friend, troubled and wary. "You think I suffer?"

Lily's fists relaxed and she smiled sadly. "Yes. We all do, Piotr. If we did not . . . would we need aid to find the Light we once spurned so thoughtlessly?" She touched him gently on the shoulder. "As once you taught me, I shall now teach you. Hear my words and attend me, Piotr, for your very soul, listen well: the lost souls of children are no longer our duty. The Riders you began are no more. We must spurn the Lost. We have more important goals now. I know that, and so do you. One day Elle will know that as well."

"One day I'll know what?" Elle's approach through the front doors of the hotel had been soundless and swift. She'd shaped her essence into a flashy red-fringed gown for her meeting upstairs, her bobbed blonde tresses clinging to the sides of her head in elaborate pincurls. Careless of Piotr's presence, Elle hiked up her already short skirt and adjusted her left stocking, rolling it just above her knee and pinning it there.

"That's better," she said and swished her hips, grinning at the rustling fringe.

"Indeed?" Lily drew away from Piotr and crossed her arms across her chest, still half-clothed in shadows. "How was hunting?"

Elle threw her hands up and spun around. "There's one hell of a rub going on up top."

"Indeed?" Piotr asked dryly. "Do go on."

Rolling her eyes, Elle ignored his tone and spoke to Lily instead, nearly gushing with glee. "The band is laying down some smoking licks and every snifter is the real McCoy—Kentucky Mountain Gold!" She giggled and flapped a hand at her face. "I swear, I'm flying off fumes alone!"

"The crowd is indeed thick," Piotr murmured. "We can hear them from here."

"It's a real crush," Elle agreed. "Every spirit up there is over-flowin' with years and I haven't seen so many folks cutting a rug since I was alive."

"Such revelry seems imprudent. I wonder why they celebrate so," Lily mused.

Elle shrugged. "Makes sense to me. Everyone's been in hiding since the White Lady claimed this chunk of the city, right? But since the Lightbringer blotted her out even the babbitts want a night out on the town. It's a real dead man's bash up there!"

"If there is so much revelry," Lily said slowly, "and safety, then the Council is most certainly making no end of profit off these endeavors."

"The sawbucks are falling like rain," Elle agreed. "When I had a chance to squeeze past the hoofers and get a word in, I spotted better than two or three hundred thousand in trade piling up behind the bar. Most of it was hard scavenge too, useful stuff like heaters and ice. Bone knives. Even a couple of copper pipes, polished up nice and weighted." She knocked her knuckles against a temple. "Take a Walker down quick."

"The Council is collecting guns and weaponry?" Piotr frowned. "Without bullets, what is the point?"

"Who knows? So long as they can't point 'em in our direction, or, more specifically, your direction, who cares?" Elle shrugged and slung a companionable arm around Lily's shoulders. "Anyway, Pocahontas, the big cheeses wanna invite you and Petey-the-grind here upstairs for the ballyhoo. Feel like cutting a rug?"

Lily glanced down at her *manta* and moccasins. "I do not believe I'm attired properly for such a gathering."

"Horsefeathers!" Elle declared derisively. "Half the crowd is dudded up like they never died; you'll fit right in."

"If they did indeed set Walkers after me, going upstairs seems the height of imprude—" Piotr began.

"Remind me how I managed to handcuff myself to two wet blankets like you guys, again?" Elle crossed her arms and jerked her chin toward the hotel. "Look, I went up to natter, but no dice; they patted my posterior and sent me back down like a precious little thing. It's mostly an old boys' club up there. They ain't gonna deal through a third party, Pete, especially not a tomato like me. It's you or nothing, and they went to a whole lotta trouble to see your ugly mug."

"What of Walkers?" Lily asked.

"Neither hide nor hair," Elle assured them. "You're more likely to get jumped by some hotsy with a hardon for scars than a Walker, flyboy. So, you comin' or what?"

"So be it. I shall deal," Piotr said, straightening.

Elle twirled a finger in a whoop-dee-do gesture. "Ducky. Just remember to watch yourself, and the three of us might just get out of there in one piece."

Piotr sighed. "Advice noted. I shall be wary and wise, Elle. I am not a complete child."

"Coulda fooled me," she said, but gestured for Piotr to lead the way.

"You are savoring every moment of this, aren't you?" Lily asked as they passed through the front doors of the grand old hotel and made their way across the vast, polished entryway toward the stairs.

Grinning, Elle spun again, letting the fringe fly. "Pos-o-lute-ly! I gotta level with you, it's the cat's meow to doll up and ritz it up for a night again." She played with one of the pincurls pasted to her temple. "I guess I'm just longing for a bit of the good ol' life. Or just life, period. Same thing, really."

"That seems counterproductive. We are dead. What is the point of longing for that which we have left behind?"

"Says our resident Mrs. Grundy," Elle sneered as they passed through the stairway door and began the long climb to the rooftop. "Come on, girl, don't you ever miss hunting the wild plains or . . . wait, what did you raging redskins do for fun, anyhow? Pardon me for not knowin' already, but I was a little busy livin' when I was alive. Didn't have much time for schooling or ancient history."

Shaking her head, Lily couldn't help but smirk at Elle's ignorance. "Perhaps many of our days were not as frivolous as yours appear to have been, but my people were not dull, Elle. When the crops were in, we had many hours available for enjoyment and sport. I myself enjoyed helping my parents and older sisters craft fetishes and masks for the *Shalako*, and before I passed, I was—how do you say—being courted? Being courted by—"

"*Tiho*! The both of you!" Piotr snapped from the landing above them. He waved a hand at the thin stairs that they stood on, the remnants of the hotel that had stood before a 1906 earthquake had burned it down and forced the living to rebuild. They stood upon the memory of the building that once was. It supported them as easily as if the steps had been solid wood and stone.

"Life is what it was," he said, calming and apologetic for his outburst. "It is done. We are dead. Does it truly matter now?"

"I know your oh-so-Russian posterior did not just tell us to shut up," Elle snapped back, taking the stairs two at a time to slap the back of Piotr's head. "I'm trying to do you a favor, you flat tire! Both of us!"

"Elle, please," Lily soothed, ever the mediator. "I am not

offended. Piotr is under much pressure and I know that he means no disrespect."

Scowling, Elle did not respond. Instead she pressed her lips together and tossed her head, pushing past Piotr roughly and hurrying up the remaining flights of stairs.

"Give her time," Lily urged as Piotr scowled after her. "Warrior she might be, but Elle is young yet. Barely among the dead in truth. She longs for what she left behind and yearns for all that she can never have."

"Time," Piotr sighed as Elle reached the locked door at the top of the stairs and slid through it, beyond their view. Only a few flights down, they could now hear the raucous laughter and wild musical thrumming from above. The smell of gin and whiskey made his eyes water.

"*Da*, you are right. She is yet young, and time . . . time is the one thing the Never can always offer."

CHAPTER FOUR

The Top of the Mark, though lit by dim sconces, was a multi-level restaurant, elegantly attended and packed with spirits of all ages. A portion of the wooden floor near the glassed-in wall had been sectioned off for dancing. Nearby, an eclectic jazz quartet had set up behind the wrought iron balustrade and one portly spirit perched behind the black baby grand.

Relaxing his eyes, Piotr blinked and smiled. The piano existed both in the Never and the living world, and the pianist was tickling the ivories with bright concentration. In the living lands the keys pressed down in quick succession and the distant remnant of the sound provided an eerie, dissonant echo in the deadlands, hardly heard above the hum of the crowd. Piotr was impressed; the pianist was one of the rare few who could reach past the Never and brush the living lands.

Ghosts bellied up to the shiny wooden bar. They glanced at Lily as she and Piotr passed, but none commented. The dead didn't need to drink any more than they needed to eat, but so long as alcoholics breathed in the living lands, more than a few bottles of liquor always found their way into the Never.

What amused Piotr the most was the fact that almost every spirit there was dressed to the nines—many were clad in what had passed for fancy dress in the century in which they'd lived—and more than a few were sporting the slinky styles and black-tie fashions of the current decade.

One, at first glance, didn't appear to be wearing anything at all, but she moved and her long hair slid aside to reveal the skimpiest, sparkliest dress Piotr had ever seen a woman wear . . . or barely wear, as the case may be. The man beside her, in contrast, was clad as a fourteenth-century monk, in scarlet and black from neck to toe. They appeared to be debating Revelations as Piotr neared them, though they paused their discussion to eye Lily and Piotr until they passed.

Elle had gone ahead and was waiting for them beside a long cherry wood table with an amazing view of the city spread out below. The streets were lit up like golden wefts of a spider's web and the bay glittered like starlight with distant ships' lights.

Five men and a woman lounged on the striped chairs arranged around the table, playing with a well-worn deck of cards; none looked up as Piotr and Lily maneuvered their way through the throng to join Elle.

It was the woman Piotr noticed at first—slim and dark-haired, dressed in a pale gown with a voluminous bell-shaped skirt neatly tucked under the table—she couldn't have been more than thirty or so when she'd died, but there was a vibrancy to her that many of the spirits in the room, even the loudest and most rambunctious, were lacking. As Piotr neared, she exposed her hand and the entire table groaned. The woman, smirking, leaned forward and collected the pile of chips in the middle, humming under her breath as she plucked the disks up and dropped them into a small tapestry handbag in her lap.

The closest of the men noticed them and stood, gesturing for the others to do so as well. Two of the men, one clad in regulation Navy whites and the other in modern camo, rose and abandoned their seats for Elle and Lily, moving to the bar and waving for the bartender's attention. The lady, still sitting, glanced the newcomers over with cool appraisal. Her unblinking gaze was unnerving, and when her lips pursed, Piotr felt a shiver run down his spine. He felt like a pickled specimen sliced thin and bared to the bone before her.

"Gentlemen, I think," she said, rising and tapping the table with lacquered nails shaped into perfect pale pink ovals, "that this game is done for the evening. We should leave Mr. Morris to his business."

"Ada," protested the man who had first noticed them, reaching for her hand, "you have a seat on the Council as well. I wouldn't dream of—"

Sidestepping him, Ada waved a hand brusquely. "This is your project, Mr. Morris. Have done with it." She dipped a slight curtsy and tilted her head in Piotr's direction. "I wish you good eve, sir, and good luck. May the Lord see you swiftly and safely on your way home. However, be wary. There are Walkers about."

"We're young, not dumb," Elle said, putting her hands on her hips. "We'll mind ours and you mind yours."

Raising an eyebrow at Elle's daring, Ada nodded once and started away, pausing at Lily's side. "A word, if I may? It shall only take a moment."

Frowning, Lily glanced at Elle, who shrugged. Piotr raised a questioning eyebrow, a silent signal to indicate *do what you want*. Lily nodded briefly in return and stepped aside with the older woman.

"Wonder what that's all about," the man said, gesturing left and right to the others at the table. "Women, huh? Have a seat, son, have a seat. The rest of you? Do me a favor and scram for a bit. Thanks."

Following Ada's lead, the others nodded in Piotr's direction as, one by one, they rose and drifted into the crowd. Piotr glanced over his shoulder; Lily's conversation was done. Ada sashayed away, being stopped every few feet by other ghosts who wished to speak with her. Lily returned to the table.

Uneasily, Piotr settled into Ada's abandoned seat.

"Watch it, flyboy," Elle whispered, leaning in too close, her cheek pressed against his own, and her breath tickling his ear. "Ada's got her eye on you and that ain't exactly good, if you catch my drift."

"*Da*," Piotr murmured back, making note of the men in the crowd nearby who paused to watch Elle lean forward and look their fill while she was otherwise occupied. Elle was a big girl, but she wasn't the type to appreciate people getting fresh with her unless she initiated it. "I noticed."

Now that they were alone with the man who'd gone to such lengths to meet him, Piotr found himself studying Mr. Morris. Like Ada, he couldn't have been more than thirty-five at the time of his death, sporting a full head of dark, combed back hair and a simple button-up chambray work shirt over a comfortably worn set of jeans. His features were square and regular, but it was the measured look in his eyes that prompted Piotr to sit up straighter, to smooth his own wrinkled white shirt and adjust the crease in his pants.

"Mr. Morris," Lily began, but the man held up a hand.

"Frank, please, my dear sweet dolly," he said, offering a work-roughened palm to Lily with a wink and a knowing grin. "I let all that 'Mr. Morris' crap pass for Ada because she just can't seem to get with the times, you dig it? Half the time she's still roaming around 1842." He rubbed his knuckles along his jaw. "Not that I'm much better, mind."

"Indeed," Lily said stiffly and took his hand, allowing him to turn her knuckles up and press a quick, firm kiss on the back of her hand. She shot Piotr an annoyed glare over Frank's bowed head.

"Elle, my lovely, I am so sorry for earlier," Frank continued, sweeping forward past Lily and squeezing both of Elle's hands in his own. "Comfortable, dear? Would you like a drink?"

Not waiting for her answer, he gestured behind him to a slim black-clad figure Piotr had missed before. The waiter left and returned, setting a squat glass half-filled with eye-watering amber liquid in front of Elle. "I shouldn't—" Elle began.

"Well, if it's too strong . . ." Frank said and turned to gesture again for the waiter to take the drink away. Before Piotr could protest, Elle scowled and snatched up the glass. "I didn't say that," she snapped, catching Frank's eye, and tilted her head back, quaffing the drink in three swallows.

"Good hootch," she burped, wiping the back of her hand against her lips. "But I've had better." Still, despite her bravado, her eyes twinkled, and Piotr was stunned to realize that somehow Frank had managed to make a friend of Elle. He felt a sinking in his gut. He'd counted on Elle being her normal, prickly self to help him get through this unorthodox meeting, but she seemed right at home, tapping her foot to the frantic beat as the jazz band went crazy up on stage.

Frank turned to Piotr and offered his palm.

"I am here, you have me," Piotr said, taking Frank's hand and meeting his eyes with a level gaze. "Now you promise to send no more Walkers into our lands."

"Scout's honor, Red. If it's any consolation, it wasn't just Walkers we asked to poke around for you, they just got there first. Sorry that such a nosebleed found you before some reasonable ghost, but none of the Council was up to wandering all over hither and yon waiting for you to show up. We used to know how to put a pin on you, but the territory you Riders staked out for yourselves isn't exactly clear-cut these days."

"We have no territory," Lily said, crossing her arms across her chest. "We have abandoned our ways." She glanced at Elle. "For the most part."

"So little birdies tell me. I thought maybe I'd see what your bit was these days; send in a boy or two to scope the scene, see if you kids felt like making a little mazuma." He rubbed his fingertips together to make sure they got the point. "A deal, like. A partnership. Since you're out of the saint business now."

"You wish to pay us for some deed? After you sent a beast to hunt us down?" Straightening in her seat, Lily's hands clenched into fists. "Your ambassadors are sorely lacking if you wish to bring us into some nature of business arrangement with you."

"Hey, hey now!" Frank said, holding up his hands in a genial blocking motion. "You don't have to get your feathers in a ruffle. You're all here and safe, right? What's bugging you?"

"A boy died," Piotr explained coldly, thinking of Jamie. "All because you wish to make a deal?"

"We all die someday," Frank said reasonably. "I'm not laughing at your loss, Red, but there are more important things going on in the Never than one lost little soul." Sighing, he leaned forward and tapped the table twice, waiting for the drink to be set before him before he continued. He took a long swallow, wiped his mouth, and said, "Maybe my choice of messenger wasn't the best, yeah? I am sorry about that, but you don't always get the cream of the crop volunteering to do the dirty work."

"The Walkers not only killed the boy, they tried to kill Piotr," Lily continued, quiet and fierce. "Said that it was their orders. That he'd been wandering around the Never long enough."

"That's just malarkey," Frank snapped. "We don't want Red here dead. We need him!" Realizing what he'd said, Frank grimaced and sat back. "Well, I just threw that hand, huh?" He wiped his mouth with the back of his hand. "Piotr, look kid, I've got a copy of that poster around here somewhere. We offered some prime A-grade salvage for the soul who could get you up to the Top of the Mark for a little chat. That was it. Granted, we didn't specify alive or dead, but it would be an awfully dumb ghost who thought that killing you would be the way to go."

"Dead bodies disappear here," Elle chuckled, waving for another drink, "but some of these souls aren't exactly DaVinci reborn, Frank. Those Walkers might not've thought it through." When the tuxedo-clad waiter brought it, she sniffed and sipped appreciatively. "Or maybe you should've realized that revenge can run deeper than salvage. Especially when Walkers are concerned."

Frank sat back, expression tired. "It's no excuse. It's an explanation. And I can't make what's past undone, but I can promise you— I can give you my utmost word—that if we ever put a bounty out again, I'll make sure to add a 'no one gets hurt' addendum."

"As you will," Piotr said, sitting back and rubbing his own eyes.

The Never and the living lands were flickering wildly now. The stutter-flash of the brightly lit nightclub and dimly lit restaurant were giving him a headache.

"So what do you say? Want to ride the roller coaster with me, kids?" Frank spread his hands on the table. "Feel like making a little scratch on a job well done?"

"Depends on the job," Elle said lazily. She twirled a finger through her fringe. "Depends on the pay."

Frank smiled a chilling grin. "Let's have us a little chat about the Lightbringer."

Narrowing his eyes at the older man, Piotr leaned back in his chair. "What about her?"

"It's come to our attention that you and the Lightbringer have an . . . understanding." Keeping his free hand flat on the tabletop where Piotr and the others could see it, Frank lifted his drink and took a deep swallow. "Is this so?"

Stiffening, Piotr turned his face away. Frank was sharp, too sharp, and Piotr didn't want the Council member to spot the mingled anger and dismay he felt every time Wendy's name was mentioned. "I really don't think my friendship with the Lightbringer is any of your business."

Leaning over until he was sure Piotr could see him, Frank shook his head. "Ah, son, I get you, but you see it really is my business. My business and her business," he gestured to Lily, "her business," he pointed to Elle, "and their business." Sitting back, he waved a hand at the press of people partying on the level below. "It's all of our business, son."

Piotr pushed back from the table. "I'm leaving."

"Not so fast, not so fast. Hear me out." Frank waved a conciliatory hand. "Let me explain, and if you're still feeling partial to taking a hike, I won't try to stop you."

"You couldn't," Elle retorted, suddenly stone cold sober, "since me an' Lily got his back."

"You have his back. Who has yours?" Frank glanced left and right and shadowy figures that had been hidden amid the throng shifted forward. Stomach sinking, Piotr realized that even if they were able to get past these subtle fighters, they wouldn't be able to easily escape. The barely-clad woman and the holy man lounged with arms crossed in front of the closest exits; long, sharp blades were clearly visible in ready fists. The camo-dressed soldier had the next set of doors covered as well.

Piotr scowled. They'd sent Elle up early to scout for this sort of thing, but Frank was better than they'd given him credit for. Piotr had a sneaking suspicion that Frank's verbal mistake earlier had been a ploy to keep them seated and talking so they could be surrounded. Every exit on this floor was covered and the doors, replaced within the past few decades, were the only spiritually weak spots of the rooftop bar. All the rest was solid even in the Never—they were trapped here at Frank's whim, unable to pass through the walls for a quick getaway.

"Fine." Piotr sat back down and scowled at Frank. "Let us speak of the Lightbringer. You begin."

Frank chuckled. "That little dolly of yours sure knows how to blow our jets, doesn't she? Here we are, minding our own business, and her mother's hardly in the ground before she starts rattling my cage. Not even a by-your-leave. That's gratitude for you, huh? Her mother, now . . . Mary was a classy lady, a solid straw boss."

"You knew the White Lady?" Elle stiffened.

Frank scratched his chin thoughtfully. "Not personally, no. By the time Mary was calling herself the 'White Lady' I was having no truck with her. But before?" He grinned. "Sure enough. For a broad, Mary was completely pulled together, you dig? We had an arrangement."

"I disbelieve," Piotr said dryly.

"Believe it. The Council kept all the regular-joe spirits out of her way and pumped full of the will to keep going—off the streets and cookin' at the bash, in other words—so Mary didn't have to fuss with all that nasty reaping." Frank waved a hand at the crush below. "In exchange, Mary kept our neck of the woods free of Walkers and came 'round twice a month to clean up those poor souls who'd given in or given up, who'd become Shades. Boss, right? Good deal all around."

"Reaping is the duty of the Lightbringer," Lily said stiffly, crossing her legs and eying Frank's backup closely as she looked around the room. Piotr had the sense that the instant one of them approached, they'd become fast acquaintances with her fists. Lily might be deadly with her daggers, but in their decades together James had taught her more than a thing or two about hand-to-hand. "That the White Lady would renege upon her solemn duty— allowing the likes of the Council to police this area of town in her stead—is truly reprehensible."

"Don't get your panties in a twist, girlie," Frank said smoothly. "Keep in mind that there's a difference between the crazy broad who called herself the White Lady and Mary, the Lightbringer's momma. Mary, now? Mary wasn't reneging nothing. Mary just had her hands full doing other, more important things. For example, did you three ankle-biters know that there's more than one Lightbringer in this great wide Never of ours?"

"Of course," Piotr said, bored. "Wendy and her mother. But now this is no longer, it is Wendy alone."

"Oh no, son, not even close." Frank tilted his chair back so he was balanced on the back legs and threaded his hands behind his head. "We're talking a whole battalion of ladies like your little 'friend.' Lightbringers? Might as well call 'em Lightslingers! Cousins and aunts and great-grandmothers twice removed, and damn near every last one of them has a vested interest in wiping out the dead. Dead like you, son. Dead like me."

"*NET!*" Piotr snarled, rising to his feet. In his periphery he spotted several of Frank's guards start forward, and both Lily and Elle tensed beside him, fists clenched. "You lie! Wendy would have—"

"Cool it, Red. Sit down."

"I will not—"

"I said: sit . . . down." Frank crossed his arms over his chest and gazed evenly at Piotr until Piotr, irritated and uneasy, settled back in his seat. Frank waved at the men in the crowd and waited until they'd melted back into the mass to continue. The guards on the doors, however, remained.

"Listen up, Red." Frank rapped the table with his knuckles. "I'm not claiming that Wendy knows hide or hair about her veritable tribe. Mary was known for backroom deals and playing her cards close to the vest, especially when it came to the old biddies that ran her family. Chances are, she never told little miss lovely a thing about 'em. In fact, I have it on good authority from a little birdie that your Wendy did not, in fact, have a clue from where she hails. She might now, but she didn't before. Dig it?"

"So the Lightbringer comes from a clan," Elle sneered, still tense and eying the crowd. "Whoopdy-freaking-doo. What's that got to do with the Riders?"

"Miss Mary Quite Contrary up and split," Frank said solemnly. "We've got seventeen years worth of odd-ball souls that should've been sent on ages ago wandering around this city—more than a handful of them starting to slide toward crazy with a vengeance—and a whole peck of Reapers coming home to roost. You all kept your heads so low, I'm not surprised that this is news to you."

"Your point?" Piotr asked.

He buffed his nails on his shirt. "Every sane soul in the Never from Berkeley to Santa Cruz knows through the grapevine that your little miss wasn't trained up proper-like, that she's winging it. If *we* know that, do you really think her family doesn't? They've got ears with ears plastered to 'em. Spies, Red, and lots of 'em."

Lily pursed her lips. "I hardly think it's Wendy's fault if she was not run through the gauntlet. They cannot blame her for Mary's shortcomings. Your words are wind, sir, all you do is blow hot air."

"Agreed," Piotr said, rising. "We need not stay and hear what this *zadnitza* has to say. From his mouth the truth is as twisted as lies."

Frank sneered. "Don't you take that tone with me, Commie Red. I may only be dead a handful of decades but I'm still old enough to lay you flat on your ass, even with the pretty miss here flexing those fingers at me. Oh, and by the way? Get bent."

"Enough talk!" Piotr slapped his fist against the table, making the empty glasses rattle. "Tell us what you would, make your offer, and let us take our leave, Frank. I would be done with this foolishness."

Frank shrugged. "Fine. It's your funeral." He tapped the table and waited until Piotr had sat down again to continue on.

"You've got something we want. You not only know the Lightbringer, you two were . . . close."

Piotr glared but made no comment.

"Furthermore, Mary and I had a lot of long nights negotiating the territories. We talked. I got to learn more than a little about the way those Lightbringers—Reapers, whatever you wanna call 'em—think. You following me so far, kids?"

"Boring the hell out of us," Elle said, faking a yawn, "but we're following."

"Fine. I'll speed it up for the shortbus crowd. Your girl Wendy is what's known as a 'natural' to her family. The only thing is, naturals aren't natural to them, you dig? They don't cotton to her sort."

"You think Wendy is in danger," Lily said, cutting to the heart of the matter.

Frank shrugged. "Yeah. If they follow tradition, then they're going to put your pal Wendy down like a rabid dog."

Piotr jerked and Frank smiled thinly. "Now, normally I couldn't care less about the murder of a ghost-killer, but the Council—hell, every ghost around—got used to things being sort of informal around these parts. We want it to stay that way. We want you to convince the little miss to make the same deal her mother made. That way, everyone's happy."

Lily waved a low hand at Piotr under the table, keeping him calm. "Why do you believe she would agree to the same arrangement?"

"Oh, call it a hunch. Even when the little miss was on her rampage in the autumn, she wasn't too particular about stalking us—just Walkers. The Shades she did outta pure pity, I think."

"It is Wendy's way, *da*," Piotr agreed, recalling how Wendy fretted over whether or not to send spirits on, if it really was the right thing to do or not.

"Exactly. If you stayed hidden and minded your P's and Q's, Wendy didn't hunt you down. And at the end, she started only dealing with ghosts that hunted *her* down, the ones who actively wanted to move on and sniffed her out to make that happen. That's worlds better than how most of her clan used to deal with us."

"*Da*," Piotr said heavily, pushing back from the table and glaring around the room defiantly. His head was pounding fiercely and it seemed like he'd been in this room, talking with this oily man, for decades. In reality, less than an hour had passed; the restaurant was still stuffed to overflowing with partying dead. "We understand."

"Great, Red, you're finally getting with it." Mimicking Piotr's movement, Frank also pushed away from the table and offered his hand. His eyes were serious and his smile serene. Piotr was unwillingly glad to see the calluses ringing his palm and fingers; Frank might be a cozening man but at least he worked with his hands. Piotr could respect that.

Frank smiled, catching Piotr eyeing his palm. His expression said that he understood every thought in Piotr's head and was unsurprised by them. "Glad the pair of us could eventually see eye-to-eye. *Da, comrade?*"

What choice did he have? Piotr scowled, but took the proffered hand. "Yes. *Friend.*"

CHAPTER FIVE

Parking the car and stepping into the parking garage left Wendy feeling vulnerable and edgy. Though she'd been here only a few hours earlier, the shadows of the garage seemed deeper, darker than before, and the muted shuffle of her boots echoed back strangely from the concrete pillars. It was silly, but Wendy hesitated at the edges of the last line of cars, unsure about turning the blind corner.

"Don't be an idiot," she muttered, forcing herself to move past the minivan on the end and step quickly toward the elevators. "No one is there."

The elevator arrow lit up as Wendy approached; the elevator was coming from the basement. When the doors dinged open, Wendy stopped cold in her tracks.

The elevator was filled with Walkers.

Holy crap, what do I do?! Wendy knew she could step into the Never, become the Lightbringer, and probably deal with the half dozen or so Walkers fairly easily . . . if she'd had the benefit of surprise.

But these Walkers were different, she could tell at a glance. Several of them had their hoods pushed nearly back, exposing repaired flesh crosshatched with strange symbols, weird text. These ghosts were remnants of the White Lady's Walker army, and Wendy knew better than to tangle with so many of those at once.

Walkers, especially the ones who'd worked for her mother, were well used to handling Wendy by now. They knew how to combine their attacks, how to swarm and outnumber her, and most importantly, they had quickly learned that Wendy was weakest when dropping her physical body for the Lightbringer's spiritual shape. If

they'd been normal Walkers, untouched by her mother, Wendy
might have chanced a surprise attack—but these were trained
Walkers. It was too risky. They'd be on her in an instant.

Heartbeat tripling, Wendy slowly began walking again, forcing
each foot to move in front of the other. The main stairs were behind
her, she could double back and take them, but the elevator was the
fastest way to the main floor and other living humans. She was also
afraid that doubling back might rouse their suspicions.

Then she spotted the fire stairs. Excellent!

Passing the elevator at a brisk walk, Wendy chewed her lip and
tried to sort out what to do next. Someone must have called for the elevator on a higher floor—it was going up again now, and the Walkers
would still be on it when she hit the main floor. What were they doing
here, and why were so many of them huddled in one group?

As much as she hated to admit it, Wendy knew that she had to
find out. Spying on them in the living lands wouldn't be easy—it
was late, and Wendy obviously didn't work in the hospital. She'd
stick out, but the sight of so many Walkers in one place, especially
Walkers her mother had trained, was too much. She had to follow
them.

Wendy was halfway up the stairs when she felt the wave of cold
eddying around her shins. Slowing at the turn of the staircase,
Wendy glanced down and had to bite her tongue to keep from
cursing aloud.

The Walkers had left the elevator and were following her.

What is going on here? Wendy wondered and then had to remind
herself that to the Walkers, she was just some human. No one special. Right?

Breathing shallowly, forcing herself to stay calm and keep
walking up the stairs, albeit now at a much slower pace, Wendy
inwardly chanted, *Don't panic. They have no idea who I am. I haven't
used the Light at all since the showdown with the White Lady; if I don't
draw attention to myself, it's no big deal, right? I can do this.*

Her skin was clammy at her palms and temples; Wendy felt a bead of sweat slip between her shoulder blades and trickle down her back as she glanced around the narrow stairwell. No door except up at the top of the stairs, and that one was for *Employees Only*. She still had two flights to go before she'd reach the lobby. Plenty of time for the Walkers to catch up and overwhelm her if they wanted to.

Up close, even separated by the thin veil of life from death, Wendy could smell the rank stink of the Walkers surround her like a fog. The stairwell doors closed, shutting her in. The Walkers rustled around her, their cold pressing against her cheeks and the back of her neck. They towered over her, filling the narrow passage to full with their rotten presence. The chill made her ribs ache.

Screw this, Wendy berated herself, shivering. *What are you, the Lightbringer or some sort of wimp?! This is ridiculous! You know what you have to do.*

She wasn't a novice at taking out the dead; she could gut all of them before they even had a chance to attack, right?

Right. Glad to have made that decision, Wendy prepared to loosen her hold on the Light. But, just before she could blaze into glory, a memory of her mother's brusque, sharp voice made her pause . . .

Pay attention to your surroundings, Wendy. We live in the land of the living and *of the dead—you must never, ever forget that. Always, always, WATCH YOUR BACK.*

Crap. Wendy took a deep breath and glanced up at the corner of the stairwell—*stupid, stupid, stupid*, she thought. Sure enough, there it was: a security camera, blinking red. Even if she wanted to, Wendy couldn't change into the Lightbringer now.

She could just imagine what it would look like for the security guard on duty. A teenage girl takes the fire stairs, stops halfway up, vanishes on camera, and then reappears on the main floor. Even if Wendy were so lucky that the guard wasn't watching right then, her vanishing act would still be caught on camera, most likely recorded and stored on some distant backup hard drive for who knew how long. Wendy bit her lip to keep from groaning aloud; she had well and truly trapped herself.

Realizing that she could do nothing for the moment, Wendy fought to keep her gorge down by breathing shallowly through her mouth and taking the steps two at a time now, hurrying as quickly as she could up the stairs.

Wendy hadn't flinched much when the raccoon blood had splattered her from the knees down, and had hardly winced when Jon's dinner joined the mess, but being here, surrounded by the smell of the Walkers' necrotic tissue and mealy, maggoty meat underlaid with a spicy cinnamon-rust-salt scent was almost too much. Wendy felt the burn of acid work its slow way up her esophagus. She frantically flicked a glance down the stairs, marveling as the Walkers rattled after her, silently begging for the door to the main floor to be next.

Thankfully, it was.

Holding her breath as casually as she could, Wendy shoved the door to the lobby as hard as she could.

It wouldn't budge.

Wendy stopped. The Walkers had congregated on the landing below. She could feel their cold rising up, filling the narrow walkway, icing over the guardrails.

Forcing herself to stay calm, Wendy shoved the door again and this time, thankfully, it opened with a loud creak.

Pretending everything was normal, Wendy entered the lobby and moved aside, adjusting her purse as if it were the most normal, casual thing to do in the middle of the night in a hospital entryway. Then, once she was several feet away, Wendy breathed in again, blessing the sweet, bleach-and-chemical tang of the air. Anything was better than the flat, gagging rot of the stairwell.

The guard desk was empty, Wendy realized. The gift shop was dark.

She was alone with over half a dozen Walkers.

A slow scratch of sound sent a shiver up Wendy's spine. She didn't turn to see what the noise was—she didn't have to. The smell preceded them. The Walkers had surrounded her once again.

It was colder now, Wendy realized. Much more intensely chilled than the stairs had been. Wendy's breath fogged in front of her, snot dripped out her left nostril. Wendy swiped at her face and found that she was shivering violently, teeth beginning to chatter.

Wendy looked up at the ceiling. A black bowl hung directly in the middle of the lobby, a thin red light shining within; more frickin' cameras, probably there to catch anyone shoplifting from the gift store or the pharmacy next door.

Great, just great. Wendy was tempted to flip off the camera but the Walkers were so close now and the chill pressed the very air from her lungs. Breathing too deeply caused jagged slivers of pain to grip Wendy's chest, every inhalation scraping her throat raw. Ducking her head, Wendy was startled to realize that where the Walkers stepped, small sheets of ice crackled along the ground.

Things had rapidly spiraled from bad to worse—the half-dozen Walkers from the elevator were joined by more; four others were waiting in the shadows of the gift shop doorway, their cloaks dragging the floor, their shambling gait almost synchronous as they drifted toward Wendy.

The cold was so intense now, so overwhelming, that Wendy felt her body begin to sag from the weight of the chill. Moving her head, even slightly, took immense effort. Keeping her eyes open was becoming a chore.

Stop being weak! Her mother's voice cracked across her mind like a slap, rousing Wendy from the cold-induced fugue. *Mistake after mistake after mistake; you're dying! Get it together, cover your back! Wake up! Wake up, Wendy, wake up!*

Futilely, Wendy decided that her mother's voice was right. Cameras or not, if she was going down, she was going down with a fight. A dozen to one or not, she had to do *something*. Pushing aside the sharp voice hissing orders, Wendy reached for the cords of will containing the Light within, but she'd waited too long.

The insidious cold had wormed too deeply inside. Her will was slow, drowsy, her grasp on her Light weak. There was a sniff at her neck.

Another.

Then the Walkers were on her; spectral, flaking hands plucking at her hair, thick yellow nails digging at Wendy's elbows, the stench all around gagging her as skeletal fingers raked up and down her body, pinching, pulling, twisting. Numbed by the cold, Wendy was so frozen that she was having trouble recognizing that the pack was trying to pull her apart piece by piece.

I'm going to go out like Mom did, Wendy realized dimly, in some far-off protected place deep in her mind. *The Lost ripped her apart. The Walkers are going to do the same thing to me.*

"Reaper," hissed the closest Walker, running a blackened tongue up Wendy's jaw and into her ear. "This prey tastes of Reaper!"

The other Walkers stilled for a split second, glancing at one another and shivering like dogs on point.

"Reaper?" asked another, brackish black-brown drool dripping over its chin and soaking the ragged front of its cloak. "Real Reaper flesh?"

"Move!" ordered a third, shoving the licking-Walker aside. This one was a particularly nasty-looking grey-clad woman with only half a face, the rest of her flesh soapified and sagging off her cheekbones, the remains of her left eyelid dropping over her bloodshot eye. This lady Walker pushed close, sniffed, and then chuckled. "Reaper," she confirmed. "Mine. The one I've been sent for."

At this declaration, Wendy began struggling in earnest. The fugue wasn't completely gone, but her panic was serving to push it back, to give her energy and a little hidden strength. Wendy reached for the closest Walker to her left—her Light surged just a bit, hardly more than a flicker—and grabbed it by the chin.

The Walker hissed in pain, scrabbling at her hands and twisting

Wendy's wrist free. A flap of skin came off in her hand, writhing with teeny white and black maggots, as Wendy stumbled back a step. The Walker, growling and spitting, clutched its face and cursed.

The closest Walkers dug their hands into her shoulders, mumbling in a slow, dark language, and Wendy sagged again as the overwhelming cold poured over her chest in a sheet, an intense wave of numbness that bullied every nerve into instant submission, leaving only her mind intact. Wendy lolled in their grip.

"No!" hissed the licking-Walker, pushing the Lady Walker back a step. "Ours! All ours!"

The Lady Walker rolled her good eye and straightened, grabbing the licking-Walker by his face. "Mine," she insisted and, reaching forward quite casually, snapped his neck. Then she looked at the others, pointedly ignoring the writhing Walker on the floor as he struggled to set his flopping head straight on his abused neck. "Questions?"

"Orders?" hissed the closest Walker.

"Hold her."

They hauled Wendy to her feet and the Lady Walker jabbed her hands straight out, skeletal fingers jamming into Wendy's chest. The sensation was a terrifyingly deep, tidal tug from her very core.

Nauseated by the sensation of a hand poking around in her innards, Wendy was stunned to realize that she could actually *feel* each individual finger scrape along her ribs, the icy press of the woman's hand as it brushed her heart and dug deeper in, seeking . . . something. Her Light, maybe? The cold was nothing in the face of this pain. Despite the numbing chill of the Walkers holding her down, nerves no longer deadened from cold, Wendy arched back, whimpering, and the other Walkers pressed in, forcing her to her knees.

"Found you," the female Walker whispered. "Looked and looked and here you are, where she said you'd be. At last. At long last." She squeezed an organ—a loop of intestine, perhaps?—and Wendy yelped in pain.

Piotr might never know what had happened to her, Wendy realized dimly. Or Eddie, if he ever woke, or her siblings. They'd think
she'd just collapsed again. They would bundle her up and lay her in
the same wing her mother had lain in until the day she'd died.

"Get you . . . for this . . ." Wendy forced out.

"Shhh," the Lady Walker replied, leaning forward so her slaggy
forehead pressed against Wendy's. "Sleep, Reaper. Sleep and die for
me. Like you must."

Overwhelmed, Wendy still tried to push back, attempting to
twist away so the female Walker wouldn't be wrist deep in her chest,
but the Walker moved with her. She'd found the Light, Wendy realized. Her hand grasped Wendy's core with a painful pinch, a
squeeze . . .

. . . and the world was filled with unexpected Light.

The Walkers around her hissed, the cold fading with startling
suddenness as they turned as one toward the new source of Light.
Snarling, the female Walker yanked her hands free.

"I have your taste now," she growled in Wendy's ear, her decrepit
breath scudding across Wendy's face in a foul puff of air. "Don't sleep!"

Then she was gone—and with her, the pain. Lightheaded and
nauseous, Wendy turned toward the Light, trying to make out the
shape of the woman beneath the glare.

"Mom?" Wendy whispered as the brilliant figure jammed forward with a spiral of Light, the tendrils of heat splitting the closest
Walker neatly in half. The stink of rot was joined with the sickly
sweet stench of meat charring and flame-broiling in an instant, the
smoke rising in thick grey-black clouds.

"Hi," Wendy said to the figure and, now freed of the Walker's
intense, numbing grip, flung loose her Light within.

The Light poured out of her like an explosion of cold-heat-fire-
ice, circular pulses of noiseless thunder that pounded into the
Walkers around her and broke them apart, shattering their yellow
bones, liquefying their mottled, cross-hatched skin, each subsequent

burst slicing through them until they were as dust and shattered shards upon the floor.

The sensation was familiar and horrible and wonderful all at once. This was what it had been like to destroy a room full of ghosts in the basement of the Palace Hotel. This had been what it felt like when the orb of her Light, her soul, her abilities, cracked on the ground and every bit of her was free to expand, to stretch, to obliterate any and all dead around.

And, just as before, when the Light was done, it collapsed inward and Wendy, staggering, reined it in once more. How could such immense heat remain banked within her? Wendy didn't know. All she knew was that coming back into her body was like balancing *en pointe* on the edge of the Hobart Building, peering down into the vertiginous void.

Her stomach lurched.

Helpless to do otherwise, Wendy turned and retched into a potted plant, clinging to the tall black plastic with everything she had as the waves of nausea hit and hit and hit again until she was shaking and dripping sweat. It seemed that she purged for hours, though it could have only been a minute or two at most, and when she was done Wendy hugged the cool plastic, marveling that she was alive, much less relatively intact.

A cool, soft hand brushed her hair back from her temples. The touch was gentle, kind, and another hand offered Wendy a silver flask.

"Drink up," Wendy's savior said. "Or at least rinse out your mouth. You don't want your teeth to get all puke-scummy."

"What . . . what is—"

"Water. Nothing more, I promise." Strong hands guided Wendy into a sitting position against the wall as Wendy, eyes closed, gratefully glugged the water from the flask.

"Slow down there, sport," the voice said, chuckling. "Or you're going to blow chunks all over again."

"Sorry," Wendy said, wiping her mouth and sighing. "I was just . . . that was . . ." Struggling for a way to describe how shaky and *wrung out* she felt, Wendy finally opened her eyes.

"Um. Hi. Nice hair," she managed as the girl stood, turning away from Wendy, arms held loosely open and fingers curled, facing the dark hallway from which the Walkers had come.

Wendy meant the compliment—the girl's hair was electric blue, a chin-length bob that shone under the hospital lights. In fact, the girl looked like she'd just come from a club—no more than eighteen or nineteen at best, she was clad in skintight black jeans, strappy silver high-heel shoes, and a loose scoop-neck blouse over an intricately inked bare back with corset ties up her sides. Silver jangly earrings dangled all the way to her shoulders, glimmering like scales in the light of the lobby.

Done examining the hallway, the girl turned and, grinning, rested a fist on her hip. Her upper arms and collarbone were looped with an intricate, lacy mesh of Celtic tattoos, several of which Wendy recognized from her own skin.

This girl was a Lightbringer too.

"Thanks," the girl said, shaking her head and offering Wendy a hand up. "You good to stand? Because Mr. Jim Security Dude is due back from his smoke break any minute and we don't exactly paint a good-lookin' picture right now."

"Right," Wendy agreed, letting the girl pull her to her feet. She wavered, trying to find her balance. "I'm Wendy."

"I know," she said, nudging Wendy toward the side stairs. "Let's go this way. Less chance of bumping into anyone."

Wendy waited for the door to close behind them to ask, "How did you know who I am?"

The girl grinned and rolled her eyes as if she thought Wendy was teasing her. They were halfway up the stairs on their way to the next floor and the girl was taking the stairs two at a time, despite her heels. "Seriously?"

"Yeah." Wendy stopped on the landing. "Seriously."

"Oh." The girl, frowning, stepped down so she was eye-to-eye with Wendy. "Um, well, hi, I'm Jane." She paused as if this name were supposed to mean something to Wendy. When Wendy continued to look at her questioningly, Jane frowned. "You know, Jane? Emma's cousin? You know, your mom's replacement for this part of the Bay Area?"

"My mom's . . . what?" Wendy couldn't help the sudden wrench of fear that yanked deep in her gut. "Wait . . . Emma? Emma Henley? The intern on my mom's floor?"

"You didn't read the letter, did you?" Jane shook her head, disgusted, and started up the stairs again. "Or, knowing Emma, you might not have even gotten the letter. She's stupid-busy with her rounds these days; she probably forgot. Typical. So typical."

"Letter . . ." Wendy trailed off, struggling to keep up with Jane's rapid pace. "That *sounds* familiar. I got . . . something. From my sister, she said it was from Emma and I never really got a chance to read it. Is it on my desk? Maybe . . . I think? I've been a little busy."

"Well Emma should've made sure you got it." Pausing at the top of the stairs on Eddie's floor, Jane rolled her eyes. "Long story short: again, I'm the new Reaper for this part of the Bay Area. Hi."

"Whoah, whoah, hold up a minute!" Wendy grabbed Jane by the wrist. "Says who?"

"Says Grandmother? You really should've read that letter, huh?" Jane tsked, but smiled, showing that she meant no harm. "But I guess you were too busy, with your mom dying and all. It's cool, I would be too."

"Exactly," Wendy snapped, stung despite the soothing smile. "My mother just died. Okay, you're like me, but what gives you people the right to waltz in here and—"

"Why were you here again? This is your usual floor, right?" Jane gestured to the door. The long-term ward was just beyond; Eddie's room was close to the end of the corridor, thankfully far away from the main nurse's station. With luck, Wendy would be able to sneak in and sneak back out again with minimal fuss.

"I'm here to see my friend," Wendy grumbled. "He's not near his body. I thought . . . there's this buckle, and . . ." Wendy trailed off. "I just had an idea that I thought might help him."

Jane raised an eyebrow and, digging in her pocket, pulled out a piece of powerfully-scented grape bubble gum. She popped it in her mouth and chewed broadly before saying, "You're kidding."

"No," Wendy replied testily, "I'm not."

"Well, lead the way." Jane stepped away from the door.

"You're coming with me?"

"Yep. If there are any wandering spirits in my jurisdiction, then I need to know about 'em." She held up a hand. "Walker bonanza or not, I think I've got enough juice left to handle a couple regular ghosts. If not, well, it's not like they're going anywhere. Probably."

"I don't—" Tired of fighting and still shaky from the Walker attack, Wendy sagged. "Fine. This way."

Eddie lay as she had left him—nearly motionless on the narrow bed, the soft beeps of his machinery a quiet counterpoint to the barely discernable rise and fall of his chest. Stripping off his jacket, Wendy sat beside him on her usual chair and took his hands. "Hi Eds, long time no see," she whispered. "I thought I might, I don't know, leave this for you, okay?"

Digging in her purse, Wendy pulled out the buckle and tucked it in his right hand. She wasn't sure what she was expecting to happen—maybe a dramatic flash of light or possibly the swelling of some instrumental song in the dim reaches of the Never—but she was disappointed. Eddie rested as he had before, only now with a buckle in his hand.

"It was a long shot," Wendy sighed, shaking her head and standing up. She didn't know why she'd thought that introducing her hospitalized friend to the buckle would make a difference in his condition, but it had *felt* right.

Jane, tucked into a corner of the room, had been silent this entire time. "What exactly was that supposed to accomplish?" she asked curiously.

"Nothing," Wendy replied, dejected. "It was just a thought. A dumb one."

"You know . . . you know that this dude's spirit came home with Emma, right?" Jane pushed a hank of blue hair off her face and blew a bubble. "Weeks ago, actually. He's been hanging around, deading up the place. Great-grandmother wouldn't let any of us touch him, though." She popped the bubble. "I guess this answers the question of why not."

Wendy felt her throat close. "Eddie's spirit is with Emma? How? And what the *hell* is he doing there?"

"Yep. I mean, technically he's with all of us, seeing as we all live together, but yeah." Jane raised one eyebrow. "You really are out of the loop, huh?"

"It just doesn't make any sense," Wendy said. "Why would Eddie go home with Emma when he could have stayed here and waited for me?"

"You really need me to answer that question for you?" Jane snorted and gestured to the sterile, plain hospital room. "Just take a look around, girlie. Emma: hot doctor. Your buddy here, Eddie: teenage boy—specifically, a teenage boy with the newfound ability to poke his head through walls. Hospital: boring place to hang out, nothing much going on, mostly a bunch of dead folks and tired nurses. Emma's house: a building that holds many rooms like showers and bedrooms and a veritable cornucopia of our attractive cousins in various states of dress any time of day or night. Get my drift?"

Wendy scowled. "You think he'd go with her just for a chance to be a peeping pervert? Eddie's not like that, he . . . okay, well, he's totally like that, but it'd be a joke."

Jane laughed. "Yeah, I figured that one out on my own. He got

a little more than he was bargaining for with that trick, though."
She patted his foot and addressed Eddie's still form. "No harm, no
foul, kiddo. Even alive, you're cute enough to pull it off."

Wendy sighed. "So what's next, then? What do I do to get him
back? He can't stay with you all forever."

"Ah, at last, a plan!" Jane stretched until her spine crackled and
glanced quickly out into the hall. "Okay, no one's coming, let's
move. I'll take you home with me. You have your car, right? You
drive, I'll direct. You get to pick up your buddy and I can get in
some quality 'net time before I have to haul my butt up in the
morning. Win-win-win, so far as I'm concerned."

"I don't think—"

"Wendy," Jane said sweetly, wrapping a companionable arm
around Wendy's shoulders, "not to sound cliché, but like your boy
toy here, sometimes it's best just to let those in the know direct the
flow . . . so to speak. Get me home and let me handle it so we can
get some shuteye. Graveyard shift in the long-term ward sucks and
we both need our beauty rest."

CHAPTER SIX

San Ramon wasn't the ritziest neighborhood in the Bay Area, but it wasn't cheap either. Wendy felt nervous pulling the beat-up old Charger up to a large, sprawling house with a steep six-car driveway. Not waiting for Wendy to stop, Jane silently jumped from the passenger side and strode into the house, leaving Wendy to quickly kill the engine and hurry behind.

"This better not be some joke," Wendy breathed out loud, scanning the front porch as Jane, lit by the thin silver moonlight, slid her key into the lock. "Eddie, you'd better be in there."

"Dude, where else would I be?" a familiar voice asked as Eddie stepped through the wall separating the garage and the front walkway. "I was beginning to think you'd forgotten about me!"

Stifling a yell, Wendy spun on her heel and found herself face to face with her best friend's spirit.

"Eddie!"

"One and the same." Eddie grinned and opened his arms wide. Wendy, forgetting that she was corporeal and Eddie most certainly was not, flung herself into his embrace and banged her forehead loudly against the doorjamb.

"Ouch!"

"Smooth move," Jane grumbled. "I *was* trying to sneak in and not wake the entire house." She jiggled her keys in the lock and sighed loudly. "Damn it, the key's not working!" Jane hissed. She turned and waved a hand at Eddie. "Hey, you, spirit guy. Did Annabelle change the locks again?"

Eddie shrugged as a lamp flicked on upstairs, bathing the side yard in dim yellow light.

Wincing, Wendy probed her tender forehead; she could already feel a lump rising on her temple. Eddie grimaced as a corgi—or, rather, the ghost of a corgi—poked its inquisitive face through the front door and barked twice before vanishing back inside. "Hope you like dogs. This place is lousy with them."

"You can say that again," Jane agreed sourly. She smacked the doorjamb. "Work, damn it!"

A volley of barks echoed throughout the house.

"And they're loud too," Eddie added.

"Hell," Wendy sighed. "Nothing's ever easy, is it?"

"Nope." Eddie leaned against the pillar and grinned. "But hey, cheer up, most of the house sleeps the sleep of the dead. Only a couple of them are light sleepers. Aaaand, to kill the time, I've got one for you. Why did the psychic medium cross the road?"

Wendy groaned. Eddie was telling jokes *now*, of all times? "I don't know, Eddie. Why?"

He slung a chilly arm around her shoulders, hovering it a quarter inch above her skin. "To get to the Other Side! Other Side! Get it?"

"Oh my god." Wendy buried her face in her hands and shook her head. "I should leave you here just for that."

"Speaking of leaving me here—three weeks? Seriously? It took you three weeks to come and get me? I'd hate to see what happens if you ever become a soccer mom. You'd drop the kids off in kindergarten and remember them sometime around fifth grade."

Jane, still struggling with the lock, snickered.

"Shut it. I was sick two of those weeks, myself," Wendy said, deciding that now wasn't the time to tell Eddie she'd been unconscious that entire time. "And I've been at your coma-ridden bedside nearly every day that *I've* been out of the hospital. AND you haven't had to deal with your mother, either." Wendy crossed her arms and leaned against the post. "At least I showed up as soon as I learned where you were. I could've left you here until morning."

"Point. Sorry."

The front door swung open. Emma Henley, as regal as ever even in a silky bathrobe, pursed her lips at the three of them and frowned. Wendy was irritated to note that Emma's hip-length strawberry-blonde hair cascaded down her back with nary a tangle to be seen. Even flush from sleep, she looked flawless and radiated calm confidence. Damn! That was irritating.

Emma glanced at her wrist, where a slim, gold Rolex proclaimed the time in quiet, even ticks. "While I appreciate you finally coming to fetch your friend, Wendy, is this really an appropriate time?"

"Need the toilet. Move," Jane said brusquely, pushing past Emma and hurrying into the recesses of the house.

"San Ramon isn't exactly up the street," Wendy said. "And I've been kinda busy lately." Wendy didn't know why she didn't want to let Emma learn that she hadn't read the letter yet. All she knew was that Jane hadn't been lying. She'd said Eddie would be here, and here he was. Feeling absurdly grateful, Wendy made a mental note to treat the blue-haired girl to a movie or something. She'd barely met her, but Wendy already owed Jane a lot.

"Obviously."

Her palm itched; Wendy wanted to slap Emma so badly she could practically feel the sting of it on her skin. Jane had said that Emma was supposed to keep Wendy in the loop, but obviously she'd done a piss-poor job of it. It was strange enough to learn that her mother's neurology intern was related to her, much less to learn that the competent and cold woman knew all about Wendy, while Wendy knew nothing about her.

Another—thankfully stronger—part of Wendy knew that she had to bide her time, if not for her own emotional fortitude, then for Eddie's sake. Wendy gestured to Eddie's midsection—his empty midsection.

Eddie's cord was gone.

"Believe me, Emma, I'd love to snag a spirit and run but I notice that something . . . oh, let's say something important . . . is missing from my best friend. My best friend who was in one whole corporeal piece last time I saw him. Care to explain why?"

"Hmmm. Yes." Emma stood back from the door and waved them inside. "Come in. I've been looking into that, and we've got things to discuss."

"Obviously," Wendy snarked, but stepped inside. As she passed Emma she felt the burning heat of the doctor press against her like a blast from a blow dryer. She couldn't see or hear Jane anywhere.

The foyer of Dr. Henley's home was as lush and elegant as the exterior. Closing the door behind them, Emma strode past Wendy and led the way into a spacious living room with vaulted ceilings and mahogany floors. The couches were low-slung, camel-colored suede and the lamps were wavy carnival glass; a sepia-toned tapestry of a many-branched tree hung across from a massive fireplace and ceiling-to-mantle mirror. The tapestry stretched from corner to corner across the entire wall, each branch of the tree a confection of delicate needlework etched thin in fine black thread. Wendy squinted and made out names and dates sewn onto each leaf. There were thousands upon thousands of them.

"I'm a light sleeper. My schedule requires," Emma said, gesturing for Wendy to sit and careless of her scrutiny of the room, "that I'm available at all hours. The others, however, sleep like zombies and would've missed you entirely." She smirked. "Perhaps that would have been a good thing."

"The others?"

"My various cousins, including Jane. Grandmother and Great-Grandmother," Emma said, indicating the tapestry with a nonchalant wave. "My mother and aunts. The others."

Emma crossed her legs and part of her robe fell away, exposing intricately tattooed ankles and legs. The elaborate Celtic knots stretched halfway up her shins and tangled down the tops of her feet in a riot of purple, blue, and green. Seeing the riot of ink on strict and prim Emma was deeply surprising. Wendy's fingers brushed her own collarbone tats, hidden beneath Eddie's leather jacket.

Emma spotted her eying the ink. "Useful, aren't they? Not much of a deterrent if a soul really decides to fight, but good for keeping the riffraff away."

"You—you and Jane—are both like my mother," Wendy said, glad of Eddie's chill beside her. The cool of his soul had a calming effect, especially compared to the heat baking off Emma in a wide and uncomfortable radius. "You're like me."

"Your mother Mary was a second or third cousin," Emma replied. "A few times removed, I'm certain." Glancing at the tapestry, she made as if to get up. "I can check the exact relation, if you'd like."

"No, that's okay." Wendy hesitated, unsure of her footing now. Emma was young for a doctor, really only a handful of years older than Wendy was—no more than twenty-three or twenty-four—but facing her like this, in her luxurious parlor, those years seemed like decades, centuries more. Emma, cool and confident and on her own turf, had the upper hand. Wendy was the interloper here.

"Jane said . . ." Wendy's voice dropped. "Jane said she was here to take over for my mom. Is that true?"

For the first time, Emma seemed uncertain. "Not exactly," Emma hedged. "Possibly. Probably, but there are . . . options available."

"Then if you're not here to take over for her, why *are* you here?"

"Girl's got you there, Emmaline," chuckled a raspy, thin voice from the archway across the sitting room. "Took her long enough to get here, but she's plenty quick on the uptake, yeah?"

"Great-Grandmother," Emma said, jumping to her feet and rushing to the shadow's side. "You shouldn't be up at this time of night!" She bent down and offered her arm to the figure, leading the shadow into the light.

Great-Grandmother turned out to be a thin, sharp-eyed old woman with a shock of wispy blue-white hair and teeth like tombstones. A large mole dominated the lower left of her face, sprouting several coarse white hairs that bristled out far enough to cast a shadow on her chin. Like Emma, she wore a bathrobe, though hers was faded red flannel, mended at the elbows and knees, and worn thin from years of use.

"Pish-posh," Great-Grandmother exclaimed. "These old bones don't need half the sleep they used to. Besides, it's chilly up in my room and I like this time of day. It's quiet." She eyed Wendy and Eddie. "Normally."

"I'm sorry if we woke you," Wendy said. "We'll go."

"Bah, it's nothing," Great-Grandmother said, waving a hand as Emma settled her in a cream wingback chair close to the couch and fireplace. "Keep sitting, child, I'd be up anyway." She coughed harshly, fumbled in her pockets, and wrangled out a thick blue handkerchief, also mended and worn, to spit in. She waited until Emma turned away, hunting for a box of Kleenex, before stuffing the hankie back in her pocket. "So. You're Mary's girl. Winifred. Wendy."

"Um," Wendy said, glancing between the old woman and Emma, amazed at the similarities. Emma's cheekbones and eyes might as well have been carbon copies save for the wrinkles and creeping white film of cataracts. The gaze was different, though; her Great-Grandmother had a vast nest of wrinkles bracketing her eyes and mouth while Emma's skin was smooth and unsullied. One of them had spent unknown years grinning at every opportunity while the other looked as if anything more than the smallest of smiles might crack her face like porcelain. "Y-yes, ma'am. I am."

"None of that 'ma'am' stuff," Great-Grandmother said, snorting and flapping a hand at Wendy. "You can call me what that there boy does—Nana Moses."

Wendy glanced at Eddie, who tucked his hands behind his back and rocked on his heels, staring at the ceiling and pretending to whistle innocently. "Nana Moses?" she mouthed, horrified. The name, obviously an invention of Eddie's, seemed so undignified, but the old woman clearly liked it.

"Nana Moses," Wendy repeated slowly, tasting the name. Beside her, Emma grimaced, and that slight motion alone convinced Wendy to use the moniker every chance she got.

"Ayuh," Nana Moses said. "As in 'older than.' Now then. About your boy, here."

Eddie sat up straighter.

"How's his body?" Nana Moses pointed to Eddie with one yellowed finger. "It's starting to go, ain't it? Muscles starting to atrophy a bit sooner than those doctors expected? Maybe he's losing a little hair here, a little hair there? No matter what sort of chemicals folks like my Emmaline here pump into him, maybe a tooth or two is getting loose?"

"A little," Wendy admitted, frowning at Nana Moses and not looking at Eddie. Even out of the corner of her eye she could tell he had stiffened and was frowning; he hadn't known his body was degrading. "The doctors say—"

"Pshaw!" Nana Moses slapped the arm of the wingback chair so hard the lamp beside it tinkled. "Doctors! Doctors don't know nothing about death, girl! Not *real* death."

"But Eddie's not dead," Wendy protested. She turned to the soul beside her and waved a hand wildly, fingers passing through the slightly thicker air that made up his shoulder. His soul was chill to the touch. "He's right here!"

"Hey, ouch!" Eddie complained. "Give a guy a little warning, hey? That stings!"

"He will be," Nana Moses said, waving her finger. "Mark my words, Wendy. If you don't slap him back in his body posthaste, he'll be stiffer than a boy's—"

"Great-Grandmother!" Emma interrupted, scandalized.

"He'll be dead," harrumphed Nana Moses, rolling her eyes at Emma. "Dead-dead, none of this hangin' near his comatose body for years crap. Wendy, child, I know you ain't been at this long, but don't you got eyes in that pretty little head of yours? Look at the edges of him, girl! Does he look solid to you?"

One of the ghost-dogs trotted by with something white and thick clamped in its jaws. It neatly darted past Eddie's attempt to pet it, outlining his arm against the parlor lamplight. Though she hated to admit it, Wendy *had* noticed that Eddie was hazier around the edges than he should be. Most spirits, unless they were Shades, were crisp at the edges of their bodies, almost as if they were stamped into the Never by some ethereal hand. But Eddie . . . it was as if his soul were a watercolor slowly blurring from the outside in, a centimeter at a time. Exactly like a Shade.

"I'm here now," she said stiffly. "I'll help keep him active and awake and happy until—"

"This ain't about the will to keep going on," Nana Moses continued. "That's different from soul to soul, and nothing keeps a body willful like seeing your own perfectly good flesh going to waste. This is more complicated than all that, and this boy ain't even dead yet." Her voice, steadily rising, was almost a shout. "His damn cord's gone, girl! Or hadn't you noticed with all your runnin' around?"

Emma shot Wendy a dark look and grabbed her great-grandmother's hands. "Shh! You'll wake the house!"

"Let 'em wake, buncha layabeds," grumbled Nana Moses, but her voice dropped down to a manageable level. She sighed deeply and glanced shrewdly between Wendy and Eddie.

"Girl, why didn't you follow procedure?" Nana Moses asked abruptly, rubbing the handkerchief across her mouth. "All this mess with your mother being sick, her soul being torn apart, could have been handled by now. The boy here could have been handled by now too, if you'd just contacted us as soon as he fell sick, instead of letting Emma find him wandering around the hospital like a lost puppy. We take care of our own, you know that."

Not wanting to make her mother look bad, Wendy hesitated in

replying. Mary had done the best job she could training Wendy, but there had only been the two of them and, as the White Lady had pointed out time and time again when Wendy encountered her during her dreamwalks, Wendy never thought to ask the right questions.

"I didn't know you guys existed before tonight," Wendy finally whispered, licking her lips nervously. "I thought that, with my mom dead, it was just me."

Emma and Nana Moses exchanged a troubled look. "How could you think you're alone?" Emma asked coolly. "I sent that letter along for you, explaining the current situation, and your studies alone should have—"

"First of all, everyone keeps going on about this stupid letter you supposedly sent, but I have no clue what it said, okay? I think it's safe to say that it got misplaced. And secondly, studies?" Wendy barked, suddenly aggravated. At the hospital, after being overwhelmed and nearly drained by the Walkers, Jane had looked at her with pity and a kind of sisterly exasperation. Emma, on the other hand, seemed to be implying that any problems Wendy was having were entirely her own fault.

"*What* studies? You think I had an opportunity to study up on sending ghosts into the Light? So far as I knew, Mom and I were the only ones. I see them, and if they want to be sent on, I reap them. What's there to study?"

"I . . . you . . ." After a moment of fumbling for a reply, Emma rubbed her forehead, clearly confused. "Wait a moment. You're telling me that Mary administered the Good Cup without making you go through a dreamwalk or teach you our history or . . . anything at all?" Though she did her best to hide it, Emma was obviously outraged at the prospect.

"No," Wendy said, jutting her chin out and crossing her own arms across her chest, mimicking the haughty woman's stance as best she could out of simple mulishness. Her tactic worked. Emma's lips tightened, her eyes narrowed, and she took a step forward, balling her fists. Wendy braced for a potential punch. "Got a problem with my mom, doctor?"

"Girls. GIRLS!" Nana Moses slapped the armrest. "Enough of that. Wendy, you stop provoking Emma. Emma, you stop jumping to conclusions and let the girl explain herself." Nana Moses honked into the handkerchief again and flapped the faded rag in Wendy's direction. "Go ahead, now. You tell us how you became a Reaper. Leave nothing out."

"I saw his dad die in a car wreck," Wendy said simply, gesturing to Eddie ruefully. "It was several years ago. After that, I could see ghosts and send them into the Light. I didn't drink anything or eat anything or fall down some mystic rabbit hole. Mom said I was just born this way. That's all."

Stepping back, Emma sagged and sat on the edge of the closest armchair. One hand crept up and pressed against her mouth, fingers trembling. Dimly, against the deep silence, Wendy could hear a grandfather clock ticking away the seconds, the sound of water rushing through pipes in the distant recesses of the upper floors, and the creaking groan of the house settling around them.

"Looks like we've got ourselves a natural, Emmaline," Nana Moses said baldly, and coughed into her handkerchief. She dragged it across her lips, the raspy sound of it louder than the words that followed. "May the Good Ones preserve us all."

CHAPTER SEVEN

"**W**hat a complete pill," Elle griped as they set out for the Pier and her old turf; she'd asked to pick up a few things before they left for Mountain View. The Riders were well used to roaming the city but they'd done a great deal of traveling over the past few days and Lily wished to take the MUNI rather than hoof it. Snorting at Lily's weakness, Elle led them down California Street, raving about Frank the whole time.

"Can you believe the nerve of that piker? After that earful, and he still don't know from nothing. Threatening you, trying to bribe the Lightbringer. Guards. Like we would've even bothered with a snooty little man like him." She blew out an aggravated breath, ruffling her fringed bangs. "I oughta've cleaned his clock for him."

"He was simply doing as he thought was best for the spirits who follow the Council's lead," Lily said reasonably, "though I agree that he overstepped his bounds overmuch." Piotr watched as, in the living lands, the shadow of her spirit stepped through a bush and paused, frowning, on the other side, plucking the remnants of crumbling leaves from the edge of her skirt. The Never was strange here, so close to the Top of the Mark, the deadlands and living world sliced in paper-thin layers that hurt when he looked at them too closely.

"Says you. That's the understatement of the year," Elle grumbled. She glanced at Piotr. "Why so glum, chum? Did the wet blanket actually rattle your cage?"

"Somewhat," Piotr murmured, rubbing his eyes and wishing that he knew what to do, how to sort this all out before they reached Wendy. She had so much going on in her life right now, the last thing he wanted was to become an unwelcome complication. "Before, when the Lightbringer and I parted, my decision was *ochyen kharasho*, it was good. Wendy is strong; I had no worries, no qualms about leaving. But now my concerns, they nip at my heels with sharp teeth. I wonder if she is safe. I wonder if she is happy." He gave Elle a troubled smile. "I wonder many things."

"So her family's maybe not quite on the level, maybe they're poking their noses in a little bit," Elle breezed, waving a hand and stopping to kneel beside the road, examining a discarded and forgotten leather clutch. She rose, rolling the leather, and pocketed the clutch, continuing on, "You and I both know the Lightbringer isn't a pushover. I've never seen a tomato like her in all my years—living or dead—and I ab-so-lute-ly guarantee that your bearcat will give anyone who tries to pull a fast one on her the bum's rush."

"Even her *sem ya?*" Piotr asked. "I have concerns about this family of hers; I am not so sure."

"Yeah, we're going to warn her, yippy-skippy, but Wendy's one smart cookie. If her family's contacted her—which Frank doesn't even know if they have yet, remember—I bet the Lightbringer's already on to that busload of fake fakersons."

Lily, who'd been walking in silence as Elle and Piotr conversed, stopped suddenly. "Look," she said, and pointed up Montgomery Street. "Do you see it?"

"What in the holy hell is that?" Elle shaded her eyes with her hands. "No. It can't be."

The night sky was blotted out less than a block down, long trailing tendrils of grayish-white Light dangling from the tops of the buildings all the way to street level. Up high the Light was woven into a thin, fine mesh, the interlocked wires glittering high above the Financial District. The webs filled the sky still, effervescent and bright, their long waving fronds wrapped spiderweb-like around over two or three dozen souls. Most seemed to be Shades. All were mummified by the webs, slung high and hung by ankle and wrist, more than half twisted into pretzel-shapes and mummified lumps, stripped down to their very bones and dangling above the street like grisly, awful egg sacs. Closer, where the bulk of the webs weren't so dense, small bushes of spirit webs clung to ceilings and the tops of cars, wound around lampposts and stoplights in far-flung films just barely reaching one another to wind thin tendrils, rounded like the roots of a tree, together in dripping braids and waving strands.

"They are dense up high," Lily whispered, "but see how they send roots down? This is new."

"I've never seen so many spirit webs in one location," Piotr agreed, stunned. "It's like a *taiga* . . . a forest!" He turned to Elle. "Surely our eyes are playing tricks on us? This must be some sort of optical illusion, *da*? It is gigantic!"

"Best illusion these peepers have ever settled on, then," Elle said. "I'm gonna get a closer look."

"Elle, no!" Lily cried, grabbing Elle by the wrist and tugging her back. "Why must you always thrust yourself without thought into danger?" she scolded, shaking a finger under Elle's nose. "If it is indeed a forest of webs, then who is cultivating them and why? We would be approaching their territory—this is something you simply mustn't do without caution and stealth."

"Yeah, well, James ain't exactly among the dead anymore," Elle said sharply, yanking her wrist free. "So I figure I'm the best we've got for stealth right now."

"Elle," Piotr rebuked her softly. "That was cruel." He didn't need to look at Lily to see how stiff she'd become. Though Elle couldn't know it, referring to James was highly unfair, as Piotr had used him to try and distract Lily earlier in the evening. That, too, had been mean.

"Cruel or not, it's the truth." Elle's chin jutted out as she glared at Lily. "And I don't take kindly to little Pocahontas here orderin' me about."

"As you wish," Lily said, stepping back and crossing her arms over her chest. She looked stricken and tired, bone-weary and ready to walk away from the entire mess. "But don't say that I did not give adequate warning. You simply did not heed it."

"Ladies, *puzhalsta*," Piotr begged. "Please do not disagree like this."

"Pipe down, flyboy, I'm not mad at her," Elle said, rolling her eyes and starting off down Montgomery in the direction of Pine at a good pace. "And if you stopped to look a minute, you'd see she's only a little ticked at me. We'll have words later maybe, but it's none of yours."

Confused, Piotr followed at some distance, with Lily—daggers drawn—stalking behind.

"Heaven above," Elle breathed, stopping at the stoplight at Montgomery and Pine. She sagged against the pole and tilted her head up, gazing at the jellyfish-thin tendrils floating high above. Piotr, his sight painfully flicking between the living lands and the Never, saw that the Dress Barn door beside them was completely hidden behind the thick webs and the title company across the street was a morass of thin sections of deadspace and living lands, layered with tangled spirit webs that grasped and sucked at the few living passersby, mostly homeless, but also a few late partygoers, slurring drunkenly as they staggered down the street.

"I thought it was too dotty to be true," Elle whispered. "Those really are spirit webs."

"These must be the remnants of the White Lady's spirit snares," Lily murmured, coming up behind them. "Though I cannot see how such a thing came to be. I was under the impression that they needed living energy to survive, yet these appear to have burrowed into the buildings themselves. Yes, they are feasting on passersby and the Shades, but look where they are the brightest . . . their roots have sunk into the bricks."

"It is impossible," Piotr agreed, "but yet, there it is."

"Hey, you don't figure the White Lady fussed with those webs somehow, do you?" Elle asked suddenly, pushing off from the pole and pacing the sidewalk nervously. She passed through several of the living homeless; they flinched away from her cold but Elle, so entranced with the mystery before her, hardly winced at the living heat. "I mean, we know she could change the Walkers, twist their skin, make 'em whole or strip 'em down; maybe she could do the same for the webs?"

"It would not be unlike her," Lily agreed slowly, "but to what ends? What could cultivating an entire forest of planted spirit webs gain one such as she? This is so far beyond the Palace it is unreal. But look . . . these webs fall in orderly rows, like trees. They were set here. This is not natural growth."

"Who knows. The White Lady was off her rocker. She started off by breeding the stupid things in Walkers, who knows what else she did to 'em?" Jittery now, Elle scrubbed the back of her hand against her chin. "I'm gonna go in."

"What?" Piotr cried. "Madness, Elle. Why would you do such a thing?"

"Well, for one, it's a straight shot to Market Street if we go this way, and I don't know about you, but I'm not exactly thrilled with the idea of 'tralalala'ing my way around this mess. Secondly, aren't you at least a *little* bit curious? This is the sort of thing no one's ever seen before, Pete! Look at it! It's huge!"

"It is the size that concerns me," Piotr replied dryly. "Imagine it to be a real forest. We have no living modern conveniences, no GPS or cell phones to guide us north or south. We are alone, the three of us, amid essence-plundering creatures that would strip us to our bones if they could but get close enough. What if we were to get lost, Elle? Or stray off the safe path? Of course, that is assuming that the *bezumnym* White Lady thought to make one when she planted these abominations, or that they haven't overgrown the safe way since her passing."

"Damn you, flyboy, always with the logic," Elle grumbled. "I don't even have to ask Pocahontas what she thinks. It's written all over that stick she's got shoved up her—"

"Elle," Piotr said sternly. "Enough. *Umolyayu*. Please."

Elle threw up her hands. "Fine, fine. I'm done trying to convince you to come with me. But you two wet blankets can't stop me from taking a peek inside."

"You are being foolish, Elle," Lily warned as Elle stepped toward the thinnest section of spirit webs, her unstrung bow upraised in preparation to shift aside the first wave of tendrils.

"Please, Mrs. Grundy. Nothing's going to happen," she sneered.

Just then, from the depths of the forest, echoed a long, wailing howl, like a tortured coyote's cry. A flock of seagulls burst from the top of the webs, most dripping essence and flying erratically toward Alcatraz.

"Well, ain't irony one hell of a pill? That answers that question," Elle said, yanking backward and glaring into the wavering forest, paler than Piotr had ever seen her before. "Not going in there, no way, no how."

"Our sweet savage sees reason," Lily said, bemused, sheathing her knives. "*Yanauluha* be thanked."

"Rub it in, sister," Elle said. "I'm just not up to tangling with hell-dogs today."

"As you say," Lily said gravely. "Then by all means, as you are skilled in stealth and know the shortcuts this area has to offer, I beg of you, please lead the way."

Mollified by Lily's request, Elle tossed her head and turned southwest, moving to skirt the mass. They'd made it no more than a tenth of the way around the edge, just past St. Mary's Square, when Sutter opened up onto Grant and they stepped into a thin place in the Never while coming face to face with a trio of Walkers.

Startled, Elle fell back a few steps. Her bow was unstrung, her knives sheathed. Lily's knives were out but they looked pale and dull here, in this strange, uneasy place. Piotr sensed that if he drew his own knife his blade would have suffered the same fate—the living world was leaching from them, weakening them all.

"What have we here?" hissed the nearest Walker, shorter than the others by several inches, and slimmer, swaying left-right, left-right in a way that emphasized how much smaller it was. There were long vertical rips in its grey cloak and Piotr could see surprisingly intact legs beneath, muscles whole and flexing, flashing its pale, mold-riddled skin. Other than the mold the legs looked strong, good for chasing down prey. Piotr shuddered, trying not to imagine this particular Walker not walking, but running, after him; hunting him to ground like a beast.

"Three Riders out past their bedtime? So late at night. What are you doing awake?" It chuckled roughly, and the menace of it raised the hairs on Piotr's arms. This Walker wasn't nearly as mindless as it ought to be, he realized, and it didn't seem as affected as they were by the thin spot of Never.

"It's one of the White Lady's, too," Elle said softly. "Look, its hands are all scarred up."

"How many of you escaped?" Piotr demanded suddenly, exasperated. "It seems we cannot turn around before bumping into another one of you!"

"Perhaps Piotr walks in the wrong parts of town then?" suggested the lead Walker, drawing its hood partially off its face. Piotr winced when he saw that half the Walker's face was gone, the left eyelid drooping deeply and the flesh spongy and soapified on the left side.

The lips drawn back were bloodless and chapped and the eyes were unnaturally wide, but something about the Walker's features struck a chord deep inside. It took Piotr a moment before he realized why this Walker wasn't quite as tall as the others, why it was so slim, why it looked so different than the others—he was a she.

Recoiling back a step, Piotr grimaced. He knew that, in theory, some female spirits became Walkers, but it wasn't usual. He'd always gotten the impression that they just didn't last as long as the men, and they hardly ever lasted long enough to reach a position of dubious power among the Walkers. It wasn't that women were incapable of being just as cruel and cold as a Walker had to be, it was simply that even dead, prejudices persisted. Most of the Walkers had been living men in a time when most women were subservient and cowed—any woman who became a Walker had to be twice as cold and cruel just to survive. The fact that these other Walkers were following her was almost unheard of. Of course, since the White Lady, many previously unheard of things had been occurring at a disquieting rate.

One of the other Walkers chuckled when Piotr fell back a step, and the lead Walker stiffened, raising her head sharply and squaring her shoulders. "Problem, girl-flesh?"

"You appear to know Piotr's name, or perhaps Piotr himself," Lily said. "This was unexpected."

"Pooey on knowing Pete, he's got a face no one'll forget any time soon. What I'm interested in is the factola that *you* just happen to be a lady *and* a Walker," Elle said, snorting derisively. "Why are you hanging out with these palookas, girly? The afterlife's that boring for you? You shoulda gone up the Top o' the Mark way. They at least have some appreciation for a nice pair of gams like yours."

The Walkers behind the leader shifted silently in place. The leader shook her head once, holding out her skeletal, scarred hands.

"Was female," she corrected. "Now, I am Walker. And you are Rider. Understand me, I am a Walker." Then, faster than Piotr's eyes could track, her other hand darted out, arcing quickly outward and upward. Without thinking, Piotr stepped into the path of the motion.

"Brave, idiot Piotr," the Walker hissed under her breath, twisting the sharpened hook in his side. Piotr gasped—the pain hadn't been immediate, but as she twisted and worked the point, his essence felt as if it were being scraped free of his very bones, like she was gutting him alive. For all he knew, she was; the bulk of the weapon was sunk into his gut. Who knew the damage she was doing? "You never change. Never, never. It will be a pleasure to feel you die." She leaned forward and ran her dry, raspy, rotting tongue across his facial scar. "Again."

An arrow punched past Piotr's face, embedding itself deeply in her stabbing arm. "Step away from Piotr," Elle said coldly, another arrow already notched and ready. She'd stepped out of the thin place and her bow buzzed with bright, fierce energy. "He may be a piker, but he's our piker, and I don't take kindly to anyone manhandling him. Understand?"

"Toys," the Walker sneered, using her free hand to yank the arrow free. It ripped a large, gaping hole in her essence, releasing a puff of foul air like spoiled meat and rotten eggs.

She pushed back and, shaking her head so that the rest of the hood fell down, revealed spare strips of dirty blonde hair that clung wetly to the grisly remains of the vertebrae slanted at the top of her spinal column. "I thought perhaps it was a sign, now that we see one another again, that a deal could be made."

"I don't know who you are," Piotr said. "I've never seen you before in my life."

"Lies," she sighed. "All from your lips are lies and lies and lies again. I see now how wrong I was. Fine. Worthless boy. Worthless girls." She glanced over her shoulder, and jerked her chin at the other Walkers. "I am done with these things. Teach the boy a lesson; hurt his girls. Suck their fingers to the bone. Chew on their soul-meat until all the flavor is gone."

One the others darted forward, pulling weapons from hidden pockets, sharpened fingertips raking the air as they massed toward Lily and Elle.

Then, surprisingly, the woman drew Piotr close, using the hook in his gut as leverage. "The White Lady taught them many things, Piotr," she whispered in his ear, "but I watched. I learned. She did not know how much, how long I watched. She had no idea how long I've known you, or how young she really was."

Gasping, Piotr struggled but couldn't move. Small as she was, she was far stronger than she looked; his toes barely brushed the ground. Behind him he heard Lily scream, though whether in anger or pain he couldn't tell. Elle yelled too and there was a loud, sharp clatter as someone knocked over a trashcan on the corner.

"I don't know what you're talking about," Piotr ground out, twisting painfully on the hook, trying to push his hands against her shoulders and give himself enough leverage to push up and off, to flee the immense pain.

"I hungered. No children, no Lost, for many months; I had become nothing but a shadow, walking the highway. I regretted my choice to take the souls but they were so tasty and I was so scared of becoming nothing before my time. Again and again and again. All your fault."

"I don't . . . I can't . . ."

"I hated you . . . you never had to worry about tasting the flesh. For you, unending Never. For me? Only pain." The Walker pressed her rough lips against the cup of Piotr's ear and the smell of her enveloped him in a rancid, rotting cloud. "Cursing my luck, I hunted in the rain, walking the highway, waiting for the death I could smell on the wind. And then the bus crashed."

She was talking about the accident that had created the White Lady, Piotr realized, horrified, the one where Wendy had to reap the Lost for the first time.

"The Lightbringer took my prey—oh so many young souls!— but I was patient. I watched . . . I learned." She chuckled. "I saw what you did for her, Piotr, how you came when she called, and pulled her soul together and stitched it back together after the children ripped her apart. I knew you. So long apart and you were almost exactly the same!" She brushed a hand across his face, fingering his scar, and chuckled. "So much the same."

"I don't remember—"

"Lies. Lies get you nowhere. But I expect your lies. They are natural as breathing, as sleep. I waited here for many days. I knew you would come back. You always come back, you can never keep away from them, can you? So I offer you this deal: I will call off my Walkers, once *her* Walkers. If. IF. If you do this for me. Make me whole again, like you did for the White Lady. Stitch me back together and your friends can go free. I will go my way and you yours, like before. We will be nothing to one another again. Do this little thing for me, boy. If it weren't for you, I wouldn't be trapped here. You owe me."

"I do not remember," Piotr said again, this time with more force. It was the wet-meat smell of her that was finally getting to him, the rotten sewer smell combined with her rancid breath and the insistence, the blind, chilling certainty, that Piotr knew something that he didn't, that he was holding out on her.

How did she know him?

He wished he could remember that night. He wished he could remember half the nights he'd had for the last ninety-plus years that Elle swore she'd known him in, or the centuries Lily promised that they'd been friends. Past a certain point—the seventies? The fifties?—it all faded into nothingness . . . and Piotr hated that. He worried that, if this kept up, one day his memories of Wendy would drift away just as everything else had. He didn't want to forget her.

"I don't remember doing anything to you," Piotr ground out. "And people keep telling me that I did it, but I don't remember how I put the White Lady together again, either. I don't *remember* anything! Why can't any of you understand that? *I don't remember!*"

Then, drawing on unexpected reserves of strength, Piotr lifted up his legs and, jamming his feet into her solar plexus, shoved violently backwards. He felt his essence rip, felt the unimaginable pain of jerking himself free of the hook, and hit the ground with a wet thump.

"So be it," the woman said coldly. "Have it your way, for now. But you still owe me, and I do not forget your debts as easily as you do."

Spitting on his prone body, she turned on her heel and fled, leaving Piotr to wonder why she'd run. He certainly wasn't in any shape to hurt her. As he was about to sit up, a second figure leapt over his body—one of the other Walkers—sprinting for the forest.

"You bastard! Come back here!" Elle shouted, dropping to her knees at Piotr's side for balance and letting another arrow fly.

It soared across the distance, cutting cleanly through the air, and embedded itself deeply in the Walker's back. He staggered but kept running, zigzagging down Sutter Avenue as quickly as he could. He was almost to the corner of Sutter and Post, just skirting the edge of the spirit web forest, when a humongous, hulking figure leapt from the darkness. Before Piotr had the time to blink, the creature—what looked to be an impossibly huge wolf, but twisted, somehow *wrong* —snapped up the Walker and shook him in its mouth like a pet poodle might do to a chew toy. The Walker shrieked, a long undulating sound that wavered in the air, but within seconds the scream was replaced by a series of wet, ripping noises accompanied by hideous growls.

"Go-go-go," Elle hissed.

Piotr flipped over to his stomach as fast as he could, but the second he put weight on his right foot his leg buckled beneath him. "I can't," he hissed back, trying to keep an eye on the beast and stay inconspicuous at the same time. It seemed busy for the moment, but Walker meat couldn't be tasty. Who knew how long before it smelled the essence pouring out of Piotr in a river, and came to investigate?

"Oh, hell!" Elle grumbled, yanking Piotr up and over her shoulder in a fireman-carry, half-dragging him as far from the beast as they could manage, as quickly as she could stagger. Piotr was uncertain how long he was jounced along on Elle's shoulder, but she didn't stop until they'd reached the intersection of Mission and Market. There, gasping, she dropped him onto a bus bench and slumped down beside him, swiping the sweat off her brow with a shaking arm. Nearby, the BART rumbled.

"She sure worked you over, didn't she, Petey?" Elle said, coughing as she knelt by his side. "Can you get up?"

"The others?" Piotr asked weakly, waiting for the waves of pain to subside. "Lily?"

"I am fine, Piotr," Lily said, kneeling on his other side. "It was close at times, but I gave as good as I received. They will not choose to engage us again, mark my words. But how do you fare? Do you need aid in rising?"

"He boogered up his ankle," Elle explained. "And we've gotta hoof it all the way to Mountain View with Petey-Sore-Paw. We are well and truly up the creek."

Lily chuckled. "So negative, Elle! This is unlike you. We are called Riders, are we not? Why should we do such a thing as walk?"

"Well, I don't know if you've noticed, but there aren't exactly a surplus of horses wandering these parts anymore, Pocahontas. How, exactly, do you think we should catch a ride with Piotr unable to jump on a car, especially all the way down to Mountain View? Caltrain's not running yet and BART will only get us so far."

"Simple," Lily said, pointing down the street where a faded ghost of an image was slowly making its way toward them in the living lands. "We catch the last bus."

Thankfully it was so late at night that boarding was painless. They slid through the side of the vehicle as it stopped for a brief moment while the driver noted the stop as empty on her log. Huddling in a pair of seats near the back of the bus, Piotr allowed Lily to examine his wounds. When she sat back, her expression was grave.

"You are healing," she said carefully. "Not as fast as I would like, but there is certainly some closure at the back. I would prefer that we had a Lost to help with the process, but for now you shall be fine if you do not engage in another battle. How do you feel?"

"Achy," he said honestly. "Somewhat off, woozy . . . but I think you're correct. It's just a scratch."

"And your ankle?"

Piotr gingerly twisted his foot from left to right. "Hurts, but not as badly. I have dealt with such before."

Lily nodded. "Your will is strong; were I to know of these injuries on another Rider, I would say that they would be laid up for many days. I do not think this will be the case with you. You heal quickly."

Thankful that Lily hadn't chosen to probe *into* the wound, Piotr sat back and tried not to wince too much as Lily went to check on Elle's cuts and scratches. He felt badly about hiding the full extent of his injuries from Lily, but he knew there was no way she'd be able to open him up and examine what he was sure were cut organs inside. Thankfully, he had no need of organs anymore. The pain would slow him down until he healed the damage, but so long as his slow leak of essence was kept to a minimum and he maintained a bright and strong will, he was sure he'd be fine.

Getting to Wendy, warning her of what he'd learned from Frank, was more important.

Breathing so that the pain ebbed with the movement of air within him, Piotr allowed himself to rest. He didn't know how long they traveled, only that they were heading steadily south, and the thrum of the wheels on pavement beneath him was soothing. Still, it seemed cold, even for a winter night.

After long minutes Piotr shivered, slumped, and slept.

"Petey? Hey, flyboy, wakey-wakey!"

Piotr jerked aside as Elle shook his shoulder again. "Do not touch me, witch. I'll cut your lying tongue from your head!" he snapped, and then immediately regretted his sharpness when Elle, stiffening and angry, raised both hands and took a step back. "My apologies, Elle," he said, rubbing knuckles against his tired and gritty eyes and wishing his terrible dream would fade faster. "I was sleeping. I am . . . weary."

"Yeah," she said dryly, relaxing. "We noticed. Better wake up in a hurry, though. We're just about at our stop."

Wendy lived about a mile from the main bus route. Thankfully, Piotr knew the way by heart and was able to navigate toward her house even in his tired stupor. Perhaps it was due to Wendy's mother, or Wendy herself, or perhaps they had just settled in a particularly spiritually rich neighborhood, but many of the trees and plants were unnaturally dense here, many of the homes as solid in the Never as they were in the living lands. He was glad that there were no thin spots; he wasn't sure he could stand the flickering pain behind his eyes much longer.

"Piotr?" Lily asked quietly when Elle stopped to examine a lush bush overflowing with pungent honeysuckle. "Do you need help? You seem to be in some distress." She looked up at the sky above them and frowned. "This does not appear to be the right direction."

"Of course it . . . isn't," Piotr said, shaking his head. Even though he could have walked to Wendy's blindfolded before, the exhaustion was finally getting to him. "We just turned down a street early. My apologies."

"Do you wish me to lead? I am sure that I can find—"

"I'm fine," he swore. "I am . . . I am just nervous."

Lily nodded, understanding, and dropped back a few steps, letting Piotr once more lead the way. Again Piotr felt the guilt gnaw at him. He wasn't nervous. It wasn't what she thought. Piotr rubbed his fingertips against his palm. Part of him was grateful for Lily's concern. Another part of him was uncommonly furious that she was poking her nose in yet again.

Silently Piotr berated himself for an ungrateful fool. His friends cared greatly about him; they only wished to know that he would be fine dealing with his love.

He wished they didn't have to be there, but Wendy deserved to know what she was facing. That was all. She'd illuminated so much about him, about why he was the way he was, why he drifted through the Never like an unmoored raft, tossed by the waves of chance.

Wendy needed this warning about her family. He owed her that much.

"Perhaps just Piotr should meet with the Lightbringer first," Lily suggested as the three of them finally reached Wendy's front yard. She looked meaningfully between Piotr and the house. "Entering her abode in this manner, without warning or request to enter, seems somewhat rude."

"I used to feel the same way, but Wendy made it clear many times that her door is always open to me," Piotr replied simply, dodging the suggestion. He approached the tree beneath her window and prepared to pull himself up into the branches. Part of him did want to go into Wendy's home unaccompanied but another part of him quailed at facing Wendy alone. It was better this way, with Elle and Lily by his side. "Let's go."

CHAPTER EIGHT

"**Y**ou have to leave," Emma said abruptly, pushing to her feet and glancing quickly over her shoulder at the dark hallway leading to the back of the house. "Both of you. Get out. Now."

"Whoa, whoa," Wendy protested. "What about Eddie's cord? What about the fact that you all have a bunch of Reapers traipsing around the city without even a—"

"Your mother was an idiot!" Emma snarled, grabbing Wendy by the shoulder and shoving her a few steps toward the door. They passed through a set of matching corgis relaxing by the couch; their chill was minor compared to the heat of Emma's touch. "I don't care how good a Reaper she was, or how talented she was, she never should have been allowed to watch this town by herself!"

"Now, now, Emmaline," Nana Moses soothed, running the tips of her fingers along the armrest, "relax yourself, girl. Look at her. Stop, breathe a moment, and *look* at her."

Emma's head dipped down, her chin resting briefly on her collarbone, and she shuddered. When she raised her head again the frantic panic was replaced by cool, measured consideration.

"Why is being a natural, whatever that is, so bad?" Wendy asked, glad that Emma was calmer now, though the narrow-eyed speculation was equally unnerving.

"Do you want the truth?" Emma asked. "Or an excuse?"

Surprised at the underlying venom in the question, Wendy cocked an eyebrow at the doctor and wrapped her arms around her torso. She felt stripped to her bones all of a sudden, exposed to her core by the harsh question. Emma had been condescending before,

107

but not hostile. Her unexpected chilliness worried Wendy. "The truth."

Emma rose and moved to the tapestry on the wall, running her fingers along the bumps and whorls of the thread and fabric. Eddie followed her, joined her, his eyes tracking the places she touched. When she squatted down to prod a particular branch, he looked closely at it.

"Only a small percentage of the women in our family are capable of being Reapers," Emma said softly, running her thumb over a long, arching branch. "But there is a lot of power inherent in working with the dead. It is important that power like that isn't squandered, is used appropriately. Do you agree?" She flicked a glance at Eddie and rose, meeting Wendy's gaze with icy equanimity.

"Maybe," Wendy replied, eying the pair of grinning corgis in the entryway. "Depends on the power, I guess. Depends on the girl."

Clicking her teeth, Nana Moses chortled. "Smart girl."

"We prune branches of our family tree that can't—or won't—follow the rules." Emma tapped a branch. "These family members were cut off in the 1890s." She tapped another. "These were cut off in the 1750s." Then, crouching lower down, she ran her finger along a long, black branch outlined in silver thread. "These . . . this family cut themselves off."

"As in, they defected and quit?"

Emma's smile was sharp; it stretched too widely and showed too many blindingly white teeth. "As in, they let a natural-born Reaper, their daughter, live."

Standing up to join Eddie and Emma at the tapestry, Wendy struggled to form the right question, her mother's admonitions echoing in her head. *You never ask the right questions*, the White Lady jeered from her memories. *Don't take everything at face value!*

"'Let' her live?" Wendy asked pointedly.

A creak behind her alerted Wendy to Nana Moses' standing up. She shuffled to the tapestry and rested a withered, spotted hand on the fabric. "We kill naturals, Wendy. Kill 'em dead."

"Kill*ed*," Emma correctly quickly, voice pitched low, eying the dark shadows of the hallway once again. "Past tense. Obviously, we don't do that anymore. It'd be barbaric."

"Why?" Wendy rasped past a throat that felt parched and tight. She licked her lips but her tongue felt thick, furry in her mouth. Only Eddie's calm presence beside her kept Wendy from bolting then and there.

"Ever been fishin', girl?" Nana Moses asked, leaning forward and peering at Wendy closely. Up close her eyes were bloodshot and the whites of her eyes were aged yellow, but her expression was searching, sharp.

"Not really," Wendy said. "Dad tried to take us once, but Mom had to bail halfway through and go to work."

"I have," Eddie said, patting a thigh to entice the dogs closer. They gladly crowded round to receive his attention. "What about it?"

"You know about deep sea fishin'?" Nana Moses tapped the middle of her forehead. "Down deep, where it's so cold and dark that man can't go, there're fish that live without ever seeing the light of the sun. And there're fish that light up their own sort of sun and dangle that light in front of 'em, fishes that go fishin' for other fish, if you will."

"Angler fish," Emma supplied. "They can, for the most part, protect themselves handily."

"Usually, yes," Nana Moses said, "but sometimes those lights, they call more than just the little fish for the angler fish to eat up. Sometimes those lights catch the attention of deeper, darker things."

Wendy shivered. "You're saying that I'm like an angler fish," she said. "That the Light is my way of calling ghosts to me so I can send them into the Light."

"No, girl," Nana Moses said sadly. "A regular Reaper, trained the way we've been trainin' em since time began, those girls are like angler fishes. You? You're a whole new creature, like if some deep-sea fisherman dropped a spotlight at the bottom of the ocean. Maybe one or two fish would swim up to a regular angler. You? You'd get half of the ocean floor in one go."

"By the end of the training period, regular Reapers have an ultimate hold over their powers," Emma clarified. "But naturals don't have to take things tiny step by tiny step. They learn everything all at once. It's just handed to them, so they don't have nearly the control."

"I have control," Wendy protested, stung. "Mom made me practice on Shades all the time!"

Nana Moses snorted. "Shades! Pah! She was draining your Light, girl, the safest way she knew how. Never had you reap Walkers, did she? Or a normal spirit? Or even, Good Ones forbid, a Lost?"

Unwillingly, Wendy remembered . . .

. . . *the stutter-flash of the ambulance's lights, the crumpled school bus half-on, half-off the road, and the small mob of Lost spirits milling around as the firemen and police officers and EMTs tried to separate the living from the dead. Wendy, moving as a shadow amid the chaos, sending the Lost on, feeling the tug deep inside of herself, the cramping pain and achiness that accompanied sending on Lost after Lost after Lost. Thirteen in all, and in the end, her mother's body, crumpled on the February-slick pavement, red curls plastered against her cheeks as Wendy knelt down and wept at her side.*

Emma snapped her fingers in Wendy's face and Wendy jerked back, simultaneously annoyed and embarrassed that she'd let her mind wander like that.

"No," she said, swallowing rapidly and fighting the pinprick of tears in the corners of her eyes, "I didn't reap a Lost until after my mom was . . . until after she collapsed."

Uncomfortably, Wendy remembered her first reap. Her mother had made her spy on the ghost of a grandmother pushing her granddaughter on a swing; even now Wendy clearly recalled the feeling of her filthy, scabby knees encased in itchy hose and wishing that she were anywhere but there at that particular instant. She remembered the warmth of that first reaping, the overwhelming burning sensation that kindled in her core and demanded to be released, the last words of the grandmother, that desperate request for help for the child.

How old is that little girl now? Wendy wondered. *Hopefully her stepfather never got custody back.*

"I only sent on one normal ghost before that," she whispered. "It . . . it was my first reap."

"Your mother knew better," Nana Moses said with a knowing nod. "Knew what might happen if she let you work with the Walkers or the Lost. What eventually *would* happen, most like, no matter her precautions."

"Which is?" Wendy asked testily. Her mother had slapped her after that reap, had told her that it was time for Wendy to grow up.

Cover your back, she'd hissed as Wendy pressed the hot, stinging flesh of her cheek with one hand. It had been the litany of her childhood and adolescence from that point onward: *You give the dead seconds of your life every time you send them on; give them nothing else! Protect yourself, Wendy, watch your back!*

"What could happen? Well, girl, normal Reapers build up their powers slowly. A normal Reaper can only send on so many souls in a night. Too many and she gets drained, tired, sloppy. She leaves herself open to attack, you understand me?"

"It takes years to extend your powers to a larger capacity," Emma added. "I'm one of the best Reapers in this house and I can only send on a dozen or so a night. And it takes more energy and skill to send on Walkers or Lost."

"Mary could send on fifteen or sixteen a night when she was your age," Nana Moses added, "but she was truly something special. Even then, though, she'd have to rest up for a day or so to replenish her stores."

Nana Moses tapped Wendy on her shoulder. "That's why we split cities into sectors, girl. Because it's nearly impossible for a Reaper to keep a city under control on her own. The fact that Mary managed it alone for so long was a miracle, honestly. I'm not surprised that she went the way she did. It was just a matter of time."

Wendy blanched. There had been times, when Piotr and she had been separated, when she'd been hiding out from her family and friends, that she'd taken down two or three dozen Walkers an evening, easily. Sure, she'd been worn out at the end of the night, dropping into bed with subsequent nightmares as if diving off a pier into deep water, but she'd never really felt completely drained, just tired.

"Naturals . . . don't have that limit?"

"You tell me," Nana Moses said and then shook her head. "No, don't say anything, girl, you're no good at lying. Look at you. A dozen regular ghosts is nothing to you, yeah? Two dozen? More?"

Emma shook her head. "How many of those were Walkers?"

Flushing, Wendy shrugged. "I don't know. A lot." She tried not to brood on the mass of Walkers at the hospital, how they'd over-whelmed her so easily. If they'd been normal Walkers—untrained and hungry—she would have taken them down easily . . . but they'd been something more. *How many special Walkers would I be able to handle at once?* Wendy wondered.

"Naturals burn hot, Wendy," Emma said softly, warningly. "If a regular Reaper is a candle in the darkness, you're like . . ."

"A bonfire?"

"Worse. Like a nuclear explosion." Emma frowned faintly and crossed her arms across her chest, staring at the tapestry moodily. "And nuclear explosions, even small ones, blow out windows for hundreds of miles. They draw attention."

"So more ghosts come to see me. I'll reap them, no fuss, no muss, right? If I don't let myself get surrounded like my mom did, I don't see what the big deal—"

"Control is more important than you're realizing and, more importantly, time adds up," Nana Moses interrupted. "You lose a second of your life for every spirit you send on. You're young and I know it doesn't seem like much to you now but, speaking from expe-rience, every heartbeat counts when you reach the other end, yeah?"

"I understand the risks," Wendy said softly. "If a spirit needs me, I'm willing to give up some of my life to send it on." She shrugged. "Apparently it's what I was born to do."

"Oh really? Do you understand that the brighter someone like you burns, even if it's only for a brief instant, the further your Light goes? There are spaces between the worlds, girl, spaces where deep, dark things exist. I wouldn't call it livin' exactly, but they stay there and bide their time. But if some light reaches 'em, well, they start heading in the direction of that light, yeah?"

"You're dangerous," Emma said coldly. "Even standing here, right now, in my house, you are dangerous."

"Dangerous?" Wendy rolled her eyes. "Seriously? Look at me! I'm not dangerous."

"The more we use our powers, the more ghosts can sense us," Emma said sharply. "It's feedback that Lost souls are especially sensitive to. We're like . . . candy to them. And they haven't eaten in years."

Wendy thought of the Lost spirit Specs, the feeling of his fingers stripping her soul from her flesh, of him holding her Light in his hands, and the vertigo of Piotr taking her from Specs and pressing her soul back into her body. Wendy shivered. "I figured that one out on my own."

Emma raised an eyebrow. "Oh really?"

"Hush girl," Nana Moses said. "You had a point there. Finish before I get any older."

"Sorry Great-Grandmother." She turned to Wendy. "We're at our most vulnerable going from solid to ethereal. If you're not fast enough, that moment between solid and not is the best time to take down a Reaper."

"I know that, too." Wendy thought it was best to wait and let Jane explain the mob of Walkers that had followed her into the hospital lobby. "If you don't shift into the Never, though, they won't necessarily—"

Nana Moses snorted. "Beacon, girl. You can avoid all you want, but if you reap enough souls in a row, eventually they'll find you.

They can smell you, and the stronger you are, the louder that siren song, even if you haven't reaped in weeks or months. The more you *practice*—especially the more you practice on the stronger ghosts like Walkers—the brighter you burn. No matter how you cover it up." She hawked and spat again, point made.

Eddie and Wendy exchanged a worried glance. By the end of the previous school semester Wendy had been reaping so many Walkers and spirits that the ghosts *had* begun hunting her down and bothering her during all hours of the day or night, at school and home, begging her to send them into the Light even if they found her on the toilet or showering. They hung around, staring and weeping, until she gave in. More than once Wendy had wondered how they'd found her no matter where she was. Now she knew.

Eddie leaned down and buried his hands in the corgi's fur, allowed it to nuzzle his cheeks and neck soothingly.

"Okay," Wendy said slowly, licking her lips. "So what can I do? What if I just stop using my powers completely?" The thought of all those needy souls pained her, especially the Shades, but she'd done it once already. If she kept her reaping to only the most extreme cases . . .

"Our records state that if a girl is a natural . . ." Emma clasped her hands together nervously, "even one who never uses her power, the ghosts will eventually find her even if she can't *look* in the Never anymore, much less reap."

Startled, Wendy glanced at Eddie. Seeing into the Never had become second nature to the point where she didn't even have to concentrate anymore; it was like glancing at a twisted black-and-white photograph just beneath a bright and sunny snapshot. "That's possible? Not seeing into the Never?"

"Oh ayep," Nana Moses said shortly. "Once there was a natural-born Reaper who had her eyes put out for being a witch. Couldn't see into the Never, but the Never could sure see into her. And how."

Wendy swallowed thickly. "What happened to her?"

"Well, she did the best she could to stay out of everyone's way, but because she didn't use her powers often enough she lost the ability to control 'em."

"Family legend states that the Light began seeping out of her pores," Emma added. "You could practically see it in the living world."

"That's how it works," Nana Moses agreed. "You use the Light or the Light starts building up. Without a pressure release it'll start to burn. It's bad for a normal Reaper; it's terrible for a natural. All that excess, a normal Reaper can last weeks or even months, but a natural? She'll burn up in days, if not hours."

"Sounds painful," Wendy said, wincing.

"Her family, though, they weren't willing to do what a thousand year tradition told 'em to . . . told the rest of us to mind our own business and kept her alive."

Peering at the wall, Nana Moses tapped the tapestry at the branch outlined in silver. "This was her family, this whole big branch. Wiped out in one night."

"What happened?" Wendy asked nervously.

"Her family caught and brought her ghosts to reap, but eventually she couldn't anymore. No more will to keep struggling on. She burned herself from the inside out and that Light called every ghostie for miles around."

Nana Moses rubbed a hand across her eyes. "The records say that they were found the next morning. Their shells were untouched—scattered on the ground of their cottage like garbage—but their souls were shredded like cheese, and every spirit in the area was glutted with power. Most of 'em were able to combat the Reapers that came to send 'em into the Light. All of 'em became Walkers after their feast; most escaped. Some are undoubtedly still out there."

Wendy shivered and Emma nodded, smirking. "I'm glad to see that you're finally starting to understand."

"They ate the natural, too?"

"Not a trace of her left, not even bones or hair," Nana Moses said. "Takin' her in gave those Walkers the ability to reach into the living world some. To touch us in our human shells the way we can touch any ol' spirit. Like so." She poked Eddie in the shoulder and he winced.

"Ouch! Come on, Nana Moses, that stings!"

"It's just . . ." Wendy hesitated, uncertain how to explain her confusion. "If a natural is so strong, if she's got the Light on all the time, I don't understand how they could overwhelm her. You're so warm that you just hurt Eddie simply by poking him. When I'm the Lightbringer my Light burns; if this blind chick had such an excess of Light that she couldn't even turn it off in the end, then why didn't her Light hurt them, too? Why didn't they burn up just getting close to her?"

"It did a little," Emma patiently explained, "but ghosts attracted to a natural, especially ghosts like the Lost or the Walkers . . . they are nearly mindless. They're already dead. More pain is nothing to them. All they are is desire—desire for the Light, desire for the bringer of the Light—and, given enough of them, they can easily overwhelm her and all the Reapers around her."

"Feeding frenzy," Nana Moses clarified.

"You saw what happened to your mother. Now imagine it a hundred—no, a thousand—times worse than that. The soul of a natural Reaper in the hands of spirits, or worse, is bad."

"Deep water things?"

Nana Moses chuckled. "Exactly. There are beasties in the darkest depths of the Never that would turn every curl on your head white. Banshee. Dvergar. Gwrgi. Or worse. Balderkin."

"Great-Grandmother!" Emma hissed. "Shhh!"

"Bah," Nana Moses sniffed. "If it's my time, it's my time. I'll be glad to go." She waved a finger under Wendy's nose and then poked her painfully in the shoulder. "But you, girl, you need to keep your fool self out of the hands of beasts like that. A Walker munching on a natural is bad enough. A Bad One having a snack on the likes of you is worse. The Bad Ones are bad business."

"Then what the hell am I supposed to do?" Wendy cried, nettled. "I can't live my life in a box, and if I don't use my powers there'll be buildup, right?"

"Yes," Emma said. "Which is why I want to train you."

Wendy blinked. "Excuse me?"

"I wish to train you," Emma repeated slower and louder, as if Wendy were mentally deficient. "To most of our family, you will be seen as an abomination, as a freak, as a base creature that should not be allowed to be. If we can prove to them that you are none of these things, that you may indeed be an asset to the clan, then they will leave you be."

"Fabulouso," Wendy snapped, "but what's in it for you?"

Nonplussed, Emma pursed her lips. "Who says that I need to gain anything from helping you?"

"Call it a hunch," Wendy replied shortly. "Maybe you have my best interests at heart, but you're still the type of girl who wants to maximize her profits. Two ghosts, one Reaper, that sort of thing."

"Fine. I don't like living in California," Emma replied. "Very few of us do, to be honest. It's expensive here, and the drivers are rude. The medical staff at every hospital I've encountered are unaccountably arrogant. It smells."

"So?"

"Your mother held this territory by herself for nearly fifteen years. No help was needed from any Reaper to keep the Bay Area ghost-free." Emma smoothed the hair back from her temples. "Only someone extremely talented or extremely powerful could hope to follow in her footsteps. Mary was talented."

"And I'm extremely powerful." Wendy shook her head. "But if you leave me here to handle everything on my own, I might get eaten unless I learn some control, forcing you to come back all over again." She snorted. "You're a real piece of work, you know that? All of you."

Emma shrugged. "There's also the matter of Eddie here, of course." She looked him slowly up and down, an inscrutable expression on her face. "His cord issue intrigues me on a professional level."

"Um, thanks?" Eddie said, shifting a step further away from Emma. The dogs crowding around him shifted as well.

"I want you two to allow me to help discern what happened to him," Emma said, raising an eyebrow. "If it is possible to separate a soul from the body in this manner . . . well, the research opportunity for the family is invaluable, not to mention the medical opportunities it provides."

"You want to experiment on me?" Eddie squeaked.

Emma rolled her eyes. "Hardly. I merely wish to ascertain how this particular malady of yours came to be. Imagine the medical aid I could give the wounded; disconnect the cord and slap an at-risk patient out of their shell before surgery and pop them back in as soon as they're safe. There's absolutely no risk of the patient waking during surgery if their soul is standing beside you. Most likely, there would be even less risk of accidental death."

"You should worry more about the actual dead and less about the living," Nana Moses harrumphed. "Medical opportunities, indeed."

"Grandmother approves," Emma said.

"She would," Nana Moses retorted.

"I would what?" asked a voice, and Wendy realized why Emma had been glancing nervously down the hallway their entire conversation. A woman, no more than sixty, with an elegantly coiffed head of stark-white hair stepped from the shadows. Her satin night-apparel was more pantsuit than pajamas, though it gaped enough at the neck for Wendy to make out an intricate pattern of faded Celtic knots and dense runic whorls completely unlike any she'd ever laid eyes on before.

"We woke you," Emma said apologetically.

"My bones woke me," the woman replied, flicking her attention to Eddie and Wendy only briefly before noting Nana Moses at the back. She frowned. "Mother, you should be sleeping at this hour."

"And you should be dead," Nana Moses quipped. "Funny how these things work, huh?"

"Mother," the woman sighed, "your humor is falling quite flat this morning. Our guests might think you're serious."

"People think funny things without me saying a word. But you've got a point. It's late. I'm going to bed," Nana Moses said, waving a hand in Wendy and Eddie's general direction. "Come get me at dawn, Emmaline. Bring coffee."

The woman stiffened; her expression hardened, turning into not so much a scowl or a frown as a narrowing, an inward disapproval. Wendy had the feeling that this discussion was a familiar one for the two of them. "Mother, your heart—"

"My heart won't stop if I have a cup of coffee, Elise Anne," Nana Moses snapped, clapping a hand against her chest in mock aggravation. "Not after all these years. It might stop if I *don't* have a cup, however. Keep your nose out of it."

Wendy, watching this exchange, was troubled. Why did the name Elise seem familiar to her? The woman herself was striking enough that Wendy was sure she'd recall if they'd ever previously met, but it was her name that was striking a quiet chord deep within.

Elise tried again. "Mother—"

"The day I let my youngest boss me around is the same day I give up this mortal coil. Enough, young lady. You mind your business and I'll mind mine."

Chastised, Elise graciously inclined her head and stepped aside, allowing Nana Moses to bully her way past. "G'night!" The old woman crowed, stopping only long enough to add, "And Eddie? You come visit me any time." With that, Nana Moses thunked away, moving down the hall Elise had just come from, muttering to herself under her breath the whole while.

Then, out of the blue, it came to her. Wendy could clearly remember her mother once, during training, chastising Wendy.

Mom, she'd whined, *I can't do this. Shifting through a tree? It's impossible!* Her mother, shaking her head and rolling her eyes, had slid through the tree easily and turned on the other side with an exasperated expression.

You're lucky I'm not Elise, Mary'd said, shaking her head and gesturing for Wendy to try again. *Moaning like that would've gotten you twenty laps and all night practicing. Do it again.*

Stalling, Wendy'd asked: *Who's Elise?*

No one . . . important to us right now. One day you'll see.

Now she had her answer.

Waiting until Nana Moses was well down the hall and out of earshot, Elise smiled thinly and turned to Eddie, snapping for the ghost dogs at his feet to disperse. They quickly jogged over to kennels in the corner and slid through the walls, settling on the remnants of blankets with both real and ethereal bones to chew on.

"I see your ride is finally here."

"Yep," Eddie said, edging toward the door.

"Then, as you've long overstayed your welcome, it's best you left, yes?" Elise smoothed one hand over her hair and glanced at Wendy. "We shall talk soon, Winifred, but it is late and, like my mother, I think it is time to return to bed. You may let yourselves out."

"Sure thing," Wendy agreed readily, glad to finally be on her way.

"I'll see them to the door, Grandmother," Emma said.

"As you wish." Elise patted Wendy on the shoulder before turning away and Wendy had to bite her lip to keep from hissing in pain. Elise's touch was intensely hot, as sharply painful as if she'd just finished running her hand across a stovetop. If Elise noticed the pain her touch caused, she made no mention of it. She merely strolled back into the shadows as if nothing were amiss at all.

Emma guided them to the door, forcibly guiding Wendy out with hardly a glance. "I'll be in contact," she promised in a breathy whisper, barely allowing Wendy past the archway before the door clicked shut and locked behind them.

CHAPTER NINE

nsulted, Wendy made her way across the dimly lit yard to find that Eddie was already waiting for her at the Charger, leaning casually against the driver's side and staring at the stars. "Some adventure, huh?"

"You've really been with them this entire time?" Wendy could hardly believe it. "How did you stay sane?"

"It wasn't all that bad."

"Color me surprised. With people like Elise around, I'd have figured you for walking home long before now."

"She's just a tightass, no biggie. I've dealt with worse. Speaking of worse, give me the quick and dirty about your mom. *She* turned out to be the White Lady? How the hell did *that* happy crappy go down?"

Speaking quickly so she didn't have to dwell on the past few months, Wendy unlocked the driver's side as Eddie slid through the car door and gingerly settled into the passenger seat. Starting the car and backing out of the drive, Wendy explained how her mother's soul had been ripped apart by twelve Lost souls at the bus wreck the previous February. Called by her pain, Piotr had helped put her back together again, and was then drained of the memory of the event by the newly created White Lady. Since Wendy had sent the guilty Lost into the Light, the White Lady decided to gather up twelve other souls to mend her soul completely. The final step in returning to her body was devouring Wendy's Light.

"But wouldn't that hurt you?" Eddie asked as Wendy stopped at a stop sign at the edge of Emma's neighborhood.

"It would have killed me," Wendy said quietly; the retelling had brought her to tears. She wiped a hand across her face and fumbled one-handed in her purse for a Kleenex to blow her nose. "It almost did, actually. Mom was so conflicted at the end. Being shredded by the Lost like that made her go insane, Eds. She kept going back and forth between Mom and the White Lady, trying to warn me one minute and then the next saying that she had you captured and if I didn't give up my soul then she'd kill you."

"But she didn't," Eddie protested. "It wasn't her."

"Yeah, she eventually admitted that. Later." Done with tears, Wendy coughed to clear her throat and straightened in her seat, all business now. "Of course, now the question is who *did* knock you out of your body? Do you remember what happened at all? And how did you end up at Emma's?"

"Not a clue. One minute I'm minding my own business and the next there's this immense . . . I don't know . . . pressure? Around my chest. I came to in the hospital, standing outside my body. Mom was freaking out and there were doctors swarming everywhere. It sucked big time."

"I'd imagine," Wendy said. "But you obviously kept it together long enough to find help."

"Help found me." Eddie scrubbed his hands across his face. "I'm sitting there by my body, waiting for it all to be over and the Light to pick me up the way you always said it would, when Jane pokes her head in my room. Doing rounds, I guess. She's always up at the hospital these days."

"Jane?" Wendy frowned. Jane had claimed that *Emma* had found and helped Eddie. Wendy wondered why she was being so humble about aiding her friend. Though, if Wendy thought about it, "helping" wasn't exactly the coolest thing in the world for someone like Jane to do.

"Jane. She takes one look at me and says, 'Hold up a sec. You're not dead. Like . . . really not dead.'"

Eddie sighed and leaned forward, motioning with his hands. "I was all, 'Nope! Care to help a guy out?' and she gave me a funny look and told me to follow her. Took me straight to Emma and Elise—they were downstairs in the lobby—and Elise decided that they'd take me home with them. Emma finished writing some kind of letter to give to you, and we bailed."

"I'm so sorry," Wendy groaned. "I should have been there. You must have been . . ."

"Terrified out of my ever-lovin' mind?" Eddie asked. "Yeah. You could say that. And I kept falling through stuff when I didn't want to."

"I'm sure you've figured this out by now, but staying cohesive and moving around in the Never is a matter of willpower. Once you can wrap your mind around that, life—well, death anyway—gets a lot easier."

"Emma showed me that. I guess your mom taught you?"

Wendy stiffened, using the excuse of piloting the Charger to think over her reply. "Piotr, actually. Mom and I didn't spend a lot of time in the Never together."

Eddie was silent for an equally long moment, digesting this. Then he sighed and said, "Right," clasping his hands in his lap and grudgingly asking, "How is old Pete, anyway?"

"I wouldn't know," Wendy said. "He dumped me."

Eddie jerked in the seat as he lost his concentration, and he started to sink through the cushion. "What? You're kidding me!" He scowled thickly, grabbed the dashboard, and pulled himself back up. "What happened?"

"It's complicated," Wendy said, merging carefully onto 680. It was early yet, not even dawn, but already the early morning gridlock had begun as all the Silicon Valley bigwigs who lived outside the valley commuted in to work.

Grinning, Eddie poked himself in the chest. "I think I've got time."

"He wanted to figure out where he came from," Wendy said, shrugging and sitting forward in the seat to try and get a better vantage point on the traffic.

"Um, Russia?"

"Yeah, but according to Mom and his friend Lily, Piotr's been dead a lot longer than even he realizes, Eddie. Maybe he was from Russia once, but he hasn't been there in at *least* five hundred years. Probably more."

"Weird," Eddie said. "I didn't know ghosts didn't have to stick around the place they died."

"They can travel just like we can." Wendy merged into the center lane. "And speaking of traveling . . . nice job, leaving my gift before you bailed to go spend Hanukkah with your family. I would've liked you to be there."

"So you did get the buckle and my note." Eddie scrunched in his seat, blushing. "I didn't want to ask."

"It was an amazing gesture, Eds. Of course I read your letter. And I can't imagine what you had to go through to get that buckle." Wendy didn't want to tell him that his buckle was now at the hospital, grasped in his shell's hands. Her futile gesture seemed silly now.

Turning his face to the window, Eddie was silent for a long moment before replying. "I didn't do that much, actually. After Dad died, Mom threw me in therapy and the counselor kept suggesting that I find something to be angry at other than my dad for a bit. Because I was in denial."

"And you decided on the buckle that didn't save him?"

"No. I just wanted a piece of the car; even the gas cap would've worked. I asked around and it turned out that my Uncle Arthur knew the guy at the lot Dad's car ended up at. Once the CSI-types were done making sure there was no foul play, he went and got me the buckle." Eddie shrugged as if it was no big deal, but Wendy knew that the retelling was bothering him.

"Then what?"

"Well, I yelled at it; hours screaming at that dumb buckle for not saving him. I threw it. If you look closely you can even see the corner where I took a hammer to it once. And then, one day I realized that it wasn't the car's fault. It was an inanimate object. It was no one's fault. It was an accident. It wasn't fate or kismet or karma or any of that stupid crap. Figuring that out . . . it was like a light had flicked on in my head, chasing away all those nasty, grimy shadows. I didn't need the buckle after realizing that. Not really."

"Yeah?"

"I relapsed once or twice. It wasn't overnight. But it was like that one realization was a lancet hitting some big boil I didn't know I had. I still needed time to heal but it didn't ache anymore, yeah? I wasn't all this pent-up rage walking around pretending to be a person."

Merging onto the 101 was simpler than merging onto 680 had been. It was busier but calmer here. Wendy began to relax. All the talk of the accident that had killed Eddie's father was making her nervous about her own highway driving, especially during the early morning rush. "Okay, I understand that. But then why give the buckle to me?"

"Because I love you."

Wendy, startled, hesitated over her reply. Eddie had said he'd loved her before, but never so plainly. Normally he flirted up a storm and approached the subject with winks and nudges and playful laughter. This was bald and fresh and raw; completely unlike her best friend.

"Eddie—"

"No, look, I said in that note I wasn't going to bug you with it and I'm not, okay? So don't panic. It's just . . ." Eddie licked his lips, pausing over what he was going to say next, "It's just that it's the truth, okay, all unvarnished and out there. I love you. And it's all well and good to write that down in a letter that I wasn't even there for you to read, but it's completely different when I tell you face to face, you know?"

He crossed his arms over his chest and took a deep breath. "I love you. I love you. I love YOU, Wendy. You're the only person in the world who went through what I went through that night and, even more importantly, that night—what happened to Dad—that was what shoved you into this ghost-thing. If it hadn't been for that accident maybe you would have no idea why your mom collapsed, you know? That car flipping over made us both completely different people. And, as much as it sucks to say this, because we've been through a lot of crap in the past year, maybe it made us better people. Overall, at least. Maybe. And maybe we'd both be a pair of jerks if we hadn't gone through that. Maybe we wouldn't even be friends; people grow apart, it happens all the time, you know?"

"Eddie—"

He sighed loudly. "Don't. Just . . . don't. I don't want your pity and I don't want your 'I love you like a buddy' or 'we talked about why this would never work out' speech. I know you're not interested in me and you've probably still got the mega-hots for Petey the Russian Ghosty. I just wanted you to know. It's important to me."

Wendy quirked a smile and decided that if Eddie wasn't ready to really talk about this weird thing between them, then she wasn't either. "Actually, I wanted to know if you wanted me to drop you off at your house or if you're coming home with me. Or I can run you by the hospital if you want to check out your amazingly sick abs in that flimsy little hospital gown."

Eddie laughed. "Pervert."

"Hey, like you wouldn't peek. Your mom has you in a delightful pair of Superman Underoos by the way."

"Okay, now I know you're joking."

"Piotr wanted me to go with him," Wendy said suddenly.

"Yeah?" Eddie's voice was carefully neutral. "And?"

"I said that I couldn't. I couldn't just walk out on Chel and Jon and Dad like that. So we parted ways. That's all that happened. It's that simple. And that complicated."

"So no big dramatic fight? No cheating on you with Zombie Cleopatra?"

She snorted. "Hardly."

"Damn."

"He's gone, Eddie. And just because I thought—in the past—that you and me being together wouldn't be the best of ideas, that doesn't mean that I don't really care about you. I love you too, you stupid . . . head . . . guy."

"Couldn't quite make that one work, huh?"

"Shut up." Wendy shook her head. "The point is, I don't know what I want. Maybe that'll be you. Maybe that's someone like Piotr. I don't know. But I do love you. Not entirely as a friend. Not entirely as something more. It's love though. I'm just not ready for serious right now."

"What about Piotr?"

"What about him? He left, I stayed, you're here, and it's not like love is this all or nothing thing, right?"

"It is, in fact, complicated," Eddie agreed.

"I have to be reasonable, Eds," Wendy pressed. "Piotr's dead and when we find your silver cord you'll be one hundred percent alive. Maybe then, after I've figured out where your cord is and how to get you back in your body, then we can talk about . . . us. This. Whatever this thing is." She see-sawed a hand back and forth between them.

Eddie snorted. "Oh, you did not just tell me that I might win out your heart because the first place guy skipped town and happens to be dead. I'm insulted!"

"No!" Irritated, Wendy pounded the steering wheel. "Stuff your pride and *listen* to me, Eds. Before, I always said no because you didn't get where I was coming from. You had no clue what it was like to live in my world. Right?"

"Right . . . oooh. I get it." Eddie smacked himself in the forehead. "Dummy, Eddie, dumb-head! You didn't want to be with me because I kept telling you to quit Reaping and give up on your mom." He frowned.

"And now?"

"And now . . . the shoe's on the other foot and wow, do I feel like an ass. I'm so sorry about that, by the way. You're not going to give up on me the way I wanted you to give up on your mom, are you?"

"Of course not. And thank you for admitting you were acting like a jerk."

He paused for a long moment. "Why didn't you belt me again? I would have deserved it."

"Because you were just alive." Wendy shrugged. "You couldn't know any better. You hadn't been there."

"No kidding. Time . . . everything is different over on this side. Sometimes it's so slow and sometimes it's like everything is whizzing by. So what day is it anyway?"

She thought a moment. Sometime during the night, late had turned to early . . . "New Year's Eve."

He whistled. "That late? Crap."

"I'll find your cord, Eds. Don't panic. Maybe after I get a nap in we'll crack the mystery by this afternoon. You could be back in your body by midnight, just in time to booze it up. And if not, Emma's apparently interested in helping, so there's that. Not that I'd trust her any farther than I can throw her. Though, on the other hand, she's awfully skinny."

He waved a hand. "No, it's not that. Your birthday is in like a week."

"Yeah, your point is?" With a relieved sigh, Wendy took the El Camino Real exit, glad to finally be well away from the highway.

"Well, that means we've got a week to put me back in my body or I'm going to miss lighting my dad's *yahrtzeit* candle." Eddie scowled and clenched his fists on his thighs. "I've never missed it before."

"Oh no! Oh, Eddie, maybe—" Wendy gingerly reached over and brushed a careful, comforting hand across his upper arm. He hissed in pain and she jerked her hand back. "Damn, I'm sorry! Maybe Nana Moses is right—I need more control. I'll be more careful."

"No," Eddie sighed, rubbing his arm, "it's fine." He chuckled. "Pete didn't have this problem, right? He must've been one of those gnarly bearded manly types that scoffs at pain." Eddie flexed a muscle. "Grrr."

"Hardly. No, he just could touch me when no other spirits could."

"Do you know why?"

"No clue." Wendy recalled how the White Lady had mocked her relationship with Piotr, belittling his memory loss for every instance of touching a Reaper. She'd hadn't needed to belittle Wendy for every kiss she and Piotr had ever shared, Wendy had done it to herself.

Remembering this, Wendy wondered if Nana Moses or Emma knew about Piotr, and she was suddenly glad that he'd chosen to skip town when he did; she had a feeling Emma might consider Piotr another interesting specimen to study. Lost in thought, Wendy pulled into her driveway. "We're here."

Eddie waited for Wendy to kill the engine and stepped out onto the driveway. He moved to her right. "Wendy?"

"Yeah, Eddie?" Was that movement in the bushes under her window? Squinting at the shadows against the wall and not really paying attention, Wendy half-turned toward her friend. "What's up?"

Eddie, taking advantage of the moment, leaned in and kissed her. Wendy, startled, stiffened for an instant, and then leaned forward, deepening the kiss. Eddie's lips were cool to the touch and his hands framing her face were supple and soft, his thumbs brushing her curls off her cheeks. Wendy found herself breathless, her heartbeat thudding in her chest and pounding in her ears, every inch of skin zinging and tingling.

"Wow," she said, pulling away after several long seconds. She shivered and tried to put her thoughts in some kind of reasonable order. "That was . . . wow! Just wow. Eddie. Um . . . that was unexpected."

"Indeed," said Piotr from beneath the tree. "In that, Wendy, I would have to agree."

CHAPTER TEN

After unknown years existing in the Never, Piotr was a realist. He hadn't been expecting a tearful, overwrought greeting from Wendy; he knew that, after the way they'd parted, she was unlikely to dive into his arms with passionate kisses and demands for him to never leave her side again. But what he hadn't been expecting was to find her passionately kissing her best friend.

Elle and Lily, eying the troubled expression on Piotr's face, carefully moved to flank him. He knew they were doing it for his own good—just as he knew that Wendy would never hurt him—but purposefully pissing off the Lightbringer was a foolhardy action at best, and Piotr was profoundly grateful for their friendship.

"Piotr?" Wendy drew back from Eddie and Piotr was bitterly glad to see that Eddie bore the marks of their kiss; his essence was thinner where her fingers and lips had been, and the hands that had been tenderly cupping Wendy's face were thin as paper and nearly translucent.

Either he didn't feel the pain, or he had a strong will. Eddie hardly noticed his wounds, instead twisting quickly to face Piotr, his flesh quickly thickening and darkening as he shifted slightly to edge between Wendy and Piotr. He looked to Wendy. "This is Pete—er, Piotr? I thought you said he left town?"

Beside him, Elle smothered a snicker and Lily sighed.

"He did," Wendy said, brushing her hair back from her face and approaching him, wary as a fawn. She nodded once at Lily and Elle, but did not greet them. "Piotr, why are you here?"

"I had come for you, to speak of important things. My thinking was that our earlier connection, your invitation to visit anytime, still held true. I can see now that this was false." Piotr sneered. "From another girl, one who is of more relaxed morals, from one such as this I could believe being replaced so quickly. But from you, Wendy? Finding you like this with one such as him is a shock."

"Wait a second, did you just call me a slut?" Wendy demanded, stunned.

"Hey now," Eddie said, scowling and angry on Wendy's behalf, "one, I don't see a ring on that finger, ghostly or not. Two, Wendy's fully capable of kissing whoever she wants." He snorted. "'One such as him'? Really, dude? And three, bucko, you left her, remember? *She* didn't go into your hospital room and bail the second *you* woke up. You took off; so don't go flinging blame."

"How cute," Piotr snapped, "the boy thinks his opinion matters. *Past' zakroi*, little man."

Glaring, Eddie leaned forward, nose to nose with Piotr. "Dude, I just met you and you are stepping all over my last nerve. Whatever the hell you just said, say it again."

Thrilled at the opportunity to shove his knuckles through this annoying boy's face, Piotr's hands balled into fists and he grinned. "Loosely translated, I told you to shut it, boy. Or I will shut it for you." He fingered his scar and leered at Eddie. "Perhaps with a very, very sharp weapon, *da?*"

"Okay, you two, that's enough," Wendy snapped, suddenly between the two of them, shoving them apart. The instant Wendy made contact it became clear that she wasn't taking care with her abilities. Where she touched Piotr, their flesh misted, fogging faintly, but he was too angry to care; where she touched Eddie, he burned.

"I'm not some spiffy new toy for the kiddies to fight over," Wendy declared angrily. "*I* get to decide who I'm in a relationship with, who I kiss—hell, whoever I want to do damn near *anything* with. *Morally* or not, Piotr, this ain't the Middle Ages, you frickin' prude. And furthermore, I don't appreciate being snapped over like a piece of meat. I'm a person, not a possession. Got it?"

She poked Piotr in the chest, the heat of her forcing him back a step. "*You* left *me*, it was all amicable and everything. I don't know how they did it back in whatever century you come from, but this is now, which means that I can kiss whoever the hell I want. I'll prove it if I have to." She looked tauntingly at Elle. "You wanna kiss a Lightbringer?"

Elle threw back her head and laughed, leaning over so Wendy and the others could see the curve of her chest peeping out the top of her bodice-blouse. "Not the most romantic of proposals, but sure, you're cute enough. I'd be willing to neck a little to put our flyboy Pete in his place."

"Hey now," Eddie said mildly, both irritated and amused at the suggestion. "That's hardly fair."

Lily, shaking her head, put a warning hand on Elle's shoulder. "Do not aggravate him. This is not funny."

"To me you would do this thing?" Piotr asked Wendy, outraged. He limped to her side, examining her face closely. "You would kiss one of my best friends, one of my *only* friends, in front of me? Without a care to our past?"

"Just trying to get a point across," Wendy replied coolly. "You don't own me, Piotr." She jerked her chin up. "And when you left, you'd already hurt me the only way you can. So back off, buddy. You won't win a fight here."

It was as if the world spotted red. Heart thudding in his ears, Piotr trembled with rage, watching the spots dance in front of his eyes. He concentrated on the streetlight across the way, trying to train his head and heart on the glass bulb within to keep calm. As he watched, the bulb popped and popped again, glass cracking into a glittering spiderweb. Destroyed in the real world, it began to take shape in the Never.

Piotr had to close his eyes for a moment, but still the Never and the living land merged, separated, merged again, and the lights flickered frantically behind his eyes as Piotr struggled to reason with himself, to keep calm, to remain sane and logical.

He failed.

Furious, Piotr's mind snapped. Without thought, guided only by frustrated fury, he shoved Wendy as hard as he could. She staggered back, falling right through Eddie and hitting the Charger's bumper with her thigh, twisting hard as she tried to catch herself from falling on the driveway.

"PIOTR!" Lily shouted, grabbing him by the shoulder as he stepped toward Wendy, icy cold pulsing from his hands. Elle grabbed his other shoulder and then yelped in surprise. Piotr struggled with them briefly as Eddie hurried to Wendy's side to make sure she wasn't seriously injured.

Piotr, snarling, swung hard at his friends; Elle blocked with a knee, catching Piotr off guard and in the groin. He folded up wordlessly, the terrible red pulsing in his head fading as the pain caught up with his brain and shut down his incredible, terrible rage.

"I was wrong before. His hurt is not mending," Lily said, clearly and quietly, forcing Piotr to lie on the floor as she examined the Walker-inflicted wound in his side. He hissed and thrashed in her arms for a moment before his eyes rolled back in his head and he passed out.

"Look at the edges of his cut," Lily exclaimed softly, resting his head on her knapsack and lifting his arm aside so that Elle could get a better look at the wound. "It is as if the very essence is being eaten away. And the back, I missed it before . . . that awful hook gored him all the way through. What did that Walker do to him?"

"Has to be poison," Elle said, rubbing her knee and frowning. "Spirit webs and all, the White Lady had some nasty stuff at her disposal. Knowing her, she probably left some of it behind when she bit it. Whatever it is, look at it, it's eating him alive. Dead. You know what I mean, he's being pulled apart." She held up a hand and a trail of Piotr's essence stretched between her fingers and his body like sticky, gummy spider webs, oozing life and will all over the sidewalk.

"Piotr's hurt?" Rubbing her hip, Wendy knelt down by his head. A car drove slowly by, heading for the apartments at the end of the block; Wendy knew that she had to look strange, hunched over and kneeling on her driveway in the middle of the night, but she didn't care. "When did this happen?"

"Earlier this evening," Lily said, explaining briefly about their encounter with the group of Walkers outside the spirit web forest. "When their leader ordered them to fight, it was like nothing I have ever seen before in Walkers. Like wolves, working in an elegant pack formation to take us down. We would have succumbed in the first attack had it not been for Piotr. He engaged the leader right away, leaving us to fend off the others."

"Dummy here got in the way of an attack headed for me, and he's been balled up ever since," Elle added, frowning. "Erratic, edgy, getting lost. Totally not Piotr. Dumb Dora me, I thought he just had the heebie-jeebies about meeting up with you again, but it looks like maybe whatever the Walker used got to him, made him crazy with pain or some such." She pressed a gentle hand to his side and hissed. "It's freezing."

"Oh, I'm so dumb," Wendy muttered, hand hovering over Piotr's head. "I mean, I'm pissed he swung at me, and if he didn't have a damn good reason I'd be feeding him his head right now, but . . . but Piotr always has it together." Aggravated, Wendy shook her head. "I should've known losing his cool like that was totally unlike him."

"So you're saying loverboy here's not normally a judgmental, jealous psychopath?" Eddie asked from behind them. Elle shot him a scornful look and he shrugged. "Hey, this is the first time I've ever actually met the guy and he threatens to disembowel my face. Maybe it's a passionate Russian alpha-male thing, or maybe he's just a dick. I'm allowed to ask."

"Normally Piotr is very caring and kind," Wendy defended him, stripping off Eddie's motorcycle jacket and pushing back the sleeves of the lightweight hoodie beneath. "But not crazy. No, I have to help him."

"Is that wise?" Lily asked. "We do not know what effect pouring your power into him would do at this time. He is severely wounded —perhaps such power would hurt him rather than heal him?"

"At the very least, he'll lose a memory, right?" Elle asked. "That's how this weird thing you two cats have going works, right?"

"I'm confused," Eddie said plaintively. "What are you three blabbing about? Lose a memory? Like what your mom did to him when he healed her that one time?"

"Yeah, sort of. Before, when Piotr and I were together," Wendy explained haltingly, "kissing him would drain me. I would become more ethereal, he would become more real."

"Excuse me?" Eddie drawled. "You're telling me that he made you more like a ghost? And you're seriously *not* seeing the creepy factor in that?"

Wendy glanced at her friend and shrugged, shamed that she'd never thought of it that way before. Being in Piotr's arms had seemed so natural, so right, at the time. Though Piotr worried about their closeness, Wendy refused to believe that Piotr might drain her completely. She trusted him implicitly. He was *Piotr*, protector of the Lost and her friend. That was all she'd ever needed to know . . . before now.

"The effect was always temporary for me," Wendy said stiffly, "and energizing for Piotr. When we went to fight the White Lady, she explained that Piotr's ghost has been around my family for centuries."

Careful not to touch his flesh with her own, Wendy tenderly brushed the hair off of Piotr's forehead, exposing the twisting scar at his temple. "He's always been here, on the sidelines, helping us out, healing us when we needed it. It's how he knew my mom was hurt at the bus accident; it's how he knew to go to her. He couldn't help himself."

Remembering the way her mother had mocked Piotr's weakness, Wendy scowled. "Awful as it is, the White Lady described Piotr like a battery. You put power into him and later you can take it out again when you need it; when you're sick or hurt."

"So, does powering up the Energizer Ghostie hurt you guys? Reapers, I mean."

"Not for long," Wendy promised, gingerly pulling Piotr's head into her lap.

The three bystanders held their breath as Wendy, supporting Piotr's head, leaned forward and tenderly slanted her mouth across his. White steam billowed from their touch, obscuring their kiss.

After several long seconds the steam cleared and Eddie, rubbing a hand nervously along his arm, intervened. "So, Lady Smoochalot, did the Princess Charming kiss-o-magic work or what?"

Wendy drew back from Piotr, tears in her eyes, and settled his head back on Lily's knapsack. "No," she whispered, pulling away from Piotr so that the others could see what her touch had done. Fresh purple-red palm prints marred his face where her hands had pressed. His lips had blistered and the side of his nose was red and angry-looking, seeping essence slightly. "It didn't."

Lily gasped and turned her face away.

"I'd be pissed, but there's no way you knew that'd happen," Elle whispered. "Holy hell, girl, that's new. If *you* can't even touch him, how in the hell are we supposed to stop him from getting eaten alive by the poison?"

"A Lost," Lily said, turning back to them as she wiped her eyes with the heel of her hand. "We must find a Lost or a wise woman. If the Lightbringer cannot aid him, a Lost may yet be able to. At the very least, they might be willing to pump him full of the will to keep going." She shuddered. "We must do all that we can, even if his form ends up as the Walkers', naught but flesh-covered bone."

Weary and frustrated, Wendy stood up. "Carry him to my room," she told Lily and Elle, as Wendy headed for her climbing tree. "Eddie can lead you there and I'll sneak in my usual way."

Once they were all safely in her room, Wendy closed the window and began pulling down the blinds. It was a good thing she hadn't come in through the front door; already she could hear Chel downstairs, starting up the treadmill in the living room.

"Every Lost skipped town weeks ago," Elle said as Wendy finished drawing the blinds shut. "We sent 'em on their merry way ourselves."

"Sad as it is, death is a part of life. Many children die every day," Lily said grimly. "We need only find one of them."

When Eddie made a disbelieving sound, Lily narrowed her eyes and jerked up her chin. "You have been living, and are still living, yes? Then you cannot hope to understand our ways. With the Riders a Lost is always protected and in return they heal us, give us the energy to keep on in this bleak hell that is the afterlife. It is our pact. One such as you, not even yet dead, can have no idea how the wheels of the Never work. Hush your ignorant mouth."

"Sorry," Eddie said, chagrined. "It just seems so . . . mercenary."

"Welcome to the Never," Elle snorted. "Leave your scruples at whatever nasty bit'o'business dropped you off in this hellhole to begin with."

She hugged herself loosely, arms crossed across her stomach, and shivered, eying Piotr's lolling body with resigned sadness. The wounds caused by Wendy's kiss were rapidly healing but the hole in his side was still seeping and raw.

"After I crossed over, Petey here was the first one to find me; he gave me purpose, introducing me to the other Riders, explaining about the Lost. If it weren't for him . . . I owe him one. More than one, if I'm bein' honest. So let's do this thing."

"He is in good hands with you," Lily told Wendy, tenderly lifting Piotr's head from her knapsack and settling it back on the floor. "When he wakes, wrap his wounds—ankle, side—and apply a salve to his burns if one can be found."

"I've got supplies we can use on him, but I can't fix him up myself," Wendy protested weakly. "Even for a second. I'll hurt him."

"Then your friend must do it," Lily said gravely. She turned to Eddie. "Can I trust you to take care Piotr, of my friend, even though he threatened you earlier? It was clearly not him talking, but this sickness, this poison's madness. You have my word on that."

"Yeah," Elle agreed. "Petey can be a bit of a bluenose every now and then, but overall he's good stock."

"Oh geeze, of course I'll help," Eddie grumbled. "I'll fix him up if for no other reason than a guy can't stand the three of you looking all mopey at him. One of you, maybe, but all three is just overkill."

"I thank you," Lily said, nodding once at Eddie and then stepping through the bedroom door.

"You're pretty keen, you know that?" Elle said and, leaning up, bussed Eddie on the jaw, letting her lips linger in the hollow of his cheek. Behind the cover of their bodies, Elle pressed a dagger into Eddie's hand. "This is for you. Take good care of it."

Eddie nervously slid the sheath into a belt loop. "Um, thanks, I guess?"

"No thanks needed, handsome," Elle said, winking at Wendy as she drew away but still addressing Eddie. "If you end up staying here in the Never, you and me can have a bit of a talk later. And if you're really lucky maybe the bank'll be open."

"I'm sorry—and I mean this sincerely—but I haven't the faintest idea what on earth you're talking about. There're banks for the dead?" Eddie asked.

"Okay, thanks, everything's peachy, we'll take good care of him, bye now!" Wendy said sharply, scowling at Elle as she none-too-gently guided the smirking ghost through the door. She waited until she saw the two girls walking across the lawn below to shake her head in amused annoyance. "Elle's . . . a character. I'll give her that."

"Jealous?" Eddie asked slyly.

"Over you? Pshaw." Wendy tossed her head. "You can handle a short-skirted blonde any day of the week."

"Oh yeah? Well what about him?" Eddie looked pointedly down to Piotr. "What're we going to do if he wakes up and he's still all 'grrr'?"

"I am awake," Piotr said groggily, opening his eyes. "And I can assure you, I am not all, uh, 'grrr.' In fact my head feels like . . .

like . . ." he laughed weakly. "Forgive me, my friends, I can't think of anything witty to say. My head, it aches greatly."

Frowning around the room, he waved Eddie over and offered his hand. "Edward, I wish to apologize for earlier. I'd never attack a man for no reason, but I am not exactly feeling myself right now. I am in great pain." He touched his side gingerly and frowned. "As you can see."

"Yeah, if I had a hole that size in me, I'd be testy too," Eddie said, kneeling down. "Lucky for you, I've got a little bit of experience patching people up. Not much, just basic first aid, but it'll be enough for now until we can get a kid out here."

"A kid?" Piotr looked to Wendy.

"Lily and Elle went to find a Lost," she explained, opening her desk drawer and pulling out a box of scavenged medical supplies she'd picked up during her rounds in the Never. *Always be prepared for anything*, her mother's voice echoed in her mind. *Always watch your back.*

"They're fools," he said, not unkindly. "Sweet and misguided fools."

"They care about you," Wendy replied simply, leaving the makeshift first aid kit on the desk for Eddie. "I say let 'em try."

"And you?" Piotr purposefully didn't look at Eddie, though he could feel Eddie stiffen at the question. "Do you care about me?"

"That depends." Parting the blackout shades, Wendy glanced out the window. Despite the obscenely early hour, a car was driving very slowly down her street. "You apologized to Eddie for threatening him, but I didn't hear an apology for swiping at me."

Piotr frowned. "I . . . I attacked you?"

"Let me guess. You don't remember." Wendy sighed and shook her head, watching as the car paused at every house.

He shook his head. "Nothing. I came to find you, to warn you, and I found you with—"

Flushing, Piotr broke off and tried again. "I was angry—too angry for reason, for logic—I literally saw red, and then . . .

nothing." He winced as Eddie used his stillness as an excuse to begin treating his wounds with the ethereal supplies Wendy had scavenged. Piotr jumped and writhed as the first splashes of the rubbing alcohol hit the open wound.

Hissing under his breath and forcing himself to talk through the pain, Piotr continued, "If I tried to hurt you, Wendy, I am truly sorry. I would never—"

"You did," Eddie said sharply. Then he sighed. "But I don't think anyone is blaming you, not anymore, at least. Or, maybe they are, but I'm not."

"You are a very confusing man," Piotr said.

"Yeah, don't I know it. Look Pete, this stuff, whatever this gunk is, it is *tres* nasty, okay? I don't think *I'd* keep my cool if this junk were inside me eating away, and considering this crap, I'm not blaming you for being a dick. Watch. Okay, I pour this here," Eddie poured another swig into Piotr's wound and Piotr hissed sharply, "I pour this here and the alcohol is doing nothing to clean out any of this black grit." He pointed into the wound, at a section that looked as if it had been gnawed at by wild animals.

"Whatever this is, I can't fix it. Maybe if I had better—what d'you all call it?—better salvage? Hydrogen peroxide, saline, a blowtorch . . . you know, something way stronger. Maybe then."

"But for now?" Piotr asked plaintively, half amused and half aggravated at how easily Eddie was taking his pain. "What now?"

"For now we'll have to wait for this kid, this Lost or whatever, to get here. It's all I can do, man. I'm sorry."

"I think Chel's still got a couple bottles of peroxide in the bathroom," Wendy suggested. "She's so attached to them I wouldn't be surprised if there isn't a Never version sitting on a back shelf."

Frowning, Eddie stepped away from Piotr and gestured to Wendy. When she joined him, he pitched his voice low and said, "Have you looked—I mean really *looked*—at that hole he's sporting?"

"Of course not," Wendy replied wrinkling her nose. "That seemed . . . rude."

"Forget rude, this is important. Go look in that hole. Hold your breath if you have to, but take a glance." Eddie sighed and approached her door. "I'm gonna check the bathroom and see if you're right about that peroxide. Maybe it'll work. Be right back."

Shaking her head, Wendy tentatively approached Piotr and knelt down as Eddie passed through the far wall. "Do you mind if I—"

"Do your worst," Piotr said softly. "For you, Wendy, I give you anything you ever want." He smiled. "Though, if you don't mind, I'd like a kiss as a reward for being so very, very brave." He winked and Wendy laughed.

"I thought we were broken up?"

"Perhaps, perhaps not," he said, pitching his voice low and eyeing the wall Eddie had vanished through. "But even if so, would you deny a man in pain such a little thing? I have not seen you in many days, after all, and I missed the sight of your face."

"Goofball," she said and glancing at the wall, pecked Piotr quickly on his lips. He hissed in pain and she nodded. "See? Not such a spiffy idea right now, is it?"

"Indeed," he agreed morosely. "This is new and unexpected. Unpleasantly so."

"I have to say that I agree," Wendy said, carefully peeling back his tattered shirt so she could see the hole. Eddie returned, a bottle in hand. Gently laying the shirt back down, she rose and rejoined Eddie at the window.

"It's swelling like some sort of boil," she whispered, troubled. "Almost like there's something growing in there. What in the heck happened to him?"

"I don't know," Eddie whispered back. "But whatever it is—and yeah, understatement of the year, I know—it isn't good."

Just then, the car wandering the streets below pulled into

Wendy's driveway and a familiar figure stepped out of the driver's side, jogging lightly across the lawn to the front door.

"Oh no, Eddie," Wendy said sharply, hurrying across the room and flinging open her closet door. "Help Piotr into the closet and hide. Finish tending to . . . that . . . stuff in there." Downstairs the doorbell rang. Wendy heard Chel move to answer it.

Eddie resisted her shoving hands. "What are you—" There were muffled words from below.

"I'm not playing, Eds! Do it now!"

"I'm not—we're not—going anywhere until you explain what's going on," Eddie protested, though Piotr, noting Wendy's frantic expression, had moved into the closet without question.

"Just trust me, okay?" Wendy pleaded as, behind her, her bedroom door opened.

Chel stuck her head in. "Wendy? You up?" She paused for a moment, frowned, and then added woodenly, "Oh. You're up. And dressed already. In the same stuff from yesterday."

"Yep, just raring to go for the day!" Wendy said as brightly as she dared, glad yet again that Chel couldn't see into the Never. Eddie, half in and half out of the closet, waved weakly at Chel while Piotr, hand pressed to his side, sagged against the door.

"Right. You have a guest. Downstairs. Waiting on the couch. At six a.m.," Chel said and then turned on her heel, slamming the door shut. Next door, Wendy heard Jon shout in surprise and fall out of bed. *Great*, she thought to herself, *now everybody's up.*

"Huh," Eddie drawled. "The buffy's a little testy today. Will wonders never cease."

"Her cardio is probably ruined for the day or something," Wendy said darkly. "I wish she didn't have to wake Jon with her theatrics."

But something about Chel's shuttered expression bothered Wendy—and then there was the fact that normally Chel wasn't big on slamming doors that didn't belong to her. Her door was fair game—it got slammed all the time—but Wendy's door stuck and Jon's had softener hinges, so they were no fun to slam at all. Chel forgot only when she was truly angry or upset.

"I should go talk to her," Wendy muttered, but then remembered her visitor downstairs. "Damn it, I don't think I'm going to have time, though."

Eddie perked up. "So, do we still have to go in the closet?"

"Just to be safe," Wendy said. "Just until I go."

"Okay, crazy lady," Eddie said, waving the bottle goodbye in her general direction. "But you owe us."

"Uh huh. Owe you ice cream in December. Bye now." Wendy closed the closet door behind them and, grabbing her purse, hurried downstairs. Emma sat waiting for her on the couch.

CHAPTER ELEVEN

"I thought you were going to text or something first?" Wendy asked, eyeing Chel who, in addition to the rap pumping from her phone headphones, was pounding on the treadmill so fast there was no way she'd be able to make out their conversation.

"And I thought you would sleep," Emma replied coolly, standing as Wendy approached. Despite the early hour and the fact that she was dressed in grey yoga pants and a plain black hoodie, Emma somehow made the whole ensemble seem as elegant as a pin-striped suit. "You're no use to me slow. I need you on your toes."

"I can handle myself." Yawning, Wendy glanced down at herself. She was still wearing her grimy, mud-splattered clothing from yesterday; a fact she knew hadn't escaped Emma's attention. She wondered if she should go change; she knew that she had to stink like day-old sweat and wet dog, and wherever they were going there was no guarantee a miniskirt would be the best choice of attire.

Screw it, she decided, after spying Emma's lip curl. She'd wear anything to get under this hoity-toity shrew's skin.

"HEY!" Wendy turned to Chel and waved wildly. "I'M LEAVING!"

"WHATEVER!" Chel shouted over her headphones, making a shooing gesture. "BYE!"

"Where are we going, again?" Wendy asked, leading Emma to the front door. There, she grabbed her grubbiest sneakers, glad that she'd left them downstairs the day before. Jon was just coming down the stairs but Emma nudged Wendy out the door before she could stop and introduce the two of them.

"That is for me to know and you to find out." As they approached Emma's BMW, Wendy realized that Jane was lounging in the passenger seat. When Jane slid out of the convertible to let Wendy in, she winked. Nervously, Wendy glanced back at her house and was dismayed to realize that Eddie and Piotr were peeking out the window. Idiots! Wendy nearly flung herself into the backseat, praying that neither Jane nor Emma would look up, as Jane settled into the shotgun seat. Piotr and Eddie were lucky; thankfully, neither of the two Reapers glanced around.

"Long time no see," Wendy said brightly as Emma slid behind the wheel. If the M6 had been Wendy's car, she would have spent several minutes caressing that buttery-soft leather interior; Emma started the car, which purred to life immediately, and backed onto the street without glancing behind to make sure the way was clear.

"No kidding. You've been busy, huh?" Jane asked, popping a bubble, lightly touching the thin silver lines of ink that crawled over her exposed collarbone and twisted in circles just above her breasts. "Get comfy, tater tot, we've got us some drivin' to do."

Having Jane along made the ride with Emma easier. Wendy sat in the middle of the back and Jane reclined the passenger side seat as far as it would go so they could talk. Wendy politely kept her eyes trained on Jane's face so she wouldn't have to notice the way every shift made Jane's hardly-there shirt shimmy further and further down.

"Ugh, why must the day-star be so bright?" Covering her eyes with her forearm, Jane popped another bubble, and a wave of faux-grape scent permeated the air between them. She dug in her pocket and pulled out a dented tin, popping it open to expose several purple-colored pellets. "Hey, Wendy, want some?"

"Um, no thanks," Wendy said, sitting back and breathing through her mouth. "I haven't brushed my teeth yet. They're feeling a little too scummy for gum." Her stomach growled. "Food and tired don't mix for me."

"Yeah, you don't look like you got a whole lotta shut-eye," Jane said, peeping out from beneath her arm and grinning. "Very meth chic, actually. That Walker attack still bugging you?"

"Walker attack?" Emma asked.

"Already over, don't worry your pretty little head over it," Jane said breezily. "We mopped 'em up."

"I'm fine," Wendy said, wondering why Jane hadn't let Emma in on how they'd met. "What about you? Did you sleep?"

"I never sleep," Jane chuckled. "It's my superpower."

"She stays up all night screwing around on the 'net," Emma supplied, swerving into another lane without signaling. "Instead of studying for her practicals." The car behind them laid on the horn, but Emma was already switching lanes again.

"Hey now, I study," Jane protested mildly. "I just don't feel the need to cram all the known knowledge in the world up my butt the way you do." She casually reached under her shirt and scratched the underside of her ribs, exposing more of the intricate filigree of ink etched into her skin.

"And Wendy, if you ever want to drive Emma nutso, misuse 'lie' and 'lay' in a sentence. Or, if you really want to get Emmaline's panties in a twist, mix up 'I' and 'me.'" Jane giggled and adopted a valley-girl tone. "So, like, me and my friends went to the mall—"

"I will get through this day," Emma said abruptly. "I will get through this day. I will get through this day without killing them both even if it gives me an aneurism, I swear on the names of the Good Ones."

"I haven't done anything wrong," Wendy protested.

"You will," Emma ground out. "You didn't sleep and you can't help yourself. And Jane isn't helping." She punched her cousin on the thigh. "Your breast is exposed and you're scandalizing Wendy. Cover it. She's got a tough road ahead of her today, she doesn't need you flashing her."

"Oh yeah, hey, I heard it through the grapevine that you were some sort of natural!" Jane said, rolling her eyes at Emma and shifting so that her shirt was back in its proper place. "Is that really true?"

"Yeah," Wendy said, not missing Emma's grimace in the rearview mirror. "Apparently I am. Why?"

"Just curious. I've never met one. I always thought they were, you know, like Bigfoot or something. High five!" Jane stuck her hand out and Wendy, feeling as if she'd inadvertently stumbled into some Alice in Wonderland offshoot with ghosts, tentatively high-fived her back.

"Ssss," Jane hissed, holding her hand limp and waving it frantically, pretending to cool it off, "Hot!"

"Haha," Wendy said, trying not to imagine the natural Nana Moses had told her about, unable to reap and burning to a crisp from the inside out. How hot had she gotten at the end? Had her flesh really burned up or had that just been poetic license?

"So you're probably wondering why I'm tagging along, huh?" Jane tweaked an earring and stretched languorously, so that her spine crackled. The pointy heels of her shoes scraped the dash.

"My car is more expensive than your skin," Emma snapped, shoving Jane's feet off the interior. "Watch it!"

"Bite me," Jane replied coolly.

"The thought had passed my mind, yeah," Wendy said.

"We're getting you marked up supa' soon, none of this pansy protection-only crap your momma laid down on you," Jane said, crossing her left leg over her right. "Great G'ma wants me to survey what I gotta work with as pertaining to that pert flesh o'yours, cuz, since I do most of the ink for the fam, don'tcha know."

"Hey now, I never agreed to that. I don't want any more tattoos," Wendy said, irritated that this strange family was already issuing edicts. "Mine work just fine."

"No. Your skin has to be redone," Emma said. "Your current tattoos hardly protect you from Shades, much less anything serious. If you're worried about future employment, Jane will keep them to your torso and upper thighs. She's quite good at concealing the ink."

"Only way, sorry, I know it sucks." Jane traced a pattern on what appeared to be a bare patch of skin on her shoulder but as Wendy looked more closely she realized that there were fine lines etched there as well. White ink.

"Maybe," Wendy hedged, marveling how closely she had to stare at the ink to see it, "white ink like yours might be okay."

"Awesome blossom. We'll do your measurements this morning before the main event, and after I see how you move I'll have a good idea how to tat you up," Jane said approvingly, tapping her shoulder and winking. "Aaand, we're here."

"Here" turned out to be Fort Funston. They parked near the beach, and Jane bounded out of the car, leaving Wendy to struggle out of the narrow backseat on her own. Emma popped the trunk and disappeared for a moment, returning with a large beach towel, a threadbare Army duffel bag, and a handful of scrunchies. She handed a scrunchie to Wendy and gathered up her long hair as she disappeared down the closest dune, heading toward the water.

"Okay, girly-girl, time to get this party started." Spinning around and around, Jane laughed as the wind picked up strands of her gleaming blue hair, and she flung her arms out, embracing the sunrise before she nudged Wendy in the direction Emma had gone. "Let's do this thing!"

"But this is Fort Funston," Wendy protested, glancing around the parking lot. It was bare of people, but several cars suggested that others were about. "People hike and walk their dogs and hang-glide just over that hill; we can't do this here!"

"You just have to know the right places in the park," Emma's voice echoed from near the water. "The bunker is this way."

"Bunker?"

Hesitating, Wendy sank as deep into the shadows as she could, nervous fingers splayed across her chest and gut. If she'd known this was part of the training, she wasn't sure she'd have been so gung-ho about doing it. Did her mother have to do something like this? It hardly seemed like the sort of nonsense Mary would put up with.

"Come on, sunshine," Jane said, not unkindly, pausing at the top of the hill. "Emma's not pulling your leg about the bunkers."

"Aren't the bunkers abandoned?" Wendy asked, following as slowly as she dared. "And locked?"

"We're Reapers," Jane said simply, guiding Wendy toward a rusted bunker door set close to the sea. It was layered thickly with bright graffiti, each colorful design outdoing the last. "You think something simple like a lock is gonna keep us out?"

"I'm not an idiot," Wendy said testily. "Even a beginner can see that the Never is strong here." She jerked her thumb toward a nearby sagging, rickety pier in the living world that was still strong and straight in the Never.

"Good eye," Jane said approvingly. "But no, I meant these." She rifled in her pocket and pulled out a key ring. Most of the keys on the ring were old and rusted, but one shone like new. "It's all legit."

"Keys? Actual keys to the bunkers?" Wendy had to forcibly close her mouth to keep it from gaping. "Do I want to even know how you got those?"

"With this family? Hah, probably not." Jane tossed the key ring to Emma, waiting at the doorway to the bunker. Emma caught it one-handed.

"Every time I think I have you guys figured out you go and throw me for another loop," Wendy muttered. She had a bad feeling about the rusting hulk and the ease with which Emma and Jane were treating this entire excursion. Part of her wanted to turn around and hike to the closest bus stop; another part, however, was desperately curious what the inside of the bunker looked like. She glanced over her shoulder at their footprints leading down the hill, noting that they'd walked in a single line, obscuring who'd gone before. *If this were one of those CSI shows*, she quietly mused, *no one would be able to tell how many of us there were by our footprints alone.*

"Come on, sunshine," Jane said, grabbing Wendy just above the elbow and forcefully steering her away from the light and sand to the rusted metal doorway. "We've adventuring to do. Here's the hidey-hole, Alice. Let's go visit Wonderland. Or Neverland. I get the two confused sometimes. Some kinda land, it don't matter much, at least not to you, not now. Ready?"

With Jane's fingers splayed against her back, Wendy grudgingly descended the creaking steps into the bowels of the bunker. It didn't look like much on the outside, just a garish, largish metal hut near the seashore, sand and scrub all around. Once you got underground, however, there was so much more. The bunker stretched in a long row of rooms for as far as Wendy could make out, dimly lit by flickering incandescent bulbs screwed loosely into wires and dangling dangerously overhead. The first room was large, larger than the first floor of Wendy's house, and empty save for a huge faded circle in old yellow paint. There were brown splotches and white streaks all over the room, but mainly in the circle.

"Is that bird poop?" Wendy asked, stepping off the last step and kneeling down to get a closer look at the streaks. Whatever creature made the mess, it certainly looked like it didn't belong underground. "How did birds get down here?"

"Mystery of mysteries," Jane said breezily. "Hey, Emma, look, I don't want one of those ancient bulbs popping and dropping glass on my head. You got the lantern ready?"

Emma, setting down a military-grade camping lantern beside the far curve of the circle, knelt beside it a moment, and then flicked a thumbs-up toward Jane. "Go."

Jerking to her feet, Wendy found herself shivering as Jane slapped a switch near the door with one hand.

The room, hardly lit to begin with, dropped into sullen darkness. Suddenly a disembodied hand squeezed her left hip and Wendy yelped, jumping aside.

"Honestly, Jane," Emma said coolly, stepping to the left of Wendy and laying down the beach towel, settling the duffel bag on top. "Must you be so vulgar? Can't you see she's embarrassed enough as it is? Must you paw at her like she's one of your little sororstitute sluts? It's hardly humorous or endearing."

"You freakin'?" Jane asked Wendy, surprised. "I'm just kidding. We're out in the middle of nowhere and it's just us three lovelies here. Scout's honor." She brought four fingers up to her forehead. "Is that how you do this thing?" she asked Emma after a moment. "I can never remember."

"You dropped out of Girl Scouts after two weeks," Emma said wearily, standing aside and shedding her clothing with a systematic ease that startled Wendy. She disrobed mechanically, stripping bare without a wasted motion. Even naked, she was the epitome of cool, flawless beauty, long copper hair drawn off her face and sleek lines lit by the steady, low lantern light. Irritated, Wendy admitted to herself that she was jealous. It hardly seemed fair that girls as model-gorgeous as Emma existed in the first place, much less that she was a relative *and* a doctor.

"You're getting nekkid?" Jane asked, hunkering down with her sketchbook. "Color me surprised. I never figured Miss Stick-Up-Her-Butt would, well, show said butt." She eyed her cousin and grinned. "Though it's an admittedly well-tanned butt for such a pale chick."

"It is only fair," Emma replied.

"Your butt?"

"My being unclothed," Emma said through clenched teeth. "If Wendy must battle disrobed, so must I."

"Wait, excuse me?" Defensively, Wendy crossed her arms over her chest. "Who said anything about fighting naked?"

Emma raised an eyebrow; her expression was cool but the set of her shoulders conveyed her irritation. "It is how it is done."

"Yeah, um, no. I would've remembered that bit in the Welcome to Our Weird Ol' Family welcome packet and I certainly didn't sign up for *this*. Especially not in a semi-public location—*'this is how it's done'* not withstanding, sorry."

"Don't be such a wimp," Jane said, yawning. "We all have to go through it at one point or another. And some of us aren't cute little things like you. You'll be fine. I won't even take pictures and load them on the Internet. Scout's honor. Never even occurred to me. Nope."

"Why is it necessary?" Wendy pressed, backing away so that she faced the room and non-nude safety was only a short sprint up the stairs.

"It takes a trained eye to see, but we bring a version of our clothing into the Never with us," Emma explained, expression purposefully bland and blank. "That clothing will hinder our activities and your training."

"That's what she said," Jane joked.

"And it's *completely* necessary?" Wendy asked, hating how whiny she sounded but unable to stop her trembling.

"Completely," Emma assured her. "It's impossible otherwise." She paused—for the briefest moment Wendy fancied that Emma felt *badly* for her—and then her expression was calm and clear again. "As Jane said, every Reaper must go through it."

"Okay," Wendy said begrudgingly, crouching down to unlace her shoes; her throat felt tight and swollen, her cheeks hot and flushed. "I hella don't like it, but . . . okay."

"Well if you two are going to go at it right away, I better measure you now, before Emma tears you into teeny tiny pieces," Jane said, hopping to her feet and grabbing Wendy's wrist in her hand as Wendy stood. She spanned Wendy's wrist with her fingers, "hmm"ing to herself under her breath. "Okay, now spin around."

"I'm confused," Wendy said as Jane circled her, occasionally squatting down and grabbing a body part—palming her ankle here, and then reaching up and squeezing the opposing thigh. "What are you doing?"

"She's feeling where the holes in your Light are," Emma explained, sorting through the duffel bag and drawing out a pair of long, slender bone knives decorated with familiar, arching Celtic knots. They curved wickedly in the dim lamplight. "To better cover your defenses there."

"You actually do have to be naked for the important parts," Jane added, "since I need to see where your current ink ends and get an idea of how the layout of your trunk goes—you know, scars and such. But this little bit, the measuring, you don't have to be bare for. I'm sorry I embarrassed you earlier, with the hip thing. You looked so edgy about the dark, I was just having a little fun."

Jane stepped back, jotting notes down on a small sketchpad and popping another bubble. "If it makes you feel any better, usually there's some ancient crone doing the booby-grabbing and I, personally, think that I'm much easier on the eyes. Plus, compared to my grandma, I'm like ten times as gentle. Grandma Elise's got fingers like a vice."

"Not really making me feel better," Wendy muttered.

"Meh, I'll ease you into it," Jane promised. "We'll do all the touchy-feely stuff clothed, okay?"

Running her hand along the dip above Wendy's hips, Jane spun Wendy to the left and Wendy felt a small, savage pinch on her hip at the height of the twirl. Wendy thought to protest but Jane was deep in concentration, leaning close enough for Wendy to examine the double-keyhole etched in white ink at the center of Jane's largest shoulder tat as she pressed hands flat against Wendy's gut and thigh. Jane must not have realized that she'd hurt her, Wendy realized, absently rubbing the sore spot.

"We've waited as long as we can," Emma said gently, checking her watch as Jane finally stepped back. "It is time to begin."

Wendy grimaced. "Last time I ask. No other way?"

"None." Emma waved the tip of the dagger at Wendy's midsection. "We're all girls here and I'm a doctor. It's nothing I've never seen before."

"And I'm an artist," Jane added helpfully. "I can't tell you the number of nudes I had to sketch in school. It'll be nothing, I promise. After I'm done you can even keep the originals."

Emma unsheathed a knife. "Disrobe."

Turning her back on them, Wendy gingerly stripped. The air was surprisingly warm, Wendy noted as she hesitantly stepped into the light. "Okay. What's next?"

Emma stepped forward and handed her the bone knives. "Take these."

"What are they? I mean, besides knives? And I should probably mention right now that I've never, ever held a knife like this before."

"They're family heirlooms," Jane said, glancing up from her sketchbook where she was drawing madly. "Don't break 'em. And stay in the light if you can."

"Don't worry about wielding them just yet. All you must do is hold them. No," Emma said, adjusting Wendy's grip, "like this. If you hold them like that you might cut your own wrist." She tapped Wendy's wrist. "Looser. *Looser*, I said! You're going to hurt yourself at this rate."

"I didn't ask for this," Wendy couldn't help whining.

"You wanted to be trained. This is what training entails. Looser! Good. Much better." Emma stepped back. "Now we stand at the opposite sides of the circle," she instructed, moving the edge of the faded arc. "You tell me when you're ready."

"Ready for what?"

"Just when you're ready."

"Don't you get any weapons? Am I supposed to come at you? Seriously, guys, I have no clue what's going on here."

"Tell me when you're ready," Emma said patiently.

After long moments of alternating between watching Emma, looking at her own naked feet, and glancing furtively at Jane still furiously drawing away, Wendy took a deep breath and said, "I'm ready."

The attack was instantaneous. It was so quick that Wendy staggered back, gasping for air, and stunned that anyone could move like that. Emma, already back on the other side of the circle, danced in a sinuous, elegant wave, darting forward and tagging Wendy painfully—a sharp tap that Wendy could feel in her teeth and bones.

The first blow, she quickly realized, had only been a test. When the next blows came she didn't even have the courtesy of seeing Emma flash forward; one moment she was there and the next her entire body stung. It took Wendy several more painful attacks to realize that while Emma was touching her with her fingertips briefly in the living world, her attacks were simultaneously coming from the Never. She was using her ribbons of Light to press into Wendy's soul and it was *incredibly* painful.

"Break! Uncle! Truce!" Wendy gasped at last, staggering over to the wall. She'd tried opening herself up to the Light in order to fight on turf she was stronger in, but every time she began the process Emma's Light would snap at her at least a dozen times, the stinging pain slowing Wendy down.

"No truce," Emma said beside her before pushing Wendy over. Wendy caught herself in time to keep from barking her shin on the edge of the lantern, but scraped her palm in the process. "The dead will not give you a break in battle; neither shall I."

"Whoa, whoa," Jane suddenly said, hopping to her feet and setting down the sketchpad, scowling at Wendy as she looked her closely up and down. She held out a hand and helped Wendy to her feet. "Wait a second. Emma . . . are you . . . are you doing what I think you're doing? Or, I guess, did? Did do? Done? Whatever."

"That depends on what you suppose I am doing or have done." Emma's face was like carved ice, her expression immutable.

"Well, I'm no expert, but it looks like you're—and look, I know you, so I'm sorry for even suggesting this—but it looks like you're binding her." Jane thrust her hands into the air in a warding off gesture. "I'm sorry!"

"Binding?" Wendy asked stupidly, feeling slow and grumpy. She was annoyed that her mother hadn't even taught her the very basics of the Reaper culture. Half the prattle coming out of their mouths was confusing and strange and the other half was downright aggravating. This latest pause was a sickening mixture of both.

"It would seem that way because that is exactly what I'm doing," Emma replied coolly, ignoring Wendy entirely. "Or, rather, have done."

"What is a binding?" Wendy demanded more strongly.

"But you can't do that," Jane protested, crossing her arms over her chest. "It's overkill, don't you think?"

"For the last frickin' time," Wendy snapped, grabbing Emma by the wrist, "what in the hell is a binding?"

"Remember that girl, the blind natural?" Emma asked, yanking her wrist free. "If this technique had existed in its entirety back then, she might have survived. As for what it is, look for yourself."

Edgy and nervous, Wendy slid into the Light and looked down. Instead of her normal, pulsing mass of incandescent power, she found that Emma had taken pieces of her Light with her knives and whips, carving a dark mesh-like pattern into her ethereal form. Her entire body was nothing but lacy scars of Light, a lightweight layer of blackness stretched over the normal fierce brightness.

"Okay, I look weird as hell. We'll set that aside for now," Wendy growled. "The key question here is WHY THE HELL WERE YOU DOING THIS OH-SO-MAGICAL BINDING WITHOUT ASKING ME FIRST?"

Groaning, Emma rolled her eyes. "I know you're new to all this, but if you'd had any training—"

"That's not my fault!"

"—any training at all, you'd have recognized this for what it is. And you'd know why it's preferable to the alternative, at least temporarily. Grandmother and Great-Grandmother ordered it done, it's done. Enough said."

"It's kind of drastic, don't you think?" Jane asked quietly. "I mean, yeah, Wendy's a weirdo freak, sure—"

"Thank you so much," Wendy snapped.

"Hey, it's not my fault you're some sort of cutesy-wootsy mutated abomination," Jane said, pinching Wendy's cheek saucily. "The point is that, weirdo or not, she's still a Reaper, right?"

"I don't count to three when I give inoculations to children," Emma replied shortly. "Sometimes they're lucky if I count to two. You do what is best, and this is for Wendy's safety. What's done is done. It's over."

"That's it?" Wendy hissed, hands grasped in fists at her side; naked and exposed, she felt as if every hair on her body was puffing out like a cat's. "No 'I'm sorry for doing something permanent to your soul, Wendy?' No 'Hey, Wendy, we had this idea we wanna try out on you'? No 'This might sting a little'? Yeah, well, thanks ever so much for the heads-up, you psycho bitch."

"Cut the drama," Emma retorted. "I never said it was permanent. What kind of a monster do you take me for?"

"A selfish hosebeastica?" Jane asked, picking up her sketchbook. "An order-taking, brown-wearing boot-licker?"

"Spare me. If Grandmother told you to jump, you wouldn't bother asking how high before flinging yourself off the closest cliff," Emma snapped, pointing an accusing finger at Jane.

"Enough! From both of you!" Wendy yelled. They fell silent and she breathed heavily for several moments, trying to find an inner calm. At long last she said, "Fine, you did this soul thingy, I can't undo it, great. Now how long is this binding for?" Wendy asked stiffly. "What did you do exactly and what's coming down the pike?"

"They usually last maybe a couple weeks at most," Jane said, licking her thumb and flicking to the next page of her sketchbook. "Nowadays a binding is usually used to teach new Reapers control of the Light. It feeds you only little dribs and drabs of the Light at a time. Not enough to stop you up, but enough to keep you from blowing it all in one fell swoop and then being helpless for days afterward."

"That's it? It just slows me down?"

"That's it," Emma said, voice heavy with disdain. "Now don't you feel bad about assuming the worst?"

"Not really, considering it's something I still would have liked some input on." Wendy scowled and concentrated. She could feel the strings of power lying across her soul, across the core of her abilities, like a series of thin ribbons woven and wrapped tightly around her chest. She could move and poke at her power but it was like pressing her hand against a fine, taut mesh, trying to grasp a shiny bauble just beyond her reach. "It's kind of uncomfortable." She shifted in place. "Like a too-tight corset, really."

"It's meant to be," Jane said, jokingly. She elbowed Wendy and winked. "Hairshirt for your powers, right? That'll teach you to be born a mutant, ya spaz."

"Quit calling her that, even jokingly. It's not funny," Emma growled. "Wendy, if you concentrate, you can still slip in and out of the Never. You won't be able to reap a spirit, but you can still train with me." She cleared her throat. "If you still want to, that is."

Wendy wanted to tell Emma and Jane both to go to hell. Instead she sighed and straightened. "Fine. I'm behind every other Reaper in actual knowledge and control. I need to suck it up and just do this. But you and me, Emma? We're not okay and we're not going to be for a long time. You got that?"

"Understood," Emma said and gestured for Wendy to raise her knives again. "Now. Come at me."

Eventually, after several more minutes or hours or days of being pummeled mercilessly, Wendy began to sort out which direction Emma might probably attack from. The tricky part was figuring out how to block her, since she pounced simultaneously from both the Never and the living world. However, just knowing the direction allowed Wendy to get the knives up in time, which would occasionally block the worst of the Light.

Then, when Wendy's legs were shaking from exertion and her heart was thudding painfully in her chest, she spotted it. It was just the barest of movements, the faintest of faltering, but even tired as she was, Wendy caught the motion. Emma was *not*, in fact, simultaneously attacking in both the Never and the living world, Wendy realized. Emma was *switching back and forth* so fast that she appeared to blur between worlds.

Amazing. Simply amazing. Stunned, Wendy took two thwacks to the shoulders before she was able to pull away.

"Okay," she said aloud. "You're not magical, you're just stupid-fast. I can do that. I think."

Ignoring Jane's chuckle, Wendy concentrated on speeding up how fast she opened herself to the Light. It was hard—Wendy had learned long ago to keep a tight rein on the Light. Her mother had insisted on it, and as such Wendy only drew on her power when absolutely necessary.

Yanking rapidly at the mental hold she erected to keep the Light safely tucked away was surprisingly painful, but Wendy kept at it until she was able to fling her hold aside in a moment. She still wasn't as fast as Emma, but each time she did it she got fractionally faster and infinitesimally more confident.

"Better," Emma said from her right and then her left. "Still not as fast as the newest of our girls, but better." She snapped a whip of Light forward and Wendy caught it with the knife.

"Not as fast as a novice, huh?"

"No. But do that two more times in a row and you'll get your truce." Emma's Light flashed forward again and Wendy felt it bite painfully into the side of her face.

"Fine," she ground out. "Block you three times in a row. Got it." Over and over again they circled one another, Emma growing bolder with her attacks, leaving herself open, and Wendy, attempting to keep from being stung again.

Finally, at long last, the knife cut through the Light a third time and Emma, sweating and pale, nodded once at Wendy as she stepped back. "Excellent job, Wendy," she said. "I am proud of you."

"Yeah," Jane added, standing up and stretching. "That only took, what, the morning to get the hang of it? Emma was razzing you there. Normally it takes newbs at least a week to figure out the trick. You're quick; I'm jealous."

Emma took the blades from Wendy's stinging, sweat-slicked hands and dried them off, sheathing them in an intricately designed set of leather sheaths that Wendy could have sworn she'd seen somewhere before.

"You'll do," she said critically, brushing coppery hair out of her eyes as, behind her, Jane gathered up their clothing to bring to the combatants. "Your mother might even approve."

"No she wouldn't," Wendy said, smiling bitterly as Jane approached with Wendy's Hello Kitty undies waving in the air and a broad smirk plastered on her face. "That I can assure you."

As Emma dressed away from them, Jane leaned over and, for Wendy's ears only, whispered, "If you get tired of that binding, call me. I can't guarantee I can fix it . . . but I can try, okay?" She held her knuckles up for a fist bump. "Reaper homegirls for life, yo."

Exhausted and amused, Wendy bumped fists. She didn't know if she'd take Jane up on her offer—the idea of precision control over her abilities appealed to the part of Wendy that still smarted over the White Lady's biting insults—but it was kind of her to offer. Terrible sense of humor or not, Jane was a pretty decent girl. Wendy just hoped that the rest of the family turned out to be like Jane and not like Emma or her Grandmother.

Unfortunately, seeing as her mother had distanced herself from her family quite effectively, Wendy had a sneaking feeling that her hopes were in vain. Well, there was Jane at least. Wendy gripped that thought tightly and quickly dressed. She needed to get home and check on the spirits in her bedroom. Who knew what they'd gotten up to in her absence?

In the ten minutes it took Wendy to feel presentable again, if still slightly skeeved out by how nude she'd been in the presence of near-strangers, Emma and Jane had topped the rise and were walking toward the beach. Jane spun in the morning sunlight, arms outflung and laughter drifting back to the bunker as Wendy hesitated by the door. Should she lock it? They hadn't left the keys.

The faintest glimmer out of the corner of her eye caught Wendy's attention. She turned and only just spotted her, peering out from around the corner of the bunker, a battered backpack clutched in one thin hand.

The little girl couldn't have been more than seven or eight when she'd died. Her clothing was nondescript—jeans and a plain white tee shirt, bare and dirty feet. The wisps of hair that tumbled out from beneath her grubby grey Giants baseball cap were dirty blonde and fine, tangled at the ends. She had a smudge across her left cheek and Wendy had to fight the urge to lick her thumb and wipe the filth away.

"Um, hi?" Wendy said and the girl flinched, staggering back a step. She was like a rabbit, all sinew and nerve, ready to flee in an instant.

"My name's Wendy!" Wendy said quickly. Hurriedly, she pawed through her purse. There, at the bottom, was a trinket she'd thought silly when she'd picked it up from Piotr's old haunt earlier in the week, but it'd reminded her of him and his Lost, of Specs in particular, and she had stashed it in her bag anyway.

"Do you like books?" Wendy asked, holding out one of Spec's battered copies of a Nancy Drew mystery. "Here. It's yours." She glanced over her shoulder; the Reapers were still walking by the water. They hadn't seen her talking to the Lost.

"What do you want for it?" the little girl asked, eying the book speculatively but not getting any closer.

"Nothing," Wendy said. "It's yours if you want it. I picked it up because the boy it used to belong to went into the Light." She smiled half-heartedly. "It reminded me of him."

The little girl tilted her head, looking Wendy up and down

speculatively. "I was watching you all in there, dancing around all naked. You're her, ain't you? That Lightbringer girl everyone's talking about?"

Wendy flushed. Was there a single soul in San Francisco who *hadn't* heard about her yet? At this rate she ought to take out an advertisement and start charging. "Maybe. Why do you ask?"

"You're different, right?" The Lost was edging slowly backwards, eyes trained firmly on Wendy's face. "You don't attack ghosts unless they want you to."

"You've got that part correct," Wendy said soothingly. "Unless you're a Walker, I only send on spirits who ask."

The girl stopped backing away and nodded. "Okay. That's cool." Then, making a face like she expected Wendy to refuse, the little girl held out a hand. "Can I still have that book? I mean . . . may I? May I still have that book?"

"Of course!" Glad that she seemed to have made a connection, Wendy tossed the book underhand to the girl. "I hope you like it . . . um . . . what's your name?"

"Sarah," the kid said, tucking the battered novel into her bag. Once it was safely stored, she straightened and scowled. "So is that it, then? The Reapers are back? This place is my haunt now. You all left ages ago; no fair with the backsies."

Horrified, Wendy realized that the girl was near tears. "Oh honey," she whispered, uncertain how to comfort the girl. "Don't cry . . ."

"It's fine," Sarah said, scrubbing her face with a grubby hand. "Stuff's gonna be like it was before? Fine. I'll manage. You seem nice, but the rest of 'em . . . nuhhuh. Not happening. I don't deal with Reapers."

"Okay, my family's back," Wendy said softly, glancing over her shoulder at Emma and Jane in the distance again. "But hopefully not for long."

Sarah snorted. "If it's anything like before, it'll be forever. Reapers like to hunker down, boss everyone around, and generally stick their noses in everyone's business. And those are the nice ones. Like you."

"So . . . you've been here a long time then?" Wendy said, choosing her words carefully. "With no Rider? On your own?"

"Riders boss you around in other ways," Sarah said primly. "I'm my own boss."

"I can see that," Wendy said wryly. "Okay, Sarah, well . . . I have a proposition for you then."

"Knew it," the girl said, rolling her eyes. "What?"

"I have a friend, a Rider, who isn't feeling well." Wendy hesitated, not sure how to explain the hook Lily had described. "He . . . he got into a fight with some Walkers and they hurt him."

Sarah scratched her neck. "Like, hurt how?"

"Stabbed him," Wendy said baldly, deciding that Sarah had most likely been dead long enough to have seen a Walker fight or two. She might still be a vulnerable little girl, but something in her eyes said that Sarah was tougher than she looked, that she'd seen more than Wendy could ever imagine. "His wound won't heal."

"Ever since the White Lady came the Walkers are twice as nasty as before," Sarah said, scowling. "I watched one rip a Shade to pieces a few days ago down by the docks. It didn't even give up any essence; the Walker just wanted to hear the poor guy scream."

Wendy winced. "I'm not surprised."

"Your Rider friend . . . he won't try to take me in or make me join his group, right?" Sarah crossed her arms over her chest and glared at Wendy. "I heard all about how those other groups of Lost got nabbed by the White Lady, even out from under the Riders' noses. That ain't happening to me."

"He doesn't have a group anymore," Wendy explained, "but if you don't want to stay with us, none of us will make you, I promise."

"And if I help him . . . what do I get? I don't work for free, you know. Will and essence ain't cheap."

"Anything you want," Wendy promised fervently, surprised at the overwhelming surge of relief pouring through her system. "Sarah, I swear to you, I will salvage anything I can just for you. And if the Reapers leave this town to me the way they want to, I will make sure you don't get sent on until you are good and ready. Is that okay?"

"Yeah, all right then. I'll help." Sarah scratched her nose. "But you know that I can't go with you in your car. Your Reaper buddies spot me, they'll—"

"I know," Wendy agreed, giddy with quiet joy. "And you're right. You have to get there on your own." She glanced up at the sky; it wasn't noon yet, but the morning would soon be over. Wendy had no idea how Piotr was faring, but she didn't want to risk waiting too long for Sarah to arrive. "I live in Mountain View. Do you know where that is?"

"Yeah." Sarah paled. "Your buddies are coming back!"

"Here," Wendy said, stepping forward so her body blocked the line of sight to Sarah. "Go into the city. Near Pier 31 there's an old abandoned bookshop, it used to be a haunt for this Rider named Elle and her Lost. Hunker down and wait there. I'll come get you as soon as I can, okay? Or I'll send someone."

"Yeah, I know the place." Sarah shook her head. "Dealin' with Reapers and Riders. I must be nuts."

"You're a saint," Wendy promised. "Now go! Hide!"

Sarah obligingly vanished into the brush behind the bunker just as Emma and Jane edged around the rise, sandy and smiling. Emma, though tired, seemed to have relaxed some, and her hair hung down in damp, salt-dripping tangles. For once the uptight doctor actually looked to be having fun and Wendy wondered for a second if she'd made the right choice by sending Sarah away.

"Got her good," Jane boasted. "Now let's head on home, ladies. There's a shower calling to me."

Tempted as she was to make sure Sarah was gone, Wendy kept her head facing forward as she and the Reapers retired to the car. It may have been her imagination, but as Emma pulled away, Wendy thought she saw a shadow of the girl creep out from behind the bunker and stand at the edge of the dune, backpack dangling from one hand and the other shading her eyes.

"Wait a second, hold up," Jane said suddenly and jammed her hand down, yanking up the emergency brake. She was shimmering with Light in an instant and out the door, speeding toward the bunker before Emma had stopped cursing.

"No," Wendy whispered and struggled to go after her, ramming the passenger seat with her shoulder and stretching frantically for the door handle as Emma killed the engine. "No-no-no!"

"What's going on?" Emma yelled as Wendy took off after Jane, running as fast as her legs would carry her.

Wendy topped the rise just as the brilliance of Jane's Light faded. The blue-haired girl dusted off her hands and threw up a peace sign as Wendy, terrified at what she would find below, trudged down the dune.

"Had a runner," Jane declared, winking and elbowing Wendy with great glee. "Good thing we were going so slow, I would've missed the Casper if we'd been moving even a little faster."

"For one ghost you abuse my transmission and possibly make me throw a rod?" Emma snarked. "If my mechanic says—"

Slowly, Wendy knelt down and eyed the area, hoping against hope that she'd spot something, anything, to alleviate this terrible dread building in her gut. Wendy couldn't see Sarah anywhere but her heart told her that if the little girl had survived she was long gone and probably still fleeing as fast as possible. Still, Wendy hadn't seen any other spirits around, not a single one. Jane must have reaped Sarah, Wendy realized, and tried not to cry with anger and despair. It was bad enough that the poor little girl had to be sent on so abruptly and clearly against her will, but there went Piotr's healing. She might have met him and decided to stay. Sarah might have liked them once she knew them; she could have been safe with the Riders.

"Yeah, yeah, I'll pay for it," Jane said, pushing past Wendy and Emma and heading up the hill back toward the car. "Come on, slow-pokes! It's not even lunch and it's going to be a bea-ooo-tiful day!"

CHAPTER TWELVE

Finally home, Wendy stood in front of Piotr, hair pulled back in a thick twist at her neck, tendrils escaping to tickle her collarbone. Smiling at her welcoming grin, Piotr reached out to brush the closest curl away but she stepped back playfully, tossing her head and laughing at his daring.

Then, unexpectedly, Wendy said gruffly, "Man, what are you doing?"

Wendy was not Wendy. Wendy was Eddie, and Eddie—while not upset by Piotr's attempts to draw him closer—wasn't exactly welcoming to his embrace.

"Don't get me wrong," Eddie said, "you're hot and all, but I don't think you're my type. Plus, until we get this thing figured out with Wendy, I don't think it'd be very fair to play the field." He winked to show he was kidding.

Shaking his head, Piotr dropped his arm and sat back, embarrassed. "Edward, my apologies. I . . . I was not in the moment. I did not mean to . . . I would not . . . please, accept my apologies. I did not realize it was you."

"Well, that's flattering," Eddie sighed. Then, eying Piotr more closely, he asked, "Are you okay?"

"I am fine." Piotr turned his face away, but Eddie took him by the elbow and guided Piotr to Wendy's desk, settling him on the chair gently and dropping to a knee beside a stack of books on the floor. "What were you seeing right then?"

"It is not important."

"Look, man, you don't have to go into details. You turned twelve shades of red so I already kinda have the idea that it must've been personal, but dude, were you hallucinating? Seeing stuff? Or was it just a wicked vivid daydream? Cuz if you were, then that's probably something to keep in mind. Health-wise, I mean. You know, in case Wendy gets back and Lily and Elle are still *incommunicado*."

"Wendy has left with her family. She cannot help me," Piotr muttered, but Eddie had a point. Wendy was resourceful and may have gathered connections he was unaware of during their time apart.

"I do not like that she left with them," Piotr said suddenly. "I do not like that, even after we warned her, after we told her of what we have learned, she would disregard our concerns so easily."

"That's Wendy for you," Eddie said nonchalantly, shrugging and plopping onto the corner of her desk, resting a heel on the tabletop. "She'll keep it in mind, no worries there, but she's got bigger fish to fry right now and she's not gonna let some dead gossip get in the way of figuring out what the deal with her family is." He sighed. "No offense, man, but I've been there. You can lead a Wendy to water but you can't make her drink." He smiled thinly. "She is a master of ignoring the obvious when it suits her."

Brooding quietly, Piotr made his way to the bed and Eddie, and taking advantage of the free space, he flopped into the desk chair. They sat in silence in the room for some time; Eddie, at the desk, idly rifling through some of the spiritual detritus that Wendy had accumulated during her time as Lightbringer—a calculator, a vividly colored scarf, a wooden-backed boar bristle brush—while Piotr lay and gazed at the ceiling, musing on the female Walker's words over and over again.

She'd known the White Lady and claimed to know him. She was better spoken than any other Walker he'd ever encountered, and smarter. There was something about the way she carried herself and the familiar way she treated him that both repelled and fascinated him—it was as if he recognized her from somewhere, but he couldn't quite put his finger on where.

Of course, considering the wreck his memories had become, that was completely understandable. Who knew, was it possible that a few centuries before, they'd been friends? Unless Piotr could find a way to stop the drain of his memories every time he encountered a Reaper, he'd never know for sure. Mostly he worried about the debt the Walker swore he owed her. What had she done for him that she would ask such a great favor?

There was no way to tell now.

Piotr closed his eyes, and when he opened them again, Lily hovered over him, carefully brushing his long bangs off his cheeks.

"*Bystro*," he croaked, then cleared his throat. "That was quick."

"Elle thought she found a trail, but I could not find the taste as she did. We chose to separate," Lily hurried to say, helping Piotr sit up, "so I brought a wise woman instead."

"Hello Piotr," Ada said, drawing up Wendy's chair and settling beside the bed. Gingerly she brushed her warm fingertips against his forehead and, glancing at Lily, frowned. "You are quite cool, Piotr. How do you feel?"

"Impaled," Piotr replied dryly. He looked to Eddie to share his amusement at Ada's blunt probing, realizing that Eddie, in all the chaos of the past few hours, seemed thinner than before, paler at the edges. Piotr frowned. Why hadn't Eddie brought their attention to the fact he was fading as well? "As if a hook has been stirring my guts. And how are you this fine day?"

"Piotr," Lily admonished, but Ada shook her head, chuckling. "I will always take a quipped reply, Lily. It shows that the spirit has not given in."

"I thought that Ada might be of service because she is part of the Council," Lily explained. "She knows everyone of importance in this town and, more importantly, she is a scientist. Doctors are so difficult to find, she seemed our best recourse."

"Well, I have heard rumors of a Lost girl by the docks, but that was many years ago. Since then, I do not know for certain where any other

Lost can be found," Ada said apologetically. "Please accept my most sincere condolences in that regard. However, I knew that I had to try to help you. You are a very important figure to the Council right now, Piotr. We very much wish to do business with you; it would behoove me to keep you healthy for the interim, yes?" She winked at him to show that she was mostly joking, lessening the sting of her words.

When Piotr did not return her levity, Ada grew businesslike. She sat back and examined Piotr's face from a distance, her fingers gingerly probing under the sides of his jaw and softly rubbing the nape of his skull, wiggling his head gently. "Lily has explained that you are experiencing vertigo, chills, and unwarranted irritation. Rage, to be blunt. Is this the case?"

"Don't forget hallucinations," Eddie added helpfully from the window where he was examining his hands, turning his fists back and forth in the dim light. "That's new."

"Hallucinations?" Ada stiffened and glanced sharply at Lily. "You did not mention . . . never mind. Let me see this wound. It may have gone septic already."

"Wait, that can happen to the dead?" Eddie asked, startled into looking up. "Oh, gross."

"That is a concern of mine. It will not close," Lily explained, ignoring Eddie and stripping the bandages expertly from Piotr's side. "At first I thought it was beginning to, but it was simply some initial swelling. His essence still flows sluggishly, see here? Both out the front and back. It thickens when it is touched."

Ada leaned forward and sniffed delicately. "Oh no," she whispered, dismayed, and pressed her hands to her cheeks. "This is . . . this is awful."

"What is wrong?" Lily asked.

"No, no, child. This . . . this is no ordinary illness like soul rot. This is poison. A very terrible poison. And worse . . . look, there is a spirit web growing within." Ada's fingers curled into a tight fist at the base of her throat, her nails digging into her flesh as she spoke.

"A spirit web?" Piotr pushed away, hands scrabbling at his mid-section, fingers straining the buttons of his shirt as if he would rip the web free that very moment with his own two hands. "This is impossible!"

"It's not," Ada said. She hung her head. "I am so, so sorry."

"Can it be removed?" Lily asked seriously, chewing on the edge of her thumb as she regarded Ada and Piotr. "We do not wish to harm Piotr."

"If it were just the web, certainly, I would be more than willing to make the attempt," Ada drawled, obviously thinking deeply on their options. After several long moments, Ada nervously shook her head, "However, the web in conjunction with the poison . . . no, it cannot be done without endangering Piotr too much. Especially not here, in such savage surroundings."

"You seem so sure," Eddie said, crossing his arms over his chest. Piotr stared at Eddie so that he didn't have to think on his own issue, and noticed how Eddie's pale fingers seemed to stand out against the darkness of his sleeves, how Piotr could just make out the hue of Eddie's shirt beneath his wrists and hands. Eddie caught Piotr examining him and gave Piotr an odd, searching glance before turning to Ada. "So how do you know that for certain?"

Flushing darkly, Ada pulled back and had the decency to look ashamed. "Because I . . . I invented the poison it has taken root within."

"What?" Lily shoved away from the bed, her hands automatically going to the knives at her hips. When Ada raised her hands in supplication, Lily's lip twisted in a sneer and Piotr tensed. Lily was not Elle; the likelihood of an altercation with Ada was slim . . . unless Ada trod heavily on Lily's sense of fair play and honor. "Explain yourself," Lily demanded, and Piotr flinched.

"I do not know if I want to hear an explanation," Piotr muttered to Lily, gathering up his wrappings and clumsily trying to rewrap his wound. Eddie moved to help him and for once Piotr didn't feel uneasy at his help. Eddie's expression was just as disgusted as Piotr felt. On this, at least, they were of one mind. If she were speaking the truth, Ada had crossed the line working with Walkers.

"Please, listen. I have no excuse to offer that can stand as a proper apology, but there are reasons!" Ada exclaimed, and the way her voice stretched thin and high grated immediately on Piotr's nerves. He fought the momentary urge to grab her by the shoulders and *shake*. "Know truly that I would never have given the recipe for my poison to an enemy of yours or any Rider," Ada was saying, and Piotr forced himself to listen to her, to take Ada seriously. She'd braved the spirit web mess to come see him. The least he could do was listen to her explanation. "You do wonderful things for the children, I would not harm them for any gain! The idea that any spirit that would do such . . . that they would use such a barbaric weapon, much less coupled with a web, at all, is reprehensible. I could not work with such a soul."

"Your job of explaining your position is poor," Piotr said stiffly. "Did you supply the Walkers—any Walkers—with this poison?"

"No!" Ada cried, fists clenched at her sides. "The Council works with Walkers on occasion, yes, but I would never give them this poison! Silly boy, do you not understand what I am trying to tell you? You are important to us! And the poison . . . it isn't even really done yet! I sowed the seeds in a safe location but I hadn't worked on it for months when Mary . . ." She stopped and sagged, rubbing her forehead. "This is tiresome."

"Mary?" Eddie looked between Ada and Piotr. Piotr wondered if he was the only one to notice the way Eddie's fingers momentarily clenched into fists, the way his disorganized focus suddenly became laser-sharp when the White Lady was mentioned. "You don't mean Wendy's mom, Mary, do you? The White Lady? You knew her?"

"We were friends," Ada said stiffly, sniffing at Eddie's questions. "Before. And then, after she was sundered by the Lost, she was a completely different soul. Insane. Wicked. No head or patience for the delicate process of distilling the . . . the spirit webs properly."

Grimacing, Ada turned away and buried her face in her hands. She walked quickly to the window and pressed her forehead against the glass and Piotr was forced to admire the theatrics of her gesture. She was obviously upset, but Ada clearly had a mind like a tack. She might feel sorry for what she'd done, he reasoned, but Piotr was willing to bet that, given the right circumstances and opportunity, she'd do it all exactly the same all over again. The science of progress didn't really care who it hurt.

"Oh my," Ada murmured sighing deeply, "This . . . this is just a dreadful mess, isn't it?"

"You grew spirit webs for distillation, spirit webs like the one growing within Piotr this very moment," Lily said, pursing her lips and crossing her arms across her chest. She tapped one foot and Piotr hid a smirk, glad that Lily was there to keep Ada in check. "What next? Please continue. You have my—our—undivided attention."

"*Net*! Let me guess," Piotr said, struggling to find a position that did not sicken him as he felt the tickle of the web coiling within. "You kept your plants, your specimen, at Moffett Airfield. And then one day you went to collect your samples and they were gone."

Straightening and turning to face them, Ada nodded brusquely. "You are quite perceptive, Piotr. Yes, I had cultivated a field of sorts out there, where the webs were high in the air and could not harm passersby."

"How noble of you," Eddie sneered, and Piotr, despite his nausea, hid another smile. Eddie might have put his grubby hands all over Wendy, but at least he appeared to be on Piotr's side in all this mess. He wasn't cheering Piotr's illness. Perhaps Wendy was right about Eddie after all.

"I learned later that the White Lady had taken the strongest of the seeds for herself," Ada said, shrugging and ignoring Eddie's aside. "She had her Walkers begin germinating the spirit web seeds in their bodies and then began implanting them in humans."

"Nasty," Eddie said, wincing. "Why?"

"She used them to create a protective maze around the Palace Hotel," Ada explained. "They grew so quickly, fed by the turbulent emotions of that area of town, they'd overtaken the blocks surrounding the hotel in a matter of days. They're still there, to my knowledge, still growing."

"Yes. A forest of them. We have encountered it," Lily said, glancing at Piotr's wound and frowning. For a moment, Piotr considered sticking his hand in the hole. Maybe then everyone would stop staring at it and, by extension, him. "Twice."

Ada laughed bitterly. "Her idea was pure insanity, as the spirit webs would be tainted by the Walkers they germinated in, but Mary wasn't exactly thinking things through at that point."

"She was quite mad." Piotr agreed.

"Are you saying that these web-things take on the flavor of the person they're attached to?" Eddie asked, waiting for Ada's nod to say, "So what's this one in Piotr going to turn out like? Russian or something?"

"It won't turn out like anything," Ada said, shaking her head at Eddie's flippant ignorance. "Germinating a seed to complete fruition . . . it requires an able participant, one capable and willing to let it have free rein of their essence. This web was planted in a wound; Piotr hasn't the energy to keep it stable, it will simply spread through Piotr's essence if left unchecked. Like a cancer it will move through him until he is . . ." she hesitated.

"Finish it," Lily said, crossing her arms across her chest. "Speak quickly and speak true."

Pale now and fidgeting, Ada pressed her lips tightly together. "Until he is torn apart."

Rubbing a hand across his lips, Piotr closed his eyes. He did not want to see Lily's stricken expression or Eddie's uncomfortable concern. "Tell us about the poison," he urged, fighting the desire to shove his fist through the wound and start poking around until he found the thing. Piotr doubted that the web would let him rip it out by the roots. The web was a weed. It had probably already dropped spores or something similar deep inside his guts. "Leave nothing out. If I am to beat this thing, I must know it all."

"It is . . . I was developing the spirit web seed poison long, long before Mary became the White Lady. I've been working on this project for years! I had no idea that when she became . . . when she . . . I couldn't have had a clue that she would take my recipe and give it to the Walkers."

Ada shook her head in disgust. "It was never meant to be used against *us* either. It was supposed to be used against—" she broke off, glancing at Piotr guiltily.

"Continue," Lily ordered coldly, fingers brushing her bone knives, and Piotr suppressed a shiver at her tone. Lily only spoke thusly when someone had far overstepped their bounds with her— this was her killing tone. "You have gone so far, it would be a shame to leave it unfinished there."

"Initially, I began my research due to the Reapers. Frank and the others convinced me that the only way we'd be out from under the yoke of their service was to 'take care' of them with such a deadly concoction that they might never recover. We would find souls willing to sacrifice themselves to administer it while a Reaper was awash with Light. The poison would eventually eat them alive."

"But then the Reapers suddenly bailed on the Bay Area," Eddie said. He leaned forward and Piotr tried not to notice the way the dim light was shining through Eddie's shoulder. "Leaving only Mary."

"Correct. And Mary, unlike her brethren, was so reasonable. She was kind and she won us over, even those on the Council who think that the living are good for nothing more than emotion to feed off of."

"Then why continue with the poison?" Piotr asked, wincing as another stab of pain threaded its way through his gut. "Were you preparing for the day Mary was no longer here?"

"We thought we had many decades with Mary at the helm," Ada

said, shaking her head. "No, I continued my research after speaking with Mary herself."

She drifted over to Wendy's desk and gestured to a framed picture on the corner of the desk. It was a snapshot from several years prior—Wendy, the twins, and her parents crouched on a pier. Wendy, no more than ten, freckle-faced, gangly, and sporting a shiny set of silver braces, sat side-by-side with her mother. Just above them her father held a twin under each arm. Everyone was smiling, happy, and almost burned as red as their hair. The picture was very solid in the Never.

"Mary came to me," Ada said slowly, "after her first born came into this world. She was exhausted—you get very little sleep those first few months, I'm told—but still reaping every chance she could. During a reap, however, she had lost control. Her exhaustion and the untapped, unsapped power caught up with her and she burned a little too brightly."

"She saw something nasty, didn't she?" Eddie said sharply. "The Reapers were all up in arms about stuff that lives between the worlds."

"What? Like a balderkin?" Lily snapped. "No! Those are . . . those are tales you tell to keep the Lost in line! Boogie men in the dark. It is impossible." She hesitated and Piotr felt for her. He didn't want to imagine that the creatures from between the worlds, from the darkest part of the Never, actually existed either. "It *is* impossible. Yes?"

"Balderkin, banshee, whatever found her, it almost destroyed her," Ada said baldly. "Despite all her protection and careful planning, Mary came away with deep, deep damage."

Ada held up her arm and, unbuttoning the prim pearl buttons at her cuffs, pulled her sleeve back and illustrated the damage with her fingers. "Mary had slices into her very essence, deeper than the wounds from that hook, from the back of her hand all the way to her shoulder. That beast swam up from the depths of the Never, punched through the layers of blackness between the levels of death itself, to try and attack a Reaper. It almost succeeded in killing her. She did not say how she survived, but it left a mark on her. Before she'd been quiet, reserved, withdrawn and almost sad at her lot in life, regretful. But after . . . after, she burned with a fierce anger. Hatred. Unbelievable fury."

"She wanted to protect Wendy," Piotr said, realization dawning. He could remember so very little of Mary—she was like the ghost of an image in his mind—but even with his faulty memory, Mary's love for Wendy seemed painfully obvious to him. "She wanted the poison to protect her family."

"Her newborn daughter, yes," Ada said, tapping the photo thoughtfully. "Such a little thing, born with a caul and curls. Mary thought Wendy might be a Reaper like she was, but had no clue that Wendy would turn out to be a natural."

Setting down the photo gently, Ada chuckled, but her laugh was bitter and cold. "Mary was so terrified the day she discovered that Wendy had been in that car accident. She spent the next evening pacing the Top of the Mark cursing her luck and making the Council swear to keep our spirits away from Wendy until she'd concocted a plan. Mary had been a good landlord, so to speak. She had well-earned her goodwill and leverage; we agreed readily."

"And the plan?"

"The plan was simple. I was to resume my work on the poison, preparing it for the day the Reapers returned to the Bay Area and learned of Wendy's natural status. Mary was preparing us for potential war—the spies the Reapers employ are so widespread Mary was certain that her family would return to California within weeks to stamp out the natural menace. Instead . . . silence. Years and years of silence."

"Mary was so certain we'd do her dirty work for her?" Lily asked roughly. "Why should we risk our existence in a familial fight?"

Ada smiled. "You Riders were always ones to stay in the shadows, to be swift and silent and cut off from the rest of the Never.

You could not have known the suffering we others endured at the hands of the Reapers. It would have taken little effort to convince most of the dead to rally to our cause." She held up a hand, palm out. "One nick, that is all it takes, and the poison seeps within."

"But what if you cut yourself by accident?" Eddie asked and Piotr silently applauded the sensibility of the question, the sheer practicality of his approach. "Don't you have some sort of medicine for if a ghost gets a little blade-happy?"

Ada frowned. "I hardly think I would—"

"*Net*, Eddie makes a good point," Piotr agreed, steadying himself against the wall. "Is there some sort of counter-poison, Ada, or am I truly damned?"

"It needs an open wound to work," Ada said primly, pursing her lips in irritation, "but yes, as a matter of fact, I did create an antidote. Do I look a fool to you, young man?"

"If a poultice exists, then why are we gathered here discussing this sordid history?" Lily asked, sharing Piotr's exasperation. "We ought to be on our way to fetch it right now!"

"The poison takes weeks to create, the antidote twice that," Ada said pointedly, grabbing a handful of her dress in a fist as if she might shake the offending fist in Lily's face otherwise. "With the proper equipment and aid—and very little rest, I must add—I might be able to distill a bottle in a week, perhaps even a few days sooner, but I would need my lab and several gorged full spirit webs."

"This can be arranged," Lily said coolly. "Where is your lab?"

"Wait. Wait just a second," Eddie protested. "Why are we taking her word for all this stuff without, you know, needing proof or something? She could be lying through her teeth! For all you know, she's working with the chick who did this to Piotr in the first place."

"Piotr," Ada addressed Piotr quietly, tilting her chin up and pointedly ignoring Eddie's outburst, "please. I feel terrible. Please allow me to aid you. I feel as if I owe you for all of this."

Piotr turned his face away, forcibly reminded of the hissing Lady Walker and all her talk of debts owed. He shivered. So cold. It was so cold. She had been so cold.

"If this potion takes so long to brew, what do you suggest in the meantime?" he finally asked. Lily, arms crossed over her chest, sagged in relief, and Piotr realized that she had been waiting for him to fight the inevitable. He smiled to himself; she knew him too well.

"Walkers survive by consuming the souls of the Lost, yes?" Ada said slowly, glancing between Lily and Piotr. "In essence, that is the exchange of years . . . of willpower."

"I do not like where this is going," Piotr said, narrowing his eyes at Ada and feeling the world shift beneath his feet. He lay back on his elbows, resting. "Surely you do not think to suggest—"

"We could donate some of ourselves," Ada hurried on. "Piotr could feed on us like a Walker and be healed."

CHAPTER THIRTEEN

"**N**et," Piotr whispered, shaking his head. "Absolutely not."

"Nothing taken by force," Ada hurried to add, wringing her hands. "It would be a gift from Lily and I. Nothing permanent, just enough to keep you stable."

"That is foul!" Piotr cried, disgusted. "To do such a thing is an abomination!"

"I cannot believe I trusted you," Lily agreed. "To suggest . . . no. No. It cannot be done. I did not bring you here for this. We are Riders. We do not act like Walkers. We are not depraved!"

"You do not understand," Ada protested. "Walkers are dark, yes, they have been forced into such a terrible predicament that they found only the most awful route to be their salvation. This is a reason to pity them, not revile them! They were once alive just as you and I were. Don't they deserve some consideration?"

"I am done with this," Piotr sneered, turning his face away from Ada. He would have turned his back on her but feared he would falter, weakening his show of disgust. "I will not consider it!"

"Um . . . I can offer some. Of me, I mean," Eddie said slowly, breaking the tension. "If eating a ghost is so bad, I can give you some of my energy, I guess. I mean, I'm not dead yet, right? So it's not the same thing. Once Wendy finds out how to put me back in my body I'll be just fine. So it's not like you're destroying someone or taking time or will or whatever off their afterlife. I'm not even dead yet. Plenty of will left in me." Eddie smiled, nervous but willing, and Piotr was once again struck by how *kind* Eddie's eyes were, how gentle his grin. Wendy would be sad to miss this, Piotr realized. She would be so proud of him.

A tiny, selfish part of Piotr rejoiced that she was gone.

Clearing his throat, Piotr turned to Eddie and held out his arms. Surely this boy was not actually this good, this sweet. It had to be some sort of act. "I'm . . . sorry?" Piotr said. "I do not understand. Please . . . please explain. Why would you do this thing for me? To give of your life-force, your essence, your will, it is a very intimate, careful thing. Only the Lost have much to give. Why would you, who barely know me—my rival, who once suggested to Wendy that I might be a bad person—do such a thing?"

Eddie flushed; he jerked his chin up and looked Piotr straight in the eye. "Look, man, I didn't know you then. And, to be honest, if you died . . . again, I mean, if you passed into the Light or whatever, then Wendy'd be heartbroken. So maybe it's not just you. Maybe I just don't dig on the idea of Wendy being sad."

Eddie's generosity, his putting Wendy's feelings first, made Piotr feel like the worst kind of cad. He worried most for Wendy's physical and spiritual safety, but he rarely took her feelings into consideration. Wendy was strong, Piotr knew. She was tough. Her feelings could survive a few harsh words said in the process of saving her life . . . right?

"You are a very thoughtful boy," Ada said gently to Eddie, "and were your situation different, I would jump at the chance to have you help Piotr. But as you say, your body is still alive and that is not conducive to aiding Piotr. In fact, giving him your life might kill you."

Ada reached forward and ran her fingers across the edges of Eddie's form, making him shiver. "You are weak at the edges, do you see? Fainter. Even Piotr, sick as he is, is firm in the Never. You are not. Your body is fading, am I correct? You are very far away from your shell." She shrugged. "Who knows how long you shall last? Hours? Days? Weeks on the outside. No more."

"Gee," Eddie said dryly, and Piotr noted how Eddie jerked his chin up, refusing to look down at his weakening body. Then Eddie smiled hugely at Ada, his teeth big and white and square in a gigantic, bared grin as he nonchalantly said, "Thanks for the vote of confidence, Miss Ada, but I'll be fine. We need to help Piotr first. He's got important crap to do and I've just got the rest of holiday break. I know Wendy'll get to the bottom of my issue in no time flat, so no worries, yeah? Let's get Piotr healed up first."

As much as Piotr despised Ada in this moment, and as much as he feared Eddie's closeness with Wendy, he knew that Eddie had a point and was shamed by Eddie's bravery and selflessness. Piotr knew that Wendy would be devastated if she were unable to help either of them; between Piotr's jealousy from before and his abandoning her in the hospital, they had left so much yet to discuss between them. Piotr did not want to leave Wendy with so much left unsaid. But Eddie . . . stubborn boy. He'd rather fade away than take that decision—whether to be with the living boy or the dead one—away from Wendy.

Eddie wasn't fighting fair.

Piotr could admire that.

"I'm starting to like you," Piotr grumbled to Eddie. "You kiss my woman, for this I am displeased, but your heart is in the right place and for that I think I shall call you friend. Fine. We shall have it your way. We shall try this transfer then, if Ada is still willing. We heal me. Then we heal you." Drawing on his remaining strength, Piotr slapped Eddie on the shoulder, perhaps a little harder than necessary. He smiled when Eddie winced.

"Um, thanks?" Eddie scowled slightly at Piotr. "Frankly, knowing you approve of me is nice and all, but I'll be honest—sometimes I still want to punch you in the face. At least once, just a quick *pop* to the nose."

"To feel this way about Piotr, that is normal," Lily said smoothly, flicking a derisive glance first to Piotr and then Eddie. Piotr tried not to smirk at his friend. Lily knew him better than she knew anyone else. Lily sighed at his innocent expression before turning to Ada. "You really mean to do this thing, then? To transfer your life into Piotr?"

"It is not desecration if willingly given," Ada said evenly. "Or so I believe."

Lily nodded. "To give of one's self is the greatest gift. So be it." Formally she held out an arm to Piotr. "You are my friend. I give myself to you."

"This is still wrong, I believe this to be true," Piotr said gravely, taking Lily's wrist in his left hand and Ada's in his right. "It feels too much like being a Walker for comfort."

"Then be uncomfortable," Ada said tauntingly, "and get on with it."

Drawing the essence from Lily and Ada was nothing like touching a Lost. Holding a Lost child was like a special communion; they always initiated the contact, and feeling their energy fill you was better than the first gulp of ice-cold water on a boiling hot day. It hurt a bit, but the relief, the feeling of their life filling you was like sinking into warmth and peace and soft, gentle, loving arms.

Every Lost had a different feel, flavor, a smell, some hint of energy that was just the barest taste of who they were. Dora had always felt like bubbling lemon-sweetness, effervescent and frothy. She tickled the nose. Hugging Specs had been like thumbing through an oft-loved book, with the slightly dusty scent and feel of soft, well-thumbed pages. Tubs had been like inhaling cotton candy, with sweetness that melted on the tongue, or bubbling ephemeral laughter hovering just on the edge of sound.

This, though, was completely different. Though Lily and Ada were willing, this was not a rush or a wave or a sinking into joy and light and love. This was pulling. This was digging his mental fingers into the meat of who they were and worrying their essence free. This was freely given, and yet he could tell that every second hurt them.

For a brief, glorious minute, Piotr felt his insides stop aching and firm up. They healed and he was glad of it, but the effort he expended to make sure that his organs were all in the right place was tremendous. His need was too great, he could feel it; it was just as when Wendy stood before him in all her Lightbringer glory, shifting from the being of Light to just a girl once more. Then she had been weak and vulnerable for a bare moment and now, his fingers deep into the essence of these women, Piotr could feel their vulnerability, their openness and exposure to his darker, greedier nature.

It was like there was some great glacier in him, one that had previously only been kept at bay by his constant energy, his purpose and strength. Now, still wounded, there were no barriers between the cold and his friends. Beneath his fingertips Lily's flesh darkened and grew bluish and thin. She gasped in pain and wriggled in his grip, but Piotr's fingers were sunk deep in now; he knew he didn't have to let go if he didn't want to.

"Piotr?" Eddie asked, grabbing Piotr's wrist and then yanking his hand back, hissing as if he'd been burned. "Ouch! Why are you so cold? Hey, Piotr, man, come on, let up. Piotr? PIOTR, LET GO!"

Horrified at what he was doing to Lily, Piotr stopped, feeling shaky and strange and icy all over. He was lightheaded and felt soiled, as if he'd just tried to do something nasty to his best friend and this near-stranger. He felt simultaneously degraded and degrading, as if he'd just tried to see them with their skirts up.

Ashamed of himself, Piotr turned his head away. Every nerve in his body pounded pain. He wished that he'd never listened to Ada in the first place.

"That," Ada gasped, rubbing her wrist, "was quite painful. Far more than I expected."

"I am cold," Piotr whispered. "So cold. My apologies, Lily. I did not mean to hurt you. Nor you, Ada. It . . . I could hardly stop myself."

"I know," Lily said, holding her wrist out and examining the place where Piotr had touched her critically. "I could feel your struggle." Her head dipped and she drew her arms back to her body, wrapping them around her torso protectively.

Ashamed, Piotr ducked his head. "If this is how Walkers feel, then I owe them a great deal of sympathy. That was a horrible experience."

"As do I," Lily murmured, rising and moving to stand beside the window. Her expression was shuttered. "At the very least you are in less pain, yes?"

"But he's still sick," Ada pointed out, rifling through Wendy's makeshift first aid kit, frowning as she lifted out an unfamiliar bottle. "And since this didn't work, my only other suggestion is that we go to Alcatraz."

"What's so special about Alcatraz?" Eddie asked, rubbing the side of his nose and taking the bottle from Ada. It was a nearly full bottle of Percocet. "I don't think either Lily or Piotr is up for traveling right now. Especially not to go on some sightseeing tour."

Finished with her perusal of the kit, Ada sighed. "I suggest no tour, Edward, and likewise I find your humor lacking. The bulk of my lab is at Alcatraz, in the basement."

Eddie laughed. "You're joking, right?" Ada's expression did not change. "You're not joking. Why would you set up shop someplace like Alcatraz?"

"I needed a place of constant, guaranteed energy, and tourist locations—especially ones with such negative histories—are particularly solid in the Never." She shrugged. "You have to deal with the occasional human in the bowels of the island, but for the most part the Shades are all gone." She slanted a glance under her lashes at Lily. "The Indian inhabitants were the ones who protested the construction of my lab the most. They have since moved on." What was left unsaid, Piotr noticed, was the manner in which she'd moved them on. Lily frowned but kept her peace.

"So, I'm no doctor," Eddie said, holding up the bottle, "but this is a pretty potent pain-killer. People get addicted to it, it's so strong. Do you think it'll work in the Never? On Piotr, I mean?"

Piotr waved a hand. "I need no—"

"Stop being stubborn," Lily replied sharply. "Take the medicine. You need not be in great pain for us to think you brave. We don't know how long our . . . melding will last."

"It looks like it's salvaged," Eddie added. "So I don't know where Wendy got it from, but it's probably better than nothing right now."

"Fine," Piotr said, holding out his hand. "So be it."

Eddie handed Piotr a Percocet and watched curiously as Piotr dry-swallowed it. "No clue if this'll be enough to help or not. I'm not a doc." He frowned at the bottle. "How does this stuff work, anyway? You guys don't even have regular blood, right?"

"The nature of being deceased is one of the mysteries I am examining in my lab," Ada said, warming immediately to the subject. "Animals can speak to us in the Never, which they do not do in the living lands. Here we have no 'blood' to guide herbs on their way, only essence that we can shape and form the outer edges of at will, but yet medicine often works. Most complicated machinery does not function here, except when it does." She grinned broadly. "The Never is a place of such extreme contradictions at times; it is truly fascinating!"

"It is aggravating," Lily replied. "To have such modern wonders at our fingertips, to see them in use every day in the living lands, and yet to be unable to work them ourselves." She frowned. "The Council stockpiles weapons of all types—including guns—and yet they can do nothing with them. Imagine the capability to destroy a Walker with but a single bullet? Think of how many would be put out of their misery."

Lily stilled then. "Wait. This lab of yours, these mysteries . . . is that what you are doing there? Trying to ascertain why certain objects work in the Never and others do not? Are you attempting to make objects such as weaponry work in the Never?"

Ada shrugged. "This I cannot say without potentially rousing the ire of the Council. But if you were to accompany me to my lab,

I would be very willing to give you a tour of my projects. Not just the Reaper poison, of course. Other things."

"I know I'm not the spiffiest science guy that ever scienced," Eddie broke in, "but is your lab really that important? Can't you just use your big brains and cook up some antidote here?"

"Hardly. On Alcatraz I have a stockpile of materials that are difficult to come by without significant time and effort," Ada explained. "I've spent decades assembling my apparatus. And, to be frank, this place makes me uneasy. It is too open, too exposed. Alcatraz was built to be a fortress and then fed with the emotions and pain of the prisoners above, causing the walls to be doubly solid, both in the Never and in the living lands. Even Reapers cannot easily breach the defenses."

"Not to mention, we must collect glutted spirit webs for your concoction, am I correct?" Lily added. "There are none to be found here, but in the city . . ."

Eddie snorted. "Yeah, that little day trip's gonna be a hoot and a half. Flesh-eating plants? Sign me up." He sighed. "I guess you can't go collect them by yourself?"

"I could," Ada said, pursing her lips, "but I've been told there is a beast in the forest surrounding the Palace Hotel. I am not a warrior, Edward. I am a scientist."

"There is indeed a great beast," Lily said. "We have seen it. No, risking Ada's skill and knowledge in such an endeavor is out of the question. We shall gather the webs for her."

"So it has been decided," Piotr said, suddenly weary of all the talk. "We escort Ada to Alcatraz, stopping by the forest to collect glutted spirit webs on our way. When shall we leave?"

"Soon," Ada said. "Your wounds might be temporarily healed, but they still worry me."

"I don't know. Maybe we should wait for Wendy and Elle?" Eddie asked, just as the door to Wendy's room suddenly swung open.

Wendy was home.

CHAPTER FOURTEEN

Overjoyed to be done with her family, Wendy waved at Chel and Jon, stumbled up the stairs and opened up her door, nearly walking through Piotr on her way to her bed.

"Are you okay?" she asked Piotr, poking his bicep as she toed off her filthy sneakers. Despite her burning touch, Piotr briefly leaned into her hand and Wendy relaxed. "You look better than you did before."

Piotr glanced at Ada. "I do feel somewhat better, *da*. It is good to see your face. I was worried at how long you had been gone."

"You went to see your family," Lily added, disapproval writ large across her face. "After we traveled to warn you against them."

"Yeah, I know," Wendy said, rubbing a hand across her eyes. She glanced at Eddie and her heart skipped a beat. Eddie's essence looked so . . . so thin. "I'm sorry, but . . . look, I kind of got ambushed. They just showed up this morning." She reached over and nudged Eddie with her shoulder. "In exchange for training me to take my mother's place, they promised to help find Eddie's cord and to help me get him back in his body. I'm not willing to piss them off right now, not if maybe they can help get Eddie back to normal."

Lily nodded once, her expression closed off, and Wendy knew that her explanation had been understood, even if the reasons behind her choice weren't entirely accepted.

"So, you're new," Wendy said, eyeing Ada and flopping on her bed. She stretched and yawned, wishing that she'd had a chance to grab a catnap earlier.

"I am," Ada said cautiously. "It is a pleasure to meet you, Winifred." She crossed her arms over her chest and stepped closer. "I am a member of the Council. Of the dead." Uncomfortably, Ada fidgeted in place and cleared her throat. "I have heard much about you."

187

"Yeah, I bet," Wendy yawned; the room was practically spinning, she was so exhausted. She tried not to think of Sarah, of the begrudgingly amused expression on the little girl's face as they parted, of how willing she'd been to talk for a while in exchange for nothing more than a battered paperback. Wendy buried her face. Eddie. Sarah. Could she do nothing right? Wendy's heart hurt. "So," she said to Ada, to take her mind off Jane's triumphant peace-sign, her wide grin and pleased swagger back to the car, "you knew my mom, huh?" Across the room Eddie sighed, and Wendy glanced furtively at him from beneath her eyelashes. One person at a time, she thought to herself. Piotr, then Eddie. Eddie wasn't poisoned, right? He had time.

Hopefully.

Ada hesitated. "I did."

"Cool. I'll want to talk with you at some point about that." Wendy yawned again and held up a hand; it was trembling wildly. "Guys, look, I want to chat and talk to you about my morning and maybe cobble together some sort of a plan of attack but I haven't slept in . . . gosh, since I don't know when. I need . . . an hour? No more. A nap. Just a little one." Wendy rubbed an arm across her face and turned to Piotr and Eddie. "Can you guys wait that long? How are you two feeling? You're . . . well, you're clearly not fixed, Piotr, but you don't look as bad as you did before. Eddie, I . . ."

"I can wait an hour," Piotr assured her. "Please, do not worry yourself, Wendy. Rest."

"Yeah, you kinda look like crap warmed over," Eddie agreed fervently. He offered an arm to Ada. "Neither one of us is going to drop any deader. We won't go far, take a load off."

"On it," Wendy mumbled, yanking off her socks, glad that Eddie knew her so well and was just so . . . Eddie about everything. "Just a bit. I'll be right with you, doing whatever I have to, but just an hour nap, okay? Okay."

Punching her pillow into a c-shape, Wendy curled on her side and rubbed her cheek into the smooth cotton as Eddie, Ada, and Lily left through the wall, Eddie glancing over his shoulder at Piotr with a frown as he vanished into the hall.

"So . . . Ada, huh?" Wendy asked Piotr, patting the space beside her on the bed. "She looks like a trip and a half to hang out with. Is she always so stiff?"

"Ada is concerned for my well being," Piotr said quietly, settling on the bed beside Wendy, "and she has brought us disturbing tidings." He touched his stomach. "She believes that, with work, she may be able to heal me of my wounds."

"Okay," Wendy murmured, closing her eyes as Piotr carefully stretched out beside her, no part of him touching her, but still spooned nearly around her like a cat. She took a deep breath and inhaled the sweetly smoky evergreen scent of him, the smell of dirt and growing things, of dark green trees in the snow, reaching branches to a sky white with heavily-laden clouds. "How?"

"We will need to travel with her to the bay," Piotr explained quietly as Wendy's eyes fluttered closed. "She has a laboratory there."

"Not gonna wait for Elle, then?" Wendy murmured. "I mean, Lily came back so fast, there's a chance Elle might still pull through. She could . . ." Wendy hesitated, thought of telling Piotr about Sarah, but decided that she couldn't talk about the little Lost yet without tearing up. "She could . . . find a Lost, still. Maybe. There has to be at least one out there."

"It is true, Elle is still searching," Piotr said and gently touched the back of her neck with one finger, then another, then another until he cupped the nape of her neck with his palm. He hissed and Wendy shuddered, but neither of them drew away. "But this is a good longer-term plan, I think. And this way we may be able to ascertain how much ill or good the Council truly holds for us."

"You should stop," Wendy said when her head was swimming and her skin was jumping beneath his palm as if he were administering tiny electric shocks to her flesh. "Your memories . . . the pain . . ."

"The pain, it is something I can handle," he replied, breathing evenly through gritted teeth. "The memories . . . I don't need them. Let them go." He pulled his hand away and replaced it with his lips, mouth grazing the back of her neck as he said, "I hated every moment we were apart."

"Then why did you leave?" Wendy asked quietly. The exhaustion was so all-consuming that even the feeling of Piotr kissing the back of her neck was soothing and not exciting. Wendy wanted to sag against him, curl into his side and sleep for a million years; only the fear of what pressing her living heat to his chill might do to him stopped her. She fought encroaching sleep but exhaustion was winning. Wendy struggled to stay awake for his reply but it didn't come.

When she realized he wasn't going to answer her, Wendy was asleep in seconds.

"Because I was scared," Piotr said at long last, when Wendy's breathing had evened out, when she lay lax across her bed. He pulled away so that they were touching no more. "And because giving you up then was easier than walking away later." He paused and then smiled. "You are asleep? Wendy?" Piotr nodded once and held up his palm. It was blistered and charred, heavily wounded from touching the back of Wendy's neck. "And because if you knew what touching you did to me, you'd never allow it again."

That said, even if only acknowledged to himself alone, Piotr stretched out beside her, careful to not touch her again, and let himself drift. Perhaps it was the poison, or his wounds, or perhaps it was simply the strain of touching Wendy again, but he was bone-weary and ready for sleep. Slowly his own breathing evened out and Piotr slid into dreams of his own.

In her dream Wendy walked and walked.

At first, the fog was so thick that she was unsure where she was, but then Wendy thought she recognized the tied boat bobbing with the tide, the rotting rope holding it to the pier, and the short stretch of rocky beach bordered with scrubland that stretched out beneath her feet. This was like the place where she'd met the White Lady for the first time, the dreamscape where her mother had tried to scare her off and punished Wendy for defying her. Later she'd ripped Wendy's tongue piercing out of her mouth in the dreamscape and Wendy had woken to find her ring gone and tongue healed, as if she'd never had the bar in the first place.

As if she'd conjured it up, a glint of silver at her feet made Wendy pause. She knelt down and there it was—her old tongue ring. The barbell was slightly tarnished by sand and sea and sun, but still recognizable.

"Gross," she said, and pocketed the ring, more for the novelty of finding it again in such a strange place than out of any actual plans to use it again.

Was this a dream or a dreamscape? Wendy didn't know. She searched the sand and scrub for the telltale door of seashells but could not see one. Of course that didn't mean anything; sometimes the doors were well hidden, sometimes they were out in plain sight. But dreams never had the doors, only dreamscapes did. Wendy could spot none and decided to assume, for now, that this was just a dream.

Above, the wind picked up, scuttling the fog clear of the beach and rock outcroppings like bones, bleached white and strange in the sand. Wendy realized that no, she'd been wrong, this beach wasn't the same. That beach had been in Santa Cruz but this was clearly not Santa Cruz at all. It was smaller, for one, and the steep scrub was much closer to shore than she'd originally thought. In fact, Wendy realized, unless she was very much mistaken, she wasn't on the mainland at all, but an island.

"Is this . . . is this Alcatraz?" she muttered to herself, twisting and craning until she could spot the familiar white washed lighthouse perched above Alcatraz Island. The tower was there, but the top of the building was thin and wavery, insubstantial and faded; the harder Wendy squinted, trying to make out where exactly on the island she might be, the thinner the building seemed to become until it looked as if the lighthouse stood alone amid the rocks and scrub, a dot adrift on the cold, unforgiving sea.

A light step nearby startled Wendy into jumping aside, but it was just her mother—not the White Lady, but Mary, feeding ravens and crows gathered in peaceful droves on the slim slope of beach. High above the tableau seagulls squawked and screamed, dive-bombing the shallow waves lapping the pier in groups and coming up with mouthfuls of struggling crabs and fish and filthy water. One nearby gull squatted over a freshly-killed squirrel and struggled to gulp it down in one bite, turning the furry corpse over and over in its bill, looking for the right angle to eat.

In the distance, from the prison behind them, a black pillar of smoke drifted up toward the clouds. A bell donged on the island and the wind picked up, hot and humid, and Wendy shuddered at the touch; the breeze felt like moist fingers fondling her skin, tugging at her skirt and yanking sharply at the loose tendrils of her hair.

"Mom?" Wendy asked, carefully picking her way through the quiet flocks of crows and ravens, "This is a dream, right? Not a dreamscape. Right? Mom?"

Her mother shrugged.

Frowning, Wendy reached her side and, taking a few pieces of stale bread from Mary's plastic bread-bag, crumbled up the food for the birds. "So I met—well, really met—my cousin Emma today and your . . . aunt? And your grandma. You won't guess what Eddie named her, by the way. Nana Moses. Can you believe it?"

Her mother remained silent, simply spreading out the bread and letting the breeze tug her tumbled red curls forward, obscuring her face. Bemused, Wendy shrugged and tried again. "I heard that you were some sort of super-Reaper. Crazy, huh? Why didn't you ever tell me?"

Again, her mother's silence. Wendy frowned. When Mary had been the White Lady, she hadn't shut up for a minute; the entire time they'd been together, the White Lady had run her mouth, talking and sniping, offering unwanted advice and picking at Wendy's choices whether she wanted to hear it or not. Reminding Wendy over and over again that she wasn't good enough, and would never, ever be good enough.

Irritated now, Wendy strode several feet away, digging her feet in the sand and wriggling her toes into the grit. Her foot caught a rock and Wendy stumbled, scraping her hand against a sharp outcropping poking up from the sand.

Hissing in pain, Wendy cradled her hand against her chest and glared around her. Where her mother rested against a large rain-sculpted grotto, the island seemed peaceful, almost sweet, but down the shore where Wendy stood, the waves were cold and filthy and rank; spotting a hole in the sand, Wendy had a mean impulse to stomp on the hole and cave it in.

Glancing over her shoulder at her mother, still resting some distance away, Wendy shrugged and stomped, relishing the squish of sand beneath her heel. Punishing the earth and possibly the clam for her own misgivings made Wendy feel simultaneously better and truly awful. For a moment she considered digging the clam out to let it breathe, but then remembered that this was a dream and even if she did, one of the birds would just crack the clam and eat its meat. Maybe it was better to leave it be.

"Mom?" Wendy called, straightening, emboldened by her stomping about. "Mom, did you really go crazy? Was it really the Lost that did all that to you? Or were you a little crazy to begin with?" No answer. Wendy forged ahead. "Piotr says he talked to some guy name Frank and that you were working with . . . working with . . ."

Wendy faltered to a stop. There was odd movement against her toes, slight scratching against the arch of her right foot. Slowly, so slowly, Wendy looked down . . . and stifled a scream.

There were spiders at her feet, pouring from a hundred holes in the sand just like the one she had stomped. Startled, Wendy tried to back away but the spiders were everywhere, large and hairy and underfoot, crawling over her toes and heaving themselves bodily out of new, larger holes in the sand. Everywhere she turned new holes were opening up, spewing out their eight-legged contents in a scuttling mass.

Fighting back a yell, Wendy scrambled back toward the grass and rock as best she could, but the spiders followed, intent on overcoming her. Overwhelmed, Wendy had no idea if they were poisonous or not, but when one dropped on her hair from above she couldn't help herself. Shrieking, she slapped at her hair, feeling the bulging heat of the hairy thing beneath her hand as she yanked fingers through her tangled curls, praying and crying that it wouldn't get caught in them. Instead she felt the slick, wet pop as it burst against her palm and the burning as what could only be its poison worked its way into the scrape.

Wendy shrieked again and flung the spider corpse away, or tried to. The large dangling legs were tangled in her hair, the cluster of eyes swinging against her cheek as Wendy, sobbing, tried to pry it free.

Just as she was about to go mad from fear a raven leapt up on her shoulder, nudged her hand aside with its beak, and gobbled the spider from her hair. It tugged painfully, but Wendy was willing to lose a few locks if it got that horrible thing off her. Imagining a pair of scissors in her hand, they appeared in the dream, and Wendy snipped the curls free. The raven flew off with the arachnid in its beak, jittering legs scrabbling at its eyes, and several of her curls trailing in the wind.

Sobbing with relief, Wendy hugged herself tightly and eyed the ground. The crows and ravens had been at work; the ground was covered in feathers but no arachnids were to be found. Here and there the birds were beginning to return from their feast; they fluttered down about her feet again, pecking at the holes and preening one another, their glossy black feathers shining in the dim winter sun.

Snorting with a combination of giddy fear and unadulterated relief, it took several seconds for Wendy to realize that the helpful raven, despite its good deed, had managed to crap all over her shirt in the process of freeing her from the spider. Staggering with the insanity of it all, with the unexpected humor of being shat upon by a dream bird, Wendy hurried to her mother.

"Did you see that? Did I imagine it, or did it really just happen?"

Pushing off from the grotto with one hand, her mother drifted away, still silent.

"Mom? MOM!" Shaky and irritated by her close call with the spiders, Wendy was unwilling to put up with any more dream drama. She grabbed her mother by the shoulder. "You don't want to talk? Fine. Just answer me this, okay? Did you know about the natural thing? Did you know that I might be in danger from our own family? Did you? DID YOU? Did you even CARE?"

Furious now, Wendy began shaking her mother's shoulder, spinning Mary around until her mom was in her arms, both shoulders gripped in Wendy's punishing hands. Angry now, furious beyond what Wendy thought she was capable of, Wendy shook and shook and shook her mother, demanding, "DID YOU KNOW? DID YOU? DID YOU!" until, suddenly, her mother's head rolled right off her shoulders.

The crows and ravens scattered.

Wendy dropped the limp body, and above her the gulls screamed in triumph and began diving down, hovering over her mother's body and pecking at her flesh with their cruel beaks, ripping long strips free like human calamari.

Horrified, Wendy waved her arms frantically at the gulls, suffering pecks and scratches to the arms and hands as the gulls fought over their new carrion. Still, Wendy was able to make her way to her mother's head and push away the one gull perched upon it. For such a little bird, the gull was surprisingly heavy; it flopped to the sand

and struggled to flip off its side. Wendy didn't care; she didn't want the gull eating her mother's eyes.

Turning her mother's head over, Wendy smoothed the red curls off Mary's cheeks and then, overwhelmed, began laughing hysterically.

"You're not my mom," she told the head, pushing a stray piece of straw back into the neck hole. "You're a scarecrow." Black button eyes glinted in the sun as if saying, *Why, you're right! I am a scarecrow! Fancy that! I wonder if your father knows!*

The cheeks were drippy red circles, still fresh and wet, and the lips were crudely sewn shut with thick black thread, twisted and knotted over and over again. The flap of extra fabric at the neck, tied with a thin green ribbon, was intricately embroidered with the same Celtic pattern Wendy sported around her collarbone. The hair alone was real, soft and silky, red curls glued to the bag in locks and then reinforced with careful cross-stitches from nape to forehead.

Disgusted and shaken, Wendy dropped the head on the sand. Let the gulls get it, she decided, rising and brushing gritty sand off her knees. Her mother had never been here. All this was wishful thinking. Just a dream after all.

A soft creak from the shore made Wendy turn toward the sea. The small boat anchored to the pier creaked as the tide tossed it to and fro, but what caught her eyes was the large raven perched on the bow of the boat. It was huge and glossy and black, spreading its wings so far they blotted out the sun.

Then it opened its mouth.

Wendy expected it to caw or croak but she was wrong. The raven took a breath and the world was filled with screams and screams and screams.

Stunned by the sudden outpouring of noise, Wendy staggered back, stumbling until she fell on her rear, painfully biting her tongue as her hand plunged through the scarecrow's thin temple, the straw and something with the texture of pudding. It squished between her fingers as Wendy grimaced and yanked her hand free with a sucking *schloop*.

"Oh nasty," she whispered. Her hand was covered with slimy grey-red goop, stray pieces of straw clinging to the heel of her hand, her knuckles coated with chaff.

"Could be nastier, I've seen worse in the ER," said a voice as Emma settled beside Wendy on the sand. She was dressed in a long black nightgown with a scoop neck that exposed a slim triangle of her intricate tattoos. Pulling her thighs tightly to her torso, Emma dug in the sand at her side and pulled out a large handkerchief, flipping it briefly to clear the fabric of sand. "You look like you need this."

"What are *you* doing here?" Wendy asked, taking the linen square gingerly between thumb and forefinger and wiping off her hand.

"Believe it or not, I hardly slept last night either," Emma said, patting her cheeks theatrically. "I figured I might as well get some business done, if I'm wasting all this precious time napping." She rested her chin on her knees. "Interesting choice of dreamscape, I might add."

"Thanks?" Wendy finished wiping her hand and hesitated. She wasn't sure if she should give Emma's fouled handkerchief back or not.

"I thought you should know," Emma continued, running the tips of her long-nailed fingers through the sand, "that I believe you're making a very big mistake."

"About what?" Wendy watched as Emma traced a lean Celtic knot into the earth, her clever fingers joining the bends and curves without error.

"Training." Emma looked up from her tracing and Wendy was startled to realize that the doctor was not smiling. Her tone was sweet, but the look on her face was ugly and dark. "You're a little idiot, you know that?"

"Wh-what?" Wendy couldn't believe her ears. "*You* were the one who offered to train me in the first place!"

"Please. As if I thought you'd honestly take me up on it. And what else was I to do? Great-Grandmother was right there, watching." Emma rolled her eyes. "That you believed me so implicitly tells me that you are clearly not proper Reaper material. You didn't think to ask any of the correct questions! You haven't even found the letter I left for you yet, have you?"

You never ask the right questions, the White Lady's voice whispered in the back of Wendy's mind.

"But . . . but there hasn't been a lot of time . . ." Wendy protested weakly. "And you said you wanted to make a deal. You said that you wanted me to take over the area like my mom did, so you all could go back home . . ."

"And you took me at my word? That we have nothing but your best interest in mind? How naïve *are* you, Winifred? Didn't anyone teach you that someone like you must take care of your own problems? Must watch your own back?"

Watch your back! Mary's voice commanded, and Wendy shivered. She balled her fists. "I thought . . . I thought you were going to help me? And what about Eddie?"

"I am helping you. Get lost, Winifred. For your good, and for the good of the family. Don't come back to the house. Stay away. It's better that way."

"But what about the binding?" Wendy asked softly. "You said it will last a few weeks, but you never said if you had to take it off or if it just fades away on its own."

"That will have to be your concern, won't it?" Emma chuckled and rose to her feet, patting Wendy on the head like an obedient dog. "If you're such a mighty Reaper that you deserve to be part of our clan, to reap this area by yourself, then you'll have to ascertain how to unravel it yourself." She smirked. "Perhaps then, if you can remove it on your own, I will reconsider my stance."

"Nana Moses—"

"Isn't here, now is she?" Emma brushed sand off her pants. "And please stop calling her that. It's disrespectful. Her name is Alonya."

Wendy shook her head. "You're . . . I don't . . ."

"Please. Stop being so weak." Emma reached down and grabbed Wendy by the chin, yanking her head up so that their noses were only inches apart. Her nails cut into Wendy's chin; the breath fanning across Wendy's face smelled strongly of mint and bourbon. "And *you* honestly believe that you have what it takes to be a Reaper? Pathetic." She shoved Wendy's face away, her long nails leaving deep scratches across Wendy's chin. "Go back to sleep, little girl. Leave the reaping to the experts."

Wendy stiffened. "You know what? Go to hell, Emma."

Emma smiled shortly. "Already there, dear. Already there." Then, glancing around the empty beach, Emma stretched and smiled. "Such a weak little dreamscape, Winifred. Weak space for a weak mind." She snapped her fingers and the sand beneath Wendy began to tremble. Wendy, a life-long resident of California, knew instinctively what was coming. She jumped to her feet.

The quake, when it hit, tore the pier from its moorings and sent great waves twice as tall as Wendy to batter the upper shore. Trees bent over backwards under the onslaught of water and wind, and the ground began vibrating in large, concentric circles, spreading out in a shockwave of buckling earth and sand.

Wendy, rather than fighting the wave, let it roll over her, absorbing as much of the brute force as she could, imagining a bubble of safety in a radius around her, picturing that the air that she breathed was calm, that the earth beneath her feet was solid and firm.

After long minutes, the chaos was done and Emma was gone. Wendy looked at her tiny space, unaffected by the disaster, and the shredded landscape surrounding her for miles around. Fish were floating belly-up on top of the water, great flocks of birds had been plucked from the sky and littered the sand and sea as far as the eye could see. The stench of rot and mold and death was nauseating.

But still, despite the ruin of much of the dreamscape surrounding her, Wendy's small space was untouched.

"You know what, bitch?" Wendy said, kneeling down and combing out a small square of shell-covered earth at her feet. "You want me to give up? Screw you. Now . . . now I'm pissed. You want to keep me from being a Reaper? Maybe, maybe if you'd asked nicely I might have thought about going some other route. But now? Now, it's on."

In his dreams, Piotr walked and walked.

The snow was knee high, sometimes as deep as his thigh, and the blood on his hands was drying from a dark red to a sticky brown. Downy feathers caught on the breeze spun around him, lifted high and drifting down again, sticking to the gummy blood on his forehead, to the tears and sweat drying on his cheeks. Piotr slogged through the snow, keeping the frozen river on the right of him, heading for the "V" where the banks of the river split and the village sat, protected on three sides by the frozen tide.

Mother will know what to do, Piotr thought as he took another step, fur-clad foot breaking through the brittle crust of ice atop the deeper softness of the snow beneath. The cloak was dragging the snow beside him, leaving thin, oddly patterned trails occasionally splattered with faint pink. The forest was intensely quiet all around; despite the great black flocks of birds weighing down evergreens as far as the eye could see, not a peep was heard.

The world was white-green-black, and then, from the corner of his eye, he spotted the motion—a flash of red, of silver-grey, and the whip-quick motion of the long red braid.

Snapping his head left, Piotr caught only the briefest hint of the shadow darting beneath the trees, gone before he was sure he'd spotted it. At first he was confused. In snow this deep, no one should be able to move that swiftly and silently. And then he remembered who—no, what—he was dealing with.

"Reapers," he whispered, hot breath puffing out in a white stream. "Harpies from the deep." He inhaled, savoring the pinpricks of pain as the icy air surged into his lungs. "I KNOW YOU'RE THERE!" Piotr screamed, his raw throat protesting every syllable. "SHOW YOURSELVES!"

Crows and ravens and blackbirds took to the sky all around him, their wings beating the air, their beaks open and screaming and cawing, their feathers spinning down through a sky briefly black with movement.

"Fool," said the woman from behind him. Piotr would have turned to face her, but he knew there was no point in doing so. If he tried to look death in the face, death would be hidden once again. The Reapers were funny that way.

"You got your wish," Piotr said, spitting on the snow beside a close feather. His spittle was bright red, the feather black. His hand tightened on the cloak. "My father's dead."

"I know," the Reaper said from his left. She leaned close and he could smell her; sweat and smoke, rich liquor mulled slowly, crisp pork cracklings, and that strange, flighty scent that seemed to belong to the Reapers alone, the smell of breezes no mortal could capture, the scent of mountain tops and flight, of blood and battle.

Her hand cupped his shoulder and Piotr hissed.

"You're close," she said, lips brushing the cup of his ear, and her breath brushed his cheek, smelling of summer flowers and sweat and tears. "It's so warm here, Piotr, and the snow is about to fall like flowers, like petals, from the sky. Lie down. Stay with me a while."

"My mother's calling," Piotr replied and forced his weary legs to take another step, no longer walking through the snow, trudging through it. The Reaper was right; he could feel his strength waning.

"Your mother's dead," the Reaper said. When she stepped in his way, blocking him from the shortest path to the village, Piotr realized that he was dreaming.

"Emma, *da?*" he asked, letting the cloak drop to the snow and chuckling with relief. Emma wore a set of leather scouting armor, well tended and well used, oiled dark in all the right places and covering her from neck to toe. A pair of long, ornate daggers hung from her hips, the tip of her braid brushing against the left one as she shifted.

Chuckling, thinking himself a complete fool, Piotr waved her a step away. Of all the people in the world, Piotr never would have expected to see Wendy's cousin in this moment, in this place. He'd never even met her in real life, only seen her from the window as she ushered Wendy into the car below. *Car*, he thought. Cars didn't belong here, in this time, in this place, any more than Emma did.

"What are you doing here?" he asked. "You haven't been born yet."

"I'm here to collect you, Piotr," she said and opened her hands. The palms were filled with Light.

"I'm not dead yet," he reminded her. Just over the rise he could see the curls of smoke from the village. A faint ringing sound, so quiet he had to strain to hear it, echoed through the trees. The black-smith had fired his forge, Piotr realized. On a clear, cold day like today, with the harvests in and nothing but maintenance to do until spring, the sound of hammering didn't bode well.

"You will be," she said and closed her palms, extinguishing the Light. "I have all the time in the world, Piotr." She turned and her hair was no longer red, it was dark and curling and cascading down the back of her armor. The Reaper wasn't Emma, Piotr realized, but Ada.

He pushed past her, ignoring the burning in his palm where he touched her leather-clad shoulder. "I didn't die this way," he told her belligerently. "I didn't die here, beside the river. I don't die now."

"I know," Ada said. "I remember."

Piotr could taste the blood in his mouth. "Do you? Do you remember? How can you, you've never been here."

"Enough for both of us," she replied and she was not Ada but Mary. Not the Mary he could recall, though; not older and worn by the stress of years, not Wendy's mother, but a young girl, hardly older than Wendy herself, with a cut high on one cheek and a bruise around her neck, dark smudges beneath her eyes. Her expression was haunted, drawn, and furious tears had dried in salt-tracks down her face.

"I remember you," he whispered, struck by the black and blue fingerprints pressed into her neck, the scabs peeling across her freshly inked shoulder. "This moment. Or . . . do I?"

"Shhh, Piotr," Mary said, reaching forward and cupping his cheeks in her palms. Up close, Piotr realized that Mary's eyes weren't brown, they were blue, and her teeth weren't straight, the canines were slightly slanted, the front teeth almost bucktoothed.

No. This wasn't Mary. This was . . . this was . . . Piotr struggled for her name, this girl he'd known once upon a time, but couldn't find it. His memories, so clear in the dream, were retreating from him rapidly now. Piotr knew that he knew her name but it was gone, buried beneath the bulk of years, beneath the decades of snow and blood and death.

The girl's hands weren't burning, they were cold as the snow and the ice and the darkness at the edges of his dream, the moving, writhing blackness Piotr could now see out of the corners of his eyes as she leaned closer and whispered in his ear. "Don't struggle. Sleep. Sleep, Piotr. Rest."

"You're not Mary," Piotr whispered as the blackness slinked closer. "Mary's dead."

"I know," the Reaper said, the girl's flesh peeling away from the skull and leaving only the bleached bone behind. Piotr reached forward, touched the bone with his fingertips, and the skull nestled its cheekbones into his palm, nuzzling his hand as if they were lovers.

"Wendy killed her," Piotr said. "She sent her on."

"I know that, too." The skull smiled as only a skull can do.

"You're dead," he said. "You're dead."

"I know I am, Piotr . . . we all are."

"This is a dream," he said. "This place is gone."

"Torn down for wood ages ago," the Reaper agreed, gathering the fabric around her so that only her skull peered out from beneath the black hood, so that the blade of her weapon glinted from the shadows of her cloak. "It is gone with the march of time. As you should be."

"As you should, as well," Piotr agreed, pressing the heels of his palms into his eyes. He was dizzy now, from blood-loss, he suspected, and every inch of his skin felt as if it were on fire. "I . . . need to see my mother. She waits for me by the fire."

"Come, take my hand," the Reaper said, offering a slim cluster of bones loosely held together, the remains of her hands bleached white by the centuries. "I will take you to her."

"But Wendy?" Piotr asked. "I cannot leave her alone. She needs me."

"Does she? Does she really?" The Reaper leaned forward and Piotr smelled the liquor thick amid the folds of cloak, saturated in the fabric, damp against his cheek. He shuddered—there had been ice and mead spilling across the floor, he remembered, and the red of spreading blood, the hair of his youngest sister fluttering on the floor as the wind blew the long shorn curls across the floor. His sister had bled but she had not begged.

Their mother had been so proud.

In the distance a bird cawed.

"Wake up, Piotr," the Reaper said, and jammed her fist into his side, the bones of her forearm jutting out like a sword. The pain was immediate and debilitating; Piotr gasped and sagged against her, letting the Reaper support his entire weight as she lifted him higher and higher until his toes only barely brushed the top of the snow. He felt the scrape of her fingers grabbing his spine, the sharp edges gouging into his guts as she twisted and wrung him from the inside out.

"Wake up, Piotr," she said again and twisted. "Wendy's in trouble. Wake up!"

CHAPTER FIFTEEN

"**Y**ou know, between the two of them, I'm not sure which one is worse off," Piotr heard as, shivering, he drifted up from the depths of his dream.

Piotr could feel everything—the burning of the flesh that had touched Wendy, the pull of the wound in his side, and the sick thump of a blooming headache, the product of his unrestful sleep.

Grudgingly, Piotr opened his eyes to find Eddie kneeling beside the bed and the room filled with thin, damp steam and saturated with rainbows and glittering, shimmering light. Piotr blinked and the shifting light vanished—some kind of mirage, he was certain—but the fog remained. His eyes watered and his head protested the sparkles of light.

"What is going on?" Piotr croaked, sitting up painfully and squinting against the glare, trying not to concentrate on the world shivering at the edge of his vision. The Never and the living lands were rapidly shifting back and forth, like a twitch, and there were dark and shadowy figures in the instant between the two realms, like the Reaper's eyes watching him, fading in and out with each twitch and pulse. He forced himself to close his eyes, an attempt to stop the hallucinations cold, but when he opened them again the visions were still there. Instead he concentrated on the clock hanging on the far wall. The cat's tail wagged, the eyes tick-tocking back and forth, and Piotr was dismayed to realize that he'd slept only half an hour at most. It had seemed like so much longer in the dream.

Ada might have been right, Piotr realized as he tried to swing his legs off the bed. His organs might have been healed by their intervention but the hook had deposited its poison and the seed so deep within him that Piotr wasn't sure he'd ever be healed. They had to get to Alcatraz quickly. If Elle didn't succeed in finding a Lost, then Ada might be his only hope.

The short sleep had done nothing for him; moving was tugging deeply at his gut, and the hole in his side was stiff and painful to the touch, but the pain wasn't the worst part. It took all his concentration to keep his vision of the Never and the living lands from swinging wildly back and forth; Piotr wasn't sure where to look to not see those dark, angry eyes that watched from the in-between spaces.

He'd been able to see into the living lands for nearly a month now, since before their encounter with the White Lady, but the malevolent eyes were new and more than a little unnerving. However they weren't *doing* anything, merely watching, and Piotr was willing to ignore the staring for the time being. With any luck, they were just another hallucination.

"I think it's a thunderstorm," Eddie said, holding out a hand and waving it through the mist. Piotr tried not to notice how the tips of Eddie's fingers were nearly as faded as the fog. "It started building right after you guys conked out." He swung his hand about the room. "I don't know if you two should be so close together, after all. Her heat plus your cold is just creating a storm front in Wendy's bedroom."

Piotr edged off the bed and sagged against the wall, blinking heavily and forcing his eyes to focus on the Never. "I had . . . such a dream," he murmured.

"Looks like you're not alone there," Eddie said, jerking a thumb in Wendy's direction. Wendy, flushed and frowning, twitched on the bed, hair matted down with sleep-sweat. "She's not exactly talking in her sleep, but that face isn't one I'd say is blissfully resting."

"Why have you not woken her?" Piotr asked, straightening as best he could and reaching for her.

"Tried it," Eddie interrupted him, flashing his burned palm in front of Piotr's face. "I wouldn't try if I were you, buddy. She's running a little hot right now."

The cat-shaped phone on Wendy's desk suddenly rang, startling them all. The sound should have been dim in the Never, distant and couched in the spaces between worlds, but instead was sharp and shrill, cutting through the air with great force. On the bed, Wendy stirred slightly but did not rouse; instead she tugged a pillow over her head and pulled into a ball, curling her free arm around her knees.

"Wow, I thought Wendy would've cut her landline ages ago," Eddie mused to Piotr as the phone jangled again. "Two more rings and then the machine'll kick in. If she hasn't shut that one off, that is. She might've."

She hadn't. The answering machine kicked on, but it wasn't Wendy's voice that greeted the caller and, laughing, told them to leave a message. It was her mother's.

"Wendy?" asked a smooth, cool voice over the line. "This is Emmaline."

"Fascinating," Ada said, moving to the desk and hovering over it, closely examining the distinct shape of the answering machine that was growing more solid by the second in the Never. "Look what just a Reaper's voice is doing to this machine!"

Piotr shushed her.

"I tried your cell phone and you have apparently turned it off, hopefully I have this backup number to your room correct," Emma was saying. "I know this is intrusive, especially after your long morning, but Jane is on her way to visit you. Grandmother insisted that we give you the first book of Reaper rules and regulations, and she would not take no for an answer. You are to study it and be prepared with any questions by this evening. Grandmother intends to speak with you as soon as possible."

The line clicked, the machine wound down, and in the Never Eddie punched the play button on the newly created answering machine on Wendy's desk. It didn't play; the hunk of plastic sat there, mocking them with its solid ineptitude.

"Typical Wendy," Eddie muttered. "Keeping something ancient around just because it was her mom's."

"The machine is fascinating," Ada said again.

"Come," Lily said when Wendy stirred. "Let us continue this conversation elsewhere. We do not wish to wake the Lightbringer." She glared at Wendy. "She needs her rest and none of us wish to be here when her family arrives."

"No kidding. I'm still alive and they know it, but you three'd probably get reaped into oblivion on the spot," Eddie said, frowning. "Man, you know, before I actually came over, I'd have been all for that too, but now . . . ? It's sort of uncool."

"'Sort of'?" Ada snorted. "So nice to learn that you can see our side of things."

"Yeah, fine, I'm a changed soul or whatever. Anyway, Wendy set her alarm, right?" Eddie glanced at the clock on Wendy's desk before grabbing a pen off the desk and a piece of paper, glad that Wendy had taken to salvaging spiritual office supplies along with medical supplies.

He flipped past several charcoal sketches of trees, of a young man with large, round glasses, and a small, tubby boy with his thumb jammed in his mouth until he found a blank sheet right at the end of the pad.

REAPERS ON THEIR WAY, WE HAVE TO BAIL IN CASE THEY COME UPSTAIRS. HEADING TO MY HOUSE, I THINK, Eddie wrote, pushing hard on the Prismacolor pencil, not noticing Piotr wincing behind him, the way he watched to make sure Eddie wasn't damaging the other pictures in the sketchpad. CHECK THE ANSWERING MACHINE ASAP. MSG FOR YOU. LUV EDS!

"Okay, done," Eddie said, tossing the sketchpad on the floor where Wendy would certainly notice it, before following Ada and Lily through the door.

Piotr lingered a moment, wondering when and why Wendy had gone back to Elle's bookshop and retrieved Dora's sketchbook. He traced the spiral spine of the pad with one hand and sighed. Dora was gone into the Light, along with Specs, and Tubs was so far away that he might as well have joined them. Still, Wendy had gone, found this memory for him, and had kept it safe. Piotr was touched.

Drawing near the bed, Piotr had to force himself to close the distance between them. Unconscious, Wendy's control was lax; the heat baked off her in visible waves and standing so near was like going toe-to-toe with a banked bonfire. Despite his immense cold, Piotr broke out in a sweat.

Was he going to let something like a little discomfort keep him from doing the right thing? No, not this time. Ignoring the heat, Piotr staggered to the bed and settled on the edge beside Wendy. Then, uncaring if the others peeked in on them, Piotr leaned forward and pressed a kiss to the hollow of Wendy's temple. His chill lips blistered from the touch—the sting was immediate and intense and faded the instant he pulled away—but he didn't wish to leave her again without this simple, quiet goodbye.

She stirred, opened her eyes, and licked her lips, clearly not fully awake. "Piotr?"

"Shhh," he replied, brushing her hair off her forehead. "We must leave for a time. Rest. Join us when you can, we will wait for you."

"Hmmm," Wendy breathed. "I had a dream . . ."

"*Da?* And of what did you dream?"

"Ravens," Wendy whispered, already drifting off again. "Or crows. A sky filled with black feathers. And my mom."

A sharp shiver raced down Piotr's spine. *A sky filled with black feathers.* It had to be coincidence that they had both dreamed of the same thing. It could be nothing else.

Wendy was asleep again, this time resting much more peacefully, he noted. Piotr rose and laboriously made his way through her door and into the hallway, brooding on feathers the entire way. He

was dizzy again, so much so that once he was in the hallway he had
to lean against the wall and rest. The world felt strange and airy
around him, as if he'd drunk copiously and then spun himself
around.

In the hall, Lily gestured for them to go downstairs, offering
Piotr an arm for support. They were only halfway down when Jon
rounded the corner going up. Jon had barely taken two steps before
he abruptly about-faced and hurried back the way he came, darting
into the kitchen and scurrying out of sight.

"Lucky for us, Jon must've forgotten his soda," Eddie said and
pointed. "If we go right through the wall we can miss him going
back up and not get burned walking through him. There's a nice
firm bench out there in the side yard. It's so solid in the Never even
I have no problems sitting on it. Piotr can rest there while we figure
out what to do next."

It took some maneuvering, but Lily and Ada escorted Piotr to
the peaceful backyard and the wrought iron bench. The bench was
old, carefully maintained and oiled, and painted on a regular basis.
It sat in a bed of silver-streaked white marble chips, cool to the touch
even in the Never, and the fence was overgrown with lush, decadent
honeysuckle, still thriving in the dead of winter. Settling himself
carefully down, Piotr turned to follow movement in the bushes; a
young raccoon with bright eyes and a curious face peered out at him
from behind the shed before vanishing with a tail flick into the
bushes between the yards.

"This is one of the few yards I've ever seen that looks as nice here
as it does in the living land," Piotr said, chuckling and holding his
aching head. "Some nights, waiting for Wendy to return from her
rounds, I would sit here and look up at the moon. She smiled down
at me, reminding me that I have so much left to do." He shivered.
Beneath him, in the Never, a rime of frost was creeping across the
bench.

"Did I ever tell you I can see in both places now?" Piotr asked

Lily, see-sawing his hand back and forth. "I am beginning to be able to control it. If I squint just right I can see into the living lands." He patted the bench lovingly. "Like a reverse Reaper."

"Truly?" Ada asked excitedly. "That is amazing! Oh, when this is all over, we really must talk! Is it in color like we remember the living world to be, or is the vision washed out as ours is? Can you make yourself seen to the living, as the Reapers are able to make themselves visible to us? And what of animals? Are you able to communicate with them in the living lands as we can here? The possibilities of being able to see into the living lands are just endless!" Spotting Lily's glare, Ada coughed quietly and crossed her arms over her stomach. "My apologies, Piotr. I grew overexcited for a moment."

"There is time for such extensive questioning later," Lily said, enunciating each word so that Ada could not misunderstand how she had erred. "For the time being, it is to be but one foot before the other."

"Right. Yes. You have an excellent point." But Ada's eyes glinted and Piotr knew that the moment Lily's back was turned she'd be pestering him about the world of the living.

"So," Eddie said, kneeling beside Piotr and looking him in the eye, "my house is only a few blocks over and my mom is a bit overprotective, so chances are that she's hanging out at the hospital right now, bugging the doctors about waking me up."

"In other words, she is not home," Ada said.

"Yep. And, even if she is, my basement is empty and pretty comfy. And Wendy told me ages ago that my place is pretty solid in the Never so, really, it's a good spot to lay low until the Reapers have come and gone." He glanced at Ada. "Then we can all pack up and go to Alcatraz together. Maybe Elle will be back by then."

"This plan has merit, but what of Wendy?" Lily asked.

"Already told her that's where we were heading," Eddie said with a shrug. "If you need me to, I can run upstairs and change the note. Either way, we have to get Piotr out of here. Just look at him."

"Are you worried for me or for you?" Piotr asked, staring at the dark men in the walls. They were crowding around him now, shadowy and colder than anything he'd ever felt in his life, some standing half in and half out of the others, the rest hovering in a circle over Piotr like athletes in a huddle.

Eddie nervously glanced over his shoulder, where the tallest of the dark shadows loomed. "Man, I really hope you're tripping out right now, because if that's how you look at people normally, I really need to stop hanging out with you."

"You did not answer the question," Piotr slurred, trying to concentrate on Eddie and not the black hands curling over his shoulders, the spaces between his thinning particles. It was like he was watching tiny universes beneath Eddie's essence wink out one at a time. "Is it my skin that concerns you, or your own?"

Irritated, Eddie shook his head and forcibly kept himself from glancing over his shoulder again. "Suspicious much?"

"It is the poison," Ada murmured. "It occasionally interferes with logical cognitive ability." She leaned forward, examining Piotr's face closely. "And I do believe he is, in fact—how did you say—tripping."

"Right. Pete's been so bloody *nice* lately that I plumb forgot," Eddie grumbled. He threw up his hands and more tiny universes faded away as Piotr watched. "I just can't win with you, can I? Just when I think we're on our way to being bros, too."

"Be calm, Piotr," Lily said softly, kneeling down so that her face was level with his. Piotr could see how earnest she was, how intent that he should trust her and follow her lead. The creature behind her lifted a strand of her hair but Lily never noticed.

Piotr forced himself to meet her eyes as she spoke. "For all our safety, Piotr, we must heed Eddie's advice and accept this generous offer. We must leave Wendy, but only for a time."

The beast closest to Piotr cupped his elbow, and for a brief, painful moment, Piotr felt the fury from before wash through him.

He bit his lip until it bled to keep from berating Lily for her arrogance.

How dare she, he thought wildly. *How dare she persist, even now, in telling me what to do?*

Piotr felt the hands recede, the low, hissing chuckle as the fury slowly abated, the swell passing but leaving the bitter taste of wormwood and ash in his mouth, the tang of dirt and ice and blood against his lips.

It took Piotr several seconds of struggling with the perfect put down to remember that Lily was his oldest and wisest friend; so long as he'd known her, Lily had always, *always* had his best intentions at heart. And he wished to wound her for daring to contradict his silly worries about Eddie and his feelings for Wendy? Insanity!

Ada was right; the poison was doing terrible things to his mind.

"I trust you, Lily," Piotr said seriously. "So be it, I shall do as you wish." His vision steadied. The shadows faded, but the living lands and the Never were back in the forefront—he didn't have that disconcerting space between them to contend with for the moment, but the way they shifted around was giving him a headache.

Gritting his teeth and willing the world to stop wobbling so, Piotr sat up. "Let us go."

As they stood to leave, Piotr quietly struggled with how to tell the others that his vision was growing worse by the second, see-sawing rapidly back and forth. With the space between temporarily abated, the Never and the living world had begun to merge into something he could only describe as a hellscape. Terrible trees with faces like screaming men loomed in the distance. One shake of their branches and their leaves tumbled down into piles like rust and crumbled paper.

The sky was red then black then red again, orange-fire and speckled with weeping stars that bled against the sky in green rivulets. He turned his head, and at the top of the hill, near the apartment complex, there waited a trio of horses with a woman astride each. They wore dresses of blood and black bile, streaming

over their naked bodies in rivers. One lifted a great horn to her lips
and the scarlet clouds themselves parted under the silent onslaught
of her long and undulating note.

"Piotr?" Ada said softly, making sure Lily was out of earshot.
"What in heaven's name are you seeing?"

"Not Heaven," he gasped, and forced a grisly smile for her. The
women were gone, the trees no longer screamed. Piotr grasped at
straws: could Ada truly counteract the madness running rampant in
his brain? He needed to think so. He couldn't go on much longer
like this. "Certainly not Heaven. Help me to safety and I shall tell
you all that I know, Ada. For this, I promise you."

In the Never the gate to the yard was significantly thinner than
the surrounding fence; passing through it was simple. Within
moments they were out in the front yard, standing beside Wendy's
father's vehicle.

Piotr, swaying slightly at Eddie's side, waited as Eddie turned
northeast and then, frowning, hesitated and turned to Piotr.

"Do you need help, man?" Eddie asked. "You don't look too steady
on your feet." He offered an arm and then, after a moment, drew it
back. "Will I get freezer-burn if I touch you? Not to be a jerk, but you
are baking cold like an oven over here and I have no frickin' clue what
to do about it. I'm worn through enough as it is, I don't dare let you
burn . . . freeze me to pieces. This is entirely me winging it."

"I am fine," Piotr said and it was only half a lie. The visions had
momentarily stilled, leaving him with the mundane sight of the two
worlds layered over one another, but nothing more. Piotr welcomed
the simplicity and bemusedly wondered how it could have ever
seemed strange and unwieldy to see them both at once.

"The sooner we travel to your home, the faster—" Piotr broke
off as the clouds above them darkened. All four of them looked up,
stunned as a huge flock of gulls spanned the sky, their cries filling
the air and the feathers spinning down in dirty white clouds.

"NO!" Ada yelled. "Run for cover!"

"What's going on?" Eddie cried, covering his head as the first bird dive-bombed the group. "I've never seen birds so big!"

"RUN!" Ada insisted and turned to flee back into Wendy's house. She made it two steps before a large flock of gulls swept down and, swarming like bees, attacked her.

In one smooth motion Lily drew her knives and strode to Ada's side, hacking and slashing at the whirling white chaos. Eddie, after a second's hesitation, drew the knife Elle had given him earlier and haphazardly stabbed at the mess as well. His thrusts were weak, however, and even with his twisted double vision, Piotr could see that Eddie was a greater danger to himself than the birds.

"Not like that," Piotr cried, disgusted. How was it that a boy his own age could have gotten so far in life without knowing how to wield a knife properly? It seemed impossible.

Despite the muddy landscape that was his vision, Piotr knew he had to help. Limping as best he could manage, Piotr twisted and tried to join them in their fight against the birds. He stabbed and stabbed, but the way his vision wavered and waved, patterns in the air twisting as he slashed and cut, Piotr knew that he was missing his thrusts. The gulls were too fast, too vicious. Though neither Lily nor Eddie had the breath to tell him, Piotr knew that he was hindering more than helping.

Struggling to stand steadily, Piotr squinted and attempted to make out which was the real world and which was the Never. The colors were a muddy mixture, the memories of the past mingling with the reality of the present and all fading in and out, jagged and red-tipped. The only steady creatures in either world were the gulls and his companions.

Pushing past Ada, Piotr tried to step between two large gulls that were dive-bombing Lily, but tripped over the memory of a bush that wavered tauntingly in the Never. He fell to a knee, ankle twisting painfully, and felt his hand punch through the thin, icy crust of snow . . . concrete . . . snow.

"Not now!" Piotr hissed, scrabbling across the ice, reaching for the nearest branch. The sky was painfully clear and bright overhead and he could hear the tattered women blowing the horn yet again.

Sensing weakness, the bulk of the gulls shifted their attention from Eddie and Lily to Piotr. Lily and Eddie, previously trying to keep the birds off Ada, were forced to move to protect Piotr.

Ada, now alone, scrabbled along the ground for some weapon, a stick, a rock, anything to use against her avian enemy, but to no avail. One bird, larger than the rest, swooped down behind her. Piotr, the only one facing Ada, was the only one to see the Lady Walker, shimmering, appear from nothing, strip off a cloak of gull feathers, and wrap an arm around Ada's waist as Ada slapped helplessly against the overwhelming tide of birds. As Piotr watched helplessly, the Lady Walker stabbed Ada in the neck with a long, silver needle and stepped back, letting Ada's body crumple to the ground, holding the scientist by her hair alone.

"Wait!" he cried, flinging up an arm against the onslaught of birds and trying to scrabble toward Ada. "Stop! *Net*! Do not!"

The Lady Walker lifted a single finger to her lips and hushed him, the curve of her half-rotten smile very clear under the hook of her filthy hood. She gestured and the remaining birds, seeing Ada helpless, dove in.

Releasing Ada's hair, the Lady Walker donned her cloak of feathers once more and vanished into the mass as the birds tangled their claws in Ada's hair and dress. Pulling powerfully upward, the huge birds worked as one and lifted Ada from the earth. They flew away, cawing and crying and shrieking their bird-cries as Piotr trembled below.

As if some signal had been given, once Ada was lost in the expanse of sky and her shadow was dim and distant, the remainder of the flock ceased their attack. As one they pulled back and flapped away, squawking and crying to one another, leaving only grisly splats of filthy white and the occasional feather to show that they had been there.

Bleeding and confused, Eddie, puffing heavily, plopped to the ground next to Piotr. His limbs were fraying at the edges, his elbows and knees worn thin and pale. "That," he said, examining the seeping scratches on his arms and legs, "was some Wizard of Oz crap right there. Do we have to go rescue her from the Wicked Witch's castle now? Isn't that how this thing goes? Where the hell would a bunch of birds take her anyway?"

"They did appear to be biding their time," Lily agreed solemnly. "But to what end? Ada is high up on the Council. I cannot imagine why gulls would do such a thing."

"We should have captured one," Piotr said bitterly. "We could have questioned it." He thought to tell Lily and Eddie about the Lady Walker, but could not convince himself that he'd truly seen her. His hallucinations were quite vivid; it was entirely possible he'd imagined her as part of the grisly scene.

"Birds are hardly more intelligent than any other animal," Lily said scornfully. "We would have gotten nothing."

"Hey, Piotr? Not that I'm not digging this whole hindsight extravaganza, but have you taken a good look at yourself, man?" Eddie plucked at Piotr's sleeve and his fingers slid through. "You're falling to pieces. And . . ." Eddie held up his transluscent hands, his essence now growing paler in a gradient from the curve of his elbow to the tips of his fingers, "coming from me, that's saying something."

He was not incorrect. Worn weak by his horrible madness, Piotr was significantly less substantial than before, his essence thin as tissue paper in places, and the tips of his fingers were rimed with frost.

CHAPTER SIXTEEN

Refreshed after her nap, Wendy stretched hugely, arching her back and feeling her spine crackle in all the right ways. She knew she had begun running somewhat of a temperature—the warmth in her eyes alone told her that—but it didn't feel quite as overwhelming after her rest.

Humming under her breath, Wendy wiggled her toes until they popped. She eased off her bed, glancing around for Piotr or Eddie or even Elle or Lily. None of them were to be seen.

"Huh," she said. "I wonder where they went?" Then she spotted Eddie's note.

"The answering machine?" Wendy said, surprised. The day after her mother had fallen to the Lost, Wendy had ferreted out the old machine and plugged it in on her desk, listening to the outgoing message over and over again with tears streaming down her face. She had tucked it away at the very back corner of her desk; it was so unobtrusive she'd entirely forgotten that she'd left it hooked up.

Pressing *play*, Wendy listened to Emma's message with a scowl. "That two-faced bitch," she muttered under her breath. "After all that crap she said to me in the dreamscape? Seriously? Yeah, if I lay eyes on her I'm going to . . ."

Wendy took a deep, calming breath. "You know what? Never mind. Not important. She wants to play this game? Fine, we'll play it. I'll memorize the *crap* out of that damn book and we'll see who's Reaper material then, won't we? Stupid fancy-ass doctor thinking she can mess me around."

Comforting herself with the fact that Emma and Jane wouldn't be there for at least forty-five minutes, Wendy drifted downstairs, led by a rich chocolate smell.

Jon, bent double over the oven and sliding in a baking sheet, didn't hear her approach.

"Cookies?" Wendy asked loudly and grinned when her younger brother jumped a foot and came down hard, knocking over the flour with his elbow. He'd donned their mother's apron to cook and it was straining almost comically over his belly. Their mother had been a tiny woman and Jon, even before he'd gained all that weight, was not delicately built.

"Don't do that!" Jon snapped, fist pressed to his chest and scowling at Wendy as she settled onto her favorite stool at the counter. "And, yes, cookies. Chocolate macadamia nut, for the Welcome Back Bake Sale. Want one?" Jon wiped flour-dusted hands against his forehead, leaving a smudge of white behind.

"Don't mind if I do," Wendy said, peeling a fresh, gooey cookie off the wax paper that covered the counter.

"Delicious," she declared. "Man, I'm not ready to go back yet. I was comatose through half of break!" Wendy leaned over, ignoring her brother's wince, and stuck a finger in the batter. "Mmm," she sighed, licking the goo off her finger. "That's good. Man, I am so frickin' hungry!"

"Did you wash your hands?" Jon asked, dampening a dishtowel to wipe up the flour he spilled. His lank hair swung against his cheekbones as he concentrated.

Wendy rolled her eyes. "Yes, Dad."

"Hey, if I get the whole school sick, no one'll let me live it down." Jon tossed the dishtowel in the sink and set the timer over the stove. "Speaking of comatose, I didn't hear you get in last night. How's Eddie doing?"

Wendy shrugged and licked a finger. "He's still breathing without any machines, which is always a hell of a plus."

Out of the corner of her eye, in the Never, Wendy spotted a large gull fly past the window and alight for a moment on the fence. It had to be the biggest bird Wendy had ever seen and, for a short moment, she was reminded of her dream, the sound of birds shrieking into the sky. Frowning, she pushed the memory away.

"Still no clue why he's out, then." Jon pushed away from the counter and kicked disconsolately at the edge of a lower cabinet. "I'm starting to wonder if doctors are just winging it, like everyone else."

"Don't fuss," Wendy said. "It's Eddie. One day he'll wake up and it'll be like nothing happened. He'll pinch a nurse's butt and hit on the orderly and they'll throw him out after a couple days of observation. I mean, hell, Dad convinced them to release me after only 24 hours, you really think Eddie's pushy mom'll let him stay in for longer than me? We'll be okay. He'll be okay. It'll all be okay."

That is, she added silently, *if I can figure out where his cord is and, once I've got it in hand, how to stick him back in his body.* Until then, Wendy was hoping against hope that Eddie wouldn't start to degrade the way her mother had.

Eager to change the subject, Wendy glanced around the kitchen. The huge stack of mail normally spread across the breakfast nook was neatly sorted, the tile gleamed, and the perpetual fog of fingerprints on the sliding glass door had been polished clean. When she sniffed the air she could make out the faint scent of Pine Sol and bleach underlying Jon's sugary cookie aroma. "It's really clean in here. You did all this?"

"Yeah right," Jon snorted. "I got home and Chel was up to her elbows in suds, scrubbing with a stack of old washcloths cuz she couldn't find the mop."

"It's in the laundry room."

"Yeah, we know that now. Chel did the laundry too; got up at the buttcrack of dawn to exercise and then kept cleaning. Been in your closet yet? Cuz she started there."

Rubbing her forehead, Wendy grumbled. "I thought something felt different in my room."

"I'm not kidding, check your closet. Guess who made me help

iron while she was—get this—color-coding your stuff? And, AND, ordering them all by size. Did it all last night while you were out."

"No." Wendy covered her mouth with her hand. "Really?"

"The red smush'em'flat corset all the way up to that wired-up blue waterbra thing." He waved a spatula at her. "In a totally unrelated note, why, sister-dear, don't you have any normal clothes? Does Dad realize that you essentially just traipse around town in your underwear?"

"Oh shush," Wendy replied mildly, sitting back and glancing at the stairs. "Why would Chel—"

"Go all OCD? No clue. But she's been like this for days, and when I try to talk to her about it she tells me *I'm* the whack job." He frowned and poked his gut. "Then she says I need to get outta the kitchen or I'm gonna get fatter. Not that she's wrong, but that's just mean."

"So she's back to central standard bitch-time?" Wendy shook her head. "I thought she'd been too nice since Mom's funeral."

"I don't think it's all about Mom, though." Jon shrugged. "I thought it was just to keep herself from getting her hands on some more Phentermine, but she's eating and she quit cheerleading and she even donated all her Twiggy-clothes to Goodwill, so I don't know anymore."

"I'll try and talk with her." Glancing at the clock, Wendy slid off the stool and ruffled Jon's hair. She still had at least fifteen minutes before the Reapers were due to arrive. "I'm gonna go to Sumi's for a trim on Saturday. You want an appointment too?"

"Sure, whatever." The timer dinged and Jon turned toward the oven, muttering, "Tupperware, Tupperware," under his breath. As Wendy turned to go, he said, "I'm borrowing Dad's car and running up to Safeway, okay? We're out of the good milk."

"Okay," Wendy said and, leaving her brother puttering in the kitchen, wandered back upstairs to find Chel.

The bathroom light was off, but Chel's room was quiet. Wendy glanced at the time on her cell. She had only napped for about an hour, so it was too early for Chel to be asleep. "Hey?" Wendy gingerly tapped on the door. "Marvelous Madame Michelle? You up?"

"Yeah," drifted Chel's voice from inside. "Come in."

For the first time Wendy could remember, she didn't have to pick her way across her sister's floor. The closet door was open and even by the dim moonlight that filtered in through Chel's windows, Wendy could make out that her sister's overflowing closet was now almost empty.

"Jon wasn't kidding," Wendy said lightly, settling on the floor beside the bed. Chel rested on top of her covers, eyes closed and fingers threaded together, damp hair dangling over the edge of her bed against Wendy's shoulder.

"I felt like cleaning," Chel replied simply. She yawned.

Flummoxed by this new, strange sister, Wendy struggled with what to say before inspiration hit. "Saturday, Jon and I are going to get a trim." Wendy tugged one of Chel's bleached curls. "You wanna come? Your roots are showing, copper-top."

Sleepily, Chel chuckled. "The roots to my ears? I hadn't noticed."

"Hey, personally I think the two-tone thing is kinda cool," Wendy said, taking a lock of her own black-tipped coppery curls and twirling it around her finger, "but you've never really been into alternative style."

"Make the appointment," Chel sighed. "But make mine a dye job. Henna maybe. I don't care. I'm done with being a buffy. Too much effort."

"Chel?" Wendy hesitated. "Are you okay?"

"Peachy keen," Chel said, scrubbing her face with her hands. "I know it seems like I'm cracking up and all but really, I'm fine." She opened her eyes and flipped onto her stomach, resting her cheek against one arm. "I'm just tired, is all. I've got some personal guy-stuff going on that I don't wanna talk about, but other than that I'm fine."

"Sure you are," Wendy agreed dryly. She knew her sister well enough to know when Chel was bald-faced lying. "You're just tired. Uh huh."

"Fine. You want to know what happened? Andrew broke up with me. That's what happened." Chel smiled tightly, more a grimace than a grin. "No, actually, he dumped my ass."

"Oh, honey. You want me to go kick him in the taint?" Wendy wrapped her hand around Chel's wrist and squeezed.

Snorting, Chel buried her head in her arms. "I wish I could tell you how awesome that would be if you pulled it off. Little ol' nobody Wendy, walking up to the king of the queeraphobe quarterbacks and taking him down a peg or two. That would be . . . amazing."

"Andy's a homophobe? Isn't his dad, like . . ." Wendy see-sawed her hand back and forth. "You know?"

"Yeah. He's got issues." Chel sighed. "It should've been me dumping him, but everything's been so weird since Mom . . . well, you know. Anyway, the jackass didn't even bother breaking up with me first. He just put his hands down Laura Dee's pants at the mall food court. In front of everyone, Wendy! Around the food! And I was all, 'What the hell are you doing?' and he was all, 'What does it look like I'm doing, you batshit crazy skank?' and everyone started laughing and . . . UGH!" Chel pounded a fist into her pillow. "I hate that school," she sniffed, her voice thick with emotion. "I hate it, I hate everyone who goes there. I'm ready to just be done, already."

"We'll be out of there in no time," Wendy promised, gingerly patting her sister on the shoulder. "Seriously, Chel, you've got only two years left. That's nothing."

"Says the senior," grumbled Chel, scowling. "You weren't the one who got dumped right before New Year's. I had mega-plans and now I don't dare show my face at any of the parties." She sniffed. "Now all there is to do is clean, clean, and clean some more."

"Yeah, Jon told me everything you did. Looking good downstairs, you really outdid yourself there. You had to vent out the frustration?"

"Pretty much," Chel said, sighing. "Hey, Wendy?"

"Yeah?"

"That chick? From this morning? Is she that doctor from the hospital?"

"Yeah," Wendy said. "She is."

"I don't like her." Chel rubbed one hand across her eyes. "She rubs me the wrong way. Maybe . . . maybe you should, like, I don't know, avoid her for a bit."

"No problem. Already in the plan." Wendy glanced at the clock. If the timestamp on the answering machine had been right, Jane and Emma were due any minute now. Wendy patted her sister gently on the shoulder. "You gonna grab a nap before the ball drops?"

"Yeah. I think so." Yawning and rolling over, Chel closed her eyes and rested an arm over her face. "Shut the door on your way out, please. And turn off the light, okay? Wake me up at like, eleven or so, if I'm still konked out."

"Cool beans," Wendy agreed easily. "Midnight with the fam. Sounds kick ass."

"Don't let Jon eat all the cookies," Chel added as Wendy shut the door. "My social life is shot; I might as well get a twin lard-ass at this point."

Feeling out of sorts and unsure whether to attribute her foul mood to Chel or to her fever, Wendy ducked into the bathroom to check her temperature.

"100.8," she noted, shaking the thermometer, tempted to try again. "That's not good."

That girl burned up, right? Wendy thought, trying to remember exactly what Nana Moses had said about the other natural. *She couldn't use her powers either.*

Slowly, carefully, Wendy tried to shift into the Lightbringer as she'd done earlier in the car on the ride home. She could feel the power there, underneath the mesh of Light Emma had woven over her soul, but it was now completely inaccessible to her. Wendy could touch things in the Never, but she couldn't completely shed her physical form. Every time she tried it hurt a little more.

Concerned now, Wendy pressed her hands harder against the thin weave, but there was very little give. Beneath her palms her chest felt hot to the touch, the Light burning brighter than before.

Jane said she'd undo the binding if I asked, right? Wendy thought, closing the medicine cabinet. It seemed like cheating, but it wasn't as if Emma had even checked with her first before binding her. "Screw this," Wendy muttered. "So what if Emma's going to be a total tool? Jane is still cool. She's got my back."

Her eyes burned; Wendy rubbed them and, irritated, filled a glass with water from the tap. Her entire face felt puffy and inflamed, warm to the touch, as she gulped the water down.

"First things first," Wendy told her reflection as she set the tumbler back in the corner of the countertop. "Deal with this Emma crap in person, tell her off if I have to. Go to Eddie's, catch up with everyone, make sure they're okay."

Wendy rubbed her wrist against her lips. "And then, what? Maybe try fixing Piotr again? It's worth a shot, right?" It seemed like the only thing she could do, honestly.

Lost in her turbulent, twisting thoughts, Wendy didn't bother to flip on the overhead light when she returned to her bedroom. She was almost at her desk when she realized that the room was significantly fuller than it'd been when she left. Eight dense shadows lined the walls of her room, their cloaks so long that they faded into the floor. It took Wendy several seconds of squinting to make out the shapes.

Walkers.

Startled, Wendy tried to step back, but a wave of bitter cold stopped her. A large shadow-Walker had settled between her and the door. "What the—"

"Lightbringer. Reaper. The Lady Walker will see you," said the Walker closest to the window. "Now."

"Uh, how about no," Wendy said sharply, mentally scrabbling up against the seal Emma had placed on her Light. She might as well have not tried at all; her attempts to free the Light were, yet again, a total failure. Without access to the Light there was no way to force the Walkers to leave her alone, she realized, horrified.

Briefly Wendy worried for Piotr and the others; thankfully they were long gone. Piotr was in no shape to handle this sort of crowd. "You and your precious Lady can go to hell, as far as I'm concerned."

The Walker who'd spoken reached out and picked up the answering machine in one skeletal hand. Then, flexing its fingers once, the Walker crushed the machine to pieces. In one hand. The metal and plastic shards scattered at her feet.

"Well, that's going to be hell to get out of the carpet," Wendy said.

"You will come," the lead Walker said softly, its voice chilling Wendy from top to toes. She remembered how, at the hospital, they had laid hands on her and had spoken in that slow, distorted language, how they'd frozen her nearly to the bone. It wasn't an experience Wendy was anxious to repeat.

"Okay," she said, holding up her hands. "Just . . . let me grab a water bottle from the fridge, okay? I've got a fever; you don't want me passing out on the way."

The lead Walker nodded once and gestured for the door. Wendy led the way as they merged through the wall behind and around her, escorting her down the stairs in a grim, shadowy march.

"So," Wendy asked, pitching her voice in a whisper so Chel wouldn't hear, "why does the Lady Walker really want to see me?"

Silence from the Walkers.

Wendy wasn't sure whether to curse or feel glad that Jon wasn't still in the kitchen. The bags from Safeway sitting on the counter indicated that he'd gone shopping and had already come back; there was one last batch of cookies slowly plumping in the oven. The timer counted down with fifteen minutes left and dimly she could make out the sound of the shower in her father's bathroom.

There was no way she'd be able to get any help from Jon, not that he'd even be able to see what was escorting her toward the back door, and Chel was most likely sawing logs by now.

Stopping by the fridge, Wendy pulled out a couple of water bottles. The largest Walker stepped forward as if to touch Wendy again and she flung the bottle at its head, knowing that it wouldn't hurt it but might at least startle the Walker enough to give her a chance to flee. Her plan, haphazard as it was, worked. The Walker ducked and Wendy spun on her heel toward the living room, taking three steps toward freedom . . .

When the frying pan hanging above the island counter slammed into her shoulder and the fridge tipped over with a huge crash, spilling food everywhere and blocking her exit. Yelling in pain, Wendy tripped, catching herself with her right knee in the cottage cheese and her left hand in the moldy leftover stuffing from Thanksgiving. She'd only just missed ramming her hand into the broken pickle jar; glass shards littered the linoleum.

The pan hovered above her, angled toward her temple this time. Wendy had to squint to see the Walker holding it.

"No game, flesh," the lead Walker hissed quietly. "You've seen what Walkers can do. You will drip red all over if you try to run again. You believe me?"

"I understand," Wendy gasped, clutching her shoulder. Upstairs the water stopped and she heard Chel's door open.

Chel's voice called down. "What the hell was that? Wendy? Jon?"

"We go now," the lead Walker said as one of the other Walkers opened the back door. "Move."

Practically frog-marching Wendy out the back door and down the side yard, the Walkers led her through the gate and across the driveway.

As they walked down the drive, Wendy twisted suddenly and dove behind the car. She might not be able to actively use her Light, but that didn't mean that she couldn't use the Never to her advantage.

"Reaper filth!" hissed the lead Walker as Wendy led them a merry, stumbling chase across her yard, into her neighbor's and back again. She had a goal in mind, and the Reapers seemed to sense her intentions; they attempted to cut her off, but despite her dizziness, Wendy was quick and sly.

Darting across her back yard, Wendy narrowly wedged herself through the thin opening Jon had left in the back shed door and triumphantly came up with the rake she'd used to stab the raccoon. It had been a wild guess—Wendy hadn't known for sure that the emotional impact of having to put the poor raccoon down would affect the rake that way—but here it was, solid and firm in the Never, fitting easily in her hands.

"Foolish Reaper," hissed the lead Walker. "You can't harm us with—" It staggered back, the rake embedded deeply in its chest, essence seeping around the tines and pattering on the floor.

"Try again," Wendy snarled, and grabbed for the shovel, hefting it deliberately. "In case you haven't figured it out, I'm going nowhere, guys."

"One Reaper," said a close Walker. "Only one."

"One Reaper," Wendy mimicked savagely. "Who's playing with you instead of reaping you. Wonder why?" She jutted her chin out and smiled sharply, hoping that her expression was as knowing and gleeful as she was trying to make it. It was all a bluff, but they didn't know that.

The Walkers stilled.

"I've got all the time in the world," Wendy said, winking and spinning the shovel experimentally in her grip. "You think your Lady Walker cares if I mess you up on my way to see her? You're a bunch of dirty child-killers. I can't *wait* to crush what little remains of you to bits!"

"Many of us," the closest Walker hissed. "Still many, many. Many more than you."

"Many of you, but no White Lady to fix up your boo-boos," Wendy retorted. "Funny how that works. No White Lady, no Lost. Just a crazy Lady Walker, I'm told, and now a whole bunch of new Reapers moving back to town . . . and, I really ought to mention, a couple of them on their way to visit me *right now*." Wendy checked her watch and grinned. "Tick tock, fellas."

"You lie!"

"Nope," Wendy declared triumphantly. "Kind of sucks to be you, huh? How do you plan on protecting your sorry, skeletal asses now with the White Lady gone?"

Wendy pretended to think. "Oh, right, you can't. And I have a sneaking feeling that the Lady Walker doesn't exactly care about you all, so much as she really likes having you around to get the beatings she's supposed to be receiving." Wendy jerked her chin at the Walker still writhing on the ground. "Like that one."

"Lady Walker guides us. She teaches us," replied the lead Walker. "She protects us."

"Protects you from what? People like me? Well, good luck, but between you and me, I'm getting a wee bit tired of messing with you all. You're just not proving enough of a challenge, I think." Wendy spun the shovel again and grinned darkly. "I spent aaaallll morning with the Reapers, getting trained up. Wanna see my newest trick?"

The Walkers fell silent and looked among themselves.

"Flesh is right," one finally said, straightening and stepping as far away from Wendy as it could manage. "There is no life here, just dirty Reaper and dirty truths."

"The Lady will howl," whispered another. "She will rend and tear."

"Let her," said another. It reached forward and yanked the rake free of its companion Walker, letting the rake clatter noisily to the shed floor. "Time grows old here. This is senseless. It lacks sense."

Wendy said nothing as the lead Walker slipped through the shed's side. The others, even the one she'd stabbed, soon followed. One, smaller than the others, waited a beat behind. "She looks for you, she sniffs the air," it warned. "She has your taste in her mouth."

"Yeah, well, I've got her rotten stench in my nose," Wendy replied, spitting on the floor. "You see her again, you tell her I'm not scared."

"Stupid girl," the Walker said, shaking its head. "When the Lady rides, we all fear her passing." Chuckling to itself, the small Walker stepped through the wall and then it, too, was gone.

Once she was sure the coast was clear, Wendy waited for a minute, then two, before relaxing enough to put the shovel down. She couldn't believe she'd convinced the Walkers to just walk away, that she'd bluffed them into believing she could beat them, that she was toying with them for her own amusement. That was something her mother would do, not Wendy-like at all.

Stepping through the shed door again took more effort than Wendy could muster. In the heat of the moment she'd been able to squeeze through thoughtlessly, scraping her back and cheek against the rusty doorway, but now, the danger gone, she had to struggle with the shed door and ease out slowly. It squealed unhappily.

The cold air hit her like a slap and Wendy stripped off her hoodie, relishing the chill. "Whoo boy," Wendy said and thumped to the grass, flopping down with legs spread wide. Her head was swimming crazily and her breath puffed out in short, staccato bursts that worried part of her. Her lungs, she dimly realized, had begun to seriously ache.

"Ow," Wendy complained, pressing a hand against her ribs. In the front of the house she could hear a car pull up.

"Great," she muttered. "Now you show up? Fabulous timing, Emma. You're just my mother-frickin' hero these days." Then, slowly, Wendy dragged herself to her feet and trudged toward the side gate. "Let's get this over with," she said. "Eddie and Piotr are waiting."

CHAPTER SEVENTEEN

Emma wasn't driving her car.

"Please, Winifred," Elise said as Jane hopped out of the passenger side and, grinning, opened the door for Wendy with a dramatic flourish, "have a seat."

"Um . . . okay," Wendy said, painfully sliding into the back as Jane settled in the shotgun seat. "Hi. So, uh, where are we going?"

"Just for a quick jaunt around the block, dear," Elise said, smoothing one hand over her impeccable 'do. The dim light caught the sparkle of the rings on her fingers; a square sapphire, an oval onyx, and a heart-shaped diamond so large that Wendy hoped it was fake, because otherwise she had no clue how Elise had the guts to walk around in public with it sparkling on her finger. "I like meeting this way, for privacy."

"Where's Emma?" Wendy asked as Elise pulled onto her street and began circling the block. "She called and left the message that you all were on your way."

"As you can see, she did not lie. However, my mother had other . . . duties for her to attend to," Elise said. "In our family, duty always comes before personal satisfaction. I'm sure you understand."

"Sure do," Wendy agreed, wondering if Elise was trying to make a pointed remark or was simply bad at small talk. "So, um, you guys have a pamphlet for me or something?"

"Rules and regs, cuz," Jane said, digging in a huge messenger bag at her feet. She pulled out a thin manual, much worn, and passed it back to Wendy. "No marks in the margins, now. It's not exactly easy to take this baby up to Kinko's for copies."

"These are the basic tenets of being a Reaper," Elise explained, slowing to a complete stop and waiting exactly three seconds before accelerating past the stop sign. "You are to memorize the first pages in their entirety, do you understand?"

"Okay," Wendy said slowly, irritated that Elise was ordering her around already instead of simply asking. "That's it? Any other hoops you want me to dance through?"

"Winifred, I do not approve of the way your mother handled your situation," Elise replied stiffly. "As I'm sure you can ascertain. It was unprofessional of Mary at best, nearly traitorous at worst. However, with that said, what's done is done and you are now a Reaper, young lady. It would behoove you to act like one."

She shot a sharp glance at Wendy in the rearview mirror and Wendy realized that Elise wasn't just talking about the actual act of reaping.

"What are you saying?" Wendy asked. "You guys agree with Emma, then? You don't think I've got what it takes to do the job?"

"How closely Emma and I see eye-to-eye on the subject of your competence remains to be seen," Elise said, pursing her lips tightly. "I am willing to allow you an attempt to prove yourself, however, which is more than can be said for some members of the family."

"You know, like the ones who *actually* think you're a total mutant freak," Jane added chummily. She dug in her pocket and offered Wendy the familiar battered tin. "Gum?"

"No, thank you," Wendy said, pushing the tin away. "So, what do you want me to do?"

"I want you to do nothing but follow orders and be initiated as any other Reaper must," Elise said evenly, turning the corner. "It is only fair, yes?"

"Sure, no problem," Wendy agreed. "I don't wanna piss anyone off. That's no good."

"That's actually something I wanted to talk to you about," Jane said, twisting in her seat so she could meet Wendy's eyes. "Look, do you remember those Walkers from last night?"

"Kind of hard to forget," Wendy said.

"Yeah, but there's one particular one I'm thinking of," Jane said. "Maybe I'm wrong, but was there a chick Walker all up in your grill when I, your oh-so-stunning cavalry, arrived." She waved a hand at her face and grimaced. "Maybe she kinda looks like Two-Face, you know? Half-here, half not?"

Wendy shivered. "Yes. Definitely." She thought about mentioning the posse of Walkers she'd just sent on their way but didn't want to give Elise an excuse to shun her for not coming up with a creative way of reaping them despite her binding. Cool, competent Elise seemed the type to blame Wendy for allowing the Walkers to escape rather than rewarding her for simply surviving.

Elise and Jane exchanged a look. "Please," Elise said softly, "do not be too concerned, but this Walker is known to our family."

"'Known' being Grandma-polite-ese for 'haunts the pants off of us every chance she gets,'" Jane supplied. "I've had stalkers less pushy than this lady, and I've only seen her a couple of times. This chick is seriously wrong on, like, many, many levels."

"I figured that one out on my own," Wendy said, recalling the raspy feel of the Lady Walker's tongue sliding across her cheek. "So, uh, the other Walkers follow her pretty closely, huh?"

"Like puppies," Elise said. "She has them well-trained. However, her skill amid her own brethren is not what concerns me. What concerns me is that she is here and not back East."

"We thought we finally got her ages ago," Jane explained. "Emma said she and the Lady Walker got in a tussle back when she was a teenager. Emma won."

"At least, that is what she claimed," Elise said, hitting the brakes a shade too hard this time. Rather than coming to a smooth, controlled stop, the car jerked to a standstill in front of Wendy's house.

"My mother believed her, and raised her high within our family line in a matter of weeks for her bravery and gumption. Granted her great accolades over many other, more . . . adept and wise Reapers. Those with tenure, so to speak."

"Maybe it's a different Walker, Grandma?" Jane suggested, tapping her teeth with one fingernail. "I can't imagine Emma messing up and lying over something like that, where it's pretty easy to get caught out."

"Perhaps. Perhaps not." Elise pulled into Wendy's driveway and parked the car. "Winifred, your first official assignment for this family is to keep an eye out for this Lady Walker. If you see her, please report to me immediately. We must know for sure if she is still out there. And, if possible, engage her. Your . . . natural skill set may prove to be her undoing. It is worth an attempt at the very least."

Wendy shifted uneasily. She didn't know if she even wanted to lay eyes on the Lady Walker again, much less tangle with her. Dealing with her henchmen had been terrible enough. "I don't have your number—"

"I'll text it to ya," Jane offered, waving her phone. "I got yours from Emma."

"Wait up a sec. If she's just a Walker, then I don't see why she's such a big deal," Wendy mused, suddenly struck with the dichotomy of it all. "There are a whole lot more of you—us—than her, even with her dead posse on patrol. Why don't you reap her?"

"We've tried that," Elise said. "Generations of us, over and over again. This Walker . . . this Walker is different. She keeps coming back, generation after generation. She is our bane."

Elise gestured to the thin manual in Wendy's loose grasp. "You will find a small section on her in there. Read it well. Know it. It may save your life, should you encounter her again."

Wendy thought of Piotr, how he'd been the only one left standing when Wendy's explosion of Light at the Palace Hotel had finally faded. Were he and the Lady Walker connected somehow? The very thought of it made her ill.

"Gotcha," Wendy agreed as Jane stepped out of the car and opened the door. "Thank you."

"No, thank you," Elise said as Wendy eased out. "And Winifred?"

"Yes?"

"Welcome to the family." Elise turned and faced forward, expression drawn, as Jane shut the passenger side door.

"Come on, kiddo," Jane said, slinging an arm around Wendy's neck to guide her, "I'll walk you to your door in case there're any Walkers about, Lady-like or otherwise." She snorted at her own joke and squeezed the arm around Wendy's neck so roughly that Wendy coughed.

"Too tight, Jane, too tight!"

"Sorry, sorry, don't know my own strength," Jane apologized, releasing Wendy and pinching Wendy's cheek. "Oh, look at that baby face! You're just too cute for words, you know that? A little gothette-girlie. I could just eat you up!"

"Yeah, yeah." Wendy waved Jane off. "Enough already."

"So sensitive! You've really gotta learn how to take a joke if you want to make it in this family." Jane winked and scratched her neck. "Enough of them are pissed at us for not 'following tradition' as it is. You're really going to have to work on those peep-skills, if you get my meaning. Especially if you wanna learn from any of the old-timers. They need to know you can handle yourself."

"Hey . . . speaking of . . ."

Jane raised an eyebrow. "Yeah?"

"Well, that thing Emma did earlier. You know, the binding . . ." Wendy trailed off, unsure how Jane would take being asked to help so soon after the trial. What if she thought less of Wendy for being unable to cope with the Light's inaccessibility?

"You want it off already?" Jane said, sensing Wendy's discomfort and jumping right to the point. "Hell's bells, cuz, why am I completely not surprised?"

"You're right, I should just ovary-up and deal with the discomfort, huh?" Wendy said, dejected. "It's just, I don't feel safe like this. I feel exposed. And not in a fun way, you know?"

Again, she thought of telling the other Reaper about her tussle with the Walkers—Jane *had* to be more understanding than Elise would be—but, strangely, she didn't want Jane to know that the Lady Walker had apparently marked Wendy as prey. Wendy didn't want Jane to worry.

"Now, now. I didn't say any such thing," Jane protested, waving her hands wildly. "I'm just kind of irritated with Emma for poking holes in you in the first place. Especially without asking; it's crappy karma, if you ask this little ol' lass. It's just, well, it's tricky."

"But you think I really should do it?" Wendy thought again of the hospital lobby, of the encroaching cold, and shivered. "I just don't want to be weak if I'm supposed to be keeping an eye out for this Lady Walker."

Or more of her goons, she silently added. *She's bound to send smarter ones next time around.*

"Um, duh, yeah. That makes total sense. Hell, I thought you should have thrown a shit-fit when she did it in the first place. I would've made her take it off right then and there, Great-Grandma-approved or not. It's your Light, it's your call."

"Well, I want it off. Will you do it?"

"I can try," Jane said. "No guarantees, though. Emma's way, way trickier at stuff like this than me."

"Anything at all," Wendy said. "I'll take anything. Just poke a hole in there, something to let off more Light. Anything I can use at all."

"I'll do my best but this might hurt," Jane warned. "Try and slide into the Never."

"What . . . like, right here?" Wendy glanced around her front porch. Emma's car was still in the driveway; the side of the garage was hiding the front of the vehicle where Elise sat, so Jane's grand-mother couldn't see them, but an evening jogger was bouncing down the street and a couple with a baby were taking a stroll in their direction, only four houses away.

"Worrywart. No one's paying any attention," Jane said, waving off Wendy's concern. "Just hold still, already."

Wendy, following Jane's instructions, tried to push into the Never once again and, as had happened upstairs, was thwarted by the mesh surrounding her soul. Was it her, Wendy wondered, or was the mesh getting stronger? It was harder than before to push on it, and the fierce Light behind the mesh seemed a little brighter, a little hotter to the touch.

Ignoring all possible passersby, Jane slid into the Never easily; there, shimmering in front of Wendy in a glowing halo, she placed burning hands of Light on Wendy's chest and back. Her fingers were talented and quick but still Wendy felt a painful twinge where she touched, a sharp and sudden burning, and had to bite her lip to keep from crying out.

For several minutes, Jane's hands sought inwards, pushing against the weave, plucking and pressing against her heart, her lungs, her eyes and face, a burning-hot ribbon of Light sliding against her solar plexus, another snaking ribbon winding around her windpipe and slipping across her collarbone. Wendy whimpered despite herself, feeling the pressure quickly twist from tolerable pain to outright agony.

In the Never, Jane's voice was the sound of silvery bells. "Keep still."

Wendy obliged as best she could, but her heart was thudding rapidly against her ribs. The ribbons of Light were covering her now, sliding pervasively against every inch of skin, dipping into places kept private and close, pushing into her mouth and forcing Wendy to arch back to keep her balance as they pulled tight across her torso and knotted insistently between her thighs.

"Jane," Wendy tried to whisper as the ribbons slid tighter and tighter across her ribs, cutting off her air, "Jane . . . can't . . . breathe . . ."

The silvery bells chimed sharply, impatiently. "Wait. Only a moment more."

Wendy sagged, swaying in Jane's grip . . .

. . . and came to, lying on her front porch, Jane kneeling above her with a concerned look on her face. Elise towered above them both, a dark expression curling her lip. In the distance the couple with the baby hesitated on the sidewalk, the woman punching numbers into her cell phone.

"We are quite all right!" Elise called to the couple as the husband began to slowly cross the street, worry writ large across his face. "She just fainted! We will get her inside!"

"Neither one of us can fix it," Jane said quietly as the man paused at the edge of the driveway.

"Are you sure?" he asked. "I can call 911."

"Low blood sugar," Jane said smoothly, jerking on Wendy's elbow. "Get up," she hissed.

"I'm fine," Wendy said woozily, sitting up. "Really. I'm fine." She waved a hand at the woman across the street. "I'll eat a cookie and be great. I promise."

"Well . . . okay," the man said. "If you're sure."

"We've got her, thanks," Jane promised him and waited until he and the woman had turned the corner to sigh and pat Wendy on the shoulder. "Nosy neighborhood, huh?"

"We keep an eye out for our own," Wendy said, stung at the derision in Jane's voice. She patted her legs and chest. "So it didn't work?"

"Nope," Jane said shortly. "Emma did something really, really weird to you. You're wrapped tighter than a Thanksgiving turkey. I've never seen anything like it."

"She is not answering her cellular phone either," Elise hissed softly, snapping her phone closed with one hand. "I have no idea what my mother was thinking when she bid Emma to do as she did, but this nonsense must stop immediately. If your soul isn't released soon, you may begin to burn up! Trapping a natural in a feedback loop of this nature, binding them this tightly . . . what was she thinking?!"

"You can't do anything at all?" Wendy asked tentatively. She felt tender and sore in all the wrong places, uncertain and on edge. When Jane reached for her to steady her, Wendy nearly flinched back. Jane had only been trying to help, she reminded herself, but the thought of those intrusive, invasive bands of Light touching her again made Wendy wince.

Unaware of Wendy's shell-shock, Jane shook her head. "We both tried. You're gummed up but good, cuz."

"Go inside," Elise ordered, grabbing Wendy by the elbow and guiding her toward her front door. "Relax. Rest. Nap, and if you can, do not fret overmuch. I will look into this and be back with you as soon as I may."

Then, in a surprisingly motherly gesture, Elise smoothed a curl off Wendy's forehead. "Above all else, do not tamper in the Never, Winifred. Any use of your abilities will speed up your degradation."

"But don't worry, okay?" Jane told Wendy in a whisper as Elise strode down the walkway back toward her car, punching numbers into her phone furiously.

Waiting until her grandmother was out of sight, Jane hugged her loosely, her blue hair tickling Wendy's nose. "Emma's a bitch right now, but the rest of us, well, we're family, right? We've totally got your back."

Watch your back, Mary whispered in Wendy's mind.

Watch your back, Emma whispered from her dream and Wendy, shuddering, closed her eyes and rested her forehead on Jane's warm, comforting shoulder. She wanted to weep at the kindness of the older girl.

"Thank you, Jane," Wendy said and Jane squeezed her warmly, helping her steady herself. "I owe you one."

"Nah," Jane said. "You find that Lady Walker and prove Emma's a huge ol' liar-head, and we'll call it even." She pressed a grape-scented kiss to Wendy's cheek. "You just take care of yourself, yeah? Stay healthy. You're the first Reaper I've met without a stick up her butt. I'd love to keep you around."

"Yeah," Wendy said and opened the door behind her. "Will do."

"Sleep," Jane said, and waved her phone in Wendy's direction, backing down the walkway. "Grandma will figure out what the hell Emma did to you, and I'll be in touch."

CHAPTER EIGHTEEN

The downstairs was empty, the house quiet except for the hiss of a shower upstairs, when Wendy stepped back inside. She paused for a moment in the kitchen, eying the terrible mess left behind after her tussle with the Walkers, and wondered how in the hell she was supposed to right the fridge all by herself before Chel and Jon found out.

"Hell," Wendy said after several minutes of staring. "Screw it." She knew she ought to feel badly about leaving the food splattered across the floor but honestly she was too tired and aggravated to care much about anything at this point. When Jon or Chel found the mess she'd get up and handle it, but if they discovered her cleaning the kitchen they'd want to know what happened. Wendy didn't have a good answer for that; claiming ignorance seemed to be the best option for now. After all, saying "a bunch of angry ghosts did it" wasn't likely to be taken seriously.

Decision to shirk her familial duties made, Wendy drifted into the living room and settled on the couch, tucking her feet beneath her. Part of her ached to run upstairs and shower, to slough a loofah against her flesh until her skin no longer felt like it was crawling with the invasive Light, with every fine hair standing on end and the air slowly slipping away, but scrubbing down seemed disrespectful to Jane and what she'd tried to do on Wendy's behalf. Wendy couldn't bring herself to do it.

"Manual for the dead," Wendy murmured instead, shaking her head and turning on the table lamp beside the couch. "Nutjobs, the whole lot of them." But the thin paperback was much worn, the pages wavy at the edges. It had been read many, many times. Had her mother held this book? Had her mother's mother?

"Okay, fine," Wendy said, licking a finger and flipping the cover open. "You all want me to memorize some rules and regs? Fine. Let's see what you've got to say."

The paper was thick, heavy, and the font a slightly staggering type that had to go back to the turn of the century or before. Wendy found herself squinting to read it and paused to flip on a second light.

"'Point one, tell no one of the Reapers, lest they find you mad.'" Wendy stopped to roll her eyes. "Well, duh. What moron would go shouting *that* from the rafters?"

The house creaked around her and Wendy paused again, glancing quickly around to make sure Eddie or the others hadn't returned. She knew that she ought to run upstairs and pack a bag, to hurry and meet her friends at Eddie's place, but her curiosity was too great. The idea stuck with Wendy that the Lady Walker might be like Piotr, and the book was thin. It wouldn't take her long to skim it through just once, and then she could catch up with the others.

Point 1 – Tell no one of the Reapers, lest they find you mad and all further Reapers suffer for it.

Point 2 – To be a Reaper is to hold allegiance only to the greater family and none other. No lover, no child, no duty or country shall break the bonds between Reaper and family.

Point 3 – The soul is weak, the flesh unwilling. Bind and send on all souls, no matter how they cry or beg. Such is the Good Work and those who are chosen to engage in it.

Point 4 – Let not the Natural walk free, for she is an abomination unto our kind. Kill her kindly and quick, bind her soul tightly until she burns with the Light of a thousand suns, so that she may not doom us all.

"Sonnuva—" Wendy hissed sharply. "Yeah. Thanks, guys. No wonder Emma was such an a-hole about it in my dream." Irritated, she flipped the page and continued on.

Point 5 – A single exception is to be for the Natural one who burns too brightly. A binding may serve as a test alone, but only for those of great strength. Should she pass, training may be provided. The Good Mercy on her soul—one such child must abide alone in the Good Work henceforth or risk the family's demise. Bless and keep this girl, she knows not what she shall struggle with.

Wendy paused. "Wait . . . what?" She read the rule again and frowned. Her thoughts were slow and muddied, confused. "So, a natural must be destroyed unless the family really thinks she—I—can handle working alone? Holy crap. But that's not what Nana Moses said at all. So which is it?"

Closing the book, Wendy frowned and stared at the mirror across the room. She knew that she looked a sight. Her face was flushed, her hair ragged and tangled, and her clothing filthy.

"Who's right?" Wendy wondered. "Jane? Or Emma? But Emma was so *insistent* in my dreamscape." Wendy rubbed a fist across her face. "She told me to quit while I was ahead. To give up. But . . . what if it was part of this test? What if they're all in it together and Emma *isn't* being a total cow? What if I'm being tested right now?"

A horrible thought occurred to her. Wendy sat up straighter. "Oh crap, what if by asking Jane to fix me, I ruined everything?" But no, Jane and Elise had seemed as aggravated with Emma as Wendy was.

"I don't know," Wendy whispered, staring at the messy girl in the mirror, wishing that her mother was upstairs so she could run to her, let her fix everything as she always had. "I just . . . I just don't know what to do."

Slowly, turning back to the book, Wendy took a deep breath and continued on.

Point 6 – Be wary of the Unending Ones, those spirits we cannot reap. All scarred and battle-worn—none are your friends, none your enemy. They

come with gifts in their hands and knowing in their mouths but they are as
serpents and are not to be trusted. Do the Good Work and mind them not.
They cannot greatly harm us and we cannot greatly harm them—a circle is
formed at the touch and the touch alone. Hide from them if you must, engage
them not, for they know not what they've done, nor where they've been, only
that they can taste a Reaper on the wind.

This was definitely referring to Piotr, Wendy thought, turning the
page with a shaking hand. She could see how if someone like Jane or
Elise had never met Piotr she might be wary of him and what he
could do but, then again, her mother had called to Piotr, had used
him to put her soul back together when she couldn't. So who was
right?

    Point 7 – Cleave unto the family, for we alone understand from whence
we came and the dangers in the spaces between the Dark and the Light. Do
not turn your face away, do not seek to lie or cheat. Listen always to the
matriarch and follow her guidance as if it were law. Such is always as it
has been, such is always how it should be.

    Point 8 – Follow the tenets of our family closely. Follow the steps of
awakening honestly. Drink from the Good Cup when it has been passed into
your hands and not before, lest you awaken more than your Sight. Pity those
born with the Sight—Naturals and Seers—for they cannot control their
will, and the Darkness and Light shall take them, the Never shall swallow
them whole.

Wendy stuck her tongue out. "Well poo on you, too," she muttered
and shifted uncomfortably on the couch. It had been a long time
since she'd curled up down here to read. The tough upholstery was
scratchier than she remembered, and the cushions seemed to be all
lumps.

    Whatever, Wendy thought. First world problems. She'd just
deal.

There were several more rules along these lines and Wendy was rapidly growing bored reading them. Instead she decided to flip through the rest of the book and skim around a bit, to see what was interesting.

"Blah, blah, blah, ghosts, types of ghosts, Shades, blah," Wendy said, rubbing her dry eyes. "Walkers . . . eww, that picture's grosser than an actual Walker, I think. Oh, hey, the Lost and Riders."

Startled, Wendy blinked and peered closer at the page, squinting to keep the cramped words from swimming around so drastically. "Wow. That's Lily."

The resemblance to the spirit Wendy knew was uncanny; if it wasn't Lily, Wendy would be surprised. Thankfully the blurb below Lily's picture only called her an "elusive spirit seen escorting Lost souls" and suggested that the Reaper in question might wish to consider waiting for the Rider in question to be alone before engaging them in the Good Work.

"Because she'd kick your ass," Wendy chuckled to herself. "Oh, no: because apparently the Riders stick together and gang up on Reapers. Huh. They're kinda fractured; they don't do that now. You know, unless you force them to."

Seeing Lily in the book had been mildly entertaining, but Wendy was rapidly growing bored. Her head was beginning to ache a little and she really wanted a glass of water, but she was too tired to bother getting up and nabbing one from the kitchen.

There'd been no mention of Piotr or the Lady Walker, beyond the rule at the beginning. Wendy was starting to believe that Elise and Jane had only dangled that carrot before her to get her to read the manual more quickly.

"'How to see into the Never,'" Wendy read aloud, paging through the last, most weather-beaten pages, "how to reap a spirit, how to transmute a silver cord, how to shift through solid objects . . ."

And then she stopped.

How To Transmute A Silver Cord.

Squinting at the passage, Wendy felt her throat dry up. She hurriedly read further.

The transmutation of a silver cord is neither simple nor desired. To do so to another is to do a great disservice to the Reaper in question and might be considered an attack upon a fellow member of the family. However, in some cases, it may be necessary to move about the spiritual realm without arousing suspicion from the spirits.

In order to hide amid the dead, it is necessary that the cord of the living be spun very fine, almost as if weaving the thinnest shroud about one's person, cleaving it tightly to the flesh-essence itself. This is difficult to do to oneself, but not impossible. Know no mistake—the nature of this act is quite destructive. Maintaining this unnatural curvature of the cord will leach the essence and Light from the Reaper in rapid time, weakening both their spirit and living body permanently. The Reaper will fade slowly over the course of months as the pull of their cord binding them in the Never drains their abilities and spiritual power away. NEVER TRANSMUTE A NON-REAPER'S CORD—THIS WILL KILL THEM IN SHORT ORDER (weeks).

Wendy closed the manual. Was this what happened to Eddie? Had someone—some Reaper—snuck up behind him and twisted his cord up, spread it thin, until it seemed like it was missing? Why? What would the point of that be?

And, furthermore, this stuff was in the frickin' *beginning Reaper's manual*! Emma was a smart chick, why wouldn't she have known already that it was possible to do this to someone? Why would she ask to study Eddie if the answer was right there in "Reaping for Dummies" all along?

Unless. Unless she *did* know and had been playing dumb about it. But would Emma do that? Wendy didn't know.

"Whatever. It doesn't matter," she said, setting the manual on the coffee table and stretching. It was so warm in here . . . had Chel turned up the thermostat again?

What was important now, Wendy decided, stripping off her hoodie, was finding Eddie. Finding him and fixing him, if that transmutey-thing was what was really wrong with him. She hoped it was. It sounded . . . sort of simple to fix? And maybe Jane could help if Wendy couldn't do it alone.

Wendy reached into her pocket, searching for her phone. She'd just call Eddie up and have him meet her . . .

Wait.

"Wendy, you dummy," Wendy sighed, running her tongue over dry and cracked lips. "I'd like to see the rate plan on cell service in the freakin' Never."

Grumbling, she stood up and headed for the side door. A sick headache was beginning to pound at her temples and her neck felt like a pillar of solid, painful, stone.

Thankfully Eddie's house was just a short walk away, Wendy soothed herself. With any luck he and the others would still be there—where else did they have to go, after all?—and she could lay hands on his spirit, try and fix whatever nastiness had been done to him. She might not be able to step into the Never now, but Wendy'd been able to grab that rake. Grabbing Eddie's cord the same way might be a piece of cake . . . she hoped.

Crossing her backyard left Wendy feeling exposed and wondering if her bluff had truly scared off the Walkers or if they were cleverly laying in wait somewhere else in the yard. She rubbed her hands up and down her arms against the light evening chill.

Wendy thought that they might have been chased off, but if the Lady Walker was as scary as everyone seemed to think she was, then she wouldn't take too kindly to her boys running away after only a few pokes with a garden rake, no matter how pointy.

Wendy would worry about it later. First Eddie and Piotr, then deal with Miss Phantom-of-the-Opera-Face. After that . . .

Wendy was near the back shed when a sudden, unexpected heavy pressure shoved her forward, sending Wendy sprawling to the ground.

"What the hell!" Wendy struggled to her feet and then the shove came again, twice as powerful this time around. Her hand smacked against the side of the shed, her forehead banged against the window. Twisting and cursing, Wendy managed to flip over, expecting to have to kick out against her assailant, to scratch and scream . . .

Nothing.

There was no one there. Not in the Never and not in the living lands. No Walkers, no Lady Walker, nothing.

Perplexed, Wendy began to sit up when the pressure forced her back to the grass, a heavy weight that pinned her down from her collar to her hips, shoving down with so much force that Wendy struggled to breathe.

Spaces between worlds, Nana Moses' voice whispered in the back of her mind. *Creatures and creatures again, drawn by your Light.*

The world began to grey around her, just as it had when Jane's ribbons of Light had twisted so tightly.

Reaching forward, Wendy concentrated on where the bulk of the pressure was, where Jane's ribbons had twined the tightest. She didn't know if this would work, but it was her only chance.

There. There it was. Her Light.

Wendy felt it, right there at the edge of her fingertips, banked and roaring deep inside her, a bonfire somehow swept into a little hearth that promised to burn the house around it to cinders. She could feel how the mesh of the binding had been twisted tight and knotted, a wrap around the heat, threatening to burst and break her apart in the process.

Tapping into the Light, wedging her fingers under the very thinnest of mesh edges, Wendy was able to bend the bindings on her power just a little. Not enough to break them, no, but the heat of

her power blazing on the other side was just enough to wriggle a fingernail's width of space free. Not much, a miniscule amount, but
enough for the moment.

With hands encased in Light, Wendy reached into the invisible,
punishing mass and *squeezed*.

A terrible shriek ripped the air above her and for a brief, glorious
second Wendy was able to breathe as the invisible pressure loosened.
Then, before she could do more than gasp a few mouthfuls of air, it
was back and gripping tighter than ever.

Marshalling what energy she could, Wendy squinted into the
Never, hoping against hope that *this time* she'd be able to make her
enemy out.

It wasn't some terrible monster from the deep, she realized, just
a bird: an enormous, furious seagull with dirty, stinking wings,
mostly camouflaged by the shadows and the night and gripping her
torso with all its might. It squawked and tightened its immense,
mutated talons around her chest. Where she had touched it, the
essence smoked. The scaly leg burned from her touch.

The gull was a fighter, though. It wasn't going to let Wendy get
away. When she tried to twist free, it flapped foul, sea-rotted wings
in her face and darted downward, tearing a large chunk of Wendy's
arm in a deep, jerking gash. For a brief moment Wendy thought that
the awful bird had actually cut her corporeal flesh, but then she felt
the hole where her outer essence should have been.

What little of her banked power she'd been able to grab was
now almost gone. Wendy squeezed harder and was rewarded by the
nasty beast pecking at her eyes and gouging her left cheek. Wendy
buried one hand in the bird's chest, futilely yanking out only a
handful of filthy feathers.

The world began to dim, and just as Wendy gave up, she heard
a sharp, loud chittery growl and smelled a clean, evergreen scent.
Forcing her eyes open, Wendy spotted a huge black shadow darting
as a raccoon slammed into the gull, pinning it down.

The gull screamed and Wendy, at a loss for how to help, used the very last of her remaining power to *squeeze* the gull's leg again. The gull made an almost-human yell of pain and surprise and flapped off her chest, choosing to combat the raccoon over its weakened and torn-up prey.

Scuttling over the ground in fast, darting motions the raccoon and gull went at each other with a startling fury, the raccoon darting in and out of the fray with sharp, quick swipes, the bird doing its best to peck the raccoon's eyes out. The gull was strong but the raccoon was quick, and within moments the gull was missing great patches of feathers from its chest and neck. The air was filled with dirty white-grey fluff. The bird's skin was speckled with red.

Finally, realizing that it was outmaneuvered, the gull managed to take wing and escape. The raccoon, hissing furiously, leapt into the air after the gull and tried to snatch it back down, catching only a few tail feathers for its effort.

The raccoon, clutching the feathers in one paw, waited until the gull was long gone before it sauntered over to Wendy and began grooming its paws and face.

"Hello again," Wendy said, coughing painfully. She thought about trying to sit up, but even the idea of moving made her woozy. "I thought you were done with me. Decided to stick around for some more giggles, huh?"

Wendy ran her hand along the raccoon's back, luxuriating in the strangely slippery feel of its dense fur coat. The raccoon, dropping the feathers, preened under her touch and Wendy got the impression that if it could purr, it would have. "Thank you," she whispered. "I appreciate your help."

The raccoon flicked an ear at her: *Chips? Crackers? Tacos? Chocolate chip cookies?*

"I still don't have a snack for you," Wendy apologized, chuckling helplessly at the situation until a sharp spike of pain along her temples made her stop. "At least, not one you can eat in your cur-

rent, you know, dead state. I'm really sorry. Though . . . I don't
know . . . maybe we can salvage some nommables for you later?"

She coughed again and this time was dismayed to feel a thick
bubble break at the corner of her mouth. Her eyes were dry and hot
in their sockets.

"I really am running a temperature now," Wendy told the raccoon. "Whoo-nelly, I feel sick."

*A normal Reaper might last weeks or days but a natural would burn
up in a matter of hours*, Emma's voice reminded her. How long had it
been since the binding? And how long since Jane had tried to
remove the binding?

Wendy shivered. Time seemed to be speeding up, and not in a
good way.

"I know you're hungry," Wendy said aloud, staggering to her
feet. "Believe me, I know. I promise, when I can I'll . . ." She
coughed again and wiped her wrist against her damp lips, ignoring
the pink tinge in the faint streetlights.

"Actually," Wendy told the raccoon, rubbing the back of her
neck, "now that I come to think about it, maybe I'll take that
shower, after all. Eddie's not going anywhere, right? Right. Cool off
a touch, then go fix him right up."

The raccoon said nothing, merely bounded across the yard and
through the kitchen wall, leaving Wendy to follow. When she
entered the house the raccoon was waiting patiently on the stairs. It
flicked an ear at her and darted to the second floor, leading the way.

CHAPTER NINETEEN

S tumbling upstairs, Wendy staggered into the bathroom and slammed open the cabinet door, pawing through the jumbled morass inside until she found the old thermometer. It was ancient and probably hardly worked, but if all else failed she'd go looking for a newer one in Dad's bathroom. She was alarmingly dizzy. Small grey spots were beginning to swim at the edges of her vision. How *hard* had that gull hit her, anyway?

Using the old thermometer seemed to take forever. Wendy squinted at the readout and then shook the thermometer.

102.9.

That can't be right, Wendy thought. Her temperature had sky-rocketed far too high, far too fast.

And that was going-to-the-hospital temperature, wasn't it? Wendy wished she could ask her mom what to do. Mary had been an EMT for years; she'd know how to handle this.

Slumping to the bathroom floor, Wendy rested her cheek against the cool tile. Her mind was a tangle of thoughts and worries and missing her mother. She'd never really had the time to mourn Mary; she'd been in the hospital, unconscious, until the day after they'd buried her.

"What did Emma *do* to me?" Wendy asked the floor tiles, absently rubbing a spot of dried gunk under the cabinet door lip, cleaning like Chel might if she'd known it was there.

Rolling over onto her back, Wendy dug in her pocket for her phone. She pulled out her old tongue ring, stared at it a moment in confusion, and then pocketed it again. She knew she was forgetting something important about the ring, something about where she'd seen it last, but right now contacting Emma was more important. It seemed silly to think that Emma was working against her. It seemed crazy.

Wendy laughed at the absurdity of calling the only doctor she knew over a panic about a little fever. "Be all like, 'Yo, Emma, I gots a temp, guuurl, and it's all yo fault. Now whatchoo want me to do 'bout it?' Oh yeah, she'd looove that."

The raccoon said nothing, but it leapt down off the toilet and nudged the hand holding her phone.

"Oh, hey," Wendy said as image after image of travelers at a nearby rest station appeared clearly in her mind. They were holding their phones up, obviously trying to get reception.

"That's a great idea. Sicker than snot? Smartphone to the rescue!" Wendy patted the raccoon on the head. "You, little guy, are one smart . . . mammal . . . thing."

The raccoon said nothing but preened under her petting and licked its snout again.

"Here we go," Wendy muttered, pulling up Google and checking WebMD. "High temp," she typed, rolling so that her other cheek now lay against the melting tiles and cold floor while she waited for the page to load.

"Have to save Eddie," she said. "Have to cool off, have to save . . . Sarah? And Piotr. I can do this. One step at a time. No problemo. I am Wendy, hear me roar. Or whimper. Whatever." She coughed. "Did I save Sarah? I didn't, did I? She got . . . she got sent on."

Squinting at the screen was making her dry, raspy eyes water, and the salt tears stung. Looking away eased the discomfort; Wendy was dismayed to realize that glancing back caused stabbing pain behind her eyes.

"Light sensitivity, fever," Wendy muttered, shading her eyes and trying to read the WebMD article in quick, snapping glances. "Skin tight? Yeah. No sweat? Damn it, yes."

Heat stroke.

Wendy thumbed her phone closed and flipped it upside down, setting it face down on the tile. She waved weakly at the light switch and, to her surprise, the raccoon hopped up on the countertop and scrabbled at the switch with its paws until the light, blessedly, turned off.

"Did not know you could do that," Wendy said and pressed herself as flat to the floor as she could manage. It kept the world from spinning quite so rapidly. "Well, you learn something new every day, huh?"

Now only the dim light coming in from her father's bedroom window down the hall lit the bathroom; Wendy used this weak illumination to twist the cold knob and flip the stopper, resting her hot forehead against the cool fiberglass while the tub filled and the world melted and spun.

"Gonna throttle Emma when I get my hands on her," Wendy whispered to herself. "Gonna show her."

Stripping her jeans and shirt seemed to take forever; by the time she was done the water was lapping the overflow hole. Easing into the icy tub, Wendy grabbed for the towel rack for support and sent the towels sliding to the floor. She thought about picking them up but instead welcomed the cold water slinking up her legs and caressing her hips, tummy, chest.

Once she was sunk up to her shoulders, Wendy tilted her head back and reveled in the cold shiver that ran chilly fingers up the base of her skull to her temples. Groaning, Wendy sank again as deeply into the bath as she could, until only her nose was above the water. When she opened her eyes the bathroom ceiling was distorted and wavery, but Wendy had a feeling that it wasn't just the water causing her vision to drift.

Surfacing, she stared at the wall and nodded; yep, she was definitely beginning to hallucinate. Her father had last painted the bathroom when she was ten, maybe eleven. Wendy was positive that she'd remember if he'd decided to spray paint pink stripes and swirls above the toilet, especially ones that had the disconcerting habit of forming into glaring, malevolent faces in her peripheral vision.

Finally dragging her eyes away from the faces in the walls, Wendy was stunned to realize that the air was steaming above her. "Didn't I run cold water?" she whispered plaintively.

Ice melting in a Styrofoam coffee cup, watering down the bitter liquid flung on the side of the road.

"No. No-no-no, I know what to do," Wendy said, sitting up so that the water sloshed over the side, drenching the tiles and towels. She waved at her raccoon and chuckled maliciously, grabbing for the driest washcloth to wipe her hands. "I really will ask Emma."

It took her three tries to punch in the number correctly. It rang and rang and rang, and just as Wendy was certain it was going to voicemail, Emma's familiar cool voice answered. She was annoyed. "Wendy, I'm about to eat for the first time all day. What is it?"

"You. Bitch," Wendy slurred.

There was a pause on the other end. "Excuse me? I beg your pardon?"

"You heard me. You bitch." Wendy was shaking now in the water, her teeth chattering. "You haul me out to the middle of nowhere, strip me down, and bind me up without even asking per-mission—"

Immediately Emma's voice dropped and grew further annoyed. "Wendy, please, we discussed the reasons behind this already."

If she'd been in the same room, Wendy would have slapped her. "And then you have the nerve—the nerve!—to tell me that you don't think I'm good enough to be Reaper material? You come into *my* dreams and try to push me around? What the hell, Emma? Who *does* that?"

"What?"

"But I can handle that, you know? It's just stupid high school buffy crap all over again, just from an adult. So I can handle you thinking you're better than me because you're all hot and older and a smarty-pants doctor. Eddie thinks you've got good legs. Who cares? I've got legs too, you know. But it's not—"

Wendy broke off to cough. Her entire torso twisted under the shuddering shape of the wracking coughs, and her throat felt like razors were shredding her insides apart. Every inch of her flesh ached.

"Wendy?" Emma's voice was no longer pitched low or cool. She actually sounded *concerned*. "Wendy, what's wrong?"

"What did you *do* to me, Emma?" Wendy whispered, scooping up a palm full of bathwater and drinking it down. "Jane couldn't take off the binding. *What did you do?*"

"Wait-wait-wait," Emma was nearly pleading now on the other end. Her voice had gone high and quiet. "You saw Jane again today? When?"

"I hate you," Wendy said baldly. "I hate you so much. You guys . . . everyone, all the ghosts, they say I killed my mom but it was really you. You did it. 'Cause if Mom had her cord transmuted the way Eddie's cord is probably transmuted then she'd be alive, right? Yeah. She'd have walked around those Lost like it was nothin'."

Wendy coughed again. "You're the doctor, Emma. Emma*line*. Emmaline, thinks she's soooo fine. You could have saved her. You could've taken her after Piotr put all the pieces together again and you could've put her head back on straight. She just had to go back in her body. No biggie, right? You knocked Eddie out of his easily enough."

"Wendy?" Emma said softly. "Wendy, I don't know what you're talking about. Did you take something today? Are you drunk? Did you drink alcohol in conjunction with—"

"I'M SICK!" Wendy screamed into the phone, making the raccoon jump and flee the bathroom. "Don't you get that, you crazy bitch?! I'm . . . I'm running a fever. I'm staring at the walls and the walls are staring at me and the bath was so cold but now the water's warm-warm-warm."

There was another long pause. Wendy thought that perhaps the phone had cut out, that Emma had hung up on her, when Emma quietly said, "Have you taken your temperature recently, Wendy?"

"One-oh-three-ish," Wendy said stiffly. Then she laughed crazily. "And I'm getting hot-hot-hot!"

Cursing quietly on the other end, Emma quickly began speaking with someone else. Wendy shook her head. Silly Emma. Silly, stupid, back-stabbing Emma.

"I'm coming over right now," Emma said, returning to the phone. There was a strange echo in the background now; Wendy thought it might be the sound of Emma's running steps echoing around the hospital's concrete parking garage. "Stay there. Stay cool if you can. Dump out the bathwater, run a cold shower. Get ice packs if you can manage it."

"Why should I listen to you?" Wendy demanded. "You got me into this mess."

"Because, one, I'm a doctor, and two, I put the loosest binding possible on you, Wendy. You should *not* be reacting this way. You said that Jane tried to remove the binding? Are you sure?" Emma broke off and quietly cursed. "Where the hell is my car?"

"Elise has it," Wendy giggled. "Jane had her feet all over the dashboard too."

"She . . . what?!" Emma made a noise somewhere between a growl and a gurgle. "I . . . I just don't . . ."

"Emma?" Wendy whispered. "I think I'm gonna be sick."

"Jesus. Look, just lean over the side of the tub," Emma demanded and Wendy did so. The sick splattered across the tile was nothing but spit and bile; Wendy realized that the only thing she could recall eating all day was one of Jon's cookies.

Setting the cell on speakerphone and resting it on the toilet lid, Wendy carefully straightened and flipped the stopper on the tub. The water began to drain as she crawled out, easing over the side of the tub as slowly as she could manage. Her knee slid on a tiny puddle and Wendy cracked her funny-bone painfully on the side of the toilet. She moaned.

"Wendy? Wendy, are you still there? Wendy, are you okay? Answer me, damn it! WENDY!"

"Mmmhmmm," Wendy whispered. "No more bath. Tired."

"Wendy, okay, I want you to listen to me. Are you listening? Wendy, tell me you're listening."

"Listening," Wendy obediently repeated, taking the phone between her chattering teeth. It took all her energy to straighten up and rest against the wall, but she managed. It was time to crawl.

Tilting away from the bathroom wall, Wendy lifted one leg and then the next, then an arm and then the next, forcing her rebelling body to shuffle down the hall until she reached the relative sanity of her own room. Her comforter was half on/half off the bed, her gothic Hello Kitty throw pillow peeking from beneath the dust ruffle. Wendy hooked a finger into the black tassel and pulled the pillow close, jerking the rest of the comforter off the bed to wrap over her shivering, naked form.

"I can't hear you," Emma was shouting into the phone. "WENDY! SAY SOMETHING!"

"Sorry," Wendy whispered, watching colors pulse against her eyelids, a kaleidoscope of red and green and blue. "I don't really think you're a bitch. I'm just mad."

"Listen closely, Wendy. I'm getting a taxi and I'm coming over, okay? Where are you, Wendy?"

Wendy pinched the bridge of her nose. "I'm glad I'm a Lightbringer. I'm glad I'm not a Reaper. I'm new. I'm different. I'm my own."

"Where are you?"

"My room. Upstairs. End of the hall."

Emma's voice dropped; she was relieved. "Great. Fabulous. I'll be there as soon as I can but in the meantime I want you to try and take the binding off yourself, okay? Do you think you can do that?"

"You can take a binding off yourself?"

Emma hesitated. "You can try."

"You still don't think I'm good enough," Wendy accused her, voice breaking. If she weren't so dry, she would have cried. "You still think I'm trash."

"Wendy, I never said that." Emma was almost pleading now. "Please, just try to take off the binding."

It was worth a shot. "How?"

"Thank heavens, she finally sees reason. Fine, okay, here's what you do. Try and slide into the Never. You won't be able to do it, but try anyway. This will make seeing into the Never easier, yes?"

"Uh huh," Wendy said, remembering Jane's ribbons of Light and how they'd wrapped around her, pinching and pinning her down, twisting her all up. She closed her eyes and followed Emma's instructions. It was still difficult to push past what felt like layers of cotton pressing down beneath her skin, layered on her bones and ligaments in soft, twisted tangles, but she managed. "What else?"

"Once you can see your Light as well as feel it, look at it closely. Feel the cool spots, the black parts of the Light, woven through the holes in the brighter parts of your Light. Like . . . like one of those silly potholders you'd make in school, with a handloom? Feel the holes? Those are the spots where you can force open the binding."

Far away on the other line, Emma could have no idea how hard it was for Wendy to even see the Light, much less force anything.

"I . . . I can't . . ."

But then, just as Wendy was about to give up, she felt it. It was nothing at first, just the slightest twinge against the underside of her too-sensitive skin, nails rasping faintly across her nerves. Wendy paused and returned to that spot, her hands hovering on the outside of her body while inwardly every coherent thought was concentrated on that narrow slice of skin and sinew and bone.

Emma was right; it was Light, but Light like no other she'd ever felt before. It was Dark Light, cool to the touch, the texture silky but strong, the feel of it almost like brushing her fingers through Piotr's hair.

"You see?" Emma asked from forever away. "Can you feel it? Now rip it if you can. Tear. Pull."

Brushing her inner senses along the deftly woven strands of power, Wendy pried her fingers into the weave. It hurt and she dimly realized that she had to be causing some sort of damage to herself by trying to pull free on her own. Emma had made this dark stuff out of Wendy's own spirit, carving into her soul and weaving it back together again— yanking on her soul could only rip her apart piece by piece.

Then Jane had twisted the weave so tightly that there were hardly any holes left.

"Harder," Wendy whispered, digging her mental fingers in. "Ignore . . . it."

"You can do it," Emma was saying. "Keep trying!"

Wendy knew she was crying freely now, but she didn't care. This agony was like nothing she'd ever felt before; worse than the time she'd shattered her wrist, worse than when she'd been attacked by Specs and had her soul stripped whole from her body, worse than the vaguely remembered pain of the car accident that ushered her into this bizarre give-and-take existence with the dead in the first place.

"Hurts," she whispered, finally giving up. The binding hadn't budged, not really, and she felt the failure sticking in the back of her throat in a lump of disappointed tears and frustrated anger.

"Wendy? Wendy?" Emma's voice was growing smaller and smaller as the lights in Wendy's room stuttered and dimmed.

"Wendy?"

She coughed; it was the best reply she had.

Emma's voice was rapidly fading.

"Wendy . . .

I'm . . .

on . . .

my . . .

way . . ."

CHAPTER TWENTY

"There are birds everywhere still. We don't dare go to my place," Eddie said, laboriously straightening and scowling at the overcast sky. They'd taken sanctuary under the bridge of the Tot Lot playground, but raucous calls in the distance made it clear to all three of them that it was only a temporary shelter. "And we know heading back to Wendy's house is right out. So what do we do?"

Edgily looking around, Eddie patiently watched as Lily knelt beside Piotr. She brushed a hand across Piotr's knuckles and winced; her fingers passed through his flesh as if she were living and Piotr were only the faintest of Shades.

"What's up?" Eddie asked.

Lily held up her palm. "It is completely numb. I can feel nothing . . . Eddie, I am at a loss," she said, drawing back and shaking her wrist sharply to wake the deadened hand. "Perhaps we should have listened to Ada and traveled directly to Alcatraz. Stopped by and grabbed a couple of webs on the way."

"No use. Without her. No antidote without her. It was a trap," Piotr roused enough to say. "If it looks like a trap and tastes like a trap then it is a duck. In a trap." He chuckled weakly and shook his head, trying to hook fingers in the dappled diamonds of the swaying bridge. His fingers passed through. "Where is Wendy? I came here for Wendy."

"She's not here, man," Eddie said uneasily. "We don't want her here right now anyway, remember? The Reapers are coming. If they spotted us . . ."

"We could go to one of the Riders' haunts." Lily suggested. Frowning, she glanced at the road, hands restlessly sifting through the sand at her feet. "If we could catch a ride going north, Piotr's

Treehouse isn't far. We will be safe there for a time, until we can regroup and plan our next step."

Eddie stuck his hands on his hips, grimacing. "Treehouse? Right. Like, what, an actual treehouse? He lived up in a tree?" Eddie shook his head. "Good one."

"No." Lily smiled and shook her head. "It is just a nickname. No treetops. A warehouse and a steel mill. They are both abandoned. Near the canal."

"Okay, no trees. But how are we gonna get him to this mystical land of tetanus and safety? You can hardly touch him and I'm not entirely sure that if he *could* walk, he'd stay stable enough to ride the whole way in a car."

"A travois, perhaps?" Lily asked, glancing around the playground. "It may take some time to scavenge the material."

"You mean like a stretcher? Yeah, I guess so. But how would he . . ." Eddie drifted off. "Oh, wait a second! Hang on just one minute." Glancing furtively over his shoulder at the treetops, Eddie hopped to his feet and darted through the fence toward the closest house, returning a minute later with a multi-patterned quilt bundled in his hands. It was nearly solid in the Never, brighter than most of the surrounding wildlife. He beamed broadly.

"How did you—" Lily began.

"Wendy said the more emotion you pour into an object, the likelier it's gonna make a dupe in the Never, right? Well, that house right there belongs to the Perkins family," Eddie said, flopping the quilt into Lily's lap.

"You know them well?"

"Oh yeah. I babysat for them every Saturday night for almost a year. This, my dear lady Lily, is their wedding quilt. Or, rather, Mrs. Perkins *first* wedding quilt."

Lily rubbed the luxurious, rich quilt between her fingers. "What is the significance of this first wedding that the quilt would be so thick, so real?"

"She and my mom were great friends for a while there until her first husband, Mr. Horowitz, passed. He was a cop, you know? But his beat was up in Oakland and he ran afoul of some dealers. She lost it when they brought the news. I mean, seriously. Lost. It."

"She loved him a great deal."

He tapped the quilt with a sad, knowing smile. "Yep, you don't spend that kind of time with a family without knowing their treasured possessions. When Mrs. Horowitz became Mrs. Perkins, she packed the blanket away for her kids . . . but it was still hanging on the wall in the Never."

He pointed across the street. "Speaking of treasured possessions and knowing your neighbors far better than is entirely healthy, that family over there is a flock—a gaggle?—a bunch of hippie Rennies. I bet they've got a staff or two in their back shed."

"Rennie?"

"Renaissance Faire nuts. They do the circuit every year. Wanna go check?"

"Stay here," Lily said, eying the sky. "It is my turn to risk my skin."

Quickly darting across the street, she vanished through the fence into the backyard. She was gone far longer than Eddie thought was prudent. He was about to try and tuck Piotr beneath the low slide and go after her when Lily scrambled back through the fence hauling a large canvas-wrapped bundle in her arms.

"What did I tell you, huh? You found the staves?" Eddie asked.

"Better," Lily said, a twinkle in her eye, as she unrolled the canvas, exposing a network of deftly braided cables and what looked like thin, flexible sticks. She picked up two and began screwing the ends together. "Camping gear."

An hour later, Eddie was still marveling at Lily's ingenuity. The crude travois he'd been envisioning had become a lightweight circle of durable flex-frame lashed with the thin twine. Piotr rested easily on the quilt; he was faint to look at, but the quilt was so dense that it held his weight easily and even seemed to lend him a little bit of substance. They waited until sunset to move and then scurried quickly toward Castro Street, hauling Piotr behind. Eddie had thought briefly of swinging by Wendy's to change the note and let her know where they'd be, but figured that it was too risky. They'd have to figure out a way to meet up later.

"I don't understand what you're trying to do," Eddie said, panting as Lily stopped only momentarily at a streetlight to allow him to rest.

"We head north," she replied simply. "Here. Hurry. The Caltrain comes." She grabbed her edge of the stretcher and began speeding toward the tracks, Eddie grabbing up the foot of the travois and hurrying after. They barely made it.

Eddie was glad to see that the Caltrain was nearly empty of passengers, but Lily had them squatting with Piotr amid the bicycles for safety anyway. They stayed there all the way to the airport, where Lily made them dismount and hitch a ride on the back of a catering van puttering up the 101.

"You're disturbingly good at this," Eddie said as they hopped off near the San Bruno canal. "Do all Riders ride around like this?"

"It used to be easier," she said absently, eying the moon rising above the treetops. It was winter, the sun had set early, and it couldn't be any sooner than seven, Eddie realized, amazed that so much had happened in a day. It seemed like years ago that Wendy had fetched him from Nana Moses and Emma, not a hair more than half a day.

"What?" Eddie joked. "Did you all used to ride horses or something?"

"Yes, actually," she said. "It is how we got our name. This way."

Guiding them in the rising moonlight, Lily skirted the edge of the canal, leading Eddie unerringly through the least debris-strewn path of rubble. Still, despite her caution, Piotr was jostled fiercely along the way. Moaning, his head rocked from side to side, and he muttered in his delirium, alternately crying out for Wendy and cursing extensively in what Eddie could only assume was Russian, though it sounded different from his normal tone, more guttural and strange.

"Is this place close?" Eddie asked when they paused to rest, his voice pitched low and worried. "Because I don't think he's gonna make it much further. Look at him. Even hugging that quilt like it's his last friend, he's barely a shadow." He frowned and examined his hand. Eddie was pale nearly to his shoulder now. "Though, to be honest, I'm not much better off."

"We will be there soon," Lily assured him, rising fluidly and doubling their pace. "Do not concern yourself overmuch on Piotr's behalf; he is strong, he will abide."

Much to Eddie's chagrin, Lily had been telling the truth. Piotr's "treehouse" turned out to be an abandoned steel mill in the nexus of crumbling office parks.

Keeping an eye out for Walkers, Lily led Eddie inside. Eddie realized that Piotr and his Lost had squatted amid the squalor on the cleanest level available, the thirteenth floor. He wasn't a particularly superstitious person, but the idea of a bunch of dead guys picking the thirteenth floor to hang out on amused him. It was like Piotr had no sense of irony whatsoever. What did Wendy *see* in this guy anyway?

Still, thirteenth floor or not, Piotr in his prime must be tough as nails; huge sections of the stairs were broken away and had to be traversed carefully. Eddie struggled to do his part in carrying Piotr over the holes. He couldn't imagine having to carry kids over the gaps by himself as Piotr must have done time and time again. Undaunted, Lily urged them on, though she was the one to carefully gauge the distance and crab-crawl over the smaller gaps or leap the larger ones. Once across, Lily waited for Eddie to pass the handles of the stretcher across the divide as, together, they hefted Piotr further up and up again until every muscle in Eddie's body blazed.

"I'm practically dead," he panted as they rested on a creaky, rotting landing. "This shouldn't hurt this much. Man, I am out of shape!"

"This task would be arduous even for a brave; carrying the kill back to the huts was often aided by horses or other hunters, rarely a hunter alone or in pairs, " Lily said. "Do not fret; I have run you harder than I would have at any other time. You have done well, Eddie. You should hold your head with pride."

"Really?" Eddie flushed. "Geeze, Lily, uh, thanks."

Lily paused and then, suddenly, held out her hand. "Give me your palm."

Eddie blinked in surprise. "What?"

"I . . . I wish to help you. You have been a great boon to me, to Piotr. It is the least I can do. Give me your hand."

"I don't understand. Help me? Like how?"

Lily scowled and, leaning forward, snatched up Eddie's hand, cradling it between her palms. "Like this."

When Lily poured her essence into Eddie it was the purest form of giving—something like what she'd done for Piotr but . . . different. Piotr had begun gulping her essence at the end, taking what Lily had been willing to give in great yanking, starving jerks. Whereas Eddie, either too young a soul to know what to do or too confused to take advantage of the situation, simply held very still as Lily pressed his palm between hers and poured herself into him. Through their connection Lily could feel him—thin and rapidly weakening and tired and scared—and Lily marveled at what a generous, sweet soul Eddie was deep down inside.

He hid, she realized, behind his sarcasm, behind his flippancy, because words were a wall and Eddie was a master at turning words to his advantage. Lily inhaled deeply, opened her hands wider, and felt him tense beneath her grip, straining against her and caught in the waves of her essence, lifted up and gently twisting beneath her hands, yearning in her touch. Moved, Lily leaned forward and tugged Eddie closer. Moving under her guidance, Eddie drifted closer, until they were nose to nose, palms clasped close, and Lily could breathe in the spicy scent of him, feel the hidden, wiry wrestler strength beneath his jacket, could taste the heart of who he was as she poured her soul into his.

"I . . . I . . ." Eddie whispered and Lily opened her eyes staring directly into his. His pupils were huge; Eddie's lashes swept down when he recognized Lily's regard. He swallowed deeply. "I . . . I don't know what to . . ."

"You love her," Lily replied serenely. "More than anyone else. I know. I can taste it."

"I do," he admitted as if it were a shameful thing. And then, as if gasping for air, like a shadow yearning toward the light that would destroy it, "She's . . . she's *Wendy*."

Lily nodded. "She is."

Lily kissed him.

Eddie tasted of strawberries and honey and clover—simple, sweet, uncomplex. He smelled of cinnamon and smoke, of leather, and his hair beneath her fingers was crisp but soft. Lily poured herself through her palms, cupping the back of Eddie's neck and enjoying the sensation of him trembling beneath her fingertips. He was young, not terribly inexperienced, but his kiss was all sweetness and light, tenderness and gentle, delicate touch. He sent a sliver of a shiver down Lily's spine; Eddie wasn't her wonderful, passionately fierce James, but he wasn't new to the press of a lady's lips either.

In the end, when Lily felt that she'd reached a good stopping point either moments or millennia later, they both shuddered and Lily drew back, her hair falling across her cheeks, her eyes downcast as she assessed her rapidly thrumming heart, the tingle in her palms, and the pleasant ghost of pressure against her lips. "How do you feel?"

"Better," Eddie sighed and held up a nearly solid hand. "Much, much better."

"Good," Lily said, smoothing her hair and straightening. "This is right." She turned to gather up her side of the travois.

"Wait," Eddie whispered desperately, "aren't we . . . aren't we going to talk about . . . what just happened there?"

He was such a sweet boy, Lily thought. James would have approved of him immensely.

"No," she said and cupped his cheek. "Accept the gift I gave you, Eddie, and speak of it no more. We have much work to do and time is wasting." Then, glad he was not the type to press, Lily knelt down and gathered up her end of the travois. She could feel that she was much weaker than she was previously, but she considered her temporary weakness worth it to help both Piotr and Eddie. James, she knew, would have been proud of her sacrifice.

"Let us continue our journey."

Lost in thought over what had just transpired, Eddie was unsure how much longer it took to get where they were going, but when they reached Piotr's floor, he knew it.

Perhaps it was the sense that, not too long before, someone had lived and loved in this space. The walls of the offices were papered with immature but effective drawings and sketches of the landscape glimpsed through shattered windows, peppered occasionally with pictures of Piotr, a towheaded toddler, or a gangly boy with glasses. Or perhaps it was just the fact that this floor was debris-free and what few day-to-day items could be seen were well-organized, stacked neatly against walls and covered with threadbare comforters or tattered tarps.

Touched and vaguely creeped out at these remnants of a family as threadbare as the scavenged supplies, Eddie brushed a finger against a yellowing page, old enough to have curled up at the bottom corners. Piotr, smiling, knelt on one knee with a jumble of fabric grasped loosely in one hand, a dagger pressed between the floor and his other palm.

"Piotr's pallet," Lily said suddenly from behind Eddie. Eddie jumped, painfully aware of Lily's presence as she brushed by him. "Bring Piotr here."

Beneath one of the few windows that still boasted intact glass, Piotr's pallet was larger than the others, the sleeping bag rolled and secured with rope at the foot of the stained mattress. There was no pillow but Lily gathered several from another corner, stacked haphazardly beside a tumbled pile of paperbacks and a cracked camping lantern.

"How do we—"

Without a word, Lily took the poles at the end of the travois, lifting Piotr up abruptly. Eddie scrambled to grab the head of the stretcher as together they lifted Piotr over his pallet and then, under Lily's silent guidance, tipped him gently on his side onto the mattress. He slumped onto his back, one arm flung over the edge of the bed.

"Nice," Eddie said approvingly. He followed Lily away from the corner, glancing back once at Piotr and wondering what they were going to do now. The gulls might still find them here, but at least no one else could be caught in the crossfire if it came down to a fight. Wendy would worry, though. Eddie wished he'd taken the time to leave her a note. Wendy was smart, he told himself, trying to reason away his concern. She would figure it out.

Making sure Lily's attention was elsewhere, Eddie wrapped his own hand in the edge of his shirt and cautiously held up Piotr's hand to the light, eying the blurriness at the edges of his fingers. The smear of Piotr's flesh was more pronounced than it had been before Lily had run him so hard to get them there.

Dropping Piotr's hand, Eddie took a deep, calming breath. He was glad of what Lily had done for him, confusing as it was, but he was beginning to feel a little nauseous. Between he and Piotr, Eddie didn't think Lily would have it in her to help him or Piotr again. Eddie shook his head and tried to ignore the worry gnawing at his own gut.

It didn't matter. Lily would be fine because Wendy would get to the bottom of it and that would be that. They'd both be completely healthy and happy in a matter of days. Wendy would figure it out. She always did.

She had to.

CHAPTER TWENTY-ONE

S ome time later, Piotr roused. He felt marginally better, though the ceiling still appeared to be made of filthy water, waving and drifting in slow arcs. The malevolent faces and wild women were nowhere to be seen.

Groaning, he sat up. This wasn't Wendy's room; her ceiling was speckled with green glow-in-the-dark stars. This ceiling was . . . Oh . . . he'd sat up too fast!

Piotr flopped back onto the bed. His head was spinning, his stomach churned, but at least he'd figured out where he was.

"Oh Specs," he murmured. "Dora, Tubs. *Zhal. Zhal, zhal, zhal.*"

He could remember the tang of fear in the back of his throat, the remorse at having to leave their nest and venture out into the city. Elle had taken his Lost into the safety of her haunt as Piotr had known she would, but it had pained him to leave them with her nonetheless. He'd sworn to protect them, even if he couldn't even recall how he'd met them. He'd been their Rider, they'd been his Lost. They'd been family.

And now they were gone.

"I should have just taken you," he whispered, resting his forearm across his eyes. "We should have just left. Gone to Santa Cruz, there are hardly any spirits there. Or headed east, perhaps. But instead . . ." he broke off and trembled. Instead Specs had been sent into the Light by Wendy, Dora had been obliterated in the battle with the White Lady, and Tubs was long gone, taken to safety by the remaining Riders along with all the Lost who hadn't been kidnapped in the last White Lady raid.

But . . . if they'd left when the Walkers had begun sniffing

around, if they'd left as a group rather than Piotr leaving them with
Elle while he planned to scout out a new haven for them, then he
never would have met Wendy.

Bitterly, Piotr laughed. "I should have left."

He loved Wendy. With all his heart, he knew they were connected. She was like no woman he'd ever met before—dead or
alive—and the fact that she'd seen something special in him was
mind-boggling. Yet, despite that, Piotr knew that they weren't any
good for one another.

Wendy had given up so much for him: school, friends, even her
job as a Reaper, as the Lightbringer. She'd nearly abandoned her
search for her mother's spirit once they'd met. Piotr had been just as
bad. He was supposed to have been hot on the trail of whomever had
been taking the Lost, but instead he'd spent all his spare time in
Wendy's room, talking about what it was to be the Lightbringer,
trying to dimly recall what it was like to be alive.

Her touch had been fire and ice, though. Her lips had been
sweet. Piotr had tempted fate every single time they touched; he
could have drained her dry and Wendy, lost in his arms, might have
let him. Likewise, when they were together her hold over her powers
was much weaker; she could have lost control at any moment and
blasted him into the Light without even realizing it.

Leaving her in that hospital room, alone and thin and freshly
roused from her coma, had been one of the hardest things Piotr could
remember doing. If he'd been smart he should have left town then. Yes,
Lily and Elle wanted time, a few days, a few weeks, to tie things up, to
scavenge and scrounge and prepare for their trip, but he could have
gone without them, waited for them in some appropriate place. Route
66 might have been nice; the Grand Canyon might have been better.

Now, facing his illness, feeling the cold pouring off him, icing
his pallet to the floor below, Piotr was finally willing to be honest
with himself. He'd stayed behind for Wendy.

It would have been madness for her to accompany him on his trek.

He had no idea of where to even begin, much less of a plan or a manner of travel or any logical, sane, reasonable way to discover his roots.

Despite that, however, he'd foolishly asked her to go with him. She would have been fresh from the hospital, and she would have had to find her own food and lodging, a safe place to rest her head at night, a way to travel in the living world that didn't involve risking herself by thumbing her way down the interstate. She would have been alone. Her mother had just died; she would have had to abandon her family in their time of need. She would have been insane to agree.

And yet . . .

And yet . . .

Piotr had hidden his disappointment at her decision well. It had only made sense, after all, to turn his wild goose chase down. But he'd lingered. He'd stayed. In the weeks following their separation he'd wandered near Mountain View in the hopes that he'd bump into her on patrol, that perhaps she might even seek him out, that she might have changed her mind.

He was a fool.

Exhausted, Piotr closed his eyes, meaning just to rest them a brief moment. He knew he slept, just not how long. When he opened them, Wendy sat by his side, her legs crossed primly and ankles dangling over the edge of the mattress.

"What is this?" Piotr asked, disbelieving the proof of his own eyes. He reached out to touch her, graze her elbow with his fingertips, and Wendy proved to be solid, firm, there. "Wendy?"

"Shhh," Wendy said, pressing a finger to his lips. "The others—even Eddie—they don't know I'm here yet. It took me forever to track you down and I wanted to see you first. How are you feeling?"

"Ill," he admitted. "So very, very cold. But . . . better. Now that you are here, much, much better."

"Flatterer," Wendy said, smirking. Then her smile faded. "Ada is really gone?"

"*Da*," Piotr said. "The gulls, the Lady Walker, took her. We do not know where."

Frowning, Wendy threaded her fingers through his. Her touch was warm, reassuring. Unlike Lily or Eddie, Wendy was unbothered by his chill. Perhaps the heat of the Lightbringer offset it, or perhaps she could feel it but simply wasn't showing the discomfort. "She wanted to go to Alcatraz. That's as good a place as any to start."

"Ada . . . your mother . . . she did these things for you."

"I know." Wendy brushed hair off her face and smiled wryly. "Mom sure knew how to get around, huh? It seems like there wasn't a ghost in this town she didn't have some sort of backroom deal with."

"She was certainly persuasive," Piotr agreed. Then, smiling wickedly, he added, "But not nearly as lovely as you."

"Oh really?" Wendy poked him in the side. "Remembering what my mom was like before she became the White Lady, huh? You finally starting to get your memories back?"

Piotr grabbed her poking hand and caressed the back of her knuckles until Wendy's fist relaxed. He pressed her palm to his cheek. "I do not know. What do you think?"

"I think you're a mystery even to yourself, Piotr," Wendy replied seriously, brushing the pad of her thumb against his cheekbone. "She took your memories. They all did, even me, though I didn't know I was doing it at the time. Over and over and over again. Don't you ever wonder how? Or why? There has to be some beginning, right? You haven't been like this . . . forever. Right?"

"I . . ."

Piotr closed his eyes. Dreams and dreams and dreams again. Snow. Ice. He was so cold, so sick, so cold. What had those Walkers done to him? What was this terrible poison, to bring such horrible, icy visions dancing between the spaces of worlds?

"I do not know," he admitted. "Even now, I do not know."

"That's okay." Lying beside him, resting her head in the crook of his shoulder, Wendy pressed her palm against his chest. "It's okay to not know."

"Can you feel a heartbeat?" Piotr asked her, curious.

"No," she whispered, craning her neck and pressing a soft, sweet kiss beneath his jaw. Her breath tickled the fine hairs at the nape of his neck. "You're dead, Piotr. Rotting in the ground. Remember?"

Twisting in her arms, Piotr yanked Wendy close and kissed her. No, if he were honest with himself, he did more than just kiss her. He punished her. For her smartass quip, for her refusal to go with him when he'd asked, for kissing Eddie, and for being better than someone long dead—someone like him—deserved. It was the moment she revealed herself to be the Lightbringer all over again; Piotr hated her and loved her and loathed himself all over again for not being able to walk away.

He was brutal and fierce and not gentle in the slightest. He pulled her hair back at the nape, he ground his lips against hers, his fingers curved cruelly into her hip as if he would bruise and punish and hate her for all the darkness in the world, in the Never. As if it were all her fault.

Wendy, after a brief moment of shocked stillness, growled in the back of her throat and then, unexpectedly, gave as good as she got. He felt her nails rake his back red and raw beneath his shirt. There was a billow of steam where her nails cut and her heat and his chill mingled. Her knee jammed between his legs, pressing painfully into his thigh, her thumbnail gouging the hollow beneath his ear as her teeth tore at his lips, her tongue forcing between them. He could taste her hate, so like his own, and knew that as he punished her, she punished him—for not being alive, for not saving her mother, for walking away without a glance back. She loved him and hated him and loathed herself just as much, if not more, and Piotr helplessly felt his skin begin to blister under her palms.

Piotr couldn't breathe beneath her onslaught. Gasping, he pulled back and was both relieved and disappointed when she let him go.

They were both left damp and shaking from the steam. Wendy took his jaw in one hand and twisted gently until she could see the extent of the damage along his neck. She brushed the pad of her thumb along a stinging ridge. "I was mean to you."

"We were mean to each other."

"I should've been a little nicer, huh?"

"I started it." Back stinging with each tiny movement, Piotr relaxed against the mattress, closed his eyes, and luxuriated in the counterpoint warmth of her, the oranges and smoke perfume that clung to her hair and cinnamon-mint that scented her breath.

"Did you?" Wendy curled into his side again and rested her hand on his chest. "I lied. I can feel your heartbeat."

Smiling, eyes closed, Piotr pressed his palm against her chest, waiting for the comforting thump. "*Da?* Well, I can . . . can . . ." Piotr drew his hand away and sat up.

Wendy was gone.

Frantically, Piotr's head whipped left and right, desperately searching the room. Had she hidden in a corner? Had he fallen asleep again and she'd gone to find a private spot to take care of living nature's business?

His bed was still rimed with frost. Piotr ran a hand under his jaw; there were no scratches. The flesh on his back, on his face, didn't protest even slightly when he shifted. His blisters were no longer there.

A dream, Piotr realized. Wendy's visit had been nothing but a wonderful, terrible, agonizing dream.

"Such a fool," he whispered, contrite and aggravated with himself. "I am such a stupid fool."

"Piotr?" Lily peered around the doorjamb, black hair dappled grey and silver in the remains of the dim light. "We heard you call out. How do you fare?"

"Tired," he said. "I had a dream." He glanced around the room. "*Spasibo*, for watching over me, and for bringing me here. It was a wise choice. We shall be . . . should be . . . safe here. Momentarily, at least."

Lily tilted her head in silent acknowledgement. "Do you wish to continue resting?"

Though he knew now that the kiss was all in his mind, Piotr wanted to see Wendy again, even if it were nothing more than his own fevered imagination. "For a while," he said and curled on his side as Lily retreated.

Freed to dream, Piotr slumbered, drifting easily into sweet dreams and sour, tasting Wendy on his lips, feeling her fingers curl through the nape of his hair, the tips of her nails experimentally brushing against the twisting scar from temple to jaw. Piotr shivered under the onslaught, willing himself to hold perfectly still. If he roused she would be gone again. He would be alone.

Time passed, possibly minutes, probably more, before Piotr woke again from his dreams.

He'd dreamed of ice floes, of snow banks, of pressing on through drifts as high as his hips, leaving his heat in a red trail behind. He'd dreamed of the Reaper again and he hurried. He hurried. He hurried and when he woke Piotr knew that . . .

. . . knew that . . .

Knew that this place had once been his. The bare soles of his feet recognized every board, every creak, each thin space in the Never so that he could pass unseen through walls and find those others huddled below.

He felt alert now, rested, but as he stood, Piotr left ice in his wake, not just in the Never, but on the mill floor in the living lands, small pools of ice in spreading circles each place his bare feet touched.

He hunted in complete, effortless silence.

Kneeling in Pandora's room at the end of her pallet, Lily struggled to keep her eyes on Eddie as he spoke. He ought to have her full attention, she knew, but resting here brought back uncomfortable memories of not just Piotr's young charges, but her own Lost as well. Her heart ached at the emptiness of the room, the walls papered with Dora's sketches and the warped door resting on cinderblocks as a makeshift desk, bare save for a few curls of colored pencil and faded paint splatters.

"I still think Piotr needs a doctor," Eddie urged. He gripped the back of the folding chair Dora had left tucked beneath the desk until his knuckles turned white. "You can't tell me that *every* dead doctor goes right into the Light." Behind him Dora's pictures flapped on the walls, caught in a suddenly chill breeze. Shivering, Lily rubbed her arms and considered shaping the essence she'd draped into a simple shift into a longer-sleeved garment, one that would protect her from the clammy air of the Treehouse.

"Of course not," Lily replied, rubbing her forehead. Eddie clearly meant well, but he was missing the point entirely. Piotr's issue wasn't just his sickness. Lily took a deep breath and began trying to explain. "But there is more to it than just his physical—"

"Trying to get rid of me?" Piotr demanded, appearing suddenly through the wall.

Despite herself, Lily flinched back; Piotr's tone was icy, sharp, and high. She'd known Piotr hundreds of years at this point, and he'd never spoken like that before . . . unless you counted the crazed minutes after he'd found Eddie and Wendy kissing.

Casually, Lily moved to place herself between Piotr and Eddie.

"I knew you would one day," Piotr snarled, striding closer. Like Eddie had once been, Piotr's edges were now flickering like a dim light, only he seemed to be growing thinner and less substantial before their very eyes. "It was just a matter of time. *YA nikogda ne doveryal tebe.*"

"What?" Eddie glanced at Lily, confused.

He was flush, Lily realized, either with anger or dismay; despite their kiss she still didn't know him well enough to tell. This was terrible—the last thing she needed was all her good work with Eddie undone by Piotr's temper as her gift of energy and will was sapped away by whatever was draining Eddie slowly dry.

"What are you talking about, man?" Eddie asked nervously. "We're trying to *help* you."

Piotr," Lily said, calmingly, disregarding Eddie's paleness in favor of calming Piotr. Once Piotr was relaxed Eddie would calm as well. She hoped. "You are fading in and out. Please, Piotr, please sit. Rest."

Piotr, apparently, was having none of it. He pounded the doorway with the side of his fist and glared at Lily. "You won't trick me this time," he snapped. "Where is she? What have you done with her?"

"Who, Piotr?" Lily asked, patience personified, though she felt that the situation was rapidly spiraling out of her control. "Who are you seeking?" "

"I . . . I . . ." Piotr hesitated, an expression of momentary confusion darting across his face before he clenched his fists and glared at the ground.

"Are you looking for Wendy?" Eddie asked cautiously.

"No. Yes. *YA ne znayu!* I do not know!" Moving in a jagged jerk, Piotr ripped one of Dora's sketches off the wall—a picture of the tree outside in full, glorious summer bloom—and crumpled it, throwing it at Eddie's head.

"Man, chill out!" Eddie shouted. "Just . . . relax, okay?"

"I've waited for her for so long," Piotr said coldly to Eddie. Lily frowned; the cadence of Piotr's speech was changing, his body language was shifting. He had come in raging and now he was moving, rocking, from side to side, as if singing a slow song with his words. "So long. Centuries and centuries and centuries again. You can't take her from me, *hooyesos*, with your sweet words and kind eyes, your friendship of years masking your intentions. I have waited for her decades beyond your years! I have the greater need! I won't allow it!"

"Why do I get the impression that what he just said was extremely mean?" Eddie whispered to Lily as she eased further in front of him, pushing him back into the shadows behind her with a nudge of her hip and shoulder. Piotr was radiating a kind of sinuous seriousness that worried her.

"Piotr, do you remember something from before?" Lily held out one hand, palm up, fingers slightly curled and gestured to the room slowly. "Do you remember your life now?"

"Of course I remember," Piotr said, snapping out of his back and forth daze and glaring at Lily. "A fool, you think I am. No more! I always remember!"

"Not always," she reminded him softly, not wishing to shame her friend in front of his rival for the Lightbringer's affections. "Sometimes you forget."

"I am not confused!" Piotr shouted, pounding the wall again, this time with both fists. "I am not a child to be coddled!"

"No," Lily quickly soothed, wishing briefly that he *were* a child. That she could just reach out and pull Piotr into her arms as she might one of her Lost, that she could rock him in her lap until the memories surfaced or whatever terrible fears he harbored subsided. Piotr, however, had the right of it: he was not a child, not a Lost. He was her equal and Lily knew that he needed her guidance, not to hide in her embrace. "No one thinks you are. Please. Please, Piotr, please. You are angry once more. There is no reason to be. We are your friends. We are your allies. Talk to me, Piotr. Tell me what you know."

"The hearthstone," Piotr said, his sneer sending chills up Lily's spine and raising the fine hairs on the nape of her neck. "Where she kept her cloak of fur and feathers. The feasting hall, the great fire in the center, stone rough-scorched and charred black at the edges. We huddled close, together, waiting for the others, and she told me stories of battle and blood, of how she rode and rode for days on end until her hunt was done, until the soul was gathered. All these things, these important things, I remember. I remember her."

"Has he gone nuts?" Eddie whispered in a *sotto* voice, rolling his index finger in a 'cuckoo' gesture around his ear. "I thought he had some kind of Wendy's-Mom-induced-amnesia? That not the case anymore?"

"Hush your mouth," Lily hissed quietly, wishing that it were Elle at her side for this and not this jester dressed in silver and grey. "Tripping over these words does us only ill." She stepped toward Piotr and gingerly reached for his hand. "Please, Piotr, go on."

Piotr, seeing her intent, yanked away.

"Why do you care? You are a warrior, one of the fierce women! See? Even now, even in death, you walk in the halls of the dead." He spat at her feet but Lily paid it no mind. There was such fury pouring off him that she was obliquely grateful she wasn't actually the real target of his rage.

"I wish to know because I am your friend," she said softly. "You have to know that. In the light of day perhaps you will not know your words, perhaps they will be lost again to the halls of memory but I, Piotr, I will recall them." Lily pressed her palm to her heart. "Allow me to remember for you."

"In my dreams I walked," Piotr said shortly, turning away and resting his forearm against the shattered window. Where his flesh touched a thin film of ice spread and crackled along the slivers and jagged triangles of remaining glass. The wood of the frame constricted as he grew close, pulling nails out of the tough, old window casing with a low screech. Beneath his palm the glass, brought to its breaking point by the incredible cold, shattered, both in the Never and in the living lands.

Eddie and Lily exchanged a glance as the tinkling shards fell. Lily was glad to note that Piotr did not seem to notice their shared concern. It might set him off once more. "I walked until I could walk no more and then, at the narrow V of the river where I tickled for summer fish when I was a boy, there I huddled in that damned cloak, that cloak of blood and feathers and fur, and I slept the cold sleep. The long sleep."

"Is he trying to say what I think he's saying?" Eddie whispered. "Because I wasn't the best with poetry, but it sounds like he's talking about when he died."

"Shhh," Lily hushed him, though he had a point. "Listen. Remember."

"There, slipping into my dreams, in the snow and wet, I knew her. I saw. Over a thousand years and a thousand years again, I've waited and dreamed, because . . . because I knew. I knew then. I know now." His voice echoed hollowly and Lily shivered again. She could almost see the years, sense them, stretching out around Piotr in a nimbus of confusion, hidden from his view but nearly tangible, lost in the annals of his mind.

"He's not making any sense," Eddie hissed through clenched teeth. "It's kinda hard to remember dithering nonsense."

Glaring at Eddie, Piotr snorted, and Lily fought the urge to grab him by the shoulders, to shake sense into his stubborn, combative head. No lover, even the Lightbringer, was worth this sort of ridiculous drama!

"I make no sense?" Piotr drawled at Eddie, gesturing rudely. "Fine. Make sense of this, *boy*. I dreamed of her hair against the snow, red like my blood dripping between my thumb and forefinger, like the hair of my mother and her shield-sisters. I dreamed of her markings, her badges of rank pricked into her very skin and soul."

He turned to face Lily and she was struck by how solid he was compared to a few moments before; denser than she'd ever seen a ghost become, dense as the Lightbringer in the midst of reaping; Piotr could have been alive.

"I dreamed of Wendy two thousand years ago," Piotr said shortly, wiping the back of his hand across his mouth. "I have been waiting for her since the day I died. And neither of you will take her from me. Not you, boy, not you, Lily, friend or foe."

"Piotr—"

"You say friend, but I say that you are playing me false. You,

Elle, warrior-women, are shield-sisters. You are one of them." Piotr
turned away from her and Lily felt her gut clench. He didn't mean
it, she reminded herself. It was the poison, the sickness talking,
nothing more.

"You are like all the rest," Piotr declared. "You wish to watch
me fail."

"One of the fierce women," Lily said, finally putting two and
two together. She felt a fool for not scenting the connections, tasting
the venom dripping from each word, sooner. "Did these women kill
you, Piotr?"

Piotr smiled grimly at Lily as snowflakes began fluttering down
from the ceiling. Lily felt them nestle in her hair, their cold kiss
upon her cheeks, and she suppressed a shiver.

"*Net*," Piotr said. "My *dyadya* did that. My uncle was the death
of me."

CHAPTER TWENTY-TWO

Groggy, Wendy opened her eyes. The sky was bright and blue above her, skimmed only lightly with clouds, and the air was dense and still. She was lying oddly, Wendy realized, with her legs stretched upward at an uncomfortable angle, ankles crossed and hands folded neatly over her ribcage. It took a moment for Wendy to realize that she was resting across the slick red backseat of an old Chevy Bel Air, head pillowed by a leather jacket.

Wendy shifted and the world around her shimmered and shivered in the strange grey light of the Never.

Wait, the Never? Wendy squinted and the Never receded, but only with some real effort. Wherever she was, the world of the dead was strong here. Even the massive trees at the edge of her vision flickered back and forth between the living lands and the Never, green and lush one moment, silvery-grey and twisted the next.

Turning toward the trunk, Wendy poked her head over the backseat and squinted at the world past the edges of the convertible. The convertible was parked diagonally in the middle of a vast drive-in parking lot, one Wendy recognized.

"The West Winds?" Wendy murmured uneasily, tasting the ghost of Red Vines and cream soda on her tongue. "How the hell did I get here?"

When she was young her mother rarely took nights off, but on the few memorable occasions that she did, the whole family would empty the Safeway candy bins, pile in the Charger, and drive down to San Jose to catch a movie. Wendy clearly remembered being small and young and crawling in the front seat to bury her head against Mary's shoulder while Dumbo's mother wreaked havoc in the circus.

Her mother had wiped away her tears and offered to cut the Disney special double feature short, to take sobbing Wendy home. Her dad had protested that it was an honor to see the classic flicks on the big screen, the way they'd been intended, but Mary had held firm—whatever Wendy wanted.

Knowing that Jon and Chel would be sad to leave, that her father was right about it being a once-in-a-lifetime event, Wendy had chosen to stay . . . and wept again when Bambi's mother died an hour later.

To this day she still hated Disney movies.

"We brought you." A greaser roughly her own age, perhaps a few years older, vaulted into the front seat from beside the car. Wendy jumped in surprise.

In the Never the screen looming behind the boy suddenly flickered. The radio of the convertible hissed loudly and static thrummed for a brief instant before a countdown began on the screen behind his head. The radio beeped with each number.

"Hang on a sec, radio's up too loud," he said, reaching back and twisting the knob so the beeps were barely heard. Just in time: the vast screen filled with dancing concession foods as *"Let's go out to the lobby!"* started playing. A long hot dog cha-cha danced with a melting Hershey's bar. A slack-eyed Coke cup tipped its lid, and as the frothing liquid filled it to the brim, it drummed its feet and grinned hugely.

There was something about the way it writhed and twisted on the ground that filled Wendy with unease. Discomforted watching the short clip, Wendy grimaced and turned her attention back to the boy.

"Popcorn?" he offered, holding up a large bucket that spilled kernels over the backseat as he tilted it her way.

Wendy wasn't hungry at all, but she got the sense he might be upset if she refused. Careful of her side, Wendy edged forward, taking the opportunity of reaching for a handful of popcorn to study the boy.

Up close he was kind of cute, in a rebel-without-a-cause sort of way. His black hair was slicked back at the top and sides but too long at the back, curling slightly at his nape. His tight tee shirt was torn at the collar and tucked into well-worn skintight jeans, the bulge of either a comb or a knife pressed against his hip. A pair of huge black glasses sat on the seat beside him, pressed against his knee, and while Wendy half-expected to see a pack of smokes rolled into his collar or one tucked behind his ear, he smelled clean. Almost like Piotr, to be honest, like evergreen and the crisp scent of autumn wind.

"Got your fill?" he asked saucily, leaning back against the door as Wendy took her handful of popcorn and leaned back. Tentatively she flicked a kernel in her mouth and was pleasantly surprised at the home-popped butter-salt taste. The before-the-movie short cut out behind him. Suddenly *The Lion King* was playing on the screen.

"This'll tide me over, yeah," Wendy said nervously, trying not to watch the movie flickering behind him. The reel had skipped the beginning of the film; she recognized the skittering, jumping rocks and the dismayed, scared look dawning on Simba's face. This was Mufasa's death scene. "Thanks."

"I meant of looking me over," the greaser said, smirking. He glanced over his shoulder at the screen and shook his head as the stampede began pouring over the ridge. "Though I suppose for a skinny baby like you, a little popcorn might fill you up. When was the last time you had a real meal, Red?"

Something about his smile struck Wendy as odd. He was stalling, she realized. "Why am I here? Who are you? What happened? I was in my . . ." She drifted off. "I'm dreaming. I have to be, because I feel fine."

"Already with the 'what's the tale, nightingale.' I bet you're head of the class with all those questions," he replied lightly, lifting a hand when Wendy began to protest. "Now, now, let a guy have a second to breathe, Red. So to speak, I mean. Cool it. I've got answers, I promise, I just gotta order 'em up right, you dig?"

Simba was weeping, curling into his father's side. Wendy turned her head aside, but not before noting that the scene had flickered and changed again. She'd only seen *Hunchback of Notre Dame* in snips and snatches while staying at friends' houses, but she recognized Quasimodo right away.

"Do I want to know why they're pelting him with rocks?" she asked, wincing.

"I dunno, doll," the greaser said, chewing his lip and tapping his fingers rapidly against the steering wheel. "You tell me. And while you're at it, have another bite."

Irritated with his levity, Wendy tossed another piece of popcorn in her mouth—this one was a widow, mostly kernel, hardly any fluffy whiteness to it—and crunched. The sound echoed around the West Winds strangely, like a gunshot, and a flock of birds took to the sky, cawing raucously. One bird broke from the mass and drifted down, flapping lazily, until it landed on the windshield and gripped the edge with large, curved talons.

It was one of the largest ravens Wendy had ever laid eyes on.

"You're a big guy," the greaser told the raven and it cawed, tilting its head left and right and puffing its tail feathers majestically. Ignoring the passengers of the convertible, the raven began grooming itself, sliding its long, pointy beak deep into the fluff and pulling hard.

Engrossed in watching the bird clean itself, Wendy almost missed the door. It was only when the raven yanked free a tail feather and let it flutter to the hood that she spotted the faintly glowing seashells rimming the hood of the car.

Seashells?

"Damn it, not a dream, another frickin' dreamscape," Wendy realized, dropping the popcorn. Half of it spilled across the floorboards, and then, as in past dreams, the dropped kernels became lovely white and yellow spotted butterflies that fluttered and danced around her head. Mollified, Wendy cupped a butterfly in her palm and felt an immense weight lift off her.

"That's how you got me here. I'm not even awake. You're in my dream."

The greaser didn't answer, but the tenseness left him and he seemed to almost sag in relief. He reached for his glasses and put them on; they made his face seem more open and vulnerable, younger than before. She realized that he couldn't be more than twenty and Wendy again wondered if Piotr had ever met this guy, if he'd been a Rider.

"Bye-bye Disney," Wendy said and pointed her index finger at the screen. "Pow," she whispered, and the bruised and bloody Quasimodo shook his fetters off, stood, and walked off screen. The screen went black for a moment and then the "let's go out to the lobby" reel began again.

"Much, much better," Wendy told the raven. "Don't you agree?"

The raven cawed and hopped from the windshield to the top of the front seat and from there to the backseat beside Wendy. It pawed at the upholstery, clawing into the crevices deeply and twisting its head up, staring at Wendy with unblinking shiny black eyes. The echoes were so strange here; in every caw she could make out the thick swell of the ocean in the distance, the screams of angry gulls and, even more faintly, a sound like the White Lady laughing and laughing and laughing.

Ill from the sound, Wendy inadvertently knocked the remaining popcorn over onto the backseat and turned toward the trees. Movement there, furtive and quick. Wendy squinted and then she saw it.

"Why is there a Walker here?" Part of the question was angry— she'd never had such a horror in her dreams before—and the other part was fear. She hadn't known it was even possible to draw a Walker into a person's dreamscape.

Noting that Wendy had spotted it, the Walker drifted forward some, and as it drew closer Wendy's heartbeat tripled.

For a moment she thought it was the Lady Walker, but once it was close she realized that it was taller and thinner than any Walker she'd ever seen before, seeming to loom impossibly tall, as if the human it'd once been had been stretched on a rack and left to perish broken-limbed in the sun. The wind lifted the edges of its tattered cloak, exposing dark yellow bones with absolutely no flesh on them beneath the flapping hem. No tendons to work the shambling horror, no skin to keep it all together; this thing was older than old, it seemed to move on will alone.

"If you're working with Walkers, I'm gone," Wendy said sharply, moving to hop out of the car as fast as the hole in her gut would allow. She'd barely moved an inch or two when the greaser held up one hand and touched her wrist with the other.

"Wait, doll. I can explain." His touch was inexplicably warm; Wendy had been expecting the cool of the dead. Beneath his fingers, her wrist tingled.

"Get your hands off me!" Wendy snapped, throwing him off. Her wound protested the sudden movement, pain rippling through her midsection and slowing her down. Gasping, Wendy had to sit back to catch her breath.

"Please, wait," he said, reaching for her again.

"Don't touch me," Wendy warned. "Too many people have put their hands all over me today."

He rolled his eyes, but acquiesced, sitting back. "Ten minutes, Red. That's all I ask."

"Fine," Wendy said grudgingly, glaring at the screen instead of him. "But I'm timing you."

"I've been in the Bay Area for a long time, Red. A lot longer than it might seem, okay? And this place, it wasn't always peaches and cream for the dead, you dig? There was a broad—not a lady, mind you, but a broad—by the name of Elise who used to run the show around here. Maybe you've heard of her?"

"Elise?" Wendy stilled.

"Yeah, you know her. I can tell." The greaser shook his head.

"Look, Red, your family is one hell of a piece of work, you know that? Some of you cats are all right but some of you . . . look, any ghost with a lick of sense in his head is gonna tell you that they get it, they dig where you're coming from. Being an angel or Reaper or whatever the hell it is that you all really do isn't the easiest gig on this wide green earth. It's pretty damn thankless on the best days and a straight-up slog on a mediocre one."

Wendy snorted. "Preaching to the choir, man."

"Indeed. All you have to do is take one look at what happened to Miss Mary Reaper to know how bad it can go wrong on a bad day. So I get it. I do."

"Should I be clapping?" Wendy asked sarcastically. "I feel like you want some sort of award for 'getting' me."

"Shut up, Red," he replied kindly. "If I only have ten minutes I can't have you slowing down my flow." He cleared his throat. "Now, where was I? Oh, right. So it's a slog, right? And any job—janitor, doctor, cop—any job that deals with the ugly parts of existence, well, it wears on a soul. Even a soul with the power of life and death. Maybe you start up with the best intentions but after a few you start to really realize how unfair it all is, how you're working your bum off and all you're getting is diddly squat in return."

"Is there a point to this?"

"The point is that after a while people like Elise maybe started looking a little harder at their job description. Searching for loopholes, if you will."

What he was saying was lining up uncomfortably with something the Riders had relayed from their conversation with the Council.

"You're saying that when Elise had control of the Bay Area, before my mom came along, things weren't that great for the dead." Wendy shrugged uncomfortably. "It's not that way now, though."

"No, I'm saying that things were fucking *miserable* for the dead back then. Elise wasn't like you or your mom, Red, she didn't do the job and get out."

Wendy turned her face away, torn. Logically, she didn't know Elise well enough to say whether or not she could be guilty of such an act, but her gut was suggesting otherwise. "I don't know what you're talking about."

"See, I think you're lying. I heard it through the grapevine that you started asking permission to do your little light show, sending spirits on. If a ghostie wants to go, you send 'em, otherwise all is copasetic to you. Is that right?"

Wendy shifted. "Maybe."

"You feeling shy?"

"No!" Wendy flushed. "It's just . . . I guess I'm not supposed to ask permission first? I don't know. Everyone's telling me something different and I never got the training I was supposed to get. I'm winging it!"

"Yeah, well just between you and me, I think asking a lady I just met for permission to do the backseat tango is a far sight better than just diving in and seeing how she takes it." The greaser shrugged. "Maybe it's how I was raised, I don't know." He glanced slyly at Wendy from beneath shuttered lashes. "You get my drift?"

"I do."

"Grand!" He rubbed his hands together. "Now Elise, she doesn't exactly have the same eye-to-eye on the subject that you and I share. Permission, and all, I mean."

"No Reaper other than me asks the dead if they can reap them," Wendy pointed out stiffly.

"This goes way beyond asking for permission before sending a soul into the great beyond, Red. Elise ran one hell of a racket while she was in charge. Ultimately she knew that all ghosties, spirits, and whatnot had to be sent along their merry way to the Light, but there was *nothing* in the rules that said *when* she had to do that little deed. So she often wouldn't send 'em on when she had the chance."

"What?" Confused, Wendy shifted carefully forward. "But if she had a ghost right there, why wouldn't she?"

"Why would a bank be a little sad that they got all their prin-
cipal back in a few months rather than a few years?"

"Uh, because they profit off of the inter—oooohhh. I get it. She
was blackmailing them?" Wendy thought of Elise's shiny rings, her
smooth hair, Emma's nice car, and frowned. She knew that a lot of
the Reapers got jobs that positioned them near the dead—doctors
and undertakers and the like—but would even a doctor's salary pay
for all the amenities she'd seen them casually using so far?

"Give the girl a cookie! The lucky ones, the powerful spirits,
yeah, you betcha, blackmail city. Elise'd threaten to send a posse of
Reapers to clean out a nest of the dead if we didn't pay up."

Confused, Wendy rubbed her forehead. "That makes no sense
though. How're you supposed to pay anything that'd be worthwhile
to the Reapers? All you have is salvage, right?"

"Do nasty little errands for her—spy on the living, say, if you
weren't all that talented moving essence or ether around, or sometimes an outright haunting of a guy if you could reach into the
living world. That fancy house up San Ramon way used to be a
prime plot of land in the 60s. That is, until she convinced a few folks
to move out of their 'obviously cursed' house. Paid them pennies on
the dollar, if I'm remembering right."

"That's . . . that's . . ."

"One of the mildest things she's done." The greaser scratched his
chin. "And if you had a disliking for doing her dirty work, Elise had
other ways to make your afterlife a living hell. She didn't like a clean
reap. Too fast and not enough word-of-mouth to further her little
agenda." He sighed, rubbed his chin, and Wendy could hear the
scrape of his palm against his stubble. "No, Elise, she wouldn't reap
unless she absolutely had to."

"So what'd she do then?"

"Torture, for one, or if she was feeling curious, experiments.
Sometimes worse. For example, that little trick the White Lady had
of breathing flesh right back onto a Walker? Elise taught her how to

do that. She could also do the opposite, and strip a regular soul down to their bare bones with only a cord left, make other folks think that they were a Walker when they were nothing of the sort."

Wendy glanced at the Walker standing still and silent at the edge of the parking lot. The greaser, spotting her gaze, shook his head.

"Oh, no, Red. She's a Walker, but there's more to that story than we've got time to talk about today. Let's just leave it at the little fact that the Never is just as complicated a place as the living lands, and just because a person's walking around without any skin doesn't make them pure unadulterated evil, you dig?"

"I just don't get how anyone would want to cannibalize—"

"No, you don't. Look, Red, that's what I've been trying to get across to you. The Never is a *complex* place and you Reapers, even the good ones who let a spirit go out with dignity, you just rage your way through it like a whole clan of bulls in a china shop."

"Hey!"

"I'm not wrong though, am I? And when Elise was in charge the whole Never was a-quiver. A few souls were just so afraid of being stripped down and tortured, or used, so frightened of winking out like a crazy Shade, or entering the Light and facing whatever awful crap they did while they were alive, that they clung to whatever possible reason they could to stay in the Never. Even if it went against everything they thought they were or ever could be. Humans are survivors, Red. Even after we're already dead."

Despite herself, Wendy thought of the Donner party and shivered. "I guess you're right."

"Of course I am. Now, the ones that got me are those Walkers that went through hell and back to keep on going—those ones that ate the babies just to survive—but under Elise's rule they figured out the only way to keep on keeping on was to turn themselves in."

"What do you mean?"

"Ever wonder why the Walkers flocked to the White Lady so quickly and stuck around despite the fact that she occasionally mutilated them instead of healing them? It wasn't just because she could mend them up, Red. They knew her before. Like I said, not all Walkers are 100 percent bona-fide evil, and while Mary pitied and loathed them, even she had to admit that they could make themselves useful every now and then."

He jerked a thumb at the Walker at the edge of the woods. "Properly motivated, that is."

"Mom wouldn't—"

"Wouldn't she? The thing is, if you can get them to work together, Walkers are an unstoppable force, an angry unsleeping army. Mary knew that. How do you think she got the Council to agree to a truce in the first place? How do you think Elise gave up her death-grip—pardon the pun—on the Bay Area?"

"I was told that Mom was able to prove that she could take care of the Bay Area by herself, so they packed up for locations that needed them more."

"It's nice to believe in fairy tales. Personally I always like the one about the fox and the grapes, myself. I think Elise might have been acquainted with that one, too."

"That's a parable, not a fairy tale," Wendy said distantly, but she got the point. "You're telling me that Mom used Walkers—*Walkers*—to make my family move out."

"One thing they told you was true: they weren't needed here if Mary could keep damn near most of Northern California clean by herself. She had the Walkers and the Council round up all the spirits from Santa Rosa to Salinas and had them hidden."

"Even the Riders and Lost?"

He snorted. "One thing I'll say for your boy Piotr, Red, back in his day he taught every single Rider to be a sneaky son of a bitch. No, they couldn't find hide nor hair of the Riders or Lost to bother rounding them up. Probably for the best, to be honest. I don't think the Walkers would have kept in line if faced with so much fresh essence. I bet Mary didn't have them looking too hard at all."

"So even if Mom had the whole place on lockdown, why would the other Reapers leave?"

"Smart girl! Mary sent the Walkers further out, like bait. She had them rage around a bit in cities back east and in the midwest. The Reapers got wind of the chaos and followed, and the Walkers, most of them at least, came back here."

"So you're telling me that after Elise left, everyone lived together for years in relative harmony," Wendy drawled slowly. "Candy corn and sweetness all around."

"Now you've got with it! But then you, little Miss Lightbringer, came along and mucked it all up."

"Excuse me! How did *I* mess anything up?"

He tapped her watch. "That, my dear, is a story for another day. My ten minutes are up and, frankly, I'm tired of flapping my jaw."

As he stepped through the car, Wendy tried to grab his wrist, but he was too quick for her. "Why did you tell me all this?"

"Are you writing a book, doll? I'm done. It's late and I need to hit the road. Miles to go and all that."

"Please. You dragged me all the way out here. Finish it." Inspiration hit. "I mean, if you're gonna drag me out here to this passion pit just to rattle my cage, you're a real . . . um . . . hep cat?"

The greaser guffawed broadly. "Nosebleed, dear. I'm a real nosebleed," he corrected, rolling his eyes playfully. "Fine, fine, I'll answer your questions. Let's put it this way: with Elise gone, a whole bunch of scared spirits realized that they never wanted to be forced into a situation like that again. So we waited, we watched, and we learned. We knew it was a matter of time before something happened to Miss Clever Mary and your family got wind that maybe you weren't up to snuff. So we made plans."

"When you say 'we' . . ."

"The Council. The dead. Maybe just plain old everyday Joe ghosts who're tired of being pushed around. It doesn't matter, the important part is that the dead don't want the wrong sort of Reapers in this town. Thanks to you and your mother, we know how to hurt your kind, and thanks to some truly amazing minds like Madame Ada, we've got the poison to do it."

The greaser snapped his fingers and the Walker approached. It drew a long, thin bone dagger from its cloak and laid it in the greaser's palm.

"If you don't take care of your family," the greaser said, handing the dagger to Wendy, "we will. What went around, comes around, you dig? This is about to be war, a war no one wants, and right now you're the only one who's got any interest in stopping it." He patted the car door twice. "Good luck."

Wendy's hand curled around the dagger . . .

. . . and she was in a dark room, underground, shelves piled high with shadowy objects—vases and knives, busts and books—with a cool breeze blowing around her ankles. The only light was flickering candlelight from a chandelier high above. White wax dripped down, splattering the floor, and Wendy's chest ached. Her eyes were beginning to dry out in their sockets once again.

She was still running a fever, Wendy realized. Her living body was still burning up even though she was safe within her dreams.

"Oh Winifred, back so soon? You really can't take a hint can you? Little idiot," Emma said, suddenly shoving her from behind. Wendy staggered against the closest stack of books. They toppled to the floor with a dry *whoomp*, sending up a great gust of dust and debris. "I thought I told you to walk away."

"You did," Wendy said, turning to watch the redhead hovering just outside the range of light. Emma was dressed in a long grey robe, her feet were bare and scabbed, and her toes were covered with dirt. A red weal marred her neck in a thin line; it oozed over her collarbone and dripped bright blood down the front of the robe.

"I didn't listen," Wendy said, frowning at the blood. What had happened there? What was going on?

"Obviously," Emma sneered. She leaned forward, her long braid dipping down, and Wendy was tempted to grab the braid and yank Emma's face into her knee, possibly breaking that perfect nose.

"Winifred the weak," Emma said, slowly stalking a circle around Wendy, leaning forward and back, her face drifting in and out of the shadows. "Winifred the whiny. Can't hack a binding for even a day, could you? Went running to Jane at the first sign of discomfort."

"So I failed your frickin' test, so sue me," Wendy spat, turning to keep Emma in her line of sight. "It was a stupid test anyway."

"Was it? Was it a test?" Emma's hand shot out of the darkness and Wendy batted it aside, her side yelling at the sudden movement. "Or was it a way to get rid of you?"

"You're a doctor. I'm sure you know a hundred ways to get rid of a person without anyone finding out," Wendy retorted, troubled. The way Emma was moving was strange; after their sparring this morning, Wendy was fairly sure she had a bead on how Emma fought, which was mostly comprised of straightforward, quicksilver attacks. This slow, sinuous slide was not like Emma at all.

And . . . and . . . Wendy struggled to remember the moments before she'd woken up in the greaser's car. Hadn't she, in her delirium, called Emma on the cell?

Hadn't Emma been trying to . . . help her?

"Winifred, alas, you assume so many things." Again the darting attack and again Wendy slapped the jab aside.

"Where'd you get that cloak?" Wendy asked pointedly. "You're not a cloak type last I checked."

"Standard issue Reaper attire," Emma retorted. "Not that you'll ever receive one."

"If that's the usual, I think I'm good," Wendy replied, unease twisting in her gut.

Where were Emma's tattoos? Emma had tattoos on her shins before, didn't she? She'd been sitting in the living room, settled on that long couch, and her robe had slipped open. Eddie had tried not to stare but her legs really were very nice . . . and there'd been Celtic swirls all up her legs.

This Emma's legs were bare. Scarred and dirty, scabbed and cut . . . but bare.

"You're not Emma," Wendy said slowly. She couldn't believe that she hadn't noticed it before. "You're not Emma. And Emma never calls me Winifred. I'm always Wendy to her."

The redhead chuckled and straightened. "Maybe you're not such a hopeless case after all." The robe slipped off her shoulders and Wendy looked away. From the neck down she—whoever she was— was nothing more than tendon and bone, yellow and white and red, her skeleton jangling in space with Emma's face perched above.

Wendy hauled back and punched her.

The skeleton stumbled left, falling over a stack of books and bringing down another stack crashing across her head and shoulders. There was a sickening crack and Wendy, moving faster than she thought possible, was in the faux-Emma's face in an instant, grabbing her by the hair and yanking her up so sharply she groaned.

"Look, I don't care who you are, but I'm sick of these mind games," Wendy snarled, jerking the face up and down as she spoke. "Everyone has been having a go at me today and honestly I'm just done, okay? You have something you need to say to me? Say it. Otherwise I'm going to peel this skin off your skull and wear it like a hat, you got me?"

"There!" cried the not-Emma. "There! There is your fire, your temper! There is the Reaper in you!" She sagged in Wendy's grip and chuckled. "I'd thought it gone. I'd thought you'd given up with your mother's death, but finally, there it is. And all you needed to do was nearly die to find your fire. Again."

"My fire? What . . ." Wendy stilled. Her hands were glowing faintly with Light. "But . . . what about the binding?"

"Is still tight," the skeleton whispered, pressing cold bone fingers to Wendy's chest. "Still close. But it's not impossible for you. You may yet slip it free. If you want."

The skeleton leaned forward, leering, bringing with it a strong mingled smell of rich bourbon and thick decay. "Go ahead. Try it."

"I'm so confused," Wendy said, drawing back to keep from gagging from the stench. "Who are you really?"

"Don't you know?" the skeleton asked, reaching into Wendy's gut and grabbing her by the silver cord. "I'm you. The best *you* that pathetic little you could ever be."

Wendy gagged. The feeling of her cord being yanked and twisted was like nothing she'd ever experienced before. The skeletal fingers digging in were sliding across her gut, dipping through the skin, and caressing her from the inside. Wendy wondered if the hand was poking out her back, like she was some macabre puppet.

"You're . . . not . . . me," she hissed, grabbing the skeleton by the wrist and pushing savagely backward, unimpaling herself with a wet *schloop* noise.

The skeleton tilted its head. "I'm not?"

Breathing heavily, Wendy shoved her fingers into the grinning skull's mouth and grabbed the two parts with each hand. Pulling up with her left and down with her right, she yanked as hard as she could until the skull slid apart like a zipper, the bones grinding to yellowing dust beneath the pressure of her hands and exposing the bemused woman beneath.

"Elise," Wendy said, shaking her head. She wanted to be surprised, but after talking with the greaser she realized that she was more disappointed than startled.

"Yes," Elise said. "And no."

Pain shot through Wendy's side. Slowly, unbelieving, Wendy looked down. A tendril of Light receded, taking with it a thin knife that dripped essence. Wendy's essence.

The pain was tremendous. Staggering back, Wendy looked down, squinting as hard as she could, and could just barely make out that her silver cord had been jogged loose of her gut. It hung loosely at hip level like a loop of intestine.

"Why?" Wendy sobbed, gathering the ethereal loop in her palms as carefully as she could. Though the knife was no wider than a knitting needle, the hole in her gut seemed gigantic, like she could shove both her fists into it. Excruciating agony rippled through her entire body as Wendy struggled with her slippery cord and tried to press its length back into her body.

"Why?" Wendy asked again, stumbling forward and sinking to the floor of the dusty tomb. "I'm a Reaper too."

Elise sneered as Jane stepped around Wendy; Jane's face was calm, still, nearly expressionless. "You're not a real Reaper, Winifred. Like every other member of your ridiculous little family, you're just in my way." She snapped her fingers. "Jane. Now."

Sliding on one foot, Jane darted forward. Her dagger swung down and Wendy flung up her forearms to block the stab, twisting at the last second. She was hoping to throw Jane over her head; instead her hand punched cleanly through the Reaper's side.

Wendy pulled back. She held a weapon in her right fist, one that hadn't been there a moment before. It was the bone dagger the greaser had given her; it had come out of his dreamscape into this dreamscape.

Unexpected hot blood gushed over her fingers and wrist, sticky and thick and nearly black in the light. Open-mouthed, Wendy dropped the dagger and scrabbled painfully backward on elbows and ass. *What had she done?*

"Jane," Elise snapped sharply. "It's just a dream, girl, stop whining so! You'll hardly feel it in a moment."

"Just tell me why," Wendy insisted, pulling herself back across the floor. "Just . . . tell me why."

"Because, as I said," Elise coolly replied, "you are in the way." She reached down and patted Wendy's cheek.

"It's not personal, dear. Just good business, just as it was nothing personal with your friend Edward. I needed you out of the way for a few days, but then you had to go and stick your nose in where it doesn't belong. I took your boy's soul and hid his cord, hoping that you'd run off after him the same way you did after your mother, but Emma managed to bring him home like a lost puppy *and* leave a note pointing you our way."

Elise shook her head, tsking. "Such waste." She pulled back and kicked Jane in the side that was gushing essence. "Say you're sorry for ruining my plan, dear."

"I'm sorry, Grandmother," Jane gasped.

"That's better." Elise wiped her hands on her hips. "Penance is good for the soul. As is pain. Just look at Wendy here, Jane. An abomination like her is still up and running despite all the pressure we've put her through today! Remarkable. Send a bevy of Walkers after her and she manages to scare them off with threats! Tie her binding in knots and she manages to free herself enough to escape into dreams. Truly, if she weren't such an obnoxious little thing, I'd be tempted to welcome her into the family."

"I don't understand. What am I stopping you from doing?" Wendy whispered, trying to keep from watching Jane twitch and sob on the floor.

"That is none of your business, dear." Elise reached down and hauled Jane to her feet. "Say goodnight, Jane," Elise ordered. "We've got much to do, and I think we've finally pinned little Miss Wendy down at last."

Jane gave Wendy a sick smile and Wendy realized that there was something seriously wrong with the blue-haired girl. Her eyes were distant, clouded over, and her expression was drawn and far away. "Bye cuz," Jane whispered. "Sleep tight."

"Wait," Wendy said, struggling to rise. Her gut twisted, the silver cord tangling around her ankle, slowing her down. By the time she'd carefully freed herself, Elise had dragged Jane into the blackness.

They were gone.

CHAPTER TWENTY-THREE

ily and Eddie darted forward, moving in unconscious unison to reach Piotr as he fell. The snow came down in flurries now, large wet flakes that filled the vision and formed clumps and small drifts on the old, rotting floors.

Indifferent to the risk of his cold, Lily reached Piotr an instant before Eddie and caught him in her arms as he tumbled down. Teeth chattering, she laid him carefully out and then quickly stepped back, briskly rubbing her arms against his chill.

"He's fading again," Eddie hissed. "Fast."

"To tend to him, to avoid frostbite, I must wrap up in blankets," Lily replied sharply. "As many as you can find. Hurry!"

Eddie loped off as Lily knelt down. The cold was so intense that she was finding it difficult to be within a foot of Piotr; she had no idea what she could do for him other than wrap him up and perhaps start a fire with Dora's drawings and the old door she'd used as a desk.

Lily was so caught up in Piotr's plight that she completely missed hearing Elle approach until her old friend was at her shoulder, kneeling down beside her.

"Care to fill me in?" Elle asked gruffly. "What in the blue blazes happened here?"

"Elle?" Lily twisted and hugged her wayward friend, stunned to see her but overwhelmingly happy that she'd finally arrived. Desperately, she squeezed tighter, not wishing to let the prickly flapper go. Eddie was good company but he couldn't handle a weapon to save his own life . . . or Ada's. "You were gone so long!"

"Well, yeah, it took me awhile to sniff out a Lost, and you will NOT guess where I found one. How's our flyboy doing?" Elle looked over to where Piotr sprawled on the floor and, glancing up, eyed the fat flakes drifting down. "You all have some sort of adventure while I was out and about?"

"You could say that," Eddie said, coming down the stairs with every blanket on the thirteenth floor piled in his arms and dragging on the stairs. "I'll admit, Elle, I'm impressed. How'd you know to find us here?"

"I figured something was up when I went by Wendy's and her whole yard was trashed," Elle explained. "This was, what, a couple hours ago? The only ones inside were her brother and sis so I thought maybe head up to the city, see if you all tried to make it to my old haunt since it's the closest completely safe zone."

"Indeed? You traveled a great distance then," Lily said, impressed, as always, by Elle's undying efficiency. "But made good speed."

"I was alone for most of it," Elle said. "Till I got to the Pier." She jerked a thumb over her shoulder. "That's where I found Sarah here, believe it or not. And get this; she already has the skivvy on Petey here. *She* was waiting for *me*."

Lily blinked in surprise and glanced at the Lost hesitating in the corner of the room, her backpack at her feet and a wary expression curling her lips. The skittishness of the girl was palpable—one wrong word and the Lost would flee. By the look of her, she'd be fast and hard to catch up with too.

"You knew of our problem, young one?"

"Walker stabbed him, pretty straightforward," Sarah said, frowning at their group. "Though if I knew I'd be laying low all day long I would've snagged another book to read. Bookstore had nothing I haven't seen twenty times."

"Get this: Wendy met her *this morning*, after we'd left," Elle whispered. "Had the kid waiting for us up at the Pier, hiding out from the Reapers. Now where is that daffy Lightbringer so I can give her a great big kiss?"

"If the Lightbringer is not at her abode then we don't know where she is," Lily said shortly. "She is, perhaps, gone. And Ada with her. Ada was taken by animals—gulls, to be precise."

Elle's eyes widened. "Ada was here? Council Ada? Why?"

"As I could not locate a Lost in a timely manner, I thought that perhaps Ada might be able to help us with Piotr's difficulties. My theory was not incorrect; Ada was able to stave off the worst of his symptoms for a short time but, as you can see, it was not long enough."

"Well Pocahontas, we got ourselves a Lost now, right?"

"You speak truly." Lily glanced behind Elle at Sarah and smiled softly. Seeing a Lost again . . . it warmed her heart. She yearned to collect Sarah to her, to hug the small scrap of girl and soothe her pains, but Lily could sense by the mere set of Sarah's shoulders that a hug would not be tolerated in the least. "It was good of you to come. I am Lily. This is Eddie. We are friends of Wendy . . . though she did not tell us that she encountered you."

Taking off her hat, Sarah toed the pile of wet snow at her feet and shivered. "I'm not surprised Wendy didn't speak up—before they left one of the Reapers nabbed a Shade not ten feet from where we'd been talking. She might've thought it was me." Sarah tucked the hat under her arm and glanced up at Elle. "You didn't tell me it was gonna be snowing."

"To be honest, short stuff, I had no clue everything was gonna get balled up while I was gone," Elle said baldly. "I figured Pocahontas here had it all under control."

"If you are done judging my competency," Lily said stiffly, "perhaps Sarah might deign to look at Piotr?"

"You think you have it in you, kiddo?" Elle asked Sarah. "Or do you need a few minutes to orient yourself first?"

Sarah scowled. "Where's my salvage?"

"Healing first, then the moolah," Elle said gently. "You can see we've got plenty, even in a dump like this. A deal's a deal, right?"

"You were talking about gulls before, right?" Sarah said, looking between Lily and Elle as she edged closer to Piotr. Eddie handed her a comforter and she wrapped it around her shoulders, shivering. Lily felt her lips quirk without guiding thought. Eddie was so considerate, it was painfully endearing.

"I used to crash up near Fort Funston, back, you know, before. Before the White Lady started looking around for Lost. And then I went back after she, you know, went away." Sarah pulled out her hat, tapped the brim absently. "I've been hanging out there since . . . what, the sixties? So I really know the area."

"Indeed?" Lily said, surprised that this little ghost had survived so long on her own. Shivering in the cold she seemed to small and fragile, so tiny, but if Sarah could remember that far back she might even be as old as Elle. Possibly older, given the odd cut of her clothing and the possessive way she handled her hat. "Were there many gulls there?"

"Around the fort? Tons. They kept an eye out, you know, for the Reapers. You had to move around at night, keep low, cuz if you saw a gull chances were that a Reaper or maybe some soul they had jockeying for them wasn't gonna be too far behind. It was like that for a long time."

Sarah yanked her cap back on and shoved any loose tendrils under until she looked like a very skinny boy. "If the gulls took your lady, she's probably up that way. The Reapers probably plucked her right up. They had a house or something up there, up near San Ramon."

"I know the place," Eddie said slowly. "Though I don't know where they'd stash someone like Ada. I mean, how do you keep tabs on a ghost?"

"Easier than you might imagine," Lily said shortly, annoyed that Eddie hadn't shared the location of the Reapers' stronghold with them already. It would have been good information to have. "But it is no matter. We will fetch Ada as soon as we can. In the meantime—"

"Your friend isn't looking so hot," Sarah finished.

Piotr was jerking on the floor, spasming up and down, back arching wildly as his head hit the floor with enough force to crack the thick layer of ice that'd formed beneath him. One moment he was nearly solid, slamming into the wood with enough force to make the old boards creak and groan and splinter beneath the ice, the next he was hardly there, his shoulders resting on the floor as his head vanished through the floorboards into the room below.

Sarah, without being asked, approached Piotr with her hands outstretched. Unfortunately, no sooner did she get close enough to touch him than his flailing tripled, and he caught her on the hip and shoulder with one wildly jerking leg. Lily darted forward to catch her but Sarah, shoved violently backward, stumbled and fell, slamming her head into the corner of the desk. Eddie was at her side in a second, lifting her carefully from the floor and examining the spreading bruise and jagged cut along her temple.

Lily gestured to Elle and Elle nodded in return. Silently, acting as one, they moved to either side of Piotr, close enough to touch him but still just out of striking range. Piotr, lost in his delirium, abruptly sat up and said something long and convoluted in Russian, eyes open but rolled back in his head, spitting and cursing as he swung his arms left and right.

"As soon as she's better?" Elle asked, dodging one of Piotr's wilder swings.

The breeze from his fist passing left Lily's flesh prickling. "On three," Lily agreed, sidestepping another swipe as Piotr, turning at the sound of her voice, spit and cursed. Lily knew very little Russian but what she did recognize was the torrent of profanity pouring from his lips. Though she did not say so out loud, Lily was willing to bet that Piotr was once more reliving his death. The now-familiar word for uncle spewed forth with such venom that her ears fairly burned.

"Are you willing to try again?" Lily heard Eddie asking Sarah. She glanced over her shoulder to see Eddie pressing a scrap of his shirt to her cut. She recognized the expression on his face—Eddie was marveling at how Sarah's flesh quickly closed beneath his palm.

"They'll hold him down this time," Eddie promised her, and Lily, despite Piotr cursing violently beside her, preened for a bare moment at Eddie's solid, unwavering assurance. Then Piotr arched forward, this time so hard his head nearly smacked the floor, and Lily immediately dropped all thoughts of Eddie to corral her friend.

"We should wrap our hands," Elle panted, wincing. "He's colder than a Sunday ice cream cone. Hey Sarah, kiddo, wait a second."

"No time. Three!" Lily declared and lunged forward, searing her palms on Piotr's freezing shoulders as she grabbed him and shoved him down to the floor. Elle, following her lead, grabbed his ankles. Piotr flailed fiercely, wildly, feet kicking and shoulders lifting off the boards with such strength that Lily ripped the flesh of her palms free to get a better grip and kneel on his torso.

Piotr, eyes frosted over entirely with white now, stilled his thrashing just long enough to twist upward and whisper so only Lily could hear, "You bitch. You know what you do is wrong, you know it is evil, yet still you abide. I will make you pay for this, if it takes me until the sun is blotted from the sky, if it takes me until your precious Ragnarok. I will destroy you both."

Then, yanking one arm free with impossible strength, he raked at Lily's face.

"Sarah! Now!"

Sarah, flinging herself forward, grabbed Piotr by the temples and sank her hands all the way into his head.

The room filled with rainbow light.

CHAPTER TWENTY-FOUR

"It worked," Lily said, wincing in pain as Sarah tended to her savaged palms. Eddie and Elle lifted Piotr up, Elle at his feet and Eddie at his head, and carried him carefully upstairs to his pallet. "Thank you, Sarah. You have no idea how special he is to us."

"He feels different from the rest of you guys," Sarah said hesitantly. "He feels . . . old."

"He is old," Lily said, running her newly healed palms over her upper arms. Piotr's chill was finally beginning to wear off and the room was filled with the drip of slowly melting water, both in the Never and the living lands. "Perhaps it is my imagination but I think he may be one of the oldest ghosts there is."

Sarah grimaced. "He's dangerous. You guys know that right? He's . . . messed up somehow. He's wrong."

"Perhaps," Lily said. She felt heavy and sad and so, so very tired. It was just all the work she'd done to lock Piotr down, Lily assured herself, but her treacherous brain kept circling to the feeling of Piotr taking too much essence, taking and taking and taking, and then, only hours later, Lily just giving essence away to Eddie, as if she truly had any extra to spare. Frowning at her selfishness, Lily banned these intrusive thoughts and turned all her attention to Sarah. "But I think he's important nonetheless. Thank-you for seeing to him."

"Elle promised me the stuff." Sarah jerked her thumb over to the alcove where Piotr and his Lost had kept their scavenged goods. "She said I could have my pick."

"You are welcome to all that is there but, please, know that you do not have to go," Lily said, secretly glad that Piotr's hard-earned salvage would find some serious use. "You could stay with us. We protect the Lost."

"Yeah, I heard, but I also heard that lately you don't do a very good job of it." Sarah found a tattered backpack amid the goods and unzipped it, quickly stuffing the main compartment full. "Don't get me wrong, you Riders have your hearts in the right places, I see that, but I know what happened with all those other kids you guys 'took care of' a few months back. The White Lady got 'em. So if it's all the same to you, I've been on my own this long, I think I can survive pretty well for a while longer."

Lily nodded. She didn't like the decision but she was not one to force the girl to come with her. Sarah must find her own way—and if she faltered, she knew where the Riders would be found. Now, Lily thought, Sarah had their scent. "I understand. Good luck."

Sarah patted the bulky bag and slung it over her shoulders as she stood. "Don't need it. Not for a bit, at least." She glanced up the stairs. "I'd be willing to help you or Elle or Eddie out, if you get hurt, I mean. But him? Count me out. I won't come for him again." Then, without waiting for Lily's reply, Sarah turned and hurried through the wall, leaving them all behind.

Piotr woke slowly. The moon was well up and the last he could clearly recall, the sun had just been setting. How long had he slept?

Gingerly, Piotr sat up and stretched. His body felt kinked all over, but strong. He was warm, all aches were gone. It took him several minutes of hard thinking but then, slowly, it came back to him.

Elle had found a Lost, and, ironically, she may have found the very Lost Ada had suggested was hanging near the docks. If only they'd listened to Ada first!

Sighing with relief, Piotr stood as carefully as he could. He could hear movement downstairs—low, familiar voices discussing their situation—and Piotr was overwhelmed with gratitude and shame.

Lily. Oh, Lily, he'd treated her atrociously. Piotr wasn't sure how he was going to make it up to her, but so far as he could recall, he'd spat on his best friend at least three times and she hadn't punched him once. Knowing Lily's fierce pride, such consideration and restraint must have taken some true self-control. Elle would have laid him flat.

Moving quietly down the stairs, Piotr waited patiently at the halfway point for his companions to notice he was awake. Eddie was the first to glance up.

"Wakey, wakey, eggs and bakey," he said, hopping to his feet and approaching the stairs. "You're looking better. How're you doing, man?"

"Much better indeed," Piotr said. "Well-rested and much healed. I owe you many thanks. All of you." He held Lily's gaze a moment before continuing on. "And you have my deepest apologies for how I acted before. I was not in my right mind. I hope you could see that."

"Have you ever been in your right mind?" Elle quipped, joining Eddie at the foot of the stairs. "I mean, hell flyboy, your head's like a sieve most days. Ain't nothin' much right about all that."

Piotr smiled gently at Elle's jest and Lily, ever observant, rose to her feet. "You remember. You do. I can see it in your eyes."

Elle glanced quickly between them. "Remember? He remembers what?"

"Many things, now." Piotr held out his hand and began ticking off points. "Elle, once, maybe a few months ago, you asked me if I could recall how you died, did you not?"

"Err, yes." Elle crossed her arms over her chest and took back a step, narrowing her eyes. "The only thing you could rustle up was that I was in red."

"You shot yourself." Piotr mimed aiming a handgun at his head for effect. "Over a boy. And you did it on his lawn to teach him a lesson about sleeping with girls and leaving them high and dry when they . . ." he drifted off politely. The memory nearly had texture and weight, it was suddenly so fresh in his mind.

"Say it," Elle said, lips thinned to a narrow line. "Finish up, Pete."

"You were Catholic and knew your parents would ship you off

to a nunnery to have the baby. You hated them, you hated yourself, and most of all you hated him. So rather than deal with the mess you'd made of your flamboyant life, you committed suicide." Piotr swallowed deeply. The red had bled even into the Never.

"Got it in one," Elle said, relaxing and smiling grimly. "And you found me, yeah? All confused and wandering, crying my damn eyes out cuz that baby was already dead inside me and I just didn't know it yet. If I'd waited maybe a few more weeks it would've passed on its own." She spat. "Such a waste."

"I found you bleeding out on his front lawn. I took you to the Pier and we watched the children play in the waves. We talked of many things—of how babies never wake in the Never. Of how they are always taken by the Light." Piotr felt the words dry up on his tongue. He could so clearly remember now—the waves in the grey Neverlight, the feeling of the pier beneath his feet, the distant sound of laughter. How tired he'd felt, standing beside this girl no older than he'd been when he'd died, and thinking what a shame it was. What a shame.

"That was a cold summer," Elle said softly. "I never knew how they could stand to dip their toes in water that cold. Toddlers like Tubs, dancing on the edge of the surf, kids like Specs and Dora keepin' an eye out for 'em." She rubbed a fist against her eye. "Boys. Ain't none of you worth it, not then and certainly not now. If I could do it again . . ." she drifted off.

They waited patiently, kindly, for her to gather herself and her thoughts.

"Well, never you mind, then," Elle finally said, shaking her pincurls roughly. "What's done is done. What I really want to know is if that sickness of yours jarred any other special memories loose, or is it all about pretty, precious little ol' me?"

"I remember much," Piotr said softly. It was the truth. The memories were so haphazard, though, surfing through his mind, searching for a hole to fill, until he felt painfully stuffed, and yet the memories kept coming and coming and coming. Hundreds . . . no, thousands of years pouring into his brain in steady spurts. "Sarah, when she touched me, she took me by the head, did she not?"

"Grabbed you right in the ol' brainpan," Elle agreed, narrowing her eyes. "Sunk in up to her wrists, or pretty close to."

"I think . . . perhaps she inadvertently fixed something wrong. Long wrong. In my head." Piotr touched his temple. He wondered if his head was bulging; it felt like it would burst under all the new pressure. "I can remember so, so many things that were missing before. So, so many things."

"Anything you want to natter about, Petey-boy?" Elle asked curiously.

"Not as of yet," Piotr said seriously. "But I will tell what comes most clearly, what I know to be most true and not the possible imaginings of a fevered mind beset on all sides. Ada, for example, is far more important than she let on, perhaps for her own safety."

Eddie crossed his arms over his chest. "How so?"

"Ada must be fetched from the Reapers," Piotr said. Flashes now, of Mary talking, of Mary explaining, of Mary waving the little test vial of the very first poison under his nose as she ranted and raved about the Reapers, about Mary's sister Tracey and her family and Wendy. Ada hadn't known Mary had stolen it. Mary had wanted a backup in case Ada failed.

"It is imperative," Piotr said, trying to push the intense memory of Mary's stalking rant into a dim, quiet corner of his mind. The edges of him felt like they were stretching painfully, like who he was was being bent out of shape . . . or into a new one. He felt bloated, like a tick, and bursting with intent. "Ada's work at Alcatraz is of great importance and must not be discovered by the Reapers." Piotr closed his eyes. He could see the thin space in the basement, hidden behind a broken mirror. Ada had been gone but Mary had known how to get in. She'd dragged Piotr to Alcatraz and showed him the thin layers of the Never, the tiny hole, the rip between the worlds.

Piotr shuddered. To Ada, it must have been some interesting anomaly. To anyone else who knew what they were looking at, the darkness with the red eyes blinking within was terrifying.

"Why, Piotr?" Eddie asked. "Is it the weapons you guys said the Council has stashed?"

"No. It is much, much greater than that." Piotr thought a moment of telling them everything he could remember, but time was short and he worried for Wendy. No, he thought, they had time for revelations later. For now . . . for now he had a job to do.

"No, we must return to Wendy's and garner her aid. This city cannot be left under Elise's control, but wresting power away from Elise cannot be done without the Lightbringer." Piotr began walking toward the far wall, instinctively sensing that if he moved quickly, with purpose, the others would tag along like ducklings in a row. "This way, I will lead you down the quickest path toward Mountain View. We must locate Wendy now."

"Pete, I was just there," Elle said, proving Piotr right by following him unquestioningly through the wall. "I know maybe you weren't all with the up and up at the time, but Wendy's place is completely trashed; feathers and bird crap everywhere in her yard, her kitchen's a wreck—in the Never, at least—and Wendy-girl's nowhere to be seen." Elle glanced back at Lily and Eddie, both keeping an even, loping pace behind but staying silent for the time being.

"That was then," Piotr said, sinking through the remnants of a door on the far side, taking the stairs down two at a time. "Not necessarily now. Wendy has a vehicle and the living move far more swiftly than the dead. She very may well have returned home by now."

When Elle began to protest, he raised a quieting hand. "By my faith, Elle, your trust I need. Wendy would not abandon us, this I know."

They'd reached the main floor. Piotr peered through the front door to make sure there were no surprises like gulls or Walkers about, and then guided them toward a nearly-hidden tangle of bushes at the back of the complex. A thin trail snaked toward the highway. The path was very thin in the Never, hardly there, but smooth worn beneath their feet; under Piotr's experienced guidance they would be traveling as the crow flies.

"No duh," Eddie said as he, wincing, walked through a particularly thin eucalyptus. He glanced uneasily up at the tossing branches above. "No one's suggesting that."

"I was just about to," Elle said, narrowing her eyes at Piotr as they broke through the brush and he led them straight up a hill toward the highway. "But someone's fancy pants knows me a little too well, I guess."

"We need her," Piotr said simply, eying the traffic. It was late in the evening, nearing ten by the position of the moon, but the airport was relatively close. All he had to do was wait for the right transport to come along.

"I don't need her."

"Fine, Elle. Perhaps you do not, but I need her. I know you and the Lightbringer have not always seen eye to eye, but she is important, this you cannot deny. Not only to us, but to them. We must reach her first."

Piotr was moving too fast; Eddie was struggling to catch up. He had to stop and say, "Look, I know everyone here is all 'grrr Reapers' but seriously, come on guys, do you really believe that Wendy's family would do all that bad stuff? I mean, come on, we haven't even given one of them a chance to explain themselves."

Eddie looked between the girls and Piotr, annoyed now. No one, not Piotr or Elle, not even Lily, was looking in his direction; they were all concentrating on the oncoming traffic. Gesturing for Eddie to join them, Piotr crouched dramatically down, tensing, as a long bus trundled up the on-ramp.

Elle grabbed Eddie's left hand, Lily his right and, as one, they flung him through the door of the bus. He skidded down the aisle and landed at the rear of the bus, clinging to the thin memory of the pole that had once been there. Seconds later, Piotr joined him.

"You were saying, Eddie?" Piotr asked, helping Eddie to his feet and guiding him to one of the empty seats near the back. Eddie flushed. Thankfully the bus was empty save for the driver and the dead.

"Ahem. That sucked, man. The train was bad enough, and hitching on that van wasn't the easiest thing ever, but I can't believe you all travel that way every day." Embarrassed at his less-than-graceful landing, Eddie shook his head. "How do you not go flying out the—You know what? Not important."

Elle plopped down in an empty seat beside him and leaned against the window. "Keep on, ducky."

"Yeah, like I was saying," Eddie continued, "we got beat down by a bunch of birds, and that sucked, and it's totally possible that they took Ada because they were, I don't know, under orders to or something. I get that."

Eddie stared at Piotr earnestly, continuing on. "But the thing is, you all haven't met Emma or Nana Moses or Jane or any of the other Reapers. Yeah, a bunch of them are stuck up, and they look down on anyone who happens to be of the, uh, well, *ethereal* persuasion, but not all of them are like that. And Wendy's one of their own. They *said* they wouldn't hurt her."

"It is difficult to think poorly of those you've broken bread with, or slept beneath their roof, this I understand," Piotr said slowly, stretching out across two seats. "But I knew Mary. We spoke many, many times. And she did not trust her family any further than she would a Walker."

"First of all, Wendy's mom is dead, Piotr. She was a nice enough lady while she was alive, but kind of a control freak, to be honest. And even when she wasn't dead, wasn't she the one who drained you like a Duracell every chance she got? Ate your memories like candy?"

"This is true. What of it?" Piotr's expression was unreadable; Eddie hoped that he'd never have to play poker with the guy.

"Even if all that poison crap was really all for Wendy's sake— which, I'd like to add, we've got no proof of, just Ada's say so—out

of all the people, well, anywhere, you're the last one I expected to
just take her at her word on anything. I mean, she's what, part of this
high-and-mighty Council? What do they do that's so great?"

"The Council has its place, just as the Riders do. As for Mary, I
do not know why she chose to take of me as often as she did in the
end, Eddie, but I can say that, in the beginning at least, she had
good reasons for it."

"It must've been some reason, that's all I'm saying."

"This place, this city, was different before. It was a darker, harder
place for the dead while Elise was in control. It seems so strange that
I could not remember this before, but if the dead did not agree to
enslave themselves under Elise's rule then they were tortured or
worse. Any Reaper that did not agree with Elise was . . . handled."

The bus stopped and two men, old, bedraggled, and obviously
drunk, stumbled on board and, staggering toward the ghosts, flung
themselves down into nearby seats. A third followed close behind
and was about to sit on Piotr when Piotr reached out and brushed a
hand against the man's wrist.

"This seat is taken," he said simply, and Eddie was in the middle
of wondering why Piotr had even bothered when the drunk man,
blinking in confusion, shivered and stepped past, joining his buddies further down.

Eddie was glad that Lily and Elle seemed just as flustered by the
encounter as he was; they exchanged a startled glance, but it was as
if Piotr didn't even notice what he'd apparently done. Elle looked
between Piotr and the man, confused. "How did you—"

"Eddie?" Piotr said. "My apologies for the interruption. Please
do continue."

Eddie grimaced. He wanted to ask about the man but his previous point hadn't been completed either. "Seriously? Then how
come none of you guys have even mentioned this before? The whole
Elise-slave/family 'handled' thing?"

Lily shrugged, eying Piotr carefully as he turned his head away.

Eddie knew she was just as troubled as he was, but she also seemed willing to let Piotr's trick go for the time being. She cleared her throat and said, "The Riders were so used to hiding that we were able to stay clear of most of the politics and problems of the age, but even we were indirectly touched. Our Lost kept us inside, hidden, but the numbers of Walkers grew and grew while Elise was in control. To be honest, I did not even know her name, only that there was a powerful human, a Seer of sorts, who had many of the spirits concerned."

"I had just squatted at the Pier so I heard some of this back then," Elle replied, still glancing askance between Piotr and the drunken man, "but I kept low so it didn't affect me. I don't gossip."

"As for myself, my memories of that time had been stripped clean and I did not recall until now," Piotr added. "At the time, when Mary sought me out, I was angry, upset, to be drawn yet again into the Reaper's machinations, into their silly family squabbles."

"I bet," Eddie said. "Who wouldn't be? But then why'd you go for it anyway?"

"Initially I was not going to help, but after learning the fate of Mary's si—" he broke off, frowning. "Mary's particular plight notwithstanding, after seeing what the city had become for the ordinary dead, how even good souls were forced to choose between becoming Shades, fading away, or donning the cloaks and teeth of the Walkers, well, how could I not help where I may?"

Piotr smiled softly and tapped his temple again, "I urged her to take it all."

"Ew," Elle said. For a moment Eddie thought she was referring just to what Piotr had said, but then Eddie noticed the shadow of the living man Piotr'd touched, vomiting up his tequila dinner in the stairwell.

Eddie could practically smell the sickness-death-rot aroma pouring out of the man as he hunched over and heaved again.

Elle frowned at the heaving man. "What did you *do* to him, flyboy?"

He looked at her blankly. "I do not understand."

"With the touchy-touchy, 'move along, Jack' bit," Elle gestured between the drunken man and Piotr. "Let me guess, you don't remember?"

"I remember but, Elle, I am unpleasantly cold to the touch," Piotr reminded her patiently. "We all are. Of course on encountering me he moved. This spot is icy and there were many, many seats to choose from."

"I dunno . . . it seemed more than that." The man retched louder and a hot splatter flew up and passed through the spot where Elle was sitting. "Oh, ew! Fine, whatever, either way, you're crazy, Pete," Elle continued, changing seats to get away from the bile.

"Indeed?"

"Yes, you're a total whackadoo. It was one thing when I thought the White Lady or Mary or whomever, was, I don't know, ambushing you and taking your brains, but knowing now that you gave it up just like that? I think I just lost a little respect for you, flyboy."

"Hush, Elle, you know not of what you speak. Mary walked the difficult line between duty and family," Lily said seriously. "This I understand. It is a truly arduous path. But why so much secrecy? If she wished Wendy to walk in her footsteps, to keep this area safe from these dark Reapers, why did she not confide in the Light-bringer herself? Why the mystery?"

"Mary called the other Reapers monsters," Piotr said. The bus stopped to let the three men off and he took advantage of the stop to step outside himself. The others followed suit. The bus driver did not pull away immediately, but leaned out the open door to berate the vomit-covered drunk, slowing her tirade only when Piotr passed near.

"The other Reapers were of her flesh, but their eyes were cold, their hands cruel," Piotr said. "Like Wendy, in their youth, Mary and a few other idealistic Reapers considered stopping reaping, what they call the 'Good Work.' The irony of the name rankled at them since, if they could do no tangible, provable good, why work for the family at all? There was no point to it but pain and degradation, both for the Reapers and for the dead. For Mary especially, who lost much in the end."

"Um, because stopping reaping hurts?" Eddie interrupted, surprising them. He knew this area as well as Piotr did; without thinking about it Eddie began moving in the direction of Wendy's house, guiding them. "Nana Moses was telling Wendy about it. It hurts to stop and sometimes stopping killed 'em. Bottled them up."

Elle grimaced. "No joshin'?"

"Naturals like Wendy had it the worst, too, because the more they used their power the more some nasty sort of boogie-man would be attracted to them, so for a natural it was a lose-lose situation. Once you wake up and get inducted into the Never or whatever, you have to reap and send on souls. Reap or die."

Piotr grimaced. "Then it is doubly important that we find Wendy as quickly as possible, to let her know of these terrible things regarding her family. Her mother—"

"Mary must have quit," Lily surmised, gliding through a short fence, "and found that the pain was too great." She frowned down at her leg and wiped the dusty remains of old roses off her thigh.

"Wuss," Elle sneered.

"Not only the pain, but the threat from her own family," Piotr said. "I hesitate to reveal this now, but her sister, like Mary, had come to the same conclusion: that their aunt was corrupt, that the noble goal of their family was rapidly degrading for profit and power. She was," he frowned, "she was eliminated."

"Wendy had an aunt?" Eddie paled, feeling whatever passed for a stomach in this ethereal body of his twist uncomfortably at the news. "And they straight-up killed her? Wow. That's . . . harsh." He scowled at Elle's derisive snort. "Hey now, you come up with a better word for 'monumentally screwed up' on short notice."

"This was, of course, before Mary found me," Piotr continued. "With the permission of her grandmother, the one you've named

'Nana Moses,' Mary and her sister delved into the books of their family, into the scrolls and ancient texts then kept in the basement of their grandmother's home. The stories and myths were well-preserved for what they were—frequently the remembrances of the Reapers, when not written down, were embroidered onto collars and the insides of sturdy cloaks—but they were women, you see, and while some were encouraged to learn to read, many . . . most . . . were illiterate."

"Clever," Elle said. They'd reached Safeway, and now even Eddie was pleased with how close they'd come. "They told their stories through paintings and some such too, I bet?"

"The few books were often transcribed and copied by the boys in the family, over and over again. Copies of copies that she found wrapped in tarps and plastic, in cloth and painted on narrow strips of ribbon or on the inside of wooden-backed brushes. This was before the death of her sister. They worked together, and when they'd found enough proof that the family was not supposed to be directed the way it was, that there was reason and greater purpose to their gift, Mary's sister approached their aunt, demanding change."

"Which she got, just not the change she was picturing," Eddie said, wincing. "Man, again, that's just . . . harsh. This way. It's shorter." Getting the hang of it now, Eddie passed through a rusty chain link fence and began heading directly down the street toward Wendy's.

"Her sister was framed by the family, so to speak, and put up on trumped up charges. They had her put to death in the old way, and Mary knew that she had to keep going to respect the memory of her own. Hidden, Mary continued researching, delving deeper and deeper into their past. Eventually she'd gone so far that the language wasn't translated; she had to go on pictures alone. And there, in smelted metals and calcified wood, in tapestries woven of hair and wool woven softer than silk, she found what she believed to be the origins of her family."

Elle shivered and sat on the narrow bus stop bench. Sensing her unease, Eddie stopped for the moment. The moon was bright and they all needed a short rest. "Okay, I'm not any kind of dumb dora, but that is creepy, Pete."

"When did she seek you out?" Lily asked, her piercing gaze never leaving Piotr's face. Eddie smirked as Piotr shifted uneasily beneath the forthright gaze. "Why did she look for you?"

Settling on the bench beside Elle, Piotr shrugged. "The stories and texts have always spoken of unending spirits who stayed near the core of the Reaper clan, but here, in those ancient texts, was definitive proof of their existence. I do not know how she found me; Mary was always close-lipped about that, but find me she did. She called me an Unending One."

"Did you remember your history before you encountered Mary?" Lily pressed as Eddie settled into a relaxed squat at her feet, examining a short stretch of buckled bricks laid in a herringbone pattern in the street. "Or was it Mary who stripped your mind clean?"

"You know this," Piotr said, his tone half-embarrassed, half-admonishing. "Not six months ago it was you yourself who told me that my memories have always been strange."

"Enough about Pete's wonky head, he's always been left holding the bag," Elle said eagerly. "Finish up with Mary. This is better than a radio drama. I want to know what happens next!"

"The history of the Reapers is not some story for you to gawk at," Piotr snapped testily. "There is much meaning here and much to be concerned about!"

"There isn't much more to tell, though," Eddie said, getting up and offering a hand to Elle. She refused it and he shrugged. He'd thought of offering it to Lily, but he worried what she might think of the offer. "A kid could figure out what happened next. You gave up memories to Mary, making her stronger. She, in turn, wiped out a bunch of Shades and then made a deal with Ada and the Council to not bug them if they hid every ghost they could get their hands on for a while. She'd take care of the bulk of their Walker problem, and hopefully she'd convince her family that she could take care of the whole Bay Area by herself, protecting herself and all the ghosts in one fell swoop. She did, they left, and then later she got married and popped out Wendy and the twins."

"*Da*," Piotr agreed. "When Wendy was discovered to be a natural—"

"Her mother must've been terrified out of her ever lovin' gourd," Elle mused. "Because, on the one hand, powerful strong kiddo that probably could take care of the whole city by herself. On the other hand, she lets Wendy get too strong, then BAM, balderkin."

"Shhh," Lily hushed sharply, glancing around furtively. They were very near where the gulls had attacked the first time, Eddie realized; the grass at their feet was still torn and spattered and foul. Lily had noticed as well. "We don't know who is listening."

"Hush yourself, Pocahontas," Elle snapped back. "The whole block is empty! We're fine! The point of the matter is, Mary had to train up an early-bloomin' daughter and take care of a city now pretty much overrun with ghosts she'd hidden from her family, all by herself. And she couldn't let Wendy use her power too much, too fast either, she had to keep her in the dark about a lot of important stuff. Am I getting all this right, Pete?"

"You have the gist of it," Piotr agreed wearily.

"So she assigns Wendy nothing but Shades, and if I'm remembering right, then she tries to take on the rest of the city by her little ol' lonesome. If it'd been my kid, I'd have been worried half to death that Wendy was getting bottled up, too, because yeah, it'd hurt, but Wendy ain't exactly the type to mouth off when she's under the weather. I don't like her much, but I'll admit, she plays it close to the vest when she's not tip-top. And all the time, Mary's having to keep an eye out over her shoulder for any family spies that nasty Aunt Elise probably sent in to peek at them from time to time."

"Wendy was quite strong the first time we laid eyes upon her," Lily said slowly. "Most likely she was growing quite competent on Shades alone, upsetting the fine balance her mother was devising. She was growing and adapting far too fast for her mother's comfort."

"Yeah, Mary was always kind of . . . weird about Wendy," Eddie agreed.

They'd reached Wendy's street; unconsciously they all slowed their pace and eyed the sky for gulls, lowering their voices so that they had to strain to hear one another.

"Especially near the end," Eddie added, feeling a little like he was admitting great dark secrets instead of info they could learn from Wendy just as easily as from Eddie. "Calling her out at psycho hours, dragging her out of class for nonexistent doctor appointments and bringing her back an hour or two later. I thought it was just her being a hypochondriac EMT at the time, cuz I didn't know what was up with Wendy right then, but looking back . . . like, she was always asking all these strange questions and stuff."

"Indeed?" Piotr asked, speeding up slightly.

Eddie sped up as well. He couldn't help himself either; kiss from Lily or not, he and Piotr were both anxious to see Wendy once more. "Oh yeah," he agreed. "She'd poke her head in while we were studying all the time, you know? I thought maybe she and Wendy's dad were worried that we were, uh," he glanced at Piotr and then, flushing, shrugged, "you know, making out or something. But we weren't, and she seemed sort of *pissed* about that."

"Cue Ada," Piotr said. "Mary's concern had grown so great that she sought out help."

"Certainly Ada, ever the scientist, would not refuse a Reaper in need," Lily said. "They devised an alteration to the original poison recipe, as Ada suggested, possibly to slow Wendy's growth, but were not able to implement it in time. Instead Mary became the White Lady and Wendy was left to her own devices."

"Not to break the dramatic tension, but we're here," Eddie said.

He waved a hand at the lopsided car in the driveway. "And if I'm not mistaken, Wendy's home."

Elle hadn't been kidding, Piotr realized as they entered Wendy's home; the kitchen was destroyed. The fridge was tipped over on its side, its innards spilled everywhere, and the floor was tacky with dried milk and exploded sour cream. A whole chicken lay half under the stool by the counter, pink blood seeping out of a crushed corner.

Jon, sitting at the other stool, was hunched over his phone, chewing on a burnt cookie with one hand and texting rapidly with the other, as Lily and Elle slid through the wall behind him.

"What the hell happened here?" Eddie asked, leading the way. Piotr found himself unconsciously picking his way across the kitchen, even though the bulk of the mess could hardly be seen in the Never. Eddie, also, moved through the debris as if it affected him, while Lily and Elle simply strode through, their feet leaving no traces in the Never of the destruction in the living world.

"Do you think Wendy's seen this?" Eddie asked Piotr. "We could go upstairs and check, I guess."

"She's gone," Jon replied, finishing his text. "Been gone for over an hour."

"Seriously?" Eddie asked. "What happ—wait." He froze, staring at Jon in utter bewilderment. "You can hear us?"

Jon looked up and, slowly, looked from Eddie to Piotr to Lily, and finished on Elle. "Yeah. Uh, miss? Your slip's showing," he said, blushing.

Elle glanced down and smirked. "It happens."

"How long have you been able to perceive us?" Lily asked, nudging Elle sharply in the rib with her elbow until Elle, rolling her eyes, adjusted her skirt so it hung a shade lower. "Were you able to before? On the stairs?"

"Yeah, I was." Jon rubbed the back of his neck. "I wasn't sure what was going on, though, you know? So I decided to keep quiet.

Honestly, the first time I saw one of you guys I thought I was going nuts. It took me most of Christmas break to realize Wendy could see you all too." He looked at Eddie and Piotr, and jiggled his leg uncomfortably.

"I sort of figured on talking to her about it pretty soon, once I figured out how to broach the subject the right way, but she started getting really squirrelly a few days ago—squirrelly even for Wendy, I mean—and then I saw you on the stairs and it all sort of clicked." Eddie held up his phone. "But I can't talk to her about it now because, surprise of all surprises, Wendy's at the hospital. Again"

Eddie stiffened. "Why?"

"Chel found her passed out on her floor. She got a message from this old friend of Wendy's—this doctor chick who used to take care of our mom—and this lady said Wendy's in danger, she needs Chel's help. So Chel, being Chel, was going to blow it off, but then she decided, what the hell, and went to check up on Wendy."

"And your sister found Wendy collapsed," Piotr said shortly. "Quite ill."

"Yep. Naked and steaming hot to the touch," Jon said. "She called 911 and apparently the EMTs flipped out at how high Wendy's temperature was. They rushed her to the ER. Chel's there right now."

"And what about you?" Eddie asked.

"I was just about to head out there," Jon jerked his thumb at a backpack on the kitchen table, "but I wanted to make sure Wendy had some stuff for her stay first. Clean undies and a toothbrush and stuff." He looked around the kitchen. "I don't suppose you guys know what happened here?"

"No, I am sorry," Piotr said. "We do not." He hesitated a moment. "How were you planning on reaching the hospital?"

"Well," Jon said slowly, "if it was just me, I was gonna take the bus, but . . . well, I've got my permit and I'm pretty safe. I drive like a turtle but . . . you all want a ride?"

CHAPTER TWENTY-FIVE

In her dreams, Wendy floated across chill grey water toward dense, high rocks. Her side ached fiercely, a slow stabbing that radiated from her hip all the way to her lungs, but the pain didn't stop her from marveling at the sight of the setting sun turning deep red as it dipped beneath the waves. When it was half gone, Wendy reached Alcatraz.

Biting back a yell of agony, Wendy forced herself to stretch on tiptoes on the edge of the boat as the side scraped the cliff face. Scraping her palms and digging her toes into the rock face, Wendy willed the cliff to provide her with handholds as she drew herself up and out, climbing as fast as she dared. Perhaps it was her power over the dreamspace, perhaps it was simply the strata of the dream, but her fingers found good climbing nooks and crannies until she was able to haul herself over the edge and to safety.

Her mother was there.

"Hey Mom," Wendy said, glad and sad all at once. Mary reached down and offered her hand and Wendy took it, relishing the cool fingers wrapped around her own as she tottered to her feet. Steadying herself, Wendy thought she heard a dim thunder boom underlined with a hiss-pop of distant lightning, but as she concentrated on the sound she realized the long echoing noise wasn't thunder but cannon-fire and gunshots.

A particularly loud crack sent scavenging birds up in droves and the sky was suddenly filled with birds—ravens and crows and buzzards—all screaming and cawing and filling the world with their raucous disapproval.

Wendy shivered. Birds . . . there was something about birds she was supposed to remember . . .

Fog rolled in from the sea, pouring over the lower cliffs like foam, rising with the eddying currents of air until the edges licked the tips of her shoes. Squinting, Wendy could just make out faint white light through holes in the fog, twinkling in the distance like starlight. For a moment she thought her mind had sent her into some sort of twisted dreamspace battle but then she realized that what she saw wasn't light, but Light. Beneath her a long line of prisoners, chained together with ribbons of Light, were trudging from the front doors of Alcatraz down into the morass of fog and sea.

"Mom? What's going on?" Wendy asked, turning to Mary, but Mary was gone. Hollow-eyed and shocked, Chel stood where her mother had been, biting her lips and roughly rubbing the gooseflesh from her arms. Typical Chel, even in Wendy's dreams she wasn't dressed for the weather, wearing only a football jersey, yoga pants, and a black pair of threadbare Hello Kitty socks. Wendy thought she recognized the socks; they used to be hers.

"Just a dream," Wendy said and sighed. Despite the peculiar surroundings, part of her had been hoping that this was not a dream but a dreamspace, and that her mother had somehow made her way back from the space beyond the Light to help her one last time. If Chel was here, this was definitely not a dreamspace. Just a dream.

"I'm cold," Chel said, and Wendy, using the skills the White Lady had inadvertently taught her, imagined a heavy cloak for her sister to wear. Chel took it gladly, shrugging into the long white fabric and pulling it close around her neck. "Thanks." She leaned past Wendy, squinting into the swirling fog at the men vanishing into the murk. "What's going on?"

"Don't know," Wendy said. "Mom was here but now she's gone. I was going to get a little, I don't know, clarification, but when I turned around, you were here."

"Sorry I can't help," Chel said, irritated.

"No, it's not you, it's me," Wendy said. "I'm missing something, forgetting something. I'm just so *tired*." She was, she realized, tired and aching and shaking from the hole in her gut. Her mouth felt dust-dry and her eyes burned.

"I miss Mom too," Chel said, taking Wendy by the arm and pulling her away from the edge of the cliff. "She could be a real bitch sometimes but she always seemed to have her stuff together, you know?" Chel guided Wendy to a nearby bench and they both sat. "I wish she'd taught us how to do that."

"She planned to," Wendy said, feeling a sudden urge to defend her. "She was just busy."

"Always busy. Too busy for us," Chel snorted and Wendy was irrationally angry with her sister, despite the fact that Chel had a point.

"Shut up," she grumbled. "Mom tried. She had stuff to do. Important stuff."

"Like you? Following dead people around? What kind of life is that, Wendy? You're giving up everything that makes you cool to go traipsing after people who already had their chance. What are you *doing*, anyway? Is this all some sort of sick game to you?"

"I have a purpose," Wendy protested. "And it's not a game. They need me just like they needed Mom."

Disgusted, Chel shook her head. "So that's what Mom was doing all those years when she was gone? Hanging out with dead people? Gross."

"You're looking at it all wrong," Wendy cried, grabbing Chel's arm and wincing as intense pain jolted across her gut. She pressed a hand to her side, trying to dull the agony with pressure, but it did little to alleviate the pain. "They need me," she said again, this time through clenched teeth. "It was her duty and now it's mine. I have to do it."

"Or else?"

"Or else they suffer."

Chel jerked a thumb over her shoulder. "Looks like they're suffering with or without you. Kind of like it was planned that way."

"You don't know what you're talking about."

Chel sighed. "Maybe I do, maybe I don't. All I know is that I'm tired of seeing the people I love end up all skinny and white in hospital beds. The sheets are always green. We're redheads. It washes us out."

"Chel—"

"Shut up." Chel rubbed the heel of her palms into her eyes. "I'm so tired. I never sleep anymore, you know that? I tried to nap this afternoon but the fridge fell over. Between waiting up most nights to see what godawful hour you decide to sneak in and worrying about Dad cracking up and Jon being all secretive—" she broke off.

"Chel?" Wendy asked quietly.

"I'm worried about you." Chel sighed and wiped a hand against her cheek. "You're the closest thing I've got left of Mom. And you're sick. Really sick."

"Is this real?" Wendy asked. "Is this a dream or a dreamscape? I can't tell."

"You're really sick," Chel repeated, burying her face in her hands and sobbing softly. "Don't die, Wendy. Please? Please don't die."

There was a howl, long and dark, and fierce ringing bells as alarms burst into song all around Alcatraz Island. The dream was ending as abruptly as it had begun; the night dropped across the sky in a billowing swath of black velvet, sprinkled with crystal clear stars.

Wendy blinked and Chel was gone. Eyes watering, she blinked again . . .

Again . . .

Again . . .

Wendy opened her eyes and found Emma kneeling beside her in the middle of a great room filled with books. It was too crowded and disorganized to be called a library; the piles teetered alarmingly with the faintest breeze. The air was clammy, cold, and smelled of must and decay. There were footprints in the dust at their feet.

"Wendy," Emma was saying, and Wendy got the impression that she'd been talking for a very long time and Wendy had only just now tuned in, "Wendy, listen to me."

"Emma?"

Emma looked up, and where her eyes were, only banked coals remained. "Wendy, you have to run. Get out of here." When she spoke, smoke curled out of her mouth, like a dragon, and Wendy realized that the skin of Emma's neck was layered in thin, etched sheets, snake-coils and dragon scales that glittered in the light.

"What's happening?" Wendy asked and flinched as a dark shadow swooped down from the ceiling, red eyes glaring, and swung back up into the rafters. A thin, heady chuckle filled the air where it had been.

"This is the space between," Emma said, coughing as more smoke poured from between her lips. She smelled like cedar chips and midnight bonfires and sulfur matches. Her hair was not just red now, but liquid fire, the braid coming undone on its own, snaking down her back and curling at her elbows. "This is the place they find you."

"They? Who's they?"

"The Dark Ones." Emma reached forward and took Wendy's hands in her own. "Go, Wendy! Get out of here. GO!"

And she shoved Wendy hard in the chest, right where her Light was brightest and yet the most tangled, the most trapped.

Wendy fell back . . .

    back . . .

        back . . .

And woke.

The daylight was almost gone, leaving the hospital room bathed in a grainy, sepia-tinted haze, like an old photograph. What had woken her? It was silent in her room except for the low beeping of monitors, the steady swish-swish of the air conditioning pumping a breeze across her pillow. Wendy licked her lips; her tongue felt heavy, thick, and furry, the skin around her mouth sensitive and scaly to the touch. Instinctively, Wendy sensed that her temperature was still high.

Drip. Drip. Drip.

Wendy squinted at the ceiling, surprised to see that there was another shell-door embedded in the ceiling tiles. Water pooled and dripped through the narrow crack between the door and the surrounding ceiling, pattering on the foot of her bed in cold, icy drops, soaking her feet with rust-colored water. Shivering from the shock of the wetness against her hot toes, Wendy drew her feet closer to her body. The damp should have felt good, but it didn't. The water was *thick* somehow, viscous, and smelled like sulfur and moss and rotten things left to decay at the bottom of a bog.

It was another dreamscape, but despite the familiar medical surroundings, Wendy could tell that this particular place didn't come from *her* mind at all. Wendy pressed against the dreamspace the way she'd been taught by the White Lady—concentrate hard enough, she'd always thought, and any dream could be hers to control. This time, however, the attempt fell flat and Wendy sagged from the mental effort. She might be strong in the Never or in her own dreams, but in this twisted place she was weaker than a kitten. It was the tidal wave and the earthquake all over again. She had very little control now, only over her immediate area.

"You're awake."

Tempted as she was to face her tormentor, there was no point. Saving her energy, Wendy kept her face pointed firmly at the ceiling, watching the water bead along the edges of the door before pattering down. "Didn't I just stab you?"

"I don't know, did you?" Jane slid her shirt aside, exposing perfectly tattooed flesh, not a mar or mark to be seen. "I feel pretty whole right now. How about *you?*"

When Jane leaned down, Wendy could smell the coconut and

strawberry of her shampoo, the sandalwood and wood smoke of her perfume, all underlined by the wet leather of her jacket and topped off by the ever-present grape bubble gum. This close, the cloying mixture of scents was nauseating.

Wendy turned her head and felt more than heard Jane chuckle above her. Wendy's fingers itched to reach up and snatch the blue-haired girl bald, but she knew that in this not-her-mind-dream-space, she was feverish and sick, no match for Jane at all.

"Should've given up by now," Jane said. "Stubborn."

"What are you doing here?" Wendy asked, irritated. "Don't you have someone else's dreams to stalk?"

"Nope. I'm here just to visit your scowling little face. This time without Grandma cramping my style." Insolently, Jane pinched Wendy's cheek. Wendy tried to pull away but Jane's long, slim fingers were deceptively strong, and pinched extra hard as punishment for attempting to evade.

Wendy shoved weakly at Jane's hands, but her fingers went through the flesh easily. Frowning, Wendy struggled to sit up, but her palms couldn't grip the edges of the bed. They faded and slid through the thin green sheets as if she were insubstantial.

"Even in your dreams you side with the ghosts," Jane said, shaking her head so that her long earrings tinkled and stepping back from the bed. "You're all faded, Wendy. Fading, fading away."

"This is a dream. I know it is. What's really happening?" Wendy asked. "What are you doing to me?"

"Nothin' much," Jane replied, fingers resting on the intricate swirls beneath her collarbone, "you're just dying. I didn't have to do anything at all. You did it all to yourself."

Wendy shoved at the dream again, trying to rip the sheet, trying to turn it red, or blue, or make it vanish. Any little bit of control, anything at all.

Nothing.

"I can feel you pushing at me," Jane said evenly. "I wouldn't bother if I were you." She held out one hand, examining her nails. "You should rest. You don't have a lot of time left."

"I'm never going to stop fighting you," Wendy warned softly. "And when I wake up, I'm coming after you."

"When you wake up? Well, hell, Wendy, I don't know that you're *going* to wake up, to be honest. You're in the hospital now, cuz, and the prognosis ain't pretty." Jane tilted her head up and looked at the pooling water on the ceiling. "They've got you tied down and damn near drowning in ice packs."

Wendy turned her face away. "You can't know that."

"Oh yeah? Well right now your little sis is outside the ER trying to get a hold of your daddy. What's her name? Chel." Jane snickered, popping a piece of gum in her mouth. "She's a real winner, Wendy. You know she can't even disguise her disgust when a Walker wanders past? Your mom sure knows how to train 'em."

"What are you talking about?" Wendy snapped. "Chel can't see ghosts."

"Riiight," Jane said, chomping her gum savagely. "Sure she can't. And I'm the mother-lovin' Queen of Bonny ol' England." She sighed. "Even now, you're lying."

"Chel has never seen anyone die in her life," Wendy insisted. "Other than my mom, I'm the only Reaper in my immediate family."

"Think again." Jane held up a hand and examined her nails. "Though, when I'm done with 'em, you'll be back to being the only one. For a few hours, at least."

"I will kill you," Wendy swore sharply. "You even think about touching Chel or Jon, I don't care if I end up dying, I will haunt your ass so hard—"

"Pshaw, whatever," Jane said, peeling her bubble gum off the knife and popping it back in her mouth. "Like I haven't heard that a million times from ghosts before." She wiggled her fingers. "Oooh, everlasting fury and thwarted revenge. Soooo spooky!"

"Is your ass ever jealous of all the crap that pours out of your mouth?" Wendy asked, and surprisingly, Jane laughed.

"Look, I'm here to offer you a piece of advice. Believe it or not, abominationy-mutant-freak or not, I kind of like you. You've got spunk."

"Geez, thanks," Wendy drawled. "If this is how you treat the people you like, I'd hate to see how you hang with the people you hate."

"Shut up, you don't have a lot of time," Jane replied, not unkindly. "Look, Wendy, my point is that Grandma might take off your binding and let you live, if you just stay in the hospital for a while and don't meddle in Grandma's business. Quit asking questions, quit talking to ghosts at drive-ins and definitely don't wander up to the city and meet with the Council. Grandma has some special plans for them, you understand?"

"Go to hell," Wendy said.

Jane smiled sadly. "Already there, cuz. Already there. But, seriously, take my advice. Emma will keep you alive, you just . . . sleep for a while. A week. Maybe two. And when you wake up this whole nightmare will be over."

An alert pinged quietly behind the bed. Twisting, Wendy glanced up at the IV stand and realized that her drip bag was empty, the tube that snaked between the bag and her arm cleanly cut. Though it seemed impossible, the IV had been doing some good; with it empty, already her lips felt drier, her skin tighter. In the far-flung distance, sounding as if the alarm were coming from half a world away, a steady, shrill beeping began to grow louder and louder. Wendy dimly realized that it was a noise outside the dreamscape. It was the IV alarm.

"That's my cue," Jane said. Winking, she blew Wendy a kiss. "And that, my dear, means it's time to boogie. See ya later, alligator."

"I hope you rot in hell," Wendy said bleakly.

Snickering, Jane reached forward and pinched Wendy's big toe.

"Sweet dreams, kiddo. Don't let the bedbugs bite." Then, not bothering to look behind her, Jane backed away several steps until she faded through the wall.

Wendy licked her lips. They were dry and cracked again, and her tongue was already beginning to feel furry. It was just a dream, but she'd learned long ago that dreams could still affect the living body, that what happened in a dreamscape could cross over into the waking world. The healed spot where her tongue ring used to be was proof positive.

"Help," Wendy whispered, laying back against her pillows and trying to think of glaciers and icy mountain lakes, of polar bears and penguins and far-flung mountaintops flush with snow unmelted for thousands of years.

In the corner of the room there was a shadow, a pair of eyes observing; they were dark and watchful. They reminded Wendy of her mom.

"Please," she said again, as the IV alarm from beyond the dreamscape began to bleat louder. "Please help."

EPILOGUE

In the beginning there was my mother.
A shape. A shape and a force, standing in the light.
You could see her energy; it was visible in the air.
Against any background she stood out.

—*Marilyn Krysl*

"Do you hear that? I wonder what's going on?" Eddie asked as the elevator doors opened. Piotr, frowning, nodded. Jon stepped around the two and, moving quickly, led the way onto Wendy's floor, Lily at his heels. They passed an empty nurse's station and several abandoned carts in the hallway.

"That isn't coming from Wendy's room, is it?" Lily asked as Jon, expression grim, slowed at the end of the hall.

"It is," he said as a tall black nurse hurried from the room, hustling past Jon without a second look and making a beeline for the nurse's desk. "Code blue," the nurse said sharply into the phone. "Get Harrison up here, now!"

Hearing that, Jon, hand pressed to his chest, thumped bodily against the wall and slid to the floor. He curled up, burying his face against his knees, and trembled.

"Code blue?" Piotr asked Eddie, but Eddie was gone, the back of his head already vanishing through the wall to Wendy's room. Glancing at Lily, Piotr followed.

"She's dying," Eddie whispered, huddled in the corner as far away as possible from the mass of nurses and doctors hunched over

335

Wendy's bed. The heart monitor behind her bed agreed with his diagnosis. It emitted a long, shrill beep to accompany the terrifying flat line that lit up the screen.

"Turn that down!" snapped one of the attendants just as the tall black nurse returned from the desk. He moved quickly and poked a dial on the side of the monitor. The sound immediately softened.

"Another defibrillator will be here any second," the nurse said. She slapped the brightly colored machine in the corner. "This piece of crap is still busted."

"Great," huffed a nurse with one knee up on the bed. She was hunched over Wendy's body, arms locked straight and fists pumping Wendy's ribcage up-down-up. "I don't know how much longer I can keep this up."

Another nurse, tucked behind the head of the bed, held a large bulb over Wendy's face that she squeezed in short intervals. Eddie didn't know what it was called, but he'd seen enough medical shows on TV to know what it did. They were breathing for her, beating her heart.

Wendy's soul, however, was still in her body.

"Come on, Wendy," Eddie whispered. "Hang in there."

"She's still burning up!" one of the nurses yelled. "Johnson! We need some fans in here! Move!" One of the green-clad attendants, a blonde, peeled off from the pack and hurried from the room.

"Gel packs from the fridge," the tall black nurse said, rushing away. The doctor shouted after, "And more ice blocks from down-stairs! Hurry!"

"We weren't separated that long," Lily said, sidestepping a bustling nurse and examining Wendy's flushed face. "What happened?"

"The damn Reapers," Elle said bitterly, hands flexing into fists as she glared around the room. "It has to be. We tried to warn her."

"Nana Moses wouldn't do this," Eddie said, shaking his head. "This has got to be some kind of mistake. I know her. She promised."

"*Eto ne imyeet bol shogo znacheniya*. Little importance now; *someone* clearly did this," Piotr replied darkly. "And we need to find out who."

"Or we can just wait a minute," Elle said, moving to the foot of Wendy's bed. "Look."

A corridor of Light was opening behind the headboard.

"*Net*," Piotr whispered, pushing past Eddie and grabbing Wendy's hand, careless of the blistering heat coming off her in palpable waves. "Not again. *Puzhalsta,* Wendy! Not again. Don't you dare!"

"This is highly unorthodox. Has anyone reached her family on the phone?" one of the nurses urgently asked as a new defibrillator was wheeled in. She was taller than the other nurses, slim and dark-haired and waving a clipboard under the nose of anyone who would stop a moment to pay attention to her. Only Eddie, standing close enough to notice, spotted the thin Celtic knot peeping out from under the collar of her scrubs.

"Unorthodox?" the doctor snorted as he pushed past her. "We're shocking her system, not playing her like a puppet. What's so unorthodox about it?"

"This is Mary Darling's girl," the dark-haired nurse replied stiffly. "I've seen this kid in here enough times to have an idea when something's up. When she was wheeled in, I checked her records!"

"Again, so? Anything important? Allergies?" The doctor nudged the IV stand. "Get me more saline in here, too! The cord on this P.O.S. is loose! Hell, it looks like it sprung a damn leak in here. No wonder she's overheating, if she's gotten any of this IV, I'll eat my stethoscope."

"She has a DNR!" the dark-haired nurse said urgently.

The doctor was frantically gesturing at the closest aide. "I need to prep the pads; where's the f'ing gel? Come ON, people!"

"I *said*," the dark-haired nurse tried again, slapping the doctor on the shoulder to get his attention. "You have to stop. She has a DNR!"

"A DNR? On a kid her age?" The doctor stared at the nurse as if she'd suddenly sprouted a second head. "Whoah, whoah, wait. Is there something I'm missing here? Is she terminal?"

"What is a DNR?" Lily asked Eddie.

"A 'Do Not Resuscitate' order," he explained, intently staring at the nurse and scowling. "It's a bunch of stupid paperwork that keeps them from saving her life if she's in an accident or something."

Elle snorted. "What, you mean like now?"

"Like now," he agreed grimly. "But I think Wendy would've said something to me if she had a DNR. This is totally news to me. And that lady, the one with the clipboard, is being pushy about it, and I think she's a Reaper."

"Piotr," Elle said suddenly. "Do something!"

The doctor was likewise perplexed, but he stopped shouting orders and frantically rushing to save Wendy. "Why would a teenage girl not want to be resuscitated? Has she been tested for pharm? Is this a self-harm case?" He grabbed Wendy's wrist and flipped it up, examining her arm expertly. "No tracks, no scars. What gives?"

"Do something?" Piotr asked, exasperated. "I do not understand, Elle. What do you wish me to do? Give her mouth-to-mouth myself? We know how that ends."

"Come on, Petey," Elle snorted, gesturing angrily to the living scrambling to save Wendy's life around them. "Playin' dumb here isn't going to help the Lightbringer. Remember the ride over to Mountain View? You and I both know you did something when you touched that drunk guy on the bus. *Somethin'*-something. And if you did it then, you can do it again. Fix it!"

"Well, she's not into self-damage that I can see." The doctor dropped Wendy's wrist and took a step back to assess the situation. "Hardly a freckle, much less a cut."

"Why is the doctor examining her arms?" Lily asked curiously. "Does he feel there may be a cure there?"

"Just the opposite, he's judging a book by its cover," Eddie replied, scowling. "She's goth-looking so, *duh*, of course she's probably an addict or a cutter. Except she's not. Judgmental a-hole."

"Explain to me again why a DNR is necessary for a teenage girl?" the doctor asked the nurse. He couldn't see it, but several of the other aides and nurses were shooting him and the dark-haired nurse dirty looks behind his back. "*Is* she terminal?"

"This girl was in a coma a few weeks ago," the dark-haired nurse replied as the attending staff, ignoring the discussion, strapped Wendy with wires and pads. "I think her family may be tapped out."

"Are you kidding me? Lack of money is no reason to—" the doctor began.

The nurse cut him off. "The reason doesn't matter. The paperwork does."

He flipped several pages on the clipboard, frowning deeply. "Well . . . you're right. Here's the DNR. Plain as day."

"Couldn't be plainer," the nurse agreed.

"It can't hurt to try, right?" Elle urged Piotr. "Please, Pete. There's so much locked up inside that noggin of yours, maybe there's a reason the Reapers have been using you for all these years. Maybe they don't want you doing to them what you did to that guy on the bus."

"As you can see here," the nurse indicated one of the pages, "her family's insurance company has already denied coverage for any further incidents of this nature."

"That is somewhat presumptive of them," the doctor said, glancing at Wendy on the table. "But my job—"

Piotr shook his head. "This is madness. I cannot . . . I . . ."

"Just try," Lily said suddenly. "Touch him and try."

The nurse shrugged but met the doctor's eyes challengingly. "Sir. The papers do not lie. DNR. Your job is to save lives of those who wish to be saved. This girl and this girl's family do *not* wish her to be saved, especially if she is going to spend her days comatose. Would you want to wither away your youth strapped to a hospital bed?"

"Well . . . I don't . . ." The doctor hesitated as the nurse flipped to another page in the file.

"This is her mother's file, and a picture of her near the end. You remember Mary? Nine months in a persistent vegetative state. Do you really think a teenage girl wants to end up like this?"

"Of course not."

"It is unnecessary," Piotr said sharply, stepping up behind the doctor and laying a hand on the back of his neck. His fingers sank into the skin knuckle deep, a thin rime of frost expanding across the doctor's flesh as Piotr pressed his hand deeper into the doctor's body. "To allow the death of a girl over paperwork is ridiculous. There is no reason to believe she will end up as her mother did. To suggest so is absurd."

"No. No matter what, a DNR on a girl this age is just absurd. Ridiculous, even," the doctor said strongly, pushing away and handing the clipboard back to the dark-haired nurse and striding to the nearest sanitation station, snatching up a pair of blue gloves from a box. "No, this is unnecessary. If her family can't afford it, I'll help them figure something out myself."

"Ridiculous or not, it's what her family wants," the nurse reminded the doctor pointedly, clutching her clipboard to her chest tightly. "Are you really going to risk your career based off of some gut feeling? This says right here—"

"You don't care about this paperwork," Piotr told the doctor, grabbing him by the shoulder as he snapped on the first glove. "She is a young girl. Too young to die."

"Paperwork can be mistaken. She's not terminal, there is absolutely no good reason to let this kid go," the doctor snapped at the dark-haired nurse, glancing at the beeping lights on the defibrillator. It had warmed up sufficiently. The nurse slapped gel pads diagonally across Wendy's chest and waved a hand, pushing away from the limp girl on the table. "She's too young to die."

Glaring at the medical team, the dark-haired nurse tried one last time. "Doctor! If you can't properly follow protocol and procedure then I'm afraid that I'm going to have to report—"

He elbowed her out of the way. "Unless you want the shock of your life, move, Jenna!"

"Doctor, please! Listen to reason—"

"CLEAR!"

ABOUT THE AUTHOR

K.D. MCENTIRE, author of *Lightbringer* and *Reaper*, lives just outside of Kansas City with her husband, children, and various pets. She spends her miniscule free time reading, writing, and battling her Sims 3 addiction (when Reddit hasn't swallowed her soul whole) and can be found online at kdmcentire.com.